THE SPARK

THE SPARK
a novel

*Every life tells a story,
tell yours with passion.*

John Kenny

JOHN KENNY

Incendiary Publications

This is a work of fiction. Names, characters, businesses, places, events and incidents are either the products of the author's imagination or used in a fictitious manner. Any resemblance to actual persons, living or dead, or actual events is purely coincidental.

THE SPARK, Copyright © 2013 by John Kenny. All rights reserved. No part of this book may be used or reproduced in any manner whatsoever without written permission, except in the case of brief quotations embodied in critical articles or reviews. For information contact the author at www.johnkennyauthor.com

ISBN 978-0-9920708-0-9

Cover Photo by John Kenny

Author Photo by Peter McFawn

For my parents,
Lorne & Olive Kenny,
who taught me the love of language.

And for Liz,
who taught me the language of love.

AUTHOR'S FOREWORD

IT'S SAID THAT WAR is 90% boredom and 10% sheer terror. If that's true, it has much in common with life in the Fire Service. The bulk of each shift in a fire hall is consumed by the mundane chores of cleaning, maintenance, training, false alarms and other routine duties. A book about that would be tedious at best, and so I have deliberately emphasized the action, adventure and drama of fire fighting in order to craft what I hope is a compelling story.

The Spark is a work of fiction. Though I have drawn from twenty-five years of experience as a firefighter, the characters and events in this book are creations of my own imagination. It is not a documentary portrayal of the Fire Service, and it is certainly not an autobiography.

Nonetheless, I have tried to give the reader a sense of what life is like both in the station and on the fire ground, and to provide an insider's view of firefighting, albeit a highly subjective one that emphasizes the action rather than the day-to-day routine.

I've also tried to portray the emotional intensity of the job, the highs and the lows. There is nothing like the thrill of a successful rescue or reviving someone whose heart has stopped. There are also moments of heartbreaking tragedy. I've sat at the kitchen table in fire halls while some of the bravest, toughest men I know have wept like babies.

Those experiences build a closeness that is uncommon in other professions. A good fire crew is very much like a family. As in every family, there are disputes and disagreements, but in the end we have a blood bond forged by putting our lives in each other's hands day after day. When it hits the fan, I know who's got my back.

Despite advances in equipment, training and techniques, firefighting is still a dangerous profession. In addition to the daily dangers we encounter, fire fighters also face high rates of cancer, heart disease and many other conditions. We give up several years of our life expectancy to do a job we love. Countless thousands of volunteer firefighters around the world accept those same risks for little or no pay. They truly have my admiration. It's not for everyone, but every firefighter I know would say they can't imagine doing anything else. I hope this book helps explain why.

I deliberately set *The Spark* in Toronto, the city I grew up in, a city I know and love. I was advised early in the writing that I might have more success if I set the story in New York, L.A. or Chicago. Though the essence of the job is the same everywhere, there are subtle differences in culture and terminology, and I was concerned that if I set the story elsewhere it might not ring true.

Regardless of whether you call the hose a "38" or an "inch and half," whether it's a "pumper" or an "engine," the deep sense of tradition and honour, the black humour and the camaraderie, the dedication to service and excellence under the worst circumstances—these things are universal among firefighters. These are the things I love, the things I have tried to celebrate.

Recently, some aspects of firefighting tradition have come under attack as "inappropriate." Some of the changes have been for the better: we are more inclusive; we are more sensitive to the damage that post-traumatic stress disorder can do to firefighters and their families. But the zeal with which political correctness and safety at all costs have been pursued has also, at times, led to the baby being thrown out with the bath water. As we move forward, we need to take special care to preserve the best of the past: the dedication to honour, excellence and service. Once you've lost those, you can never get them back.

Tonight, as you sleep, my brother and sister firefighters will stand guard to protect your community, your home and your family. It takes a special sort of person to enter a burning building when even the rats and cockroaches have enough sense to run away. We don't do it for the money. We do it for reasons that have sometimes been forgotten in our modern world. We do it with a deep sense of duty to the public we serve, and we do it with pride.

First and foremost I hope you enjoy the story, but I also hope that by the end you'll come to understand and appreciate that pride.

JOHN KENNY
November 2013

ONE
Commissioners Street

THE WINDOWS WERE black with soot. Tendrils of smoke seeped from the edges of the flat roof and wove themselves together, like a dark shroud rising into the night. *A single story industrial building — after ten, no lights on — probably no one inside this late.* It wasn't conscious thought, just something Fitz and Donny instinctively knew, just as they knew from the smell, colour and density of the smoke that the fire inside was well established.

The door was cool to the touch. The fire hadn't reached the front of the building yet. Donny pulled his hand back and drove the K-tool over the lock cylinder. He grunted and heaved. The cylinder popped neatly out of the door. He inserted a screw driver into the hole and pried the bolt back.

"Nice work," Fitz nodded.

"Some old guy taught me that a few years back," Donny grinned as he put the tools down. Fitz ignored the remark. They donned the face pieces of their Self Contained Breathing Apparatus and turned on the air tanks on their backs. Cool, fresh air flowed into the masks.

Fitz reached for the door, then paused. "Remember, the water main's shut down. No sprinklers inside, and Moose is going to have to drag the suction all the way back to Cherry Street to catch a hydrant."

"Lucky us." Donny bent to pick up the 38 mm attack line. Until the hydrant was hooked up they would have only the water they carried in the truck's tank, barely three minutes' worth — maybe a little more if they used it sparingly.

"You ready, Wedge?" Fitz asked.

"And if I said no?" Donny replied.

"I should have canned you when you were a probie."

"You should have thought of that twenty years ago." Donny's laugh sounded tinny and hollow inside the mask. Both men felt the familiar surge of adrenalin. "Let's kick this thing in the teeth."

They instinctively stepped to the side as Fitz pulled the door open, giving the fire a fresh supply of air. Dark smoke billowed out into the night. They stepped inside and were swallowed by the blackness. Once again they were blind men, guided only by touch. They groped their way down the corridor, the heat increasing as they went. The sound of their own breathing inside the SCBA was loud in their ears.

The corridor turned left and the heat grew more intense. They dropped to their knees. It was a couple of hundred degrees cooler near the floor. They still couldn't see anything but they knew they were getting closer to the seat of the fire.

Fitz held the mic of his radio to his face piece. "Pumper 6 Captain to Pumper 6, charge the line Eddy."

"On its way." Eddy pulled open a valve on the pump panel at the side of the truck. The hose running into the building surged and snapped as a hundred psi of water rushed through the line.

Donny opened the nozzle and aimed the stream towards the unseen fire that lay ahead. The heat only increased, as water turned to steam. "Feels like a pretty good fire load up ahead, Fitz; I'm not sure we're going to knock it down with this 38."

Fitz keyed his mic. "Pumper 6 Captain, we're going to need a second line in here."

"I'm at the hydrant now," Moose panted over the radio. "As soon as it's hooked up, I'll bring in a 65."

Fitz turned to Donny. "Let's move up and at least put a dent in it."

The pressure in the hose made it stiff now. Donny and Fitz grunted, dragging it along as they inched their way down the corridor. The heat was building rapidly and they began to see a dull glow ahead of them in the murky haze. They could hear the sirens of arriving trucks.

"Pump 7 on scene," the radio crackled. "Aerial 7 on scene."

"Pumper 6 Captain to Pumper 7, the main body of the fire's at the back of the building. Bring a line around to the rear and see if you can find a back door, OK, Scooter?"

"Roger, Fitz."

"Aerial 7 Captain to Pumper 6 Captain, we're heading to the roof, Fitz. We'll cut some holes and ventilate some of that smoke and heat for you."

"Thanks, Billy. It's getting pretty hot in here."

"We need that second line. I'm medium rare already," Donny commented.

"Moose will be here in a minute. Move up and see if you can lob that stream in a little deeper."

They crawled towards the orange glow.

"Jeez, I got an open door, Donny. It's burning in here too. Swing the line over and give it a wash."

Donny turned towards Fitz. He could see a hazy orange rectangle, the outline of a doorway with fire beyond. Donny swung the nozzle and sent the stream of water through the doorway. The orange glow faded but did not completely disappear.

"I'm going in, Wedge," Fitz said. "Maybe I can find a window to bust out, get rid of some of this heat. You keep the fire from coming down the hall."

"I don't think that's a good idea, Fitz. It's getting too hot too fast. I think this thing was set up."

"I'll be OK. You just protect that hallway. Trust me, I've done this before." Donny could hear the smirk in Fitz's voice even if he couldn't see his face.

Reluctantly Donny turned back as Fitz disappeared into the room. The torrent of heat pouring down the hallway was almost unbearable now. Even lying flat on his belly, it stabbed through the layers of his bunker suit. He aimed the nozzle down the corridor, swinging it in a tight arc, hoping vainly to blunt the merciless thrust of the heat.

At the time everything seemed to happen at once, though when he tried to remember it later, it all seemed to flow with the slow, relentless momentum of a glacier.

Tongues of fire began to ripple through the smoke over Donny's head. "Angel fingers," they were called. They were an indication that the fire was about to flash over, become a raging inferno that nothing and no one could survive. He swung the nozzle over his head as he rose to pivot on one knee.

"I've got a body. Shit, Donny, I've got a body," he heard Fitz call.

Moose's voice sounded over the radio. "I've got the 65. I'm coming in the door now, Cap."

"It's gonna flash, Fitz! We gotta bail!" Donny wasn't sure if he actually said it or only thought it. He lunged back towards the doorway.

"Chief 41 on scene, assuming command. Pumper 6 Captain, give me…Oh my God!"

The world blossomed in brilliant yellow. There was a dull roar punctuated by the sound of breaking glass, as flames leapt hungrily from a dozen windows. The air inside seemed to clear as the fire consumed the smoke and everything else in its path. As he fell, Donny thought he glimpsed two forms in the side room, one kneeling over the other, two beings of living flame.

His last memories were of sensations, not images. The first was a torrent of cool water, like Niagara Falls itself was pouring over him. The second was of being hauled helpless from the angry jaws of the beast by some great irresistible force.

THE SUITE'S LIVING-ROOM window looked south over the arc of parkland that made up the Toronto Islands surrounding the harbour. The pale green haze of spring swathed the trees. Beyond, the blue expanse of Lake Ontario sparkled to the horizon.

A naked man stood before the window, moving elegantly through the final postures of the Wu form of Tai Chi: turn body, double lotus swing; curve bow, shoot the tiger; step up and pound down... He was at once focused and relaxed. He moved with purposeful grace, his mind clear, his body centred.

In his mind he was not in the hotel room, but out there, balanced on the air itself, drifting with the clouds, yet ready to stoop and strike at will.

He was lean and fit, with no trace of the slow decline into middle-aged decay. His muscles moved smoothly and powerfully, from the tight bulge of his calves, through the firm round buttocks, to the deep, powerful chest and broad shoulders.

He was an attractive man, but not in the pretty boy sense; his features were in fact rather ordinary, with the exception of his vivid green eyes. It was more of an overall impression, the poise with which he carried himself and the confident strength that shone from those green eyes.

A knock sounded at the door as he completed the final posture.

"Room service," a voice called.

He moved to the bedroom and covered himself with a terrycloth robe, then answered the door.

"Your breakfast, Mr. Hubbard," the waiter announced, pushing a trolley into the room.

Yes, he was James Hubbard. At least that was what it said on the driver's licence and credit cards in the wallet he retrieved from the nightstand. He tipped the waiter and moved to the table where the dishes had been set.

He felt refreshed and invigorated. He always felt good after the successful completion of a job. He was a man who took both pride and pleasure in his work, and it was deeply gratifying when all the planning and details finally came together.

He flicked on the TV, tuned to the local news and poured himself a coffee. He reviewed the previous night in his mind as he ate his breakfast.

He had found Youssef Aziz sitting at his desk with his back to the office door, absorbed in the technical schematic on the computer screen in front of him and stroking his beard, more salt now than pepper. The office around him was a scene of creative clutter, with books and scientific journals stacked haphazardly on shelves and paper spilling out of filing cabinets. Beside the desk was a large workbench. The equipment on the bench seemed to be either partially assembled or disassembled, he wasn't sure which and it didn't matter.

Over the workbench was a window that looked out over the main assembly area. It was hard to see in the dim light, but he could make out a stack of wooden pallets just beyond the window. Perfect.

Aziz whirled in his chair when Hubbard cleared his throat. His eyes first widened in surprise, then narrowed when he saw the gun.

"Who are you? What are you doing here?" Aziz asked. His English was clear, but he spoke with a heavy accent. He started to rise from the chair, but Hubbard motioned with the gun and he sat back down.

"What do you want?" There was fear in the old man's eyes and in his voice. It was not the new fear of sudden surprise, but an old fear, rooted deep in the past, a fear that echoed with the midnight knock and the windowless grey room with a light that never went out. It was the fear of a man who knew the true meaning of the word "torment."

Hubbard wished he had more time — time to cultivate and savour the exotic qualities of that fear. But there was too much to do and a schedule to keep. Business was business.

He stepped into the room, set down the case he carried in his other hand and opened it. Wires led from the machine inside to two palm-sized adhesive pads.

The machine looked like something from a clinic or hospital. Aziz thought he recognized it. He also recognized the look in the eyes of the man with the gun. He had seen that look on the men in the windowless grey room with a light that never went out. He felt a sour taste rising in his throat.

"Take off your shirt," Hubbard instructed.

Aziz hesitated. Hubbard stepped up to him and ran the barrel of the gun lightly across the old man's lips.

"Don't make me angry," he said softly. "I know how to hurt you. You understand that, don't you? Yes, I thought so. Now take off your shirt."

The old man did as he was told. Hubbard handed him the pads and told him to attach one to his chest just below his left nipple, and the other to his right shoulder.

"You are a doctor?" The question was ridiculous and they both knew it. Only Hubbard laughed.

"No, but you're right. This is a defibrillator. At least it used to be. Normally it's used to start people's hearts. I've modified this one slightly."

Comprehension and sudden terror crystallized in Aziz's brain. As he gripped the arms of the chair to push himself up, Hubbard touched one of buttons on the machine.

Aziz felt the blinding surge of energy arc through him. His eyes rolled back in his head as his whole body arched and stiffened. He collapsed back into the chair and began panting.

"Hmm, good, that was just a test. Now, are all the plans for the system on your computer there?" Hubbard's finger hovered over the button.

The old man's brow was beaded with sweat. He struggled to swallow his fear. "You work for her? Tell her to go to hell."

"Wrong answer." Hubbard increased the power and pushed the button. The old man arched again and made gurgling sounds. "I can easily double or triple the power without killing you. Now, are all the plans on your computer?"

Aziz clung weakly to the chair for support. "Everything important is on the computer."

"And all this?" Hubbard asked, indicating the piles of paper.

"Research notes, prototypes. The blue and green folders on the desk are the final version."

"What about backup copies?" Hubbard asked. Aziz shook his head.

"Sorry, Youssef, but I don't believe you." Hubbard pressed the button several times. Aziz jerked like a marionette in the hands of a child. "I could always take the machine to your house and ask Leila. Maybe she'd be more helpful."

"No, please, leave my wife alone," Aziz said thickly. He had bitten his tongue badly, and a stream of blood and saliva ran from the corner of his mouth.

"The backup!" Hubbard demanded.

"My computer at home. That's all, I swear." There was a look of desperate pleading on Aziz's face. "I have money. I can pay you. Please leave us alone."

Hubbard ignored the offer. "And the password?"

"H-two-salaam, both the same."

Hydrogen peace — how cute, Hubbard thought. He entered the password on Aziz's computer. It didn't work. He increased the power on the "defibrillator" and stabbed at the button. The old man gave a strangled cry as his bladder and bowels emptied themselves.

"The password, Youssef. Give me the password or I swear to God I will light you up like the Fourth of July."

"I told you," Aziz gasped "The 'S', make the 'S' a dollar sign."

This time it worked. Hubbard shut down Aziz's computer and adjusted a few settings on his machine.

"I wish we had more time together," he told Aziz. He meant it quite sincerely. "But you know the pressures of the working day. Goodbye, Youssef." He smiled and pushed the button once again.

The old man's body rose out of the chair. It seemed to levitate for a moment before crashing heavily to the floor. Hubbard pressed the button several more times and Aziz's body thrashed like a freshly landed fish in the bottom of a boat. Then it was still.

Hubbard took a set of tools from his jacket pocket and removed the hard drive from Aziz's computer. He put the hard drive and the blue and green folders into his satchel. Then he picked up a stack of loose paper and carried it to the assembly area next to the office. He crumpled the paper and stuffed it into the stack of wooden pallets. Returning to the office, he stuffed more paper into several of the plastic components on the workbench.

Finally he bent over, removed the electrical pads from Aziz's body and packed up his machine. He hummed a little tune as he put the old man's shirt back on him and buttoned it up.

With a flourish, he produced a Zippo lighter from the dead man's ear. He flipped the lighter open and thumbed the wheel. A tiny shower of sparks rushed toward the wick; the flame fluttered to life and swayed seductively. Hubbard smiled at the dancing flame.

The lighter vanished with a wave. Another gesture and the lighter reappeared in Hubbard's other hand. The flame danced to life once more, only to disappear again. Aziz's face was fixed in an expression of permanent surprise. The dead were not an enthusiastic audience, but at least they were attentive. They didn't suffer from the distractions of the living. Aziz's unseeing eyes stared as Hubbard rose and sparked the lighter one more time.

It only took one, one tiny spark. The flame leapt greedily to the crumpled paper.

Hubbard shut the back door, locked it and removed his picks. He moved back into the darkness at the rear of the property. From there he fed the fire and it grew quickly. He watched the firefighters arrive, but it was too late. The fire blossomed in its full fury. It no longer needed his help.

Sadly, it was time to go. He picked up his things, climbed the back fence and walked away, past the empty lots and warehouses.

He would have liked to walk the other way, to go back and watch the fire devour the building, watch the firefighters vainly trying to quench the flames. That was an amateur mistake. Instead he walked to his car and drove to the hotel.

There it was in front of him now, on the TV. The image of flashing red lights and flames soaring into the night sky drew him back to the present. He turned up the volume.

"… was totally destroyed. One firefighter was killed and another seriously injured. A second body was also found in the rubble. No identities have yet been released. Fire Chief Allan Stevens said…"

A small gasp escaped from his throat. A firefighter killed, another badly burned? He felt himself growing hard, but he pushed the thought away. Whatever pleasure the unexpected news might bring him, he needed to think.

He got up, walked to the coffee table and picked up the Zippo lighter. He had never smoked, but the lighter was something he had treasured since his teens. It had been one constant in his life. It was a gift from his father — the final gift.

He flicked open the lid. Sparks sprayed from the wheel and the flame was reborn. The lighter vanished and reappeared as he passed it from hand to hand, marvelling at the sparks and the dancing flame. The ritual calmed him.

In the end, he decided, the news should not be a serious problem. It could even be a benefit. The death of the firefighter would distract attention from Aziz's death. That was a good thing. His planning had been meticulous. He had left no traces — none that the sheep running the investigation would recognize, anyway. They would follow their usual path, perform their usual tests, and conclude that the fire was an unfortunate accident, a tragic collision of circumstances.

That was the real magic.

He moved to the bedroom and got dressed. The hard drive and paper files he had removed from Aziz's office were already packed into his carry-on. The clerk at the front desk wished him a good day as he checked out.

The taxi sped towards the airport and James Hubbard vanished into thin air.

THE FAMILY HAD gathered, as they always did, to celebrate her birthday. Catherine watched her grandchildren frolic in the pool with happy abandon.

"Watch me, Gramma!" the youngest cried as she launched herself from the diving board, landing with an enormous splash.

"That was a tidal wave!" Catherine exclaimed as the child spluttered to the surface. She enjoyed their boisterous energy, in moderation of course. She missed the energy of her youth.

Catherine's own grandfather had come to America from England with a single sovereign in his pocket. From that he had built a successful business he named after that single coin. Her father had grown the business, transforming Sovereign into a major corporation. She in turn had taken Sovereign onto the world stage. In many ways she was at the peak of her powers. Around her stretched the impeccably manicured landscape that was one of the many fruits of her labours. It was the sort of estate most people would know only from TV and magazines.

She was at an age when most people were retired, or at least thinking about retirement, but that was a concept Catherine couldn't comprehend. The idea of enforced idleness revolted her. And to whom would she pass the reins? Certainly not to her children; their only talents seemed to be spending money and running up legal bills.

When she graduated from high school, her father had given Catherine a Jaguar E-type convertible and a copy of Machiavelli's *The Prince*. It was a watershed moment. She had enjoyed the car, but Machiavelli had changed her life. His simple, pragmatic views on the acquisition and exercise of power independent of morality were the touchstone to which she always returned.

Catherine surveyed her grandchildren. The younger ones splashed noisily in the pool. The older ones, college age, were sunning themselves on the other side from her. Which, if any, she wondered, might be a fertile bed in which to plant the seed?

Her reverie was interrupted by the approach of a neatly dressed young man. "I'm sorry to bother you at home, ma'am, especially today."

"I assume it's something important, Brendan," she stated, looking at him pointedly over her sunglasses.

"It's the Aziz matter. I thought it best to speak to you in person rather than over the phone." He glanced towards the children.

"Ah," she said. Catherine turned and beckoned to the young woman sitting a few yards away. "Carmela, take the children inside for ice cream, please. I think they've had quite enough sun for now."

Once they were alone, Catherine gestured to a chair beside her chaise. "Well?"

Brendan turned the chair to face her and sat. "It's been concluded. We just received the hard drive from Aziz's office computer as well as several key paper files. There's more at his home. I'll arrange to collect that as soon as possible."

"Very good. Send the material to Dr. Patterson for analysis. No one else is to see it but him. I want his report by the end of the month at the latest."

"Certainly." Brendan smoothed the crease in his pants, a gesture that Catherine had learned to recognize meant he had unpleasant news. "There was one, uh, complication. A firefighter was killed and another was badly burned."

"Oh, that is unfortunate." Killing Aziz didn't bother her. It was regrettable, but she had destroyed lives and careers before, even driven one man to suicide. And when one did business with third-world regimes, one could hardly claim to have clean hands. Catherine had tried every method of persuasion she knew, but Youssef Aziz had proven unreasonable, to say the least. In the end she had resolved to move swiftly and ruthlessly. It was the first time she had resorted directly to this sort of service, but she looked on it as simply one more tool in her arsenal.

The firemen were a different matter. At minimum it was a waste, and worse, it would draw unwanted attention. She had once seen a man disfigured by severe burns, his face barely recognizable as human. She shuddered at the memory.

She took off her sunglasses and stared hard at Brendan. "You assured me that this man was a professional. This seems rather sloppy."

Brendan cleared his throat. "He feels it actually might work to our advantage. The death of the firefighter will focus the investigation in that direction and away from Aziz."

Catherine tapped her fingers on the arm of the chaise. There might be some merit in that notion. Now in addition to the coroner, there would be labour inspectors, health and safety committees, workers' compensation and who knew what other agencies, all scrambling to make recommendations and justify their own existence. The more bureaucrats that were involved, the muddier the true picture would inevitably become.

"Very well," Catherine said at last, "but we need to keep a close eye on this. I need to know immediately if anything starts to go amiss."

"Yes, ma'am." Catherine watched him leave.

Every venture contained an element of risk, and this was no different; the stakes were simply higher. But if it paid off, it would transform her company from a mere player on the world stage into a dominant power. It would bear careful watching. Information, she knew, truly was the key to power. Brendan would arrange for the normal monitoring of events. In the meantime, she decided, it was time to call in a few IOUs.

She picked up her phone and called a number in Washington. "I'd like to speak to the Senator, please… I don't care. Tell him it's Catherine Rockingham calling."

TWO
Lombard

THE GRAFTS ON HIS face, neck and arms felt tight in the cool morning air. It wasn't uncomfortable, it just felt… different. A lot of things felt different. But that was OK. Wasn't that what everyone kept telling him? Like they knew? Like anyone had a goddamned clue how he actually felt?

Stop this shit right now, Donny told himself. It *was* OK. The Norton purred reassuringly between his legs. He gave the throttle a slight twist and the purr deepened to a soft growl. They swooped effortlessly into the long curve.

Under the Leaside bridge, around the bend and there it was. He loved this view of the city. From this distance, in the dawn light, it looked pure, almost unreal. The buildings gleamed softly, like some city of the future where there was no pain or loss, where everything was… OK.

He goosed it. The Norton roared and leapt out of the curve, streaking down the bottom stretch of the Parkway. He let the wind blow him clean.

DONNY TURNED INTO the parking lot behind the station, switched the bike off and sat looking at the building.

Fire Station No. 6 was a relic of the 1880s. A citizens' group had won a historical designation for the building, and it was one of the few of Toronto's original fire stations that had survived the wrecker's ball.

The bronze plaque beside the front door said that the Lombard Street station was one of the city's finest examples of the neo-something style by some long-dead architect whose name he had forgotten. Funny, Donny thought to himself, he had polished that plaque hundreds, maybe thousands of times, but he couldn't remember the man's name. He suspected that only a handful of people in the city had ever known or really cared about the architect's name. But Station No. 6 endured.

Lombard was a short downtown side street. Surrounded by office buildings and condos, the station seemed almost lost, a stodgy three-story brick and stone anachronism set among the towers of glass and steel. But it was beautiful. The station was trimmed with the same red sandstone that had been used to construct the Old City Hall, that much Donny knew. A gargoyle glared from the lintel over the main entrance on Lombard. Graceful columns framed the two large apparatus doors, from which powerful teams of horses had once issued, pulling steam pumpers and ladder wagons. Over the apparatus doors a row of deep-set windows marked the living quarters, the kitchen and the Captain's office.

Above the windows, under the peak of the steep slate roof, was the jewel of the station. There, carved in red sandstone, was a bird: a bird in a nest of flames, wings outstretched as if ready to leap from its stony perch and take flight over the city.

That image had become the station's emblem. Every engine that had borne the designation of Pumper 6, from horse-drawn steamers to turbo diesels, had been emblazoned with the phoenix. Every firefighter assigned to Lombard proudly wore the crest with the red bird on his right shoulder. And from its rocky perch, the creature stood guard as the city passed from the 19th through the 20th to the 21st century.

Donny couldn't see the phoenix from the parking lot at the back of the station. From here all he could see were the darkened windows of the dorm, and the wooden doors and hoisting post where the old hayloft had been.

He was no phoenix, but he was reborn. The months of surgery, skin grafts and painful therapy were all behind him now. In little more than twelve months he had made a recovery that the doctors regarded as miraculous. He was back — back where he belonged, back in the heart of the action. He was back with Moose and Eddy the Ladle and everything would be OK.

But not Fitz. Fitz wasn't coming back. Donny wondered if that pain would ever fade.

Thousands of people had lined the streets as row upon row of solemn firefighters marched behind the flag-draped coffin borne on the pumper shrouded in black. The procession had passed only two blocks from the hospital. Donny had asked the nurses to open the window of his room so he could hear the lament of the pipes. But he couldn't see, couldn't move his arms to salute, couldn't say goodbye. The bandages that covered his face drank in his silent tears.

Donny slammed his fist against the Norton's gas tank.

"Why don't you quit beating that antique and put it in a museum where it belongs? Get a bike that runs properly."

"Yeah, I'll do that, Eddy," said Donny, stepping off the Norton, "just as soon as you learn to cook."

Eddy the Ladle was widely acknowledged as one of the best cooks on the job. He laughed and threw his arm across Donny's shoulder. "Welcome back." He gave Donny a hearty squeeze and felt him wince. Eddy took a step back.

"You OK, Wedge?" he asked, looking Donny in the eye just a beat too long.

"Yup, fine. Just… just a little tight still. Come on, I'll let you buy me a cup of coffee."

THE APPARATUS FLOOR was a large, high-ceilinged room. It was a clean, spartan area, with a smooth concrete floor and institutional beige tiled walls. There were two bays, though for many decades now Lombard had hosted only a single pumper. The ladder wagon had disappeared with the horses.

Pumper 6 filled the front half of the right-hand bay, sitting behind the massive black wooden doors. Boots, coats and helmets were placed in readiness on both sides of the truck. A brass pole descended from a hole in the ceiling between the two bays.

On one side, two windows looked out from the floor watch room. The door beside them led to the rest of the station and the stairs going up to the living quarters. Toward the rear of the bay sat racks filled with rolls of spare hose and other equipment.

The other side was mostly bare except for a group of plaques on the wall. Over them hung the large brass and enamel phoenix that had graced the station's first steam pumper. Below the phoenix was a framed parchment inscribed with hundreds of names. The first name on the list was Firefighter William Thorton, the date November 24, 1848; the last was Captain Paul Fitzgerald. Fitz's plaque had joined eleven others surrounding the parchment: the men of Lombard who had not returned from their last alarm.

Donny and Eddy entered through the back door. A series of wire racks stood where the horse stalls and tack room had once been. They went to the one marked "A Platoon" to grab their gear. Donny stared at the crisp new bunker suit hanging in his stall. It was his, all right: "Robertson" was sewn in big shiny letters across the back of the jacket. It stood out like a sore thumb from the soot stained gear that hung in the other stalls.

Eddy glanced over. "They sent it last week. Your old suit got kind of fried."

"Yeah, I guess." Donny grabbed the pants and began folding the stiff new material down over the boots, so they could be stepped into as one piece.

"We salvaged some of your stuff for you." Eddy offered him several pieces of blackened metal, the odds and ends that firefighters filled their pockets with, things that might come in handy in a pinch. "The pliers are still OK. The screwdriver's handle melted, so we tossed it. The handle on your knife's burnt, but maybe you can get a new handle for it. Saint Florian's a little dirty, but…"

"Thanks, that's nice," Donny said, closing his hand over the medallion of the patron saint of firefighters. He wasn't religious, but most guys carried a talisman of some sort.

"And one more thing. Your hose key…" Eddy held out a metal bar about a foot long. There was a claw at one end for tightening hose connections, an opening in the middle that fit hydrant caps and spindles, and a handle with a flared end that could be used as a short pry bar.

"You know, Fitz always said those new aluminum ones weren't worth shit. Guess he was right — yours melted. Anyway, this was his."

Donny stared at the length of steel for a moment before taking it. He turned it slowly in his hand, as if seeing the familiar tool for the first time.

"The boys and me, we, well… we thought you should have it." Eddy paused. He could see the moisture welling in Donny's eyes, and looked away to the rack of clothes. "But, you know, Wedge, if it's not, you know... I mean, if you don't…"

"It's good," Donny said, cutting him off. "It's all good, Eddy. Thanks."

He slipped the hose key into his bunker pants and turned to carry his gear to the front of the truck. Christ, he thought, how long is this going to go on? Better get a grip, buddy, or you'll never make it through the day. Suck it up, or you can march right out of here and back to the shrink.

He walked past his old position on the back of the pumper to the right front seat, the captain's seat. Fitz's seat. He sighed, removed the gear of the C shift captain and put his own in its place. He busied himself with the routine of shift change: checked his air tank and the seal of his mask, put the flashlight back in the charger and clipped a fresh one to his coat, changed the battery on his radio. Finally, taking a deep breath, he put his helmet — his shiny new red captain's helmet — on the dashboard.

"I'm sorry, Fitz" he whispered. "I'm so sorry."

DONNY PAUSED in the kitchen doorway. It was like his first day all over again; it was like coming home, like he had never left.

If the apparatus floor was the heart of the fire station, the kitchen was its soul. Old black and white photos and framed citations circled the walls. An ancient, battered maple table and its flock of heavy curved-back wooden chairs dominated the centre of the room.

Three windows, set deep in the stonework, looked out onto Lombard Street. Across from the windows a heavy industrial stove had been serving up three meals a day for longer than Donny had been alive. Some things had changed over the years, of course: the air was no longer blue with cigarette smoke, and a dishwasher had been installed a couple of years back. But the kitchen was basically the same as it had been for generations.

Moose sat with his back to the door, his knitting needles clicking softly, as SportsCentre showed the previous day's highlights mutely on the TV. Two men from C Platoon sat sipping coffee and flipping through the morning paper. The other two were still in their bunks.

"Hey, guys," said Eddy, stepping past Donny, "look who I found sneaking into the hall."

"Jesus Christ, Wedge! Or should I say Captain Wedge. Welcome home!" Moose rose from the table. Donny almost disappeared in the big man's embrace.

Eddy poured coffees as they sat back at the table. There was a moment of awkward silence as they tried not to look at the scars that rose from Donny's collar.

"Jeez, Donny, it's good to see you back," said "Juice" Michaels, the C shift captain. "When it happened some of us wondered if you'd ever... I mean, you know... what a goddamned nightmare. Poor Fitz."

"Goddamned nightmare," echoed Moose. There was another awkward silence.

There it was, thought Donny, the one thing never talked about directly in any fire hall. They dealt with death every day, death in all of its horrid, painful reality. On a bad day they saw more tragedy than most people see in a lifetime. But it was always someone else's loss and you learned to keep it at a distance. Death was something that happened to civilians, or maybe other crews on other shifts. They needed to believe in their own invincibility.

They all knew the risks. It wasn't just the immediate danger of fire and building collapse. There were heart disease and cancer. Year by year the toxins seeped in through their skin, slowly poisoning them. Then there were HIV, tuberculosis, hepatitis and the dozens of other diseases they were exposed to. Statistics told them they were giving up several years of their own life expectancy to do a job they loved.

But still each man believed he was different. Maybe he could beat the odds. "Rationalizing the cognitive dissonance" was what the shrink had told Donny. You had to believe it or you couldn't go into a fire when even the rats and cockroaches had enough sense to run the other way.

Could he do it again? Sure, he had told the shrink and the pencil pushers, summoning all his bravado. Firefighting isn't something you just do, it's who you are.

Christ, he thought, I hope I'm right.

Donny looked around the silent table. None of the other guys could look directly at him, at the stark evidence branded into his skin.

Instead they were looking at the dark thing locked in the back corner of their own minds.

"Fortunately," said Eddy gravely, breaking the silence, "our new captain here has always been the ugliest son of a bitch in the entire TFD. I do believe the scars are actually an improvement."

"It's gonna make Halloween a lot simpler," agreed Moose, nodding.

"Now you got a built-in excuse for striking out with the ladies," offered Juice.

The tension drained away in laughter. Almost.

JUICE GAVE DONNY his hand-over report and the C shift men blearily made their way home. Donny, Eddy and Moose sat around the kitchen table trying to pretend nothing had changed. The table was the same. So were the pictures lining the wall. The department gossip they shared was indistinguishable from the rumors and stories that had been told in previous years. It wasn't Fitz's absence that made them uneasy, nor some sense of his ghostly presence. It was uncertainty. Something had been broken and none of them could be certain if it would ever work properly again.

"Spike" Therion arrived from Station 7 on Dundas Street to temporarily fill their empty fourth position. He had a reputation as a good firefighter – strong, willing and quick to learn. He was a lithe man in his late twenties, with bright eyes and a shaved head. He had gotten his name from the tattoos and piercings that covered most of his visible skin surface.

Spike dropped his duffle bag at the kitchen door and walked over to Donny. "You look good," he said, leaning over to have a closer look at Donny's scars. "I was thinking of having some branding done myself."

"I don't recommend it," Donny replied shaking Spikes proffered hand.

"Branding?" Eddy asked. "Like cattle?"

"Body modification, dude! Tats and piercing are old school. I had some pearling done on my junk. Wanna see?" Spike reached for his belt.

"No!" the men at the table answered emphatically.

"Listen Spike, it might be a couple of weeks until they fill our vacancy. Why don't you grab one of the empty lockers in the dorm?" Donny suggested.

"Good idea." Spike picked up his duffle bag and headed down the hall to the dorm.

"Pearling?" Donny asked the table at-large.

"Speed bumps. Like those ribbed condoms, only bigger and permanent," Moose replied.

"How do you know these things?" Donny gave the big man a curious look. Moose shrugged and resumed his knitting.

"Wow," Eddy shook his head, "and they gave me a hard time when I joined 'cause I had long hair."

"What are you going to do when one of your daughters brings home a guy like that?" Moose grinned.

"That's not funny Moose," Eddy scowled. He was the sort of guy who could pitch better than he could catch.

"What are you knitting, Moose?" Donny asked, changing the subject.

"A sweater for my Dad. He feels the cold a lot more since the stroke," Moose replied, holding up the intricate cable-stitch pattern for Donny to see. "He's learning to talk pretty good, but I'm not sure he'll ever walk again. Eddy and Kyle are giving me a hand with the renovations so we can get him out of the nursing home."

"That's nice, Moose. That's a real stand-up thing to do, moving your Dad in with you," Donny nodded.

"He's my Dad," Moose shrugged. "He changed my diapers enough times. And I got homecare arranged for days when we're on shift. It'll work out."

"So you're teaching Kyle how to be a carpenter now?" Donny asked, turning to Eddy.

"He better learn some kind of trade," Eddy frowned. "I'm not putting up with that attitude and him loafing around the house much longer."

"He's a teenager, Eddy, he'll grow out of it," Donny offered.

"Not if I kill him first, he won't. Anyway, what the hell do you know about raising kids?"

Donny held his hands up in surrender. At least the bickering had diffused the awkward tension they had all felt earlier.

"So how's it feel to be back and in charge?" Spike asked as he sauntered back into the kitchen.

Donny ran his hand over his chin and looked at the ceiling for a moment. "I don't know, Spike. I'll tell you this much, it's a hell of a lot better than being in the hospital or doing therapy."

They finished their coffee and the day settled into the regular routine. Moose washed and dried the truck, then went through each compartment, checking that every piece of equipment was where it should be and in good condition.

Eddy and Spike looked after the stoking, a term left over from the days when coal furnaces actually had to be stoked. They swept, mopped, washed and emptied. They were, Fitz had liked to say, the city's highest-paid janitors.

Donny sat behind the big oak desk in the captain's office. The room was a testament to the craftsmanship of nineteenth-century cabinet making and carpentry. A row of wooden lockers lined one side of the room, and a Murphy bed blended into the wainscoting on the other side. Like the kitchen, the office was ringed with old pictures, mostly of the nineteen men who had served as captain of Pumper 6.

It was a room Donny knew well, but it felt different. He tried to lose himself in the day's paperwork, but he found himself thinking back over the series of events that had led him here.

Donny had originally come to Lombard as a probie, fresh out of the Fire Academy. Fitz had been the Senior Man. The politically correct term was the generic "acting captain": a person waiting his or her turn on the promotional list. However, the fire service's greatest strength and perhaps its greatest weakness was its sense of tradition.

The years had passed; Fitz was promoted to Captain and helped Donny prepare for the grueling series of written, oral and practical exams that would qualify him for promotion. The wheel turned full circle and Donny became Senior Man. It had been Donny's fondest hope that he would one day return to Lombard as Captain. But not like this.

Eddy knocked on the frame of the open office door, walked in, flopped in a chair and put his feet up on the desk. "Sorry I snapped at you back there, Wedge. That boy is driving me crazy."

Eduardo Moleiro had the dark complexion, dark eyes and dark wavy hair of his Portuguese ancestors. In recent years some of that hair had begun to migrate from the top of his head to his ears and back. He was a bit shorter than Donny. Despite Eddy's love of cooking and even greater love of eating, his dedication to soccer and a part-time renovation business kept him in reasonable shape.

"It's OK. Anyway, you're right, what do I know about kids?" Donny shrugged. "Take your feet off the desk, please."

Eddy ignored him. "I don't know what's wrong with him. He's no dummy and he's good with his hands. He's just got no ambition, no drive."

Donny tapped Eddy's shoes with a ruler. Eddy shifted his feet to the edge of the desk.

"Linda's at her wits' end too," Eddy continued, "and I'll tell you, that's something when a Portuguese mother gives up on her son. I always thought the girls would be more worry, you know, but neither of them gave us any real trouble. Ah, they squabble with Linda sometimes, but that's what women do, right?"

Donny gave up on Eddy's feet and nodded mutely.

"I don't know, maybe we spoiled Kyle. He's the youngest and the only boy…"

The alert tones sounded over the PA. Saved by the bell, Donny thought. "Pumper 6, Pumper 5, Aerial 5, Rescue 1, Chief 41, respond at four zero King Street West, alarms activated on the thirtyseventh floor. Tactical channel 3, acknowledge."

They were on the pole before the dispatch announcement was finished. An uneasy feeling nagged at Donny as he stepped into his boots and pulled up the bunker pants. He knew what it was, but it surprised him just the same. Moose was setting the truck radio to channel 3 as Donny zipped up his coat and climbed into the cab. Eddy and Spike were already in the back, strapping on their breathing apparatus.

A few seconds later they were weaving their way through the morning rush hour, lights flashing and sirens blaring amid the seemingly indifferent traffic.

They knew the smell as soon as they stepped onto the thirtyseventh floor. Burnt toast in a staff room had set off the smoke detector. Donny cleared the other crews and they returned to the truck. He felt a wave of relief wash over him as they stowed their masks in the seat-back brackets.

"Let's take the scenic route home, Moose. Take a loop up Yonge Street, then we can come back down Church, stop at the bakery and we'll pick up some goodies. My treat, boys."

"Celebrating getting your cherry broke again, Cap?" asked a voice from the back.

"I guess you could say that, Spike."

"It's good to be back together," said Moose as he deftly pulled the truck into traffic. "It's going to be OK."

They rode the rest of the way in silence. Moose was a gentle giant with a heart to match. His grey eyes twinkled under a thatch of close-cropped hair. He was a man of enormous strength, with hands the size of dinner plates. A fire axe looked like a hatchet in his hand.

It was Moose who had pulled Donny out when the fire had flashed over. Moose fighting back the flames with a 65 in one hand, a hose that normally took two men to manage, and dragging Donny to safety with the other. No one else could have done it.

Donny looked over at the big man and considered the debt he did not owe and could never repay.

THREE
The Probie

DONALD MICHAEL ROBERTSON was a tall, thin man. It looked like he hadn't so much grown as a child, as been stretched. He had a narrow, protruding chin, thin mouth and button nose, but his eyes were wide and blue, and his brow was topped with a mass of tight coppery curls. His arms dangled gawkily at his sides, his neck was too long, and his Adam's apple protruded a bit too far, but this awkwardness belied a strength made of equal parts wiry sinew and sheer determination.

Donny hadn't grown up wanting to be a fireman. He hadn't grown up wanting to be anything in particular, except away — away from the small northern Ontario mining town where odd-looking little boys had to fight their way out of the schoolyard; away from the home where, beaten by life, his father had retreated into the bottle and his mother had just retreated. Donny left home right after high school to see what the world might offer other than quiet desperation.

He drifted across the country working at this and that, but there was always something missing. Donny wasn't sure what it was, but if he was going to spend the rest of his life at a job, there had to be more to it than just work and money. He'd be damned if he was going to let just living suck the life out of him as it had done to his parents.

Then one day he saw the ad in the newspaper: The Toronto Fire Department. Why not?

After a series of tests, interviews, medical exams, and what had seemed like endless weeks in the Fire Academy, Probationary Firefighter Donald Robertson crunched over the fresh January snow and walked into Station 6 for the first time.

He was early, an hour before shift change, and the hall was dark. Don't be late on your first day, they had told him in the Academy. Keep your eyes and ears open and your mouth shut. And bring food, lots of it.

The station was dark and quiet. It smelled faintly of smoke and diesel fumes. Donny gazed at the truck gleaming dully in the night lights. His truck. "Pumper 6, TFD" — there it was, written in large scrolling gold letters on the front door.

Fire coats hung beside each door, with boots rolled down waiting to be stepped into. On the floor behind the truck were stacks of rolled hose, wet and dirty with soot. A small voice somewhere deep inside told him, "This is it. This is what you've been looking for."

He found the floor watch room and put his grocery bags down. "Excuse me? I'm Don Robertson, the new guy on A Platoon."

The man slumped in the floor watch chair opened his eyes and regarded him blearily. "What?" he mumbled.

"I'm Don, the new recruit on A."

"Great. Tell someone who gives a damn." The man looked at the clock over the floor watch desk. It registered just after five a.m. "Ah Christ, we only got back to the station half an hour ago. You're way early, so why don't you go grab a nice big steaming cup of shut-the-fuck-up and leave me alone, probie."

"Sorry, I need a slim jim. My car… I kind of goofed." He laughed nervously. No one at the Academy had told him not to lock his keys in his car with his fire gear still in the trunk.

The man glared at him. "You're a real piece of work, aren't you, kid? Aldrich is just going to love you. Over the wheel well, driver's side." The man slumped back down in the chair.

Donny found the slim jim among the other tools in the

compartment. After ten minutes of fishing in his car door he managed to pop the lock, get the keys and retrieve his gear.

HE SAT IN THE KITCHEN, sipping coffee and mulling over the wreck he had made of his debut. Maybe no one would find out. Maybe the man in the floor watch chair would forget.

A silver-haired man with a neat grey moustache strode into the kitchen. His pale blue uniform shirt was crisply pressed, two silver bars shone on his epaulets, and his black tie was held perfectly straight by a clip with a golden bird in a nest of red.

Donny stood up but said nothing. The man stopped, regarded him for a moment, then turned and plugged in the kettle. He turned back.

"You would be Donald, I suppose, our new B & E artist?" He arched an eyebrow.

Donny felt himself blush. "Yes, sir," he stammered, "Don Robertson. I'm sorry about the car thing, I…"

"Hmm, yes. I'm Captain John Aldrich. I like tea in the morning, Donald. See if you can remember that. Mr. Paul Fitzgerald is the Senior Man. He is in charge of your training while you're here on probation. If he tells you something, you may assume it came directly from me or God. Any questions, Donald?"

"No, sir."

Another man entered the kitchen. "G'morning, Cap," he said, ignoring Donny. "Did you and Mary have a good New Year's?"

"It was very nice, the grandchildren were all there. How's your brood?"

"They're all fine. I'll tell you, though, I'm not sure who's worse, teenage boys or teenage girls."

"Ah, well, the reason you have children is so you can have grandchildren. You'll see one day. Oh, Fitz, this is Donald," the Captain waved distractedly in Donny's direction. "See what you can do with him. And try not to let him lock himself in anywhere."

THEY MADE AN odd-looking pair. Whereas Donny was wiry, Fitz was short and broad-shouldered. He had the look of a boxer, with dark eyes close set under a heavy brows. His broad, flat nose had obviously been broken at least once, but his chin looked like it could shatter a sledgehammer. If a bulldog were reincarnated in human form, he would look like Fitz.

Their first call was for smoke on the fourteenth floor of an office building. As the truck roared through the morning traffic, Donny tried to remember everything he had learned about high-rise procedures. He steeled himself to face the towering inferno.

Fitz sniffed once as they stepped onto the fourteenth floor. "Ballast," he said to Aldrich.

"Yup," agreed the Captain. Aldrich spoke into his radio and cleared the other trucks.

Donny wore a puzzled expression. "But there's smoke," he declared, looking at the light grey haze that hung just below the ceiling tiles.

"You smell that?" Fitz asked him. Donny nodded. "Remember that smell. Every fluorescent fixture has a ballast that controls the electrical current. When they burn out, that's what they smell like. Nothing else smells like that."

They poked their heads into the space above the ceiling tiles to make sure an errant spark wasn't smouldering in the dust and cobwebs, then they left.

"It's all about the smoke," Fitz said to Donny as they climbed back onto the truck. "The smell, colour, density and movement of the smoke will tell you a lot about a fire: what's burning, how fast, how much air the fire's getting, where it might spread to next."

As the weeks passed Donny learned to recognize the smell of burning garbage and burnt food, but he faced nothing more dangerous than a smouldering dumpster and a blackened pan of chicken.

They responded to car accidents, heart attacks and elevator rescues.

Between calls, Donny's days were split between training and cleaning the station, truck and equipment. As Junior Man he was given all the worst jobs, from cleaning the toilets to scrubbing the apparatus floor. He was also the brunt of endless practical jokes.

They responded to construction accidents, overdoses and carbon monoxide alarms.

The theoretical part of his training came out of the "Drill Book," with its chapters on hydraulics, pump operations, building construction, fire code regulations and so on. Practical training included how to use the "jaws of life," the myriad uses of rope, how to tie a dozen different knots blindfolded, and how to safely work off a ladder with saws and axes.

They responded to stabbings, suicides and gas leaks.

Fitz stood by with a stopwatch as Donny dragged the heavy suction hose off the back of the truck, connected it to the pump's intake, flushed the hydrant, connected the gate valves, and finally hooked up the suction and turned on the hydrant. They did it over and over and over until Donny could do it consistently in two and a half minutes. The truck carried enough water in its tank to supply one 38-mm hose line for barely three minutes. It wasn't much of a safety margin if something went wrong.

They responded for fallen electrical wires, helped deliver a baby and went to dozens of false alarms; everything but the proverbial cat in a tree. And still there were no serious fires.

It wasn't that he wanted anyone's house to burn down, Donny complained to Fitz one day. It was just that he wanted to prove that he could to do it, that he had what it takes, that he could face whatever the job had to throw at him.

"Be careful what you wish for," was Fitz's only comment.

The evenings were Donny's favourite part of the day. After supper, with the day's chores behind them, things became more relaxed. Aldrich, Fitz, Donny and Turk, the fourth member of the crew, would sit around the kitchen table. The dominoes would come out, Capt. Aldrich would fill his pipe and inevitably the stories would begin. Sometimes it would be incidents from only a few years back. Sometimes it would be stories that Aldrich's first captain had told him as a rookie. Other stories had seeped into the bricks and mortar of the station itself, to become part of the living oral tradition of the job.

There were stories of heroic rescues, near misses, comical blunders and unspeakable tragedies, all punctuated by the slap of the dominoes on the kitchen table and wreaths of fragrant blue smoke from Aldrich's pipe. There was always a lesson: how neglect had caused a horse harness to fail, leading to a crash that had crippled the driver; how noticing a pile of empty food cans outside the door of a burning abandoned warehouse had led to the rescue of a homeless woman...

Donny drank it all in, like a man who had been thirsty all his life and had finally been brought to the well. He loved feeling a part of something larger than himself, something that stretched back for generations, something noble and good. He loved looking at the pictures of magnificently moustachioed men, sleek horses and gleaming apparatus that lined the kitchen walls. Here was the family he had always wanted.

THE "DRY SPELL" ENDED with Donny's first month at Lombard. It was just after one a.m. when the call came in for a fire in Cabbagetown. Donny's pulse was racing as he slid down the pole, jumped into his gear and boarded the truck. Turk swerved the truck in and out of the late-night traffic as Donny checked and rechecked his gear. Please, God, he prayed silently, don't let me screw up.

Fitz reached over, patted him on the shoulder and smiled. "It's going to be OK. Just stay right on my tail. If I reach around to scratch my ass, I want to feel you there."

They were the second truck to arrive. Pumper 11 crew were attacking the fire in the ground-floor living room, and Turk went to help their driver hook up to the hydrant. Aldrich, Fitz and Donny slipped on their face pieces and took a line to the second floor for search and rescue.

The fire had started with a faulty electrical cord. A newspaper tossed onto the floor spread the fire to a side table and couch. It was a relatively small fire, and Pumper 11 had it knocked down by the time Aldrich's crew reached the top of the stairs. The heat upstairs was less than some of the training fires Donny had experienced at the academy, but the foam rubber cushions of the burning couch had filled the house with thick black smoke. Donny's flash light penetrated only a few inches into the murk.

They split up at the top of the stairs. Fitz and Donny headed to the back of the house while Aldrich moved down the hallway to the front. They crawled, sweeping their hands in front of them. They had gone only a few feet when Aldrich called out, "I've got a big one, Fitz."

"Go help the Captain. I'm going to keep searching," Fitz barked. Aldrich announced their find over the radio.

Donny had started to feel disappointed. The fire seemed to be over almost before it started. Now his heart was pounding again. He turned, took a couple of steps and stumbled over Aldrich.

"Careful. Get the legs, I've got the shoulders."

Donny groped in the blackness. "Got 'em," he called when he had secured a grip.

"Let's go," said Aldrich.

Their victim weighed a good 250 pounds, Donny reckoned. It was all dead weight, too, loose and floppy. It was awkward maintaining a grip and walking backwards down the stairs blind.

Turk met them at the front door with the oxygen kit. They set the patient down on the lawn. It was a woman, Donny could see now, clad in a nightgown. The fabric was black with soot. So were her face and body, except where Donny and Aldrich's grip had wiped it away, revealing the pale skin underneath. There were no signs of burns or charring. She looked almost like she was sleeping, her hair spilled carelessly around her lolling head.

Aldrich started compressions on the big woman's chest while Turk fitted an airway into her throat and started the flow of oxygen. "Get back in there and help Fitz," Aldrich ordered. "There may be more."

Donny heard Fitz's footsteps at the top of the stairs as he started to climb. They met halfway. "Here, take him," Fitz said simply. He transferred his burden into Donny's outstretched arms. He didn't need to see to know it was the body of a child.

Donny rushed back outside and dropped to his knees a few feet from Aldrich and Turk. He ripped off his SCBA and blew into the tiny mouth. There was a foul taste of acrid smoke. The lips were soft and warm, but totally lifeless. The sensation horrified him.

He placed his hands on the little chest and began pumping. He looked up to see Fitz emerge with another rag-doll bundle.

More crews arrived along with paramedics and cops. Donny focused on the steady rhythm of his compressions and the green and yellow teddy bears on the soot-stained pyjamas beneath his hands.

Someone tapped Donny on the shoulder and a team of paramedics took over care of the child. Donny stood and blinked dumbly at the scene around him. It was a blur of flashing lights, squawking radios and frantic activity. Fire crews were setting up lights and fans. Three bodies, two small and one large, were loaded into ambulances that wailed off into the night. Fitz appeared at Donny's side, took his arm and steered him away. They sat without speaking on the back step of the truck, steam rising from the collars of their fire coats into the February night air.

"That was a shitty call," Fitz said after a while. "That's about as bad as it gets."

Donny stared at his boots. "They just looked dirty, you know, like you could just wash them off and they'd be…" His voice cracked. Donny swallowed hard. "It wasn't even much of a fire, really."

Fitz sighed and looked up into the cold black night. "Like I said before, it's all about the smoke. Almost nobody burns to death."

A fierce anger welled up inside Donny. He wanted to scream, to smash something, to do anything that would erase the memory of the green and yellow teddy bears and the feel of those lifeless lips. He took a deep breath and felt the anger shifting towards a quiet resolve. He turned and looked at Fitz with an intensity the older man had never seen before.

"Teach me. Teach me everything. I'll do whatever you say and I won't complain."

Neither man would ever be able to put it into words, but it was a watershed moment in both their lives. Fitz shared the arcane knowledge that came from twenty years of firefighting and Donny became his disciple. Training was no longer a duty. Donny knew now that it was literally a matter of life and death.

THE PRACTICAL JOKES stopped for a while after the townhouse fire. Then about a month later, returning from a call, Capt. Aldrich looked over to see Donny's socks dripping something sticky and yellow as he took off his fire boots.

"What happened, Donald?"

"I don't know, Cap. I guess some lonely chicken laid eggs in my boots."

"Christ on a crutch!" roared the captain. He stormed out of the apparatus bay into the floor watch room and grabbed the microphone.

"Everyone in the kitchen. NOW!" Aldrich's voice boomed over the station PA.

Captain Aldrich sat at the end of the table. He was normally unflappable even at the most serious calls. Now he was livid.

"Who did it? Which one of you *idiots* put the eggs in Donald's boots?" He spat out the word "idiots" with contempt.

He looked first at Fitz but his gaze finally rested on Turk. He didn't really expect a confession. He would have been even more surprised and disappointed if any of them had ratted the culprit out.

"You know my rules. They're few and simple. You all know better than to mess with a man's fire clothes. Am I right?" He glanced around the table again. "AM I RIGHT?"

"Yes, Cap," came the chorus of replies.

"Very well, then. I want Donald's boots thoroughly cleaned and dried immediately." He looked at Donny. "Do you know who did this, son?"

"No, Cap." It was the truth. Donny had his suspicions but no proof. Aldrich knew it too, but he also knew he couldn't set the kid apart. It could turn the crew against him, and he was a good kid. He would bind them together again.

"I think you do," Aldrich stated, "and I don't like being lied to. You will all get your toothbrushes and a can of Varsol. You too, Donald. I want the underside of that truck gleaming by the end of this shift."

He stood and turned to leave, then paused and looked back at them one last time. He spoke quietly now. "That gear, your mask, a bit of hose: that's all that stands between us and the beast. You don't mess with that. I am disappointed, gentlemen, very disappointed." He left the room. His words were sharper than the sting of any lash.

After a moment, Fitz stood and glared menacingly at Turk. "I'm going to get my toothbrush. You ever pull a stunt like that again, I'll kill you myself."

Donny knew better than to say anything. He headed to the truck.

THEY WERE LYING on their backs under the truck, scrubbing away at the accumulated grease and grime, when it happened. Fitz looked over at Donny, "Hey, Wedge, pass me that can of Varsol."

"Uh, sure," Donny replied and slid it over. Turk smiled, nodded at Fitz and went back to work.

It was a tradition at Lombard that the Senior Man was responsible for the naming of new crew members. It had been over two months now and he remained not Don, not Donny, but "Donald." It was a bridge of acceptance he had not yet been allowed to cross.

Sometimes it was a simple contraction of their surname, like Fitz. Sometimes it was a mixture of humour and tough love, like Turk, whose real name, Aristedes Stavros, was about as Greek as you could get. Some names stuck like glue, others were used only occasionally. But it was a rite of passage.

Donny scrubbed quietly, but after a couple of minutes his curiosity got the better of him. "Wedge?" he asked. "'Cause I'm tall and thin?"

"Nope," replied Fitz without missing a beat, "it's the simplest tool known to man." Turk erupted in laughter, and any remaining tension and resentment melted away.

Later that evening, with the bottom of the truck as clean as the day it was built and the toothbrushes tossed in the garbage, Fitz walked into the captain's office and closed the door. He sat on the corner of the big oak desk.

"I named him Wedge."

Aldrich looked at Fitz over the top of his glasses. Fitz told him how Donny had walked face first right into it. Aldrich chuckled. "Good time for it, Fitz. I don't like seeing divisions in the crew. It's no good for anyone. That's why I put the lad under there with you. I'm sorry, I had to put you there too."

"I know."

"He's a good kid, and a hard worker. With a little seasoning he'll make a fine firefighter. You might want to keep an eye on young Wedge. You'll be getting made soon. When you get your own truck, Fitz, you'll want to gather good men around you. Sometimes the simplest tools are the best ones."

FOUR
Debrief

"IT NEVER SHOULD HAVE FLASHED."

The pastry boxes from the bakery sat empty on the kitchen table. The crew leaned back in their chairs and considered Donny's statement. They had filled in reports and statements, they had testified to the coroner's inquest, but until now they had never really talked about the fire. Not together, not as a crew.

"I tell you, boys," Donny repeated, "it shouldn't have flashed over. Not that quick."

As the temperature rises in a fire, the room contents — furniture, rugs, wallpaper, everything — begin to char, giving off flammable vapours. At about 550°C (around 1000°F), everything that can burn simultaneously bursts into flame, and the entire room instantly becomes a raging inferno. A firefighter caught in a flashover has only a few seconds to escape.

"This thing came out of nowhere. Somebody gave that fire a helping hand," concluded Donny.

"The investigator said it was clean. No traces of gasoline, diesel or any other accelerant," offered Eddy.

"How come none of the investigators look like the chicks on CSI?" mused Spike. They stared at him. "I'm just saying, you know, in real life they're mostly guys and they're all nerdy and geeky."

"What about the hydrogen tank?" Donny asked, bringing them

back to the subject. "The company was into that fuel cell, zero emissions stuff, right? I never saw it, but I heard there was a big tank of hydrogen on site."

"They checked that," Eddy said, shaking his head. "The hydrogen tank was outside, across the parking lot. The fire never got near it. All the supply lines to the building were shut down and the safety valves were good. Everything was kosher. And anyway, hydrogen explodes, right? Remember the Space Shuttle?"

"That fire just got away from us." Eddy paused for a moment, wondering if he should finish the thought. "It's not your fault, Donny. Shit happens."

Donny looked hard across the table, his whole body tensed. Eddy wasn't sure if Donny was going to take a swing at him or cry.

"He's right, Cap," said Moose quietly, putting down his knitting.

Donny looked down and sighed. "Maybe. I don't know. Just… humour me, OK?"

They gave silent consent. "So the call comes in at about ten o'clock at night, from the alarm company, right? Industrial building on Commissioners Street."

"Right," Eddy confirmed.

"OK. And the three closest stations just happen to be out already, so the fire's got a good head start by the time we finally get there. That's a handy coincidence.

"Then the water main is shut down, so there's no sprinklers in the building and we gotta run the suction all the way back to Cherry Street to catch a hydrant. That's handy coincidence number two."

"But we knew that going in," said Eddy. "We got notified about the water main that morning. I wrote it on the board myself."

"And how do you sabotage a water main?" asked Moose. "Hydrants, sure, but the mains are buried six feet deep."

"I don't know, Moose. I don't know." Donny shook his head. "Anyway, the main body of the fire was in the main assembly area, but it was also burning in the office area, where the other body was. Coincidence number three: two fires in one building. Accidental fires don't start in two places at the same time, boys."

"But they do spread, Cap," suggested Spike. "It could have travelled through the ductwork or something."

"I tell you, it was too quick. I saw the angel fingers, and whoosh! Normally you've got ten, fifteen, maybe twenty seconds, right? Fitz would have seen it. We should have had time to back out."

"I was following your hose line when it happened," said Moose. "It was like walking into a blowtorch. I had the 65 wide open but it was still blowing back along the ceiling right over my head. I don't know, maybe if I'd dropped the hose I could have got Captain Fitz too."

"Drop that hose, Moose, and we would have been burying three men instead of one." The voice came from the doorway. They stood as District Chief Joe Razzolini walked into the kitchen.

"Good morning, Chief," said Donny. He moved over as Razzolini took the chair at the head of the table.

"Ratzo" Razzolini had been in the same recruit class as Donny. They had been defence partners on the Department hockey team back when they were several years younger and Ratzo was fifty pounds lighter. He was bright and capable, and he knew which side of the political toast the butter was on. He had risen fast through the ranks and was clearly destined for the upper echelons.

"Good morning. Sit down, guys. Moose, that was the most amazing rescue I've ever seen, but you never would have made it without that line in your hand. There's nothing you could have done for Fitz." He smiled at the big man, then looked over at Donny. "Licking an old wound?"

Donny shrugged. "Just kind of going over it, you know."

"Hmm."

"Cap thinks it was set up," volunteered Spike. Donny glared at him.

"Really?" Ratzo put his hands on the table. "Let me tell you something. Everyone has been through this with a fine-tooth comb: the fire marshal's office, the coroner, the cops, Department of Labour, everybody. No one found anything out of place, no trace of arson or anything else.

"What happened that night was a terrible tragedy. It's the worst thing that can happen to us. We lost a good man, one of the best there was, a leader, a friend and a brother."

He looked around the table at each of them. "It's natural to want to find a reason for what happened. But sometimes there is no reason. Sometimes we just lose. Pray to God none of us ever has to go through that again."

His voice softened "We gotta let it go. If you want, I can arrange for the City to send a grief counsellor to help you guys work through this."

"A suit? It's OK, Chief," Eddy spoke up. "We had that already."

"You sure?" They all nodded.

"OK, good." Razzolini paused. "What do you think Fitz would have said?"

"He would have said, 'Suck it up, ladies, suck it up,'" Moose answered. They all chuckled.

"Damn right," said the Chief. "So, shall we get on with it?" He opened his briefcase, pulled out a sheaf of papers and began reading.

"Clothing orders are due. If you need to change your size on anything, you have until the end of the month to let the quartermaster know. And no," he looked around the room, "just to put the rumour to rest, I did not go up yet another waist size this year.

"There's a couple of notices from the union here. Read them at your leisure." He slid a pile of papers onto the table. "OK, here's the biggie: transfers. Congratulations, Eddy, you're being promoted to Acting Captain on Aerial 29."

"Aerial 29? You're kidding me, Chief. I'm a downtown guy — why are they sending me to Forest Hill? I'll die of boredom. I was hoping I could just stay here. I mean, we need a senior man here, right?"

"It's out of my hands, Eddy. I'd love to keep you in the district, but you know how they like to move the senior men around, broaden their horizons and all that. Let's see…" he shuffled the papers in front of him, "here it is. Richard Weber is coming here. He's from Leaside, B shift. I think they call him 'Stick.' Anybody know him?"

"He was in my district when I was a recruit out in Swansea," offered Moose. "He's OK, I guess."

"Well, that's who you're getting. And you're getting a probie next week to fill your fourth position. Susan Ko… Koza… Ko-za-ro-vitch." He sounded out each syllable.

"Susan?" asked Donny.

"Yeah, Kozarovitch, I think that's how you say it. You got a problem with that?" replied the Chief, an edge creeping into his voice.

"I guess not, as long as she's qualified."

"She's as qualified as any other probie. Your job, Captain Robertson, is to train and evaluate her fairly. None of us started out as God's gift to fire fighting."

"OK," conceded Donny. "We've just never had a woman here before, Chief. Normally I wouldn't care. Black, white, male, female, it's all the same. You could send me a green left-handed lesbian dwarf as long as she can do the job…"

"Good. I don't want to hear any more about it, then." Ratzo cut him off with finality.

Donny frowned at Razzolini and shook his head. "No. This is too much all at once. This isn't just any station, Chief, this is Lombard. I'm just getting back, and now you're sending me some guy from the god-damned suburbs as a senior man? And a probie too? A female probie? Here? I can't believe it!"

"That's enough!" roared the Chief. "In the office, right now!"

RAZZOLINI SLAMMED the door of the captain's office behind him. His face was red, and he struggled to control his anger. He paced back and forth in front of the door as Donny stood awkwardly in front of the desk.

"Who the hell do you think you are? And where do you get off talking to me like that in front of the men? You think this is the Donny Robertson Fire Department? You think the whole damned job revolves around Lombard and what you want?"

"Look, I…"

"No, *you* look. I will not put up with you sulking because you didn't get a first round draft pick. You got that?"

"I'm sorry, I didn't mean to…"

"Shut up! I went out on a limb for you. I called in a lot of favours to get you back here. I convinced the brass that it would be good for everyone to put you back with your old crew." Ratzo stopped pacing and crossed to stare out the window. "Now I wonder if that was such a good idea."

"Listen, Chief, I appreciate what you did. I was out of line."

"Damn right you were!" Ratzo turned back and leaned against the sill. He pointed to the door and the kitchen beyond. "What about them? You think this helps them any? You think that's how you build a crew — by casting doubt on new people before they even get here? Is that leadership? Fitz would puke if he saw that."

Donny's head sank. "You're right. He'd never do that." It was what he had always wanted: to carry on from Fitz and Aldrich and all the others who had gone before; to be a good firefighter and a leader of men. He had failed. His first day in charge and he had failed miserably.

Razzolini crossed to the front of the desk and sat on a corner. He gestured to the chair across the room. "Sit down. Listen, that was a cheap shot. I guess that makes us even, OK?"

"Sure, Chief." Donny couldn't meet his gaze.

"Forget the Chief shit. This is me, Wedge, this is Ratzo talking.

Look at me." Donny looked up and saw that Ratzo's anger had been replaced by concern.

"We all screw up from time to time, Donny, even the Great Ratzo. Thankfully, not too badly and not too often. And I usually find someone else to blame." He winked and Donny smiled. "So forget about it. It's over. OK?"

Donny nodded.

"You've been through hell and back, Donny. Everybody knows that. If you need a little more time off, I'll arrange it, no problem."

Donny snorted, "That's all I need: 'Hey, you hear about Wedge? He's lost it. He folded like a cheap suit on his first day back.'"

He paused. "Everything used to flow, you know what I mean? Fitz, he was like oil, smooth all the time, even when the shit was real bad. I'm all jumpy and everything feels… weird. I need to get the rhythm back, that's all. I think I just need to get back on the wet end of a hose."

"Maybe," Ratzo allowed. "But you don't have to be Fitz either. Just be yourself, Donny, that's good enough. Mostly you need to put it all behind you. That's Dr. Ratzo's prescription. If you carry this around with you, it will eat you alive."

Donny shook his head sadly. "So we put another name on the honour roll, we all salute and just put it behind us like it never happened? Is that all a man's life means?"

"I don't know, Donny. Maybe it means he stayed one fire too long. Don't give me that look. The man had forty-one years on the job. His pension was maxed out. He was working for practically nothing. Anna told me at the funeral that she had begged him for years to retire, but he wouldn't, because the job was his whole life.

"You want the hard truth, old buddy? That's one way you are just like him. You got anything else in your life besides that boat? Jesus, Donny, when was the last time you were even out on a date?"

"And you're so different, *District Chief* Razzolini?"

"Yes, I am. Sure, I got ambition. If I can make Commander, or

Deputy, or even Fire Chief, great. Maybe I can even make the job a little better along the way. But when I've got my thirtyfive years, I'm gone. I'm moving up to the lake. I'm gonna teach my grandkids how to swim. And when I'm sixtytwo, I'm sure as hell not going to be humping hose into a burning building."

They looked at each other across the no man's land of silence.

"You know what the worst part of being in hospital was, Ratzo? It wasn't the pain or the boredom or any of that. It was the itch. Sometimes I'd get this itch under the bandages. I couldn't get at it and it wouldn't go away.

"That's what it's like. I *know* that fire was set up. I know it in my guts."

Ratzo gave up. "Listen, what you do on your own time is your business. What you do here is mine, *capisce*?"

The alarm tones sounded. Donny got up and moved to the door.

"And one more thing," Razzolini shouted over the dispatch announcement. "You behave yourself with this woman probie. If I end up handling a harassment case, I swear to God you will finish your career counting paper clips in the Quartermaster's office."

FIVE
Red Bird

THE REST OF THE DAY went better. They had a small kitchen fire, a Beemer that lost an argument with a transport truck, as well as the routine medical calls and false alarms — the usual assortment of mayhem and destruction. But no one had died, civilian or otherwise, so all in all it was a good day. Things had begun to assume their normal rhythm. Donny had even managed to get a few hours' sleep, and despite the twenty-four-hour shift, he felt refreshed the next morning. It was time to get the rest of his life back on track too.

He bounced up on the Norton's kick starter and the bike snorted to life. Instead of going home, he headed east along the lakeshore to Ashbridges Bay Marina.

It was mid-May, and most of the boats were already back in the water after winter layup. Halyards chimed softly against masts as the boats bobbed lazily at the dock. The sun was just over the horizon, washing them with golden light. Gulls wheeled and squawked in the clear blue sky.

Red Bird rested in her cradle at the back of the boatyard, still shrouded in her winter cover. She had been sitting there for two winters now, since before the fire, while Donny recovered from his injuries. He parked the bike and walked over to her. He ran his fingers lightly along the waterline, and then began untying the cover straps. Before long he had the big canvas cover folded and the aluminum frame that supported it dismantled.

Red Bird was an Island Packet 35: a rugged, cutter-rigged sloop. Donny had picked her up in Florida as an insurance writeoff. *Señor Suerte,* Spanish for "Mr. Lucky," as the boat had then been named, had come loose of its mooring during a hurricane and fetched up on a sand bar. Salt water and sand had ruined the interior and electronics, but the hull and rigging were undamaged. Donny bought the boat for a fraction of its true value, had it trucked north and spent the next several years lovingly refitting it.

Sailing tradition said that renaming a boat brought bad luck, but Donny reasoned that the gods were none too pleased with *Mr. Lucky* as things stood. Still, he took the requisite precautions. He wasn't an overly superstitious man, but as any experienced sailor knows, being careful is an essential part of good seamanship.

So Donny had ritually burned the boat's old log book and disposed of anything else inscribed with the name *Señor Suerte.* He had sanded the offending name from the transom and washed the hull with rum; then, invoking the gods of wind and sea, he had broken a bottle of champagne over the bow and renamed her *Red Bird.* On either side of her bow he had had an artist paint a phoenix, wings outstretched, perched in a nest of flame.

He walked over to the marina office and booked the travel lift to pick *Red Bird* off her cradle and lay her in the water later that morning.

And then what? Where did he go from here? The question could apply on any of several fronts. It was one thing to put a boat in the water, quite another to chart a course, particularly when you weren't sure what the destination was.

While he was in the hospital, all he had thought about was getting out and getting back on the truck. Maybe Ratzo was right: what did he have in his life besides thirtyfive feet of fibreglass and teak, and a job that had killed his best friend and damn near killed him too?

"HELLO?"

"Hi, Cap, it's Wedge. How are you doing?"

"Donny! I'm doing well. And yourself?"

"I'm OK, Cap. Back on the truck, you know. It's good."

"I'm not Captain any longer, just plain old John Aldrich these days. You're the Captain of Lombard now. Congratulations."

"Thanks. Old habits. 'John' just doesn't sound right. Listen, I was wondering if you could spare me an hour or two."

"I'm retired, Donny. What do I have but time?"

"How about lunch? I'm down at the marina working on the boat, but I can hop over to the deli and pick something up for us, if you don't mind coming down here."

"Sounds great. It would do me good to get out of the house. You sure you're OK?"

Donny hadn't intended to call. The phone had just appeared in his hand, with the old man's number staring at him. Why not? thought Donny. When all else fails, go back to the beginning.

RED BIRD WAS floating in her slip and Donny was tightening the shrouds that supported her newly raised mast when he saw Aldrich pull into the parking lot. Donny stowed his tools and walked down the dock to meet him.

John Aldrich was now in his mid-seventies. His hair was completely white and his face deeply wrinkled. He walked with a limp, leaning on a gnarled and polished walking stick. Though he was beginning to stoop, he was still every inch a proper gentleman. As ever, his moustache was neatly trimmed and his clothes smartly pressed.

They shook hands and walked back to the boat. Aldrich looked at the phoenix painted on the bow.

"Ah, there's no mistaking this boat, is there? Permission to come aboard?"

"Absolutely. I guess you haven't seen her before."

"No. I think you got this one just after I retired. I was on your old boat once or twice, but I'm afraid I'm more of a landlubber."

Donny extended his hand and helped the older man climb aboard. "Let me give you the tour." Aldrich listened patiently as Donny showed him around the boat, describing the refit in the sort of detail only another sailor might appreciate.

"Very nice," Aldrich said when he had heard enough. "I don't understand half of what you've told me, but she's a fine-looking boat. May you have fair winds and calm seas. Now, I think I need to sit down."

Donny helped him back out to the cockpit. Aldrich sat stiffly. "Hmm, that sun feels nice. The arthritis devils my back and knees. It's from the Woolworths warehouse fire, before you got on. Half the building came down on us. It's a wonder we got out alive. But I know you've heard that story more than a few times. It's a terrible price we pay." He could see the distorted pink skin above the collar of Donny's T-shirt. "But then I guess you know that too, don't you?"

"I guess so. Ham sandwiches and potato salad OK with you, Cap?" Donny stepped down into the galley to prepare lunch.

"That'll be just fine, Donny."

They chatted about the latest department gossip as Donny prepared the sandwiches. He climbed back out into the cockpit, carrying a tray with the food and two beers. He held one out to Aldrich.

"It's a bit early for me, but seeing as it's a special occasion, I'll relent. Here's to old friends and new beginnings."

"Cheers," replied Donny, clinking bottles. He took a swallow and offered Aldrich a plate. "Help yourself. So how are the grandkids?"

"They're grown up. A few have started families of their own. I'm a great-grandfather as of six months ago."

"I hadn't heard. That's wonderful! Congratulations."

"Thanks. It's a pity my Mary never lived to see it. I miss her every day, you know… every day. Still, family's a great comfort, Donny." He looked pointedly across the cockpit.

"I'm sure it is. It just never worked out for me." Donny helped himself to more potato salad, and they ate in silence for a minute.

"Anyway," said Aldrich, changing the subject, "how does it feel to be the Laird of Lombard, Captain Robertson?"

"Great. Well, it's only been one day. It's what I always wanted. But I kind of screwed up." He told Aldrich about the argument with Ratzo.

"It's never wise to pick a fight with someone on his way up the ladder," mused Aldrich. "As for the crew, set your bar high, Donny. Expect the best of each person and meet that standard yourself. The good ones will be drawn to you; the others, the ones looking for the easier, softer way, will soon transfer out. That's how you build a crew."

"I know. It was just all too much right on the first day. And I've never had a woman on the crew before."

"Well, it's a different era, isn't it? When I was just starting it was recruiting blacks. Now Al Stevens is Chief of the job, and a fine Chief at that, from all I hear. Fifty years before that it was the Catholics. It's always something, but it all works out."

"You're right," Donny sighed. "I'm going to get another beer. You want one?"

"No thanks. Now, why don't you tell me what this is really about? You didn't ask me here to talk about women or your little spat with Ratzo."

Donny ducked down below and came back up with a fresh beer. "It's the fire. It's on my mind a lot."

"I thought that might be it." Aldrich leaned back and looked up at the clouds drifting lazily on the midday breeze. "When you've been hurt in a fire — badly hurt, like you were, son — it's only natural to have doubts. I've had them myself. 'Can I do it again? Can I go back in?'"

"That's not it. Well, maybe partly." Donny took a long pull on his beer and then poured out everything he had learned, thought and felt about the fire. "You've got to believe me: someone set that fire. I know it in my bones."

Aldrich ran a hand over his chin. He could see the pain in Donny's face. It was a pain that came from somewhere deep inside, beneath the scars; from the place where the brute pain of senseless incomprehension lives. "'In place of cross, the albatross / About his neck was hung.'"

Donny wore a puzzled expression.

"*The Rime of the Ancient Mariner*," Aldrich explained. "I'm surprised you don't know it, you being a sailor and all."

"I've heard of it. 'Water, water everywhere, nor any drop to drink' — is that it?"

"Yes, that's part of it too. It's the story of a man who seeks redemption." He paused and looked Donny straight in the eye. "You didn't kill Fitz…"

"Don't. Don't tell me it wasn't my fault. I'm tired of hearing that." Donny looked down the channel from the marina to the lake beyond. The afternoon westerly was strengthening nicely, and whitecaps boiled among the waves. It was the perfect wind for *Red Bird,* when other boats were beginning to reduce sail or run for cover. "They made me go see a shrink before they let me back on the trucks, you know. 'Survivor's guilt,' he called it. Like he'd know anything about it, sitting in that office. Psycho-babble bullshit!"

Aldrich stood and climbed awkwardly back onto the dock.

"Where are you going? You just got here!" Donny protested.

Aldrich stood on the dock, squinting down at Donny as if measuring him. "Come with me," he said. Retired he might be, but Captain John Aldrich had lost none of his authority.

ROSEDALE VALLEY ROAD ran like a wilderness artery through the heart of the city. Donny gazed out the passenger window at the dense woodland that clung to the steep sides of the ravine. Were it not for the office buildings and condo towers sprouting along the top, they might be driving along some remote backwoods trail.

"Do you mind telling me where we're going, at least? I've got stuff to do back on the boat."

"Did you call me up just to bitch, or do you actually want some help?"

They drove the rest of the way in silence, emerging from the soft green shade of the valley into the concrete and asphalt angles of city streets. Aldrich turned down Parliament Street and then in through the wrought-iron gates of St. James Cemetery.

They curved around the rough-cut stone chapel with its towering gothic spire, passing ivy-clad crypts and rows of mossy stones sheltering under the mantle of ancient maples.

Donny sat rigidly as they wound through the cemetery. Aldrich glanced over at him. "You've not been here before?"

"No. I was in the hospital during the funeral." Donny looked down at his hands and picked at his thumbnail. "Afterwards, I couldn't… I didn't feel…"

Aldrich brought the car to halt at the side of the narrow lane. "Don't worry. He's not here anyway. I believe Paul Fitzgerald is resting in the loving arms of God Almighty."

"Then what are we doing here?"

"Closure," Aldrich said, opening the car door. "Come on."

The grass whispered under their feet as they walked along a row of stones. Some of them were a hundred years old or more, the letters and carvings softened by a century of heat and cold, sun and snow. Aldrich sat on a bench. "Fitzgerald" was inscribed on many of the nearby stones. One was obviously newer than the rest.

"There," Aldrich pointed with his cane.

Donny sat beside him. "I'm sorry I snapped at you. I've been doing that a lot lately. Too much."

Aldrich patted him on the leg. "I've felt that anger and pain myself, and all those kind words of sympathy don't make it hurt any less. But we can't bring him back, Donny. And he has no need of our earthly help now."

Donny walked over and knelt beside the stone. He traced the letters with his fingers. The smooth, cold granite drew the heat from his hand but gave nothing in return. "I need to find out who did it. Or why. Or something. Fitz deserves that much, at least."

What was it Donny wanted from him? Aldrich wondered. Approval? Benediction? Salvation? Salvation, Aldrich knew, was for the living, not the dead. "If you're going to do this, do it for yourself, Donny, not for Fitz. And not for vengeance either. That's a fool's errand, an empty, bitter cup."

Donny considered for a moment, then walked back to the bench and sat down heavily. "I don't know where to begin," he said softly.

"Well, I'm no detective, but I'd guess you want to get hold of all the records — everything you can, the official fire report, statements from all the guys who were there. Talk to everyone involved—the coroner, fire marshal, insurance, all that. Look for something overlooked, see what doesn't belong, who stands to gain, who loses. That sort of thing. That's what the cops do."

"Will you help me?" There was pleading in Donny's eyes, and Aldrich's heart went out to the younger man.

"It's not my albatross, and I'm an old man, Donny. But my nephew is a staff sergeant now. I'll see if I can get the police reports for you. That much I can do."

"Thanks," Donny sighed. "It's going to be a lot of work, isn't it?"

"And in the end it may not lead anywhere. You may never get your answer."

"I need to try," Donny shrugged.

Aldrich rose and rested his hand on Donny's shoulder.

*"He went like one that hath been stunned,
And is of sense forlorn:
A sadder and a wiser man
He rose the morrow morn."*

"More poetry, Cap?"

"The same one. That's how it ends, Donny." Aldrich started back along the row of stones towards the car. "Take your time. I'll wait in the car."

"I thought you said he wasn't here," Donny called after him.

"Maybe he'll stop by to visit an old friend."

ALDRICH DROPPED him back at the boat. Donny tried to go back to work on the rigging, but he gave up after half an hour. He couldn't concentrate, and he knew he couldn't afford to be careless. Neptune inevitably punished the careless.

It was a big haystack, and he wasn't sure whether he was looking for a needle or a sledgehammer, but he had to start somewhere. He would have to wait until he was back at work to get the Fire Department records. In the meantime, the first link in the chain that Donny could see was the water main on Commissioners Street, the one that had been shut off the morning before the fire.

He put his tools away, pulled out his phone and called the City Public Works Department. After two more calls and several transfers he was finally connected to the South Central Works depot.

"Normally this sort of thing goes through the records department," said the man on the other end of the phone.

"I just want to talk to whoever worked on that particular job," Donny said. "Like I said, this isn't official, it's just for my own interest."

"Fire Department, eh? My wife's cousin is a fireman. Mike Cesario. You know him?" asked the man.

It happened all the time. For some reason, people assumed that every firefighter knew every other firefighter in the world. Donny had no idea who this fellow was, but he was willing to play along if it got him somewhere. "Mike? Yeah, we worked in the same district a few years back. He's a good guy."

"Really?" said the voice. "Maybe he's different in the station. He's a bit of a dick, if you ask me. Treats his family like shit."

"Sorry to hear that," Donny said, trying to backpedal. "Some guys are like that, eh? Totally different at work."

"Not your problem, anyway. Give me a minute to pull up the file." The voice clicked over to recorded music, and Donny hummed along to a song whose title he couldn't remember. The voice came back on the line. "OK, got it here. The crew from that job is starting the evening shift in a couple of hours. You can come down to the yard and see if they want to talk to you. No guarantees. You want an official response, you gotta go through channels, OK?"

SCATTERED OVER THE halfdozen acres of asphalt and gravel were backhoes, heavy duty wood chippers, compressors, snowblowers taller than a man, and a variety of other heavy equipment. There was one building, a red brick Depression-era structure that looked like a Dickensian workhouse. It housed the South Central Depot's offices and maintenance facilities. Donny looked out at the yard from the reception area with all the wonder and yearning of a kid pressed against the glass of a department-store Christmas window. He knew there were those, children and adults alike, who envied him riding around in a fire truck, but there was something about a backhoe that made Donny's pulse quicken and his fingers twitch. Just once, he thought to himself, just once...

"Captain Robertson?" a voice behind him enquired.

Donny turned from the window. An Asian woman in overalls was smiling at him. "Yes, uh, hi. Please call me Donny."

"Laurie Zhou," the woman introduced herself as they shook hands. She opened the door from the reception area and held it for him. "Come on. We'll talk while I load up some equipment, if you don't mind."

Donny followed her to a dump truck parked across from the office building. The yard smelled of diesel and grease, underlain with the rich scent of damp earth and the sharpness of rusty metal. "You were on the Commissioners Street job?" he asked.

"You were expecting some sweaty, hairy Italian guy? We got lots of them, if that's what you want." Laurie raised an eyebrow at Donny. She climbed into the driver's seat and started the truck. It always surprised people to find a woman as the foreman of a works crew, and a Chinese woman at that.

"No, but you gotta admit it's a little unusual," Donny replied, settling into the passenger seat.

"Yeah, sure, we're all supposed to be China dolls, play the violin and be good at math, right?" She laughed and tossed her short black hair in mocking seduction as she palmed the wheel. She handled the heavy truck like it was a family sedan. "Unfortunately I didn't get the China doll build, and I suck at music."

Donny cast an appraising eye across the cab. She had high cheekbones and a wide, expressive face. Crow's feet creased the corners of her eyes, but they still shone with intensity. She had a short, thick build, though it was difficult to discern anything of her figure beneath the bulky overalls.

"Hmm, and all firemen are supposed to be bronzed Adonises, right?" Donny replied, framing his own face with his hands.

"It's not that bad. Some women are into scars, you know."

Even people he knew well tended to avoid looking at, let alone mentioning his grafts. He found her honesty both shocking and refreshing. "We all have them, I guess; some are just more obvious than others."

"True, very true. You are wise, Grasshopper." She laughed again as she manoeuvred the truck across the yard. She cocked her head, glancing sideways at him as if trying to see what other wounds might lie deeper inside him, or daring him to guess where hers were. "You get those in a fire?"

"Yeah, the one on Commissioners Street."

"With the two dead guys?"

"One of them was my best friend. That's why I'm interested in it."

Laurie brought the truck to a stop in front of a heavy trailer and turned to face him, her eyes wide. "Oh shit, sorry. Now it makes sense. I thought you were just… Never mind. Did they ever find out what caused that?"

"No. Officially the cause is 'undetermined.'" Donny looked at a stack of hydrants in a corner of the yard. It seemed odd to find such a solitary species herded together.

"Listen, I'm sorry." She leaned across the cab and touched his hand lightly. "When I heard two people were killed and you were burned… Well, I didn't know it was you, but — you know. And we had shut off the water. I felt sick when I heard that. I mean if we hadn't…"

"No, listen, it's not your fault." Donny smiled at her. "How were you supposed to know there was going to be a fire? We got the notice. We knew the water was off before we got the call. Anyway, you had to. The main was broken, right?"

Laurie looked relieved. "Back me up, will you?"

Donny climbed down and directed her as Laurie backed the truck up to the trailer. She barely glanced at him in the mirror. Donny suspected that having him spot her was merely a formality.

"Everyone thinks that fire was an accident," Donny continued as Laurie got out. "They think it just got away from us, and that's why Fitz — he was my captain — that's why he got killed."

"But you don't think so," Laurie said as she secured the trailer hitch and brake connections.

"No, there are some things that just don't fit."

"Like us shutting down the water main?"

"Well, you've got to admit that would be mighty convenient if you were setting a fire," Donny said, moving to stand beside her. "Was there anything, anything at all that was unusual about that job?"

Laurie considered him silently for a moment. "Wait here." She walked over to a backhoe, started it and drove it up onto the trailer as Donny watched enviously.

Laurie climbed down from the backhoe and sat on the fender of the trailer. "Look, normally when a main goes, there's an obvious cause like corrosion or a casting flaw in the metal. Something like that."

"But not here?" asked Donny.

"That pipe was eighty years old, but the iron was still good." Laurie shook her head. There was something she wasn't telling him.

"What else?" he asked.

She started pulling tie-down chains from the storage box on the trailer and handing them to Donny. "It's kind of crazy," Laurie said, shaking her head again.

"Not if it's the truth," Donny encouraged her.

"I wasn't always in the glamour-filled world of ditch digging, you know," Laurie said, running a tie-down chain from the backhoe to a chain keeper on the trailer. "I used to be Sergeant Zhou, 2nd Regiment, Canadian Combat Engineers. Bosnia, Afghanistan, all the best tourist spots." She paused and looked up at Donny. "I know a thing or two about explosives."

"Someone bombed the water main? Wouldn't that be obvious?"

"Not necessarily. Not if you knew what you were doing." She went back to securing the backhoe. Donny followed her, handing her chains as she moved around the trailer. "You'd only need a very small charge, just enough to crack the pipe. The water pressure would do the rest. That pipe looked to me like it had been blown."

"Holy shit!" exclaimed Donny. "Did you tell anyone about this?"

"Not officially. Like I said, it's crazy. How do you strap a bomb on a water main buried six feet deep? And even if you could, who gives a rat's ass about the water supply on Commissioners Street? It's a run-down industrial area. It's not like it's a major terrorist target. I asked my supervisor if I should mention it on the report and he said no. There was no proof, you know, it was just my opinion. But there was no obvious reason for that pipe to fail, either."

"If there were explosives, wouldn't there be traces?"

Laurie shrugged, "I don't know. I'm City Works. That's CSI stuff, and that pipe is long gone for scrap metal. It's probably the fender on a Buick by now. I'm sorry."

"Damn, that's too bad. But you really think it was blown?"

"Like I said, it's only my opinion, but I do know a thing or two about explosives." She finished tightening the last chain and walked to the front of the truck. "Hop in."

Donny sat thinking as they drove back across the yard. Laurie stopped the truck beside his car, across from the office. "Listen, would you be willing to put it on the record, make an official statement or something?" he asked.

Laurie pursed her lips. "I don't know. You got anything else? I mean, how come you're doing this and not the cops?"

"Because so far this is the most solid thing I've found. But I know a thing or two about fires and this one shouldn't have gotten away. There's a bunch of pieces that just don't fit."

"Tell you what, you find something else to go on and I'll put it on the record. In the meantime, I got a street to dig up. Sorry." Donny nodded sadly and opened the door. Laurie watched him cross in front of the truck. She rolled down her window and held out a card. "Give me a call and let me know how it works out. Or just give me a call. Like I said, some women are into scars."

She winked at Donny and drove off. He stared after her and then down at the phone number on the card, his mind swirling off in several directions.

SIX
The Haystack

HE WAS STRUCK BY how ordinary it was, just like every other Fire Department incident report. Of course it would be. What else could it possibly look like? But it still struck him as odd. The data fields were all neatly filled in: address, alarm time, apparatus assigned and so on. There it was in the bottom right corner of the first page:

Fatalities, civilian – 1

Fatalities, FD personnel – 1

Jesus! He'd almost forgotten. Fitz wasn't the only one killed in the fire. There was that other guy, the guy who owned the company. What was his name? There it was on the next page: Youssef Aziz. He would need to follow up on that.

They were back in the station for another twentyfour-hour shift after fortyeight off. It was a beautiful late spring day and the sun was shining warmly on Donny's back as he sat at the big oak desk in the captain's office.

Donny scanned through the pages. There was a lot of information: names and contact particulars for the property and business owners, insurance details, police badge numbers, paramedic crews, fire marshal's investigator and others. He would have to pore over every detail and talk to every person listed. And this was only the beginning. The haystack had just gotten a lot bigger. He sighed and hit the "print" button.

The witness statements were elsewhere. Every firefighter at a fatality had to write out a personal statement, but Donny didn't have access to those files. He picked up the phone and called Ratzo.

"Chief? Hi, it's Donny."

"Hey, Wedge, what's up?"

"I need a favour. I want to get copies of the witness statements for the fire — you know, Commissioners Street. I don't have access, but I thought maybe you could sweet-talk the Division Commander and get me copies. And, you know, whatever else you can get."

There was silence on the line.

"I thought I told you to do this on your own time," Ratzo finally replied.

"I will. At least mostly, but this isn't the sort of thing I can do on my own time. I just need you to get the stuff for me, that's all."

Ratzo was annoyed. He didn't want to say no, but people would ask questions, and awkward questions were not good for a career. "And tell me why exactly I would do that. Seriously, what am I supposed to tell the Commander? That you got some crazy-assed idea and I'm just as crazy as you are?"

Donny winced. He briefly considered telling Ratzo Laurie's theory about the water main, but then thought better of it. There was still nothing solid to go on. "How about you tell him my shrink said it's a good idea. It would help me work through the trauma."

"Hmm," Ratzo thought for a moment, "that's not bad. It could work. OK, I'll give it a shot, but I'm not going to push hard on this. Leave it with me."

"Thanks, Chief. I promise not to tell anyone you're a decent guy."

Ratzo snorted and hung up.

Donny took a deep breath and let it whistle out between his teeth. It was a good beginning. The sheer monumental inertia of the thing had been daunting him, but he had made a start, and it felt good. A flicker of the old confidence warmed him. He knew he was groping in the dark. The only certainty was that if he did nothing, then nothing would happen.

He would ask for help; he would plead, wheedle and cajole. People liked to help, and he would do whatever he could to let them help him.

Donny took the printout of the incident report and began highlighting the phone numbers of all the people on it. He thought briefly about Ratzo's "do it on your own time" speech. He would. Mostly. He wouldn't let it interfere with the work that needed to be done, but as far as Donny was concerned this was Fire Department business too.

First on the list was Leila Aziz, Youssef's widow. This was not going to be easy. He took another deep breath and picked up the phone.

"Hello, Mrs. Aziz? This is Captain Robertson from the Fire Department."

The voice on the phone was high, and softly accented. "Yes, what can I do for you?"

"I'd just like to talk. Do you have a minute?"

"Is this about Youssef? I told everything to the police and the other people long ago, after the fire. What do you want?"

"Well, first let me say how sorry I am about your husband. I was there and we tried, I mean we did our best…"

"You were there?"

"Yes, I was," Donny said more softly. "My friend Paul Fitzgerald was killed in that fire too."

"You are the one they rescued? I remember your name. You are all right now?"

"Um, yeah, I'm fine. Listen, ma'am, this isn't official or anything, I'm just trying to make sense of this whole thing."

There was silence on the other end. Donny continued, "Mrs. Aziz, I have a feeling that fire was deliberately set. Do you know any reason why someone would do that?"

There was silence again. When she spoke there was a thin, brittle quality to her voice. "They tell me this was an accident. They tell me Youssef died of a heart attack, that he knocked something over when he fell and this is what started the fire."

Donny tried his best to be soothing. "I'm not a doctor, ma'am, but I'm sure your husband didn't suffer. But I do know about fires, and, well, this one was unusual."

"We don't want any trouble." There was something more than grief in her voice now.

"I'm sorry to bring this up again. I know it must be hard, but please, if there's anything you can tell me…"

"No. No trouble. Please leave me alone. No trouble."

The line went dead. Donny put down the phone and frowned. There was something very odd about her reaction; you didn't have to be Sherlock Holmes to pick that up. He circled her name and number. He would follow up later with Leila Aziz.

In the meantime, there were a hundred other leads to follow. Donny called the insurance company next. Things went much better this time.

The building had been leased by AES, Aziz Energy Systems. There was minimal insurance on the building and contents, and neither the owner nor AES had any history of suspicious claims. The insurance company had paid out. The adjuster asked Donny to let him know if anything unusual did turn up, and Donny agreed.

The Ministry of Labour inspector recognized Donny's name right away and asked how he was doing. Donny said he was fine, and asked if he could have a copy of the report. It would help him go through his "process." The inspector clucked sympathetically and said, "Sure. I hope you realize now how important it is for you guys to stay together on the hose line. Captain Fitzgerald should never have been off on his own. However, given the circumstances we decided not to lay any charges against you."

Asshole, Donny thought, but he thanked the man and hung up.

He was picking up the phone again when Eddy's voice came over the PA. "Lunch up," he announced.

THE CUP OF TEA sat untouched on the counter. Leila Aziz sat at the kitchen table and tried to get a grip on her fear.

"*Ya Allah!*" she cried aloud. Oh God, will it never end?

Saddam's henchmen had scarred their minds and bodies. The fear was never far away, but it belonged to another time and place. Leila had thought they were finally safe when she and Youssef arrived in Canada. Here they could raise Adina in peace and security. And for many years it was so.

Then Youssef had been taken from her. The week after the funeral, while she was still trying to come to grips with the reality of her loss, the men had arrived. They were better dressed and more polite than the Iraqi secret police, but Leila recognized them for who and what they were.

They represented Youssef's investors, they said. They were there to collect his research material. They were sorry to trouble her at this time, but they needed to collect it now. *All* of it. Leila would be compensated, of course, but she would also be bound by Youssef's confidentiality agreement. It would be very bad, very bad indeed if she told anyone about their visit.

The men loaded Youssef's computer into a van along with boxes of files and books. They were quick and thorough. They left Leila with a cheque and a smile that froze her to the marrow. And in that moment she knew that Youssef's death, and her fear, were only the tip of the iceberg.

The only path to safety was silence, and so she had constructed a wall of silence around Youssef's death. She would not speak of it with anyone. Even Adina respected what she thought was her mother's grief. She knew what her parents had been through in Iraq. There were some things it was simply best not to talk about.

But now this man, this Captain Robertson had breached her wall. Leila shuddered at the memory and then reached for the phone.

"Hello, Mama," Adina answered when she saw Leila's name and number on her phone. "How are you?"

"I'm fine, *habibi*, fine. I just wanted to hear your voice. It's silly, I know." Leila hesitated. How much should she say?

"You sound upset," Adina said with concern. "What happened, Mama?"

"It was nothing, really. I got a call from a man in the fire department. He was just checking some details, he said. But yes, it upset me a bit. It made me remember…"

"If they phone again, Mama, tell them to call me. I'll deal with it."

"Oh, I'm just a foolish old woman, Adina." The last thing Leila wanted to do was expand the circle of risk to include her daughter. "There's no need to trouble you. You're so busy with your work and the children. Anyway, I'm certain they won't call again. There's nothing more to tell, right?"

"Are you sure you're all right, Mama?" Adina asked. It was hard to tell with her mother, how much of her distress was real and how much was just echoes of the past.

"Your father…" Leila began and then hesitated. "You read the report."

"I'm a medical researcher, Mama, not a pathologist, but yes, I read the report and I know the man who did the autopsy. He's a very good man, one of the best."

"And… and he didn't suffer, did he?" Leila's voice quavered.

Adina had thought this might be it. After all they had been through, it was too much for her mother to picture her husband burning to death.

"No, Mama," Adina said as if she were comforting her own

children. "It was coronary arrest, very quick. There was no smoke in his lungs. Papa probably knocked something over when he fell, and that started the fire. It was very sad, but no, he didn't suffer."

"Yes, it was very sad, very sad about the firemen." Leila dabbed at her tears with a tissue.

"You want me to come over, Mama?"

"No, *habibi*, I'll be fine. Thank you. I'll see you tomorrow night for supper."

"OK, Farid will pick you up on his way home from work." They exchanged endearments and hung up. Leila felt better. The truth was still safe behind the wall. She would not allow it to be breached again.

LUNCH WAS TOASTED BLTS, bean salad and sweet potato fries. There was enough to feed a small army. There were two general rules in fire hall cooking. First, it had to be cheap. Second, there had to be lots of it. Lots of mediocre food was much better than too little gourmet fare. Eddy the Ladle went above and beyond.

"The one thing I'm going to miss about you, Eddy, is your cooking," said Moose, piling his plate high. "What are we going to do, Cap? I'm going to waste away."

"That should take a couple years," said Spike, "kind of like the retreat of the glaciers."

"Well, boys, funny you should say that. I was looking at the union contract this morning while preparing our repast." Eddy reached over to the windowsill and plopped a large binder on the table beside him. "The stuff about transfers, you know, seeing when I could get back downtown. It turns out there's a clause about promotions out of district and trading spots."

Donny swallowed a bite of his sandwich. "You think this Rick guy from Leaside will swap and take your place at 29?"

Eddy shrugged. "He's not really a downtown guy. Maybe he'd

rather stay some place a little quieter. It's worth a try, eh?" There were nods of agreement. "I'll tell him things are a little unsettled here and, you know, spice it up a little. Mind if I call him right now?"

"Be my guest," said Donny.

Eddy got up and brought the phone back to the table. "Hi, Rick, it's Eddy, Eddy the Ladle down at 6 Pump. How are you doing?"

Eddy leaned his chair back on two legs, cradling the phone on his shoulder. The rest of the crew listened as they ate.

"Congratulations to you too. Listen, I just wanted to fill you in before you got here. I wouldn't want you to just hit it cold and wonder what the hell was going on… Uh-huh… Yeah, Donny's a great guy, but you know what he's been through… Listen, I love the guy, but straight up? He's broken. I don't know what to tell you. You know they made him go to a shrink before he came back, eh?"

Donny shot him a dirty look and reached for the bean salad. "Yeah, well, I don't think it did any good… Listen, all I'm saying is you're coming in here as Senior Man and you got a Captain that's not all there." Eddy winked and Donny gave him the finger. "I thought you should know… No problem. You'd do the same for me, right?

"The rest of the crew? You know Moose, I think. He said he knew you out at Swansea… Sure, if you like 'em big and dumb, then Moose is great. Just don't ask him any tough questions, like 'what's your favourite colour?'" Moose reached over, grasped Eddy's entire skull in one hand and began to squeeze, but Eddy managed to wriggle free before his head was crushed.

"Well, it was Fitz, God rest him, who really kept the crew together. And that's when Donny was normal, too, so it was better then. It's a bit of a circus now… Listen, honestly, I'm glad to be gettin' the hell out of Dodge, but I thought I owed it to you to let you know… Hey, I'm sorry, man, but I don't make the assignments…"

Eddy pantomimed a fishing rod and began reeling in the line. "Oh, shit, I almost forgot. We're getting a probie. A woman… Uh-huh…

Absolutely, I don't care either, but I asked a buddy down at the Academy about her. Evidently she's a real ball buster and she's got the Human Rights office on speed dial. Just stay on your toes and don't even look sideways at her…"

Eddy pumped his fist in the air and smiled broadly around the table. They all gave him the finger. "Well, I don't know what you can do about it, Rick. You gotta go where they send you, right? You can always put in a transfer in six months… A mutual trade? Like you take my spot at 29 and I stay here? I didn't know you could do that." Eddy patted the binder with the contract already open to the relevant page. "Really, I didn't realize you'd been a union steward. You're sure it's in the contract, eh? Well, I don't know. I'd have to think about it… Like I said, I was kind of looking forward to a change… OK, sign the paperwork and send it to me, but I'm not promising anything. I gotta think about this. Hell, I was just trying to give you a heads up… Yeah, well, if I do this you owe me, you got that? You owe me big… OK, Rick, later."

Eddy hung up the phone, stood and bowed deeply. "Yes, gentlemen, you are in the presence of greatness."

"'As long as you like 'em big and dumb' — that was a nice touch, don't you think, Moose?" enquired Spike.

"Yeah, and I liked the simple eloquence of 'he's broken,' eh, Cap?" Moose replied.

"You're an asshole, Eddy," Donny said. "I think you're buying lunch for everyone today."

"Fair enough, but you gotta admit I'm a brilliant asshole. He was practically begging me to trade. Another minute and he would have been willing to pay me. Anyway, you said it was OK."

"I agreed you could try to get the guy to trade. I didn't say make out like we're a bunch of gimps. Jesus! What if that stuff gets around?"

"Desperate times call for desperate measures, guys," Eddy explained. Maybe he had gone a little overboard. "Anyway, the crews who run with us regularly aren't going to pay any attention to that crap, right, Spike?"

"All I can say is I'm glad I'm back at my own station next shift," Spike said, pushing his plate away. "You guys have fun with your probie."

"I wonder," mused Donny, "what Ms. Susan What's-her-name would say about that ball breaker, speed dial stuff?"

Eddy froze and his face went serious. "Jeez, I never thought… You don't think she'd find out about that, do you?"

"Hopefully not from anyone in this room." Donny doubted anything would come of it, but he liked leaving Eddy with something to think about. He went back to the office and resumed his search through the department records.

SEVEN
Spectrum

IT CAME IN AS A normal Spectrum alert. Wilkins knit his brow and studied the information on the screen.

"That's a bit unusual," he said to himself.

Commander Mike Wilkins, USN, leaned back in his chair and brought his hand to his chin. Though age had softened some of his hard edges, at fortytwo Wilkins was in better shape than most men twenty years younger. With one exception: he had lost the use of his legs. What he had not lost were his self-discipline, his mind or his resolve. From the waist up he still had the build of a linebacker. Wilkins knew the first thing people saw when they met him was the wheelchair. Few people who spent more than a few moments with him, thought of him as disabled.

He looked back at the screen. Spectrum alerts did come in from Canada from time to time, but the Toronto Fire Department? That had to be a first. He scanned down the list of highlighted files. There were some references to their Fire Marshal's Office and a few other places, but eighty percent of it was the Toronto Fire Department. The primary user was a Capt. Donald Robertson. He was Joe Public — no profile on him at all. The subject matter was a little odd too. Most of it was about some fire from over a year ago. Two people had died, but there was no indication of terrorism. Of course Spectrum did more than just track Jihadists, but there was no sign of anything at all that the National Security Agency would normally be interested in.

Spectrum was a project to gather intelligence from patterns of use on the Internet. What Carnivore and its successors were to email, Spectrum was to the web. And much more. Every person who uses the web creates a data shadow. Over time these shadows become so detailed they are akin to fingerprints.

Spectrum could of course filter for subject matter, web sites, volume of use, and several other variables. It could interpret the traffic for content, structure and significance. VOIP and Skype use added more detail to the profile. More important, Spectrum's algorithms could be tuned to pick out and link patterns from seemingly independent sources, so that a dispersed group or a single target wily enough to use different computers, even on different nodes and networks, could still be identified. It was even possible to pin down a subject's physical location by using the differences in Internet latency. Spectrum had proven key in both identifying and locating several high-value targets.

This alert didn't fit any of the usual patterns.

Wilkins turned and looked out the window. It was a small, drab office, with barely enough room for him to manoeuvre his wheelchair around the desk and filing cabinets. But at least it had a window. He could look out at the green Maryland countryside spread out around the NSA's headquarters at Fort Meade.

"What do you make of this, boys?"

He was addressing the picture that hung beside the window. It showed a group of smiling, heavily armed men standing on a beach: Wilkins' SEAL team. It was taken just before Wilkins' last mission, the one where a bullet had shattered his lower spine.

That bullet had cost him his legs and almost ended his career. But a man didn't survive SEAL training by giving up. Wilkins had used every ounce of his skill and determination, called in every favour and connection he had in the military. Against all odds, he had been able to convince the people that mattered that someone with field experience in gathering and using intelligence could be a valuable asset as a strategic analyst.

There had been a steep learning curve, but that was nothing new to Wilkins. In the end he had justified the faith of the senior officers who had gone out on a limb for him. He also liked to think he had won a small victory for others who had been wounded or disabled in the service of their country.

Borrowing the unofficial Marine motto, Wilkins had "adapted and overcome," but he still missed the old days, and he often found himself talking to the picture of the smiling men cradling their weapons on the beach. He turned his attention back to the computer screen.

This particular Spectrum file had been set to watch for traffic relating to that one fire. It had triggered on a simple volume-of-use threshold. Wilkins shook his head. What concerned him most was the routing. The alert was not addressed in house; nor was it going to the White House, the CIA or anyone else in the intelligence community. It was asking for authorization to send the information outside.

Wilkins called his section head.

"Sorry to bother you, Colonel." Wilkins explained the situation. "Aside from the subject matter it seems fairly routine. It's just the first alert I've come across that's headed to a civilian destination, and I wanted to double check with you before authorizing it."

"Go ahead," was the reply. "I remember this one, Mike. There are people and organizations that sometimes do favours for us and for our colleagues. They provide credible covers, safe houses, sometimes even raw intel. You might have used some of those things in your SEAL days. Anyway, every now and then we're asked to return the favour."

"It's a bit like using a sledgehammer as a flyswatter, isn't it, sir?" asked Wilkins.

"Sometimes our friends don't have their own flyswatter, let alone a sledgehammer. It's not for us to judge. This one was authorized at the very top. It's the cost of doing business."

"Yes, sir." Wilkins hung up the phone, turned to his keyboard and typed in his authorization code. His finger hovered over the "enter" key. Something about this made him itch. His instincts had usually served him well. They had saved his life and the lives of his team several times.

He tabbed over and hit a few more keys to tag the file. Then, with a frown, he hit "enter" and sent the Spectrum alert on its way.

A FEW SECONDS LATER a soft chime sounded on a BlackBerry half a continent away. Catherine scowled; a headache had been plaguing her for days, and the message in front of her only made her mood worse.

She read it over again, and then placed a call. "Brendan? There's a problem in Toronto. I need you to look into it."

"I'm fairly certain everything is fine, ma'am," Brendan assured her. "The investigations and hearings were all favourable as far as we're concerned."

"Were you labouring under the impression that I was asking your opinion?" Catherine asked acidly. She didn't wait for an answer. "Someone is snooping around. I'll send you the information. I want you to personally assess the situation and determine how serious this is."

"Of course. I'll book a flight immediately."

Catherine hung up. It was probably nothing to worry about, just some amateur sleuth groping in the dark. Still, it was best to be certain of these things. It would be worth doing without Brendan for a few days to have the matter resolved.

She rubbed at the low-grade throbbing in the back of her head, took two more Advil and went back to studying the briefing notes for the meeting with the Chinese delegation.

EIGHT
Susan

ORGANIC CAROB MUFFINS. She brought organic carob muffins. No bacon, no sausage, no fat-drenched, artery-clogging, traditional fire hall heart-attack breakfast, but rather health food. And even then the muffins were likely a bit of a concession, Donny suspected as he took another bite of his. It didn't taste bad — a bit dry perhaps; but it made him uneasy.

He looked down the kitchen table at probationary firefighter Susan Kozarovitch as she chattered away to Eddy and Moose. So much for the old saying about keeping your mouth shut and your eyes and ears open.

"That is beautiful, Moose. How did you get into knitting?" Susan asked.

Moose flushed. "My mom taught me. I had mono when I was a kid and I was home for months. It was driving both of us crazy, so she came up with the idea of teaching me to knit. I just really liked it. I was no good at art or that kind of stuff, and the idea that I could actually create something nice and useful too, you know, it just made me feel good."

"Well, you have a real talent. You should be proud."

"I am. A lot of men used to knit back in the old days, you know. In the Middle Ages, the knitting guilds were all men," Moose declared solemnly.

"It would be a brave man who called Moose a wimp," said Eddy. "He's made stuff for most of the guys in the district, and half their kids too."

"If I bought the wool, would you consider making a sweater for my son?" Susan asked.

"Sure," said Moose, grinning from ear to ear.

The guys looked, Donny thought, a bit like the Munchkins when Dorothy suddenly appeared in their midst, shiny, strange and exciting. The idea of Moose as a Munchkin prancing and singing "Follow the Yellow Brick Road" made him laugh out loud. They stopped talking and looked down the table at Donny.

"Nothing," he waved them off, "just thinking to myself."

"Don't worry," said Eddy in a stage whisper to Susan. "It's just the beginning stages of dementia."

"Dementia is going to be the least of your worries if we don't get some stoking done around here," said Donny, rising from the table. "It's after eight; let's get to work. Eddy will show you what's expected, Susan. When you're done I'd like to see you in the office."

DONNY SAT BEHIND the desk trying to think of what to say. He considered the things he had been told and the things he had heard said to other rookies over the years. But that was different, and times had changed. The job was the same as it had always been, yet it had morphed in a hundred subtle ways.

Some of the changes were good, Donny had to admit. Some of the rough edges needed to be smoothed, but he wasn't so sure about some of the other changes. The harsh reality of human suffering would always be part of the job. The only way to soften it was humour, humour that was often black as midnight and tinged with what might seem to the uninformed like cruelty. You couldn't run a fire department that was always politically correct; you couldn't run it as a democracy either, for that matter. Orders still needed to be given and obeyed.

One thing that had not changed was the seemingly endless requirement for forms and reports. The only difference was that most of them were done electronically now. Donny turned back to the screen and resumed wading through the day's "paperwork."

"Come in," he responded to the knock on the office door as his index fingers orbited the keyboard.

Susan poked her head around the door. "You wanted to see me, Cap?"

"Uh, yes. Come in, Susan. Close the door, please." A panicked thought crossed Donny's mind. "Are you OK with that? Closing the door, I mean?"

"Yeah, sure." Susan gave him an odd look.

"OK, good. I just didn't want you to think… Never mind. Pull up a chair and sit down."

Susan Kozarovitch was thirtyfour years old, that much he knew from her file. She was a little taller than average for a woman, and solidly built. Not heavy, Donny noted, but with a certain sturdiness you saw in pictures of pioneer women. The centrefold types didn't have the strength or stamina to make it through the Department's physical testing, and Donny thought that was just as well. The navy blue fatigues did nothing for Susan's figure. That too was just as well, as was the fact that she seemed to be wearing little if any makeup. She had a pleasant round face with thin lips and apple cheeks. Her chestnut hair was done up in a bun, ready to fit under the fireproof hood that was part of their gear. Overall she had a faintly matronly appearance.

Donny took a deep breath and spread his hands on the desk. "Welcome to Lombard," he smiled. He meant it and he hoped it showed. She smiled back and he relaxed slightly.

"Thank you," she said, "I'm really glad to be here. I wanted a busy station."

"You'll get your belly full of that." Donny tapped his fingers on the desktop. He had thought of a dozen different things he wanted to say; now he just looked at her, wondering where and how to begin.

"This is…" he stalled. "What I want to say is, you're…" He paused again.

"I'm the first woman to be posted here. I know, they told me." Susan smiled weakly.

"That's true, but that's not what I want to say," Donny said, sounding more officious than he intended to. "I want to tell you something about us, about this station. You are with the best firefighting crew in the toughest fire station in the city." He looked hard into her eyes and she nodded.

"Other stations and other crews might feel the same way. That's great; personally, I think everyone should want that. The truth is, not everyone does. Some guys look for a place to hide. We don't. We are an aggressive firefighting crew. We do our best to work smart and safe, but we go after the beast where it lives."

Susan wasn't quite sure where he was going with this. Did he expect her to shout "Hoo-ah!"? To swoon?

"Aggressive is good," she said. "Safe is good too. I'm really proud to be part of the crew."

"You're not. You are not a part of this crew — not yet, anyway. You are a probationary firefighter assigned to this station for six months of training and evaluation." Donny saw her stiffen, and the smile disappeared from her face. He didn't mean to be cruel, but it was important to explain how things worked. "You don't become part of this crew just by showing up, Susan. That's something you earn. You earn it with respect, dedication and hard work. If you think being part of a crew comes from an assignment on a piece of paper, you cheapen what it really means.

"For the next six months you will have the opportunity to learn from the best of the best. You will see more action in that time than some guys see in ten years. As Senior Man, Eddy will look after most of your day-to-day training, but everyone here has something to teach you. I suggest you make the most of it."

The excitement and joy Susan had felt walking into the station just a few hours ago was evaporating. She shifted uneasily in the chair.

"You will be treated with courtesy and respect," Donny continued. "If anyone doesn't, you let me know and I will fix it. Of course you have the right to send any complaint you have up the chain of command, but we like to solve our problems in house if we can.

"You will also be expected to pull your weight. There will be no special treatment, no corners cut and no softer ride. OK?"

"OK," Susan said. She rose from the chair and turned to go. Then she turned back. "No, you know what? It's not OK. I've been looking forward to this for a long time and now you make me feel like I'm some kind of virus."

She walked over to the desk and glared at Donny. "I'm sorry if I broke up your precious little boys' club, but I'm entitled to be here. I qualified the same as any man in my class. I'll be damned if I'll be treated like a pariah because I'm a woman!"

"Susan, this has nothing to do with your being a woman." Donny stood and paced to the other end of the office. "OK, that part's new, but you think I'm being hard on you? Christ, you should have seen what it was like when I was a probie. Recruits were lower than whale shit. Some guys wouldn't even talk to you until you made first class."

"What next?" she asked "Are you going to tell me you walked to school barefoot in the snow, uphill both ways? I mean, what exactly is your problem? I am not here to bust anyone's balls, and I do not have human rights on speed dial. Yes, I heard about that."

Donny's jaw dropped. He heard a soft "oh, shit" and muffled laughter from the hallway. He frowned. Motioning for Susan to be silent, he walked quietly to the door and yanked it open. Two faces peered sheepishly through the doorway.

"You want to explain what's going on here?" Donny glared at the two men.

"We were just passing by on the way to the kitchen," said Moose, jerking his thumb over his shoulder as if Donny had no idea where the kitchen was.

"Going to get a coffee," added Eddy.

"Want some?" asked Moose weakly.

"I don't believe it," Susan snorted derisively. "What is this, grade school? This is the 'best of the best', eh?"

"OK, you guys want to have a group hug? Come on in." Donny circled back to the desk as he spoke. Eddy and Moose shuffled along the wall beside the door. Donny sat on the corner of the desk.

How had it all gone out of control like this? He sighed heavily and looked around the room at his crew. They looked back, waiting for him to speak. "We've got a lot of new here. I'm new at being Captain. Eddy's new at being Senior Man. Susan, you're just new, period. That's a lot of new stuff."

Susan opened her mouth to speak, but he cut her off. "No, please, let me say this first. Then you can say whatever you like.

"We've been through a lot here in the last year, Susan. Some of it you've heard about; we can fill you in on the details later, if you want. What I'm saying is there's been a lot of change. It's not good and it's not bad, it just is. Maybe I haven't dealt with all of it very well.

"Now, I kind of got off on the wrong foot with you, Susan. If I offended you, I'm sorry. Really. That's not what I wanted. Sometimes the words don't come out right. But the simple truth is, your coming here is probably the biggest change in this station since they got rid of the horses. So maybe we all need to lighten up a little, me included. OK?"

Susan looked at Donny for a moment, then nodded. They all did.

"And that speed dial thing," Eddy chimed in, "um, it wasn't the Captain, it was me. Actually it was kind of funny, see, 'cause…" He gave a forced chuckle, but saw that Susan wasn't laughing. "Well, it was funnier at the time. I'll, uh, explain later."

"I can hardly wait," replied Susan drily.

"OK, bottom line," Donny continued, "there's one thing that hasn't changed, and that's what happens out there. People depend on us and we depend each other. We will do our best to teach and help you, Susan, but trust and respect are earned. It *has* to be that way, because we put our lives in each other's hands. It doesn't matter if you're a man or a woman."

"Or a moose," quipped Eddy. "Mind you, if Moose goes down it's gonna take all of us to drag his ass out. And frankly, I'm not sure it's worth it." This time they all smiled.

Donny looked at Susan. "OK, your turn."

She leaned back against the lockers that lined the wall beside the desk and looked around the room. They were like little boys, she thought, with their jokes and pranks. Somehow, no matter their age, men never seemed to get much beyond eight years old mentally. They were little boys in grown-up bodies, with big shiny red trucks, playing a deadly game.

She had heard about Commissioners Street, of course. The instructors at the Academy had used it as a prime example of what *not* to do. It all made sense now: Donny was a wounded little boy. She had seen it in her own son. She probably understood Donny better than he understood himself. The realization didn't make her feel maternal, but it took the edge off her anger.

"This isn't exactly easy for me either," she said softly. "I'm not asking for any favours. I don't want to be treated any differently, just fairly. I want to learn. I want to become a good firefighter. What I don't want is to feel like I'm under a microscope all the time just because I'm female. OK?"

Donny looked at her silently for a second, then nodded. "Fair enough."

"Is that a woman thing?" asked Eddy, grinning.

"Moose, when you have a moment, kill him for me," said Donny, scowling at Eddy.

Susan ignored the exchange. "Just one more thing: please call me Sue. That's what my friends call me."

"OK, Susan," they answered in unison. She rolled her eyes as the alarm tones sounded.

"Pumper 6, respond at 127 Adelaide Street East for a fifty-six-year-old male, vital signs absent. Tactical channel 1, acknowledge."

"Woo-hoo, start your day with a VSA," crowed Eddy. "Nice beginning to your career, Susan."

"Just try not to kill this one, OK, Dr. Kevorkian?" Moose said to him as they made their way to the pole hole.

"Hey, technically, most of them are dead before I even get started," Eddy replied.

Little boys, thought Susan as she slid down to the apparatus floor. Little boys whistling as they walked through the graveyard.

"...**SO THE GUY WAS** doing at least a hundred. No seat belt. He went through the windshield, hit the pole and just exploded. I mean, there were body parts all over. We got most of the big pieces but we couldn't find his head. We looked everywhere. We eventually found it underneath a mailbox. The thing had bounced and rolled along the pavement for at least a hundred yards. No skin left. His head looked like this." Eddy speared a meatball off his plate and held it up with his fork. He grinned at Susan, winked and popped it in his mouth.

It was a ritual of the first night. Everyone pulled out their goriest stories, each trying to top the last, the more disgusting the better. "More spaghetti, Susan?" Moose pushed the bowl down the table to her. "Some garlic bread?"

"No, thanks. I'm stuffed. And such charming dinner conversation, too. Who could ask for more?" She pushed her plate away and leaned back in her chair. "Thanks, Eddy, that was a great sauce."

"You're welcome. It's nice to have someone who appreciates good food for a change." He ignored the insults from Donny and Moose.

Moose helped himself to another huge plate of pasta and ripped a large chunk off the loaf of garlic bread. Susan suspected he might start chewing on the furniture if Eddy didn't make enough food.

"So," Moose said, tucking an errant strand of spaghetti into his mouth with his fingers, "you worked for the City before you got on our job?"

"Yup, a little over ten years in health and safety. I'm actually an industrial hygienist by training."

"What exactly is that?" asked Eddy. "I always picture someone making sure guys on the assembly line wash their hands and brush their teeth."

Susan laughed. "There's a little more to it than that. My specialty was chemical exposure."

"You should put in for the HazMat truck," said Donny.

"I was thinking of that, Cap," she nodded at him. "I'd like to get a few years under my belt on a regular truck first, but that was in the back of my mind when I applied."

"No offence intended, but why did you apply?"

"I don't know," she shrugged, "why did you? The money's good. The twentyfour's a long shift but it's only twice a week so I figure I'll end up spending more time with my son. Maybe I just needed a change."

"Who's up for dessert?" asked Eddy, setting a brick of ice cream and an apple pie on the table.

"Oh God, I couldn't," said Susan, looking at the pie with horror.

"It's not about being hungry. Just punch it into you, fatso," responded Moose.

Susan whirled on him, but Donny held up his hand to forestall her.

"It's kind of a ritual joke around here when someone says they're full. Don't take it personally."

"You guys have quite the sense of humour, don't you?"

"Tough love, baby, tough love," said Eddy, patting her on the shoulder and smiling. "You'll get used to it."

"Do you eat like this every night? Why don't you all weigh five hundred pounds?"

"I'm working on it," said Moose, patting his belly. "So how old is your son?"

"Ryan's seven."

"That's a nice age. They're still cute at that age. Mine's fourteen," Eddy sighed, "and not so cute anymore."

"If he can cook like you, Eddy, he can't be all bad." Susan turned to Donny. "I'd like to bring Ryan to visit the station one day if that's OK, Cap."

"No problem. So what does your husband think about you spending the night with three men?" Donny smirked.

Susan frowned, pursed her lips and looked down at her nails.

"Ah, come on," Donny protested. "It was a joke. Listen, I'm sorry…"

"No," Susan cut him off, "it's OK. It's just… I guess that's part of why I needed a change." She sighed. "Ryan's father decided he preferred his twenty-three-year-old receptionist."

"Oh jeez, I am sorry." *For once in your life think before you open your mouth*, Donny said to himself.

"It's OK, it was a year and half ago. But I'm still pissed."

"Can't blame you," Moose agreed. "I'm just surprised the guy is still alive, you being an expert on toxic chemicals and all."

Susan smiled. "Believe me, I thought about it. You guys might want to keep that in mind, with all your clever jokes." She pointed at each of them in turn. "I could make it look like an accident."

"No such thing as the perfect crime," said Eddy. "That's what I keep telling my wife. I think it's the only reason I'm still alive after twenty-two years."

No such thing as the perfect crime, mused Donny. The key had to be somewhere, somewhere in all those statements and reports. He just had to recognize it. He helped himself to a slice of pie and a scoop of ice cream and took them back to the office.

NINE
Sailing

DONNY'S LIVING ROOM was hardly neat at the best of times. Now there were piles of paper on the coffee table, on the armchair, on the sofa and scattered around the floor.

Aldrich, true to his word, had gotten hold of the police report, statements from several of the attending officers, and other relevant police documents. There were also printouts of documents that had been emailed to him from the insurance company, the Ministry of Labour, the coroner's office and several other agencies that Donny had contacted.

Even aside from the clutter of paper, the room was instantly recognizable — as indeed was the rest of the house — as belonging to a single man. Furniture, pictures, rugs and curios had coalesced over time, accumulating rather than following any particular design scheme. It was the decorating equivalent of a dust bunny. The place had a decidedly male air, both metaphorically and literally.

Donny had kept the house when his wife had left for the West Coast to "find herself." Whatever she had found, it hadn't led her back to Toronto. He had been more shocked than angry. In hindsight, he knew he should have seen it coming: the growing silences, both of them moving into their separate orbits.

It had been, what, sixteen, seventeen years ago? The wounds had healed. Like an amputee, he felt the occasional twinge of phantom pain, but he had grown accustomed to his single life. He was, if not happy, at least content. He had found his place at the edge of the herd with the other bachelors.

He had endured the inevitable blind dates, most of them arranged by the wives of friends who seemed incapable of tolerating the notion of a contented single man, particularly one who fit into the broad category of "a good catch." He had even asked a few women out on his own. But he had never felt that special something. Donny wasn't quite sure what that something was, and he wasn't certain he would know it if it came along. But he was also smart enough to know it was not infatuation.

And so Donny had more or less closed off that part of his life, like the unused wing of a large house that took too much effort to maintain. He had a career he loved, a few good friends, and he had *Red Bird*.

Most of all he had his freedom — freedom to come and go where and when he chose. That was nothing to be taken lightly. There was the occasional pang as he passed a playground: he would sometimes pause to watch the happy bedlam, listen to the joyful squeals, and observe the easy, satisfied smiles of the parents sitting in the leafy shade. He would smile back and then resume his spot on the edge of the herd, where the air was fresh and the view clear to the horizon.

Now, as he tried to sift through the piles of reports and statements, the thought of Laurie Zhou kept bubbling to the surface of his mind. It was only natural, he told himself. Laurie had given him his best lead so far.

But if that was so, why did he keep picturing her smile and remembering the clear musical sound of her laugh? Why was he wondering what she looked like underneath the Works Department overalls?

The ringing of the phone brought him back to reality. He moved toward the source of the sound, lifted a pile of paper and answered it.

"Is that Donald Robertson?"

"Speaking."

"Hi, it's Micah Edwards returning your call." It was a familiar deep voice with a soft Caribbean lilt. Donny had first heard it in the hospital, when the Fire Marshal's investigator had come to interview him.

"Sorry I didn't get back to you sooner," said the voice. "I was working a murder case. Anyway, what can I do for you?"

"I'm not sure if you remember me, Mr. Edwards," Donny began. "I was involved with the Commissioners Street fire…"

"Please, call me Micah, like the prophet. Of course I remember you, man. I recognized the name right away. I wouldn't be much of a detective if I didn't remember a thing like that, would I?" The Fire Marshal's investigators were recruited from the police ranks, not from the fire service. They were experienced in gathering and handling evidence, interviewing witnesses and navigating the intricacies of building a case, skills one didn't normally develop on the end of a hose. It was no easy task reconstructing events from what was left after a devastating fire. After the last several days of reading reports and statements, Donny had a new appreciation of just how painstaking it really was.

"So how are you? The burns heal up?"

"Yeah, pretty much," Donny answered. "I had to give up my career as a supermodel, but I'm OK."

The voice on the phone chuckled "Hmm, there's a pretty picture, eh? Your scrawny white ass on a runway in a bathing suit. Anyway, I'm glad you're OK. What can I do for you?"

"Well, I need a favour, Micah. I'm kind of reviewing the fire, you know, and…"

"Reviewing? What do you mean, reviewing?"

"Going over it again, you know. It just doesn't feel right. I mean, that fire shouldn't have flashed. I was hoping you could help me out, give me a copy of your notes, that kind of thing."

"So you're giving up your career as a supermodel to become a fire investigator?" A cool edge had crept into Micah's voice.

"Well, uh," Donny shifted uncomfortably, "maybe I can, like, help you out. Take a fresh look at things."

"Seriously? Fire investigation isn't a hobby. Do you want some guy off the street coming over to run your pump panel or take a hose line in for you? Huh? I didn't think so. So what makes you think fire investigation is a game for amateurs?"

Shit, Donny thought to himself, this was not how he had wanted the conversation to go. "That fire never should have flashed. Fitz wasn't just my captain. He was... I need to know why he died."

There was a moment of silence on the other end of the phone. "Donny, I am truly sorry for your loss. Now, I respect your experience; I hope you respect mine. I have looked at that fire from every possible angle, and nothing other than your feeling suggests that it was arson."

"God damn it, I was there! I know what I'm talking about."

"Don't yell at me. Now, we both know there are a lot of things that can go wrong in a fire. Isn't it possible you made a mistake? Maybe you got in too deep? That doesn't mean it's your fault. Sometimes a fire just goes bad."

"And you've never made a mistake, Micah? You've never missed something?"

"This is going nowhere. The case is still open, Donny. If you find any new information — real evidence, not just your feelings — let me know. Otherwise you can get a copy of my report through the regular channels. Goodbye."

"Shit," Donny muttered as the line went dead. He stared glumly at the piles of paper around him. He should have kept his cool. Instead he had alienated his best prospective source of information.

"Real evidence," that's what Micah had said. If he was going to convince people he wasn't crazy, he needed something concrete. Very well, Laurie Zhou was the only real lead he had. Donny pulled out his wallet and searched for her card.

The thought of seeing her again excited him and made him

nervous at the same time. He remembered the way she had looked at him, almost like she was looking *into* him. He picked up his coffee and stared at the phone.

Why did he feel like he was in grade eight again, asking Lorraine Tinsley to dance? This is crazy, he told himself. Just call her. It's business, right? She had said to call her and he needed more information from her.

He picked up the phone and dialed the number.

"Hi, Laurie, it's Don, Donny Robertson from the fire department. Maybe you don't remem—"

"I was wondering if you were going to call."

"Well, uh, here I am." He laughed nervously. "Listen, I'm sorry to bother you. I hope I'm not calling at a bad time."

"No problem, it's nice to hear from you. What's up?"

"I've got a boat, see. And I'd like to talk to you. So, um, I was wondering if you'd like to go sailing."

"Are you asking me on a date, or is this business?"

"I, um, gee, you see, it's, well…"

"I'll settle for half and half, how's that?"

"Sure. I mean great. Yeah, wonderful." He sighed. "You must think I'm a complete moron."

"Not completely. Maybe half a moron." She chuckled. What a laugh, he thought. It was the simple honesty of it that appealed to him.

"I'm sorry," Laurie said. "Maybe you're just out of practice. It's OK, it's kind of cute actually. I'm a little rusty myself. Is it OK if I bring my boys?"

"Boys?" Donny sat up abruptly. "Aghh! I just spilled coffee all over myself. Boys! You're married?"

"Not any more. Is that a problem? I'd rather find out now if it is."

"No, no. It's not a problem. I just didn't think… I mean, I never asked… It's fine, really. I… You're right, I'm out of practice — really, really out of practice. So let's try this again: Would you and your boys like to go sailing with me? Tomorrow's Sunday, would that work?"

"Let me ask them." He heard her calling into the distance. "Hey, guys, how would you like to go on a sailboat?" There were squeals and cheers in the background. "I think that means yes. I need to do some grocery shopping, and I promised my Mom we'd stop by for lunch. Is one-thirty or two o'clock too late for you?"

Donny said it would be fine, gave her directions and hung up. He reviewed the conversation several times in his head. It wasn't a complete disaster. He started wiping up the spilled coffee, feeling somewhat pleased with himself and also a little queasy.

THE BOYS SAT DANGLING their legs over the bow, laughing as the spray from the waves washed over their feet.

"This is cool, Mom," Daniel, the eldest, called back.

"Just make sure you both hang on like Captain Robertson said, OK?"

"I'm gonna make Daniel walk the plank," replied Kevin, the younger boy. There was an exchange of good-natured shoving and then more laughter as another wave sprayed their feet.

The city was getting its first taste of summer heat, but out on the lake the air was cool and fresh. *Red Bird* heeled gently, her sails full and lines taut. The water hissed softly as it washed along the hull.

Laurie was amazed at how beautiful it was. The sun sparkled off the waves. Lake Ontario was so blue, not the muddy green-brown colour you saw close to shore. The city looked completely different from out here. It nestled beneath its summer blanket of green, office buildings and condo towers reaching up through the trees to popcorn clouds.

"I can see why you love this," Laurie mused.

"Yeah, it's good." Donny looked over at her from the helm. The smile shone in her round face. She was not quite Rubenesque, not quite voluptuous, but she had a pleasing, rounded solidity, he thought. Her bronze legs were stretched out along the cockpit bench, and her shiny black hair was pulled back under her hat.

He had been nervous at first, but he gradually relaxed as they left the dock and got underway. The conversation was light and easy. They talked a bit about sailing, a bit about their respective jobs, a bit about the boys' school and hobbies. It was, Donny realized, the best he had felt in a very long time.

"So do you ever get weekends free? I mean, do the boys ever go with their father for the weekend?" Donny tried to be nonchalant about it.

"No," she said simply. She was looking at the horizon but he knew her mind was somewhere else.

"Sorry, I didn't mean to pry," he offered. Damn it, Robertson, why did you have to push? They listened for awhile to the whisper of the wind and water mingled with spurts of laughter from the boys.

"He's dead." She kept her eyes on the sunlight dancing on the water.

"Oh jeez, I'm sorry…"

"It's OK. It's not like it's some deep dark secret." She turned and looked at him. Laurie's emotions played across her face as she told her story, but she was also watching his reaction. "It was an IED. We were both in the Forces. We met in Bosnia. How romantic, eh?

"Anyway, Steve was a medic and they were in a convoy, going to this health clinic in a village in Panjwaii. The lead vehicle got hit, and a couple of guys were badly hurt. Steve got out to help them. They got him with a secondary device."

She shook her head. "It was his second tour in Afghanistan. I mean, he knew better. I don't know how many times I told him, 'You *always* have to watch out for the secondary.' He couldn't help himself, that's who he was. If someone was sick or wounded…" her voiced cracked, "he just couldn't help himself."

"I'm sorry," Donny murmured. "I know that sounds lame, but I really am sorry."

"It's OK." She waved him off with one hand and dabbed at her eyes with the other. "It was five years ago. At the time I remember feeling like I couldn't breathe, like I'd never be able to breathe again. Now, sometimes it feels like it happened to someone else. Isn't that terrible? And sometimes it's like yesterday."

She turned her head to look at the boys perched at the bow, two happy explorers embarked on a journey of adventure. "The sad thing is, Daniel and Kevin hardly remember him. I don't know, maybe it's better that way. It's true what they say: kids are so resilient. They're not weighed down by the past like we are. But still, I can see the wheels turning sometimes, when they look at old pictures."

She swung her legs down and faced him. "It wasn't perfect. I mean, we had our problems, like everyone, and it was hard when one of us was deployed. But it was good, you know? It was worth it." Laurie forced herself to smile. "Anyway, that's my sad tale of woe. What about you?"

Donny shrugged, sweeping his eyes along the horizon that separated blue from blue. "There's not much to tell, really. I was married for a few years, back in my twenties. I guess we sort of drifted apart. I think she found my schedule hard. I'd be gone a lot of evenings and weekends when other people were together doing stuff. And half the time when I was off she was at work."

"No kids?"

"A couple of miscarriages, and after a while we just stopped trying. Gradually, it was like two strangers living in the same house. One day I came home and there was a note saying she had gone to Vancouver. A year later, a bunch of papers came in the mail. I can't say I was really that upset. Maybe that sounds terrible, but it's true.

"Anyway, it was a long time ago. Like you say, it sort of feels like it happened to someone else."

"And you never got back on the horse?"

"Hmmm," Donny chuckled. "I guess I figured marriage was something I just wasn't very good at."

Their eyes met, silently asking the questions they dared not say aloud. Laurie was about to speak when Donny called to the boys.

"Anybody want to go swimming?"

"Out here?" asked Daniel.

"Yup. The water's really cold, but I'll rig the halyard so we can use it like a swing."

"Are there sharks?" asked Kevin.

"Is it safe?" Laurie asked with genuine concern. She wished he had consulted her first before making the suggestion. Now it was going to be almost impossible to say no.

"There are no sharks. Sharks live in the ocean," Donny assured the boys as they scrambled back along the deck. He turned to Laurie. "It's safe. I'll go with them."

"Yeah, sharks live in the ocean, dufus," Daniel declared as they dropped into the cockpit. "Everyone knows that."

"I am not a dufus. You're a butthead, Daniel."

"Hey, hey, that's enough of that!" Donny warned. "There will be no name-calling aboard this vessel, or no one is going swimming. Is that clear?"

"OK," the boys yielded.

"Excuse me? 'OK?' What I would like to hear is 'Aye aye, Cap'n.'"

"Aye aye, Cap'n," they declared with gusto, snapping to an impromptu attention.

"But first we need the Admiral's leave to fall out for recreation," Donny said gravely. He turned and saluted Laurie. "How about it, Admiral? Permission to go swimming?"

She instinctively returned his salute. She liked the way he dealt with the boys, but she still wasn't sure this was such a great idea. She scowled momentarily. "How deep is it here?"

"About eighty feet, Ma'am. But really, once it's over their heads it doesn't make much difference, does it? Their lifejackets will keep them up."

"Well, they don't have their bathing suits."

"We can go in our underwear," suggested Kevin hopefully.

"Please, Mom, pleeeeease," Daniel pleaded.

Donny smiled and shrugged. Laurie knew she had a no-win case, and he *was* good with the boys. "All right," she declared solemnly, "permission granted."

The three of them cheered and Laurie burst out laughing. That laugh again — it sent tingles down Donny's spine. "Get busy living or get busy dying" — wasn't that the line? Maybe it was his turn. Their eyes met again, and this time it seemed there were a few answers among the questions.

Laurie watched as Donny showed the boys how to handle the boat. He started the engine and turned into the wind, then handed the helm over to Daniel and told him to keep the wind straight on her nose.

"Look, Mom! I'm driving!" Daniel was beaming with pride and concentrating very hard at the same time. Donny showed them how to douse and furl the sails. He told Daniel to shut off the engine, and the boat drifted silently. A sea anchor, deployed off the bow, brought them to a halt.

The boys scrambled below and stripped down to their underwear. Donny got them towels, then went below to change into his trunks. Next he rigged a handle to the spinnaker halyard and adjusted the height to suit the boys.

Laurie could see the full extent of Donny's burns as he stood beside the boys in his bathing suit. His physique was good, but pink, puckered skin ran down his neck onto both shoulders. There was more on his back and calves. She shuddered, not at the sight of the scars but at the thought of the pain he must have endured.

"Who wants to go first?" Both hands shot up. Donny gave the

handle to Daniel. "I want you to run as fast as you can and launch yourself out over the rail like I showed you. Let go when you're over the water, not before — got that? I'm going to jump in now and wait for you, OK?"

Donny cannonballed over the side, managing to splash Laurie with a few drops. She squealed appropriately and the boys laughed. Daniel sprinted along the coach roof and launched himself into the air. He let go perfectly at the apex of his swing and dropped, arms and legs flailing, into the water.

Donny grabbed him as he bobbed to the surface a few feet away. "It's cold!" Daniel yelled, "but that was awesome. Ya gotta do it, Kev, it's like flying!"

Kevin splashed down a few feet away and Donny swam the boys back to the boarding ladder. "That was totally sick. Can we go again?" asked Kevin when they were back aboard.

After a couple more jumps, both boys were shivering, and Laurie declared an end to swimming.

"No arguing with the Admiral," announced Donny. "Here, take your towels and go sit in the sun. I'll make hot chocolate."

Provisioned with hot chocolate and cookies, the boys returned to their perch on the foredeck and argued over who had flown furthest and highest.

Donny went below to change back into his clothes. When he returned, Laurie reached for his hand as he climbed the companionway back to the cockpit. Donny froze for a second, then took her hand and squeezed. He settled into the seat beside her, still holding her hand. She leaned against him and breathed in the scent of his damp skin.

She wanted him to kiss her and sensed it was what he wanted too. She glanced at her boys, laughing together in the sun. She took his hand in both of hers and gently traced the pink outline that ran along its back with her finger.

"Thank you," she whispered, "for all of this. It feels… nice. Really, really nice."

"I'm glad. I'd got so used to sailing solo, I'd forgotten how much fun it is to have someone along. We can do it again if you like. Maybe a sunset cruise with just the two of us?"

"I'd like that a lot," Laurie agreed, smiling up at him. They sat quietly enjoying the moment and soaking in the sun, until the boys had exhausted their argument and their supply of cookies.

Donny set them to work helping to raise the sails and getting *Red Bird* underway once again. He let the boys take turns at the helm and trimming the sails, until they got bored and went below to play Crazy Eights in the salon.

Laurie declined Donny's invitation to take a turn at the wheel, claiming such duties were beneath her dignity as a flag officer. They both laughed easily. To stern the sun glinted off the office towers behind the broad green band of the Toronto Islands. Ahead of them the Scarborough Bluffs rose and then vanished in the distance.

Donny cleared his throat. "Do you mind if we talk shop for a while?"

"Oh dear, is the honeymoon over so quickly?" Laurie replied. "Just kidding. I was expecting this." She settled back against the cockpit cushions and faced him. "You want to talk about the water main?"

Donny rubbed the stubble on his chin. "Well, yeah. How could you blow up a water main without anyone knowing?"

Laurie nodded. "I started thinking about it after we met. First of all," she ticked off her points on her fingers, "you have to calculate how big a charge to use: just enough to crack the iron without making it obvious or creating a crater. It's not rocket science, but you do have to know what you're doing."

She watched Donny to make sure he was following. "Then you have to know how to rig a remote detonator and trigger so you don't have to be right there to set it off. That's a bit of a specialty skill too."

Donny nodded intently. Laurie pursed her lips and continued. "Here's the really tricky part: you have to plant it all on a pipe buried six feet underground without leaving a trace. We use jackhammers and a backhoe to dig up those pipes, and there's no way to hide that. You can tell when the earth has been disturbed: we'd know if anyone had been digging around that pipe, if anyone had dug or tunnelled or drilled."

Donny tapped his fingers on the helm. "But there's got to be a way, right?"

Laurie gave a small shrug. "I guess, assuming I'm right about the explosives in the first place. I'm not even a hundred percent sure about that."

She watched the boat's wake disappear behind them. When she spoke again her voice was quieter. "The Taliban could hide fifty kilos of high explosive under a road and make it look like nothing was wrong. Let me think about it some more." She smiled at Donny, but he could see the sadness beneath. "Tell you what, you buy me dinner next week and I'll do some homework."

"That's a deal, but if this makes you… well, uncomfortable…" He left the thought unfinished.

"It does. I think it makes us both uncomfortable," she said matter-of-factly. "When we first met you said some scars are more obvious than others. Well, these are mine. The past has marked both of us, but I don't want to spend the rest of my life looking in the rear-view mirror. They deserve better" — she cocked her head at the boys — "and so do I."

"I think you're the most honest person I've ever met," Donny said with admiration. "I work with some pretty courageous people, but you're amazing."

"Yes, I am. And don't you forget it, mister." There was genuine warmth in her smile this time. They sailed in silence, both of them savouring the tingle of anticipation.

"Donny," she reached for his hand, "it's not just the past that makes me uneasy. Whoever did this knows their business. If I'm right, this guy's a pro."

He glanced at her. There was a gravity in her eyes he hadn't seen before. He reached to trim the main sheet, but she gripped his hand tighter. "Don't you think this is over your head? I know it's important to you. I understand that. But let the cops or someone else handle it."

"I will, I promise, as soon as I can get someone to believe me." He pulled his hand back and turned the boat towards shore.

TEN
Pembroke Street

"SHE'S NOT MY GIRLFRIEND, Eddy. And get your damned shoes off the desk."

Dust motes danced in the sunlight that poured in through the big south window of the captain's office. The oak wainscoting around the room glowed with a soft warmth, and even the pictures of stern-faced Victorian men standing stiffly at attention seemed to flush with life. Donny, however, was definitely not amused.

Eddy brought his chair down off its back legs and took his feet off the desk. "OK, don't get all defensive. It was nice seeing you come in this morning in such a good mood. I didn't mean to ruin it. I mean this as a friend, Donny. It's about time you had a date. I'm happy for you."

"Who had a date?" Moose stuck his head in the office door. He was dripping with sweat from his workout.

Eddy waved his arm in a grand gesture of presentation. "Our esteemed Captain here."

Moose looked thunderstruck. "Really? Ah, that's wonderful, Cap. Congratulations!" He strode into the room and offered a big sweaty hand across the desk. Donny shook it somewhat reluctantly.

"Listen, it wasn't a date. I mean, not like a *date* date. We just went sailing."

"Sailing? When was the last time he asked you to go sailing, Moose?" asked Eddy.

"The last time you guys went out with me, Eddy, you got so drunk you almost fell overboard."

"That's not the point." Eddy refused to give up the offensive. "Any action? Did you at least kiss her?"

"Why would I tell you, even if it was your business?"

"He kissed her," Moose confirmed.

"A little peck on the cheek when we said goodbye. Big deal. I don't believe you guys."

"Hey, we're on your side here, Wedge." Eddy clapped him on the shoulder. "This is a momentous occasion. Our little boy is growing up, Moose: he kissed a girl!"

Donny got up and began to chase Eddy around the desk. Moose obligingly moved out of out Eddy's way, then stepped back in front of Donny.

"Moose! Don't make me go through you!"

"That would be a very bad idea, Cap."

"A kiss is good, Donny, very good," Eddy protested, keeping the desk and Moose between them. "It's the first step on the road to booty."

Susan had heard the rising commotion and came to see the cause of it. She stood in the doorway and looked sideways at Eddy. "Booty? Are you for real? What's going on?"

"Your Captain is getting hooked up," Eddy proclaimed.

Donny moved back around behind the desk as Eddy edged warily in the opposite direction. "Are we all here now?" asked Donny. "Are you sure you don't want to send out invitations to the rest of the district? How about taking out an ad in the paper?"

"Hmm," Susan mused, putting a hand to her chin, "I seem to recall someone giving me advice. Let's see: 'lighten up' or something like that. Does that ring a bell?"

Eddy and Moose copied her posture.

"Sounds familiar."

"I believe you're right."

Donny sat back down in his chair and spread his arms. "OK, here it is. Laurie's with Public Works. I wanted to talk to her about the water main on Commissioners, so I invited her and her kids to go sailing. That's it. Is that such a big deal?"

"Her *and* her kids?" Moose repeated "I'm going to have to check the rule book on this, but yeah, I think that's serious."

"It was business!"

"Of course," nodded Eddy. "I always kiss people for business. And yes, *mon capitaine*, for someone whose last date was, I believe, at the end of the Ice Age, it is a big deal. Congratulations, big guy." He led them all in a round of applause.

The alarm tones sounded as the clapping died away.

"Thank God!!" exclaimed Donny.

THEY COULD SEE the column of black smoke to the north as they turned out of the hall.

"Lock and load, guys," said Moose as he threaded the truck through traffic. "Looks like a real cooker."

It was a glorious day, the sort of day when green wasn't just a colour but a thousand different shades of bursting life on every tree and shrub. Lilacs offered their perfume on the soft breeze. Flowers bloomed in the most unlikely places, softening the hard-edged shabbiness of storefronts and rooming houses.

Donny saw none of it. His attention was fixed on the sooty arc that rose into the sky, and the cold emptiness that weighed in his gut.

"Eddy, take the nozzle. I want six lengths of 38 on the wye. This place could be a crack house. If you're crawling, watch out for needles."

Eddy reached around and put a hand on Donny's shoulder. "We've done this before, Cap. It's gonna be OK."

He was thinking too much. He was trying to plan the whole fire and they hadn't even arrived yet. He was scared. Scared was good, up to a point. Donny didn't trust anyone who wasn't a little scared going into a fire. That wasn't courage, it was stupidity, and it would get you hurt or killed. Beyond sensible caution, however, fear was just as dangerous: it led to panic, and panic was deadly.

They could see the flames boiling out of the second-story window as they turned onto Pembroke Street. A crowd of people stood gawking and pointing, and a man on the front lawn was screaming about a lady trapped on the third floor. Donny took a deep breath. Trust your instincts, he told himself.

"Pumper 6 arrived on Pembroke," Donny spoke into his mic. "We have a serious working fire in a three-story brick semi-detached rooming house. Requesting second alarm. Report of a woman trapped third floor. Pumper 6 Captain is in mobile command, attempting rescue third floor."

"Roger, Pumper 6 Captain. Second alarm. Attempting rescue third floor," repeated the voice on the radio. Pumper 7 rolled to a stop behind them as the dispatcher finished speaking.

"Scooter," Donny called to the Pumper 7 captain, "you guys better search next door. Looks like it might be coming through the wall." He pointed to the people emerging, coughing and choking, from the other half of the semi. "Can your driver get the hydrant for Moose? I want to take my probie in."

"Sure thing, Wedge," Scooter answered. "Spike, get Moose a hydrant."

"Ready to go," said Eddy. He was holding the nozzle with the hose piled loosely behind him. Susan was pulling the heavy suction hose off the back of the truck.

"Susan, you're coming with us," Donny called to her. They slipped on their masks and reached behind to turn on the air tanks. They each picked up several folds of the flat, empty hose and piled it on their shoulders. It was slack they would pay out as they made their way through the house. Donny patted Eddy on the back. "Let's go."

It was relatively cool on the ground floor but they could hear the crackle of the fire overhead. They worked by touch, groping their way through the thick smoke, stumbling over unseen obstacles, searching for the stairs that led up, listening to the fire, moving towards the heat.

"Hang on to the hose and stay right on my tail, Susan. I want you within arm's reach at all times. Got that?"

"Yes, sir." She tried to sound confident. She struggled to remember the search-and-rescue drills they had done in the smoke house at the academy. This was nothing like the drills, though. She had no idea where she was going or what she was tripping over. This was insane, her instincts told her. But the air in her mask was cool and fresh, and she was with a trained experienced crew. It would be OK, she told herself. She tried to swallow, but her throat was dry.

"Found the stairs, Wedge. Over here," Eddy called.

The smoke and heat were like nothing Susan had experienced in training. She began to see a hazy orange glow surging at them, as they climbed the stairs.

"Pumper 6 Captain to Pumper 6: charge that line, Moose!"

"Here it comes," Moose answered. He opened the valve and water rushed to fill the hose. Donny started his mental stopwatch: three minutes. After that they would need the hydrant.

Eddy opened the nozzle as they moved towards the orange glow. The hose was stiff and unwieldy now, as they circled towards the foot of the stairs that led to the third floor. The fire was licking along the ceiling, seeking a path upwards.

"Looks like the front two rooms are fully involved. See if you can hold it here," Donny said to Eddy. "Susan and I are heading upstairs to find the woman."

"Got it."

"You OK, Susan?"

"Right behind you, Cap." She was feeling more confident and the adrenalin was kicking in.

The heat funnelled up the stairs behind them. Donny could feel it gnawing at the tender skin of his grafts.

They heard a choking cough as they got to the top of the stairs. "Hello!" Donny yelled. "Fire Department, we're coming to get you."

"Oh, God! Help me, I'm burning!" a voice screamed, and the coughing started again. Donny reached behind him to make sure Susan was still there, then moved towards the voice. It seemed to be coming from the back of the building, not directly over the fire. That was one point in their favour, but the heat was still coming hard up the stairs.

They found a young woman leaning out the window in the back bedroom. She was struggling for fresh air but the open window was acting like a chimney. Smoke and heat swirled out around her. The fire would soon follow.

"Help me, please help me!" she gasped.

"We will. We'll get you out of here."

The radio crackled to life. It was Spike. "The hydrant's no good. The spindle's seized or something. I gotta get another one."

"Roger. Make it quick. We got the lady. How much water we still got, Moose?"

"Half a tank."

Donny keyed his mic again. "How you doing, Eddy?"

"Just barely holding it. We need a second line," came the terse reply.

Damn, this was not good. There was no way they could get her out alive going down the stairs.

Scooter's voice came on the radio. "Everyone's out next door. Hang tight, Wedge, we'll get you that hydrant and bring a second line."

"It's too hot to wait for the hydrant, Scooter. We're bailing."

Donny took a pouch from the pocket on his bunker pants. He pulled the end of a rope from the pouch, wrapped it around the pipe of the radiator beneath the window and clipped the rope back on itself with a carabiner. He threw the pouch out the window and the thin red escape rope snaked down the side of the house. The woman was coughing and moaning incoherently now. Sirens wailed and the radio crackled with the arrival of more crews.

"Susan, we're going out the window. Lady, I'm going to clip this rope onto Susan and she's going to take you down."

"Quarter tank, Cap." More good news from Moose. Eddy had forty-five seconds of water left at most. Donny clipped the descender that was threaded through the rope onto Susan's SCBA straps.

"I've only practised this once, Cap, and never holding someone else," Susan said nervously. "Maybe you should take her."

"You're hooked up. Now get out there. There's no time for this."

Susan climbed out the window, turned, and braced her feet against the wall. "Ready!" she called.

Donny lifted the woman towards the window. The heat hammered on them. "I can't do it, I can't," the woman moaned.

"Yes, you can, and you're going to, or I'll throw you out the window! Hang onto Susan. Hang on and don't let go for anything." He saw her clasp her arms around Susan's neck. Susan put one arm around the woman's waist and eased the rope through the descender with her other hand as she walked backward down the wall.

"I'm dry," Moose called over the radio. Donny could feel the sudden surge of heat.

"I gotta pull back till they get the hydrant," Eddy cut in. "Your best bet's the window, Donny. It's coming up the stairs."

"That's my plan once they're down," Donny answered. He lay flat on his belly, getting as low as he could under the deadly heat. The scars on his neck and shoulders were screaming. Time slowed to a trickle.

He watched the orange glow brighten in the blackness, moving closer. He knew the fire was swirling up the stairs, spreading across the ceiling, reaching towards the window. It was coming to reclaim him.

What was he doing here? They had offered him any number of

desk jobs, a training officer position, anything he wanted. Why had he insisted on coming back to the trucks?

Anger, fear and regret welled up inside him. It seemed like every emotion he had ever felt, ever denied, all surged, threatening to shatter him into a thousand glowing embers.

Then, like a towering wave, it broke. In a crystal moment, terror and remorse melted away. There was only what needed to be done. He had to wait. The escape rope was designed to hold one person; it might hold two, but it couldn't take the weight of three bodies.

The seconds stretched into eternity.

"We're down. Get the hell out of there," the radio barked.

Donny rose to his knees. The heat was a razor-edged juggernaut driving him back down. He reached for the rope, gripped it tightly, and flung himself out the window. The slick red nylon slipped through his leather gloves as he slid down the side of the building.

Suddenly he was weightless, floating. He saw the melted end of the rope drift above him, a ruby snake weaving lazily in the clear sapphire sky; then there was a thump, and the blackness closed around him.

THEY ALL LOOKED the same, the nondescript curtains and paint that seemed to have had the colour drained out of it. There was that oxygen valve thing with the clear plastic cone and the ball bearing inside. The gurneys were all the same too, not terrible, but never really comfortable either.

Donny hated hospitals. He was pretty sure that if he were taken to some alien planet in a far off-corner of the galaxy, the hospital rooms would still all look the same. And he would hate them too.

Hospital rooms on an alien planet? He looked down at the intravenous line running into the back of his hand and wondered what they were giving him. Wet dressings covered his arms and ran across his neck and back. There was a familiar pain.

A soot-stained face peeked around the curtain. "Still in the land of the living, I see." Eddy grinned at him and walked into the emergency room cubicle. Susan was right behind him.

"You're both filthy and you stink," Donny greeted them.

"We can shower. Too bad you can't wash off ugly," responded Eddy.

Donny smiled. "Moose waiting with the truck?"

"Yeah, we parked in the 'Police Only' spot. You know how they get about that sometimes," Eddy shrugged.

"How are you doing, Cap?" Susan asked with concern.

"I'm OK." Donny thought for a moment. "Yeah, I'm OK. A little sore, but it's been worse. How about you?"

"Honestly? I'm not sure. I'm kind of shaking now, but wow!" Susan shook her head. "That was incredible. It was terrifying and wonderful and… I don't know."

"Welcome to fire fighting. Don't worry, it's not like that every time." Donny looked into her eyes. There had been no panic during the fire. Sometimes it showed up later, but there was none there now either. "You did good, Sue, you did real good. I'm proud of you."

Sue. He had called her Sue, not Susan. "Thanks, Cap. I appreciate that. Lucky you were most of the way down when the rope let go."

"Yeah, lucky me." Donny closed his eyes. A ribbon of thin red rope danced like a fakir's snake.

"You sure you're OK?" Eddy asked, leaning forward.

"What, are you my shrink now?" The two men locked eyes. "I'm fine, Eddy. How's the woman?"

"Still breathing when they loaded her in the ambulance. I think she'll make it." Eddy rubbed at a red mark on his neck.

"Chalk up one for the good guys," Donny nodded. "Looks like you got a little scorched around the neck. You should let the doctor have a look at it."

"Are you kidding? After what those butchers did to you?"

"Then perhaps you'd care to leave," said a voice from the other side of the curtain. A young woman with a white coat, stethoscope and a clipboard appeared. "We try to maintain certain minimum standards of hygiene here." She wrinkled her nose at Eddy and Susan. She was young and pretty, with short brown hair and hazel eyes. She was young enough to be his daughter, Donny thought. The whole world seemed to be getting younger.

"How's the woman, Doc?" Donny asked.

"The one from the fire? Are you the guys that pulled her out?" Donny and Susan nodded. "I didn't treat her. I heard she's in serious but stable condition. Smoke inhalation, burns to about a third of her body, and some other issues I can't really discuss."

"Other issues?" Eddy asked. "Like 'you wouldn't want to exchange bodily fluids' issues?"

"Do any of you have any open cuts?"

"No," they replied.

"Then I wouldn't worry about it. I believe she's a needle user. That's all I can say," said the doctor.

"Jeez," said Eddy. "We pull them out. You patch them up. And you gotta wonder what it's all for."

"Ask the chaplain. That's not my department. Maybe it's so folks believe we're the sort of people we want them to think we are." She pointed to the exit. "I've got half a dozen patients stacked up, so now that we've solved the pressing philosophical question of the day, why don't you two go have a shower and let me do my job?"

"I think she likes me, Donny." Eddy winked at the doctor. "We'll see you later."

"Look after yourself, Cap," Susan called over her shoulder, then elbowed Eddy in the ribs. "You are such an asshole sometimes."

The doctor shook her head.

"That's just Eddy. He's a good guy, Doc, really."

"I'm sure he is," she said indulgently. "Now let me see your arms." She lifted the moist dressing on Donny's right arm. The wrinkled skin of the grafts was an angry red. She looked at the other arm, then asked him to sit up so she could check his neck and shoulders.

"Any headache? Blurred vision?" Donny shook his head. "Tingling or numbness?" she asked. She was making notes on the clipboard. "You had your mask on the whole time? You didn't breathe in any smoke?"

"No," Donny said.

"I see you were a patient of Dr. Levinson here in the burn unit?"

"Yes."

"Uh-huh," she continued, writing, then glanced up. "You know we don't give frequent flyer miles, eh?"

"Believe me, Doc, I had no desire to come back here. But it's not so bad this time, right? Can I go home?"

She put down the clipboard and looked at him. He seemed like a nice guy. She liked him, she decided. Not in any romantic way, but with a sort of collegial respect and concern. Donny sensed she was no longer looking at his injuries but somewhere deeper inside. He squirmed.

"You're a lucky man, Captain Robertson."

"So everyone keeps telling me. Please call me Donny."

"All right. You're a lucky man, Donny. Aside from a couple of blisters on your ears and the back of your neck, it's all first degree. You're going to feel like you've got a very bad sunburn for a few days, and you have a minor concussion, but the Xrays we took of your spine look fine."

"That's great. Thanks for…"

"But," she continued, putting a hand lightly on his shoulder, "luck has a way of running out. You've had two very close calls in just over a year. Should I be concerned about that?"

He felt trapped. It was one of those questions with no real right answer, like "when did you stop beating your wife?" He decided ignorance was the safest path. "I'm not really sure what you mean."

"I think you do." She waited for a response but none came. She put her foot on the chair and pulled up her left pant leg, revealing a wrinkled scar the size of a lime just above her ankle.

"That happened at summer camp when I was ten. We were toasting marshmallows. Mine caught fire and I shook it. It fell off the stick and landed there." She pointed to the scar. "I tried to blow it out, but it kept on burning. I remember screaming. I thought it was going to burn right through my leg. Then one of the counsellors picked me up and threw me in the lake. I've never toasted another marshmallow since. I don't even like sitting by a fireplace." She waited again, but there was still no response. "So why do you keep going back? Tell me."

Donny looked at his dressings, then at the IV bag's slow drip. "I guess I need the eggs," he shrugged.

"Excuse me?"

"It's an old joke. I think Woody Allen used it in *Annie Hall*. That was before your time. Anyway, this guy goes in to a psychiatrist and says, 'My brother's crazy: he thinks he's a chicken.' The psychiatrist agrees. 'Maybe we should lock him up,' he suggests. 'I can't,' says the guy, 'we need the eggs.'"

The doctor picked up the chart and started making notes again. How could he explain it? He looked at the name tag on her white coat.

"Dr. Cooke, listen. Put down the pen for a second. Do you ever go home at the end of a shift and cry yourself to sleep? Huh?" This time it was the doctor who remained silent. "But you come back anyway. And maybe the next day you get somebody's heart to start beating again, or you tell a mother her kid's going to live. And there's nothing, absolutely nothing, that feels better than that.

"We always start out behind the eight ball, you and me, but we keep playing the game. Because we need the eggs."

She picked up her pen and scratched out the previous line. "We are, as always, short of beds. Do you feel well enough to go home?" Donny nodded. "OK then, I'm going to write you a prescription for the pain and an antibiotic cream. You need to rest and heal for at least a week, preferably two. I'll have a nurse remove the IV. Can you call someone to bring clean clothes and take you home?"

Donny thanked her and asked if there was a phone he could use.

"At the nurses' station. Nothing personal, Donny, but I hope I don't see you again."

"Likewise, Doc. Thanks."

RATZO ARRIVED AN hour later, handed Donny his civvies and waited while he got dressed. They walked in silence to the Chief's van, parked illegally just outside the emergency entrance.

"I'm taking you home, Donny. Don Mills and Lawrence area, right?" Ratzo checked the traffic and did a U-turn.

"Yes," said Donny, "What about my bike?"

"The guys said they'd roll it into the station. You can pick it up later." Ratzo looked straight ahead as he drove. The sidewalk patios of the trendy Cabbagetown restaurants were filling up as the work day ended.

"Any clue what started it?" Donny asked.

"Guy on the second floor admitted he might have passed out with a cigarette. He reeked of booze. One-thirty in the goddamn afternoon and the guy's so pissed he passes out." Ratzo shook his head.

"Lucky he woke up."

"His dog woke him up. Dog's got more brains than he does. Speaking of brains," he glanced over at Donny, "you got a death wish or something?"

"Jeez, Ratzo, not you too."

"Whaddya mean?"

"Ah, the Doc was giving me a grilling." Donny looked out the window. He really didn't want to get into this all over again.

"Well, what do you expect? Your first working fire after you get back and you almost get yourself fried again, and your crew too."

Donny swung his head around and glared at Razzolini. Whatever had been in the IV was wearing off, and his neck hurt where the burn rubbed against his collar. "So it's my fault the bloody hydrant was no good?"

"Donny, I don't know whether to put you in for a commendation or drag your ass to headquarters for a hearing. You went above a working fire with a probie, without a secure water source or a backup line. What the hell were you thinking?"

"You want to tell me you would have left that woman up there to burn while you waited for a second line?"

"You don't get it, do you? You put your crew in danger. You're a captain now. Yes, we take risks, but your number one job is to make sure everyone goes home at the end of the day. You got that?"

"Just look me in the eye, Ratzo, look me straight in the eye and tell me you would have let her burn."

Razzolini pulled the van to the curb and slammed on the brakes. He was angry and the veins in his forehead were bulging. "You look me in the eye, Wedge, and you tell me what you would say if Susan or Eddy were back there lying in the burn unit. Or the goddamn morgue. Huh? Tell me what you would say to Eddy's wife or Susan's kid."

"I…"

"Shut the fuck up. This is not the old days. This is not that 'iron men and wooden ladders' bullshit. That crap they fed us when we were recruits? That's gone. If this was the old days, I'd just take you in the hose tower and beat the shit out of you!"

The rush-hour traffic was piling up behind them. A police car cruised slowly by and the cop looked over enquiringly. Razzolini pulled back into traffic and they drove without speaking.

"East on Lawrence, take the second right." Donny broke the silence when they got close.

"I remember now," said Ratzo. He glanced at Donny as he turned the corner. "I gotta know, Donny. I gotta know you've got your shit together and that you're not looking for a pumper funeral of your own."

"Hell no! I'm not crazy," Donny scowled. He needed to change the subject. "So you think you could take me?"

"What?"

"In the hose tower. You think you could take me?"

"In a heartbeat, cream puff." The van pulled to a stop in front of Donny's house, a simple post-war brick bungalow. A red maple spread its arms to the evening sun beside the flag stone path that led from the driveway to the front door. Roses bloomed in front of the bay window.

"I don't know what I would have done," Ratzo admitted. He was staring straight ahead. "About the woman, I mean, if it was me on that hose line. I don't have to make that choice any more. But I do have other responsibilities, just as serious. And I know what the book says." He looked over at Donny. There was sadness in his eyes. "I don't want to fight you. That's not how it's supposed to be."

"No, it's not," Donny agreed. Then he smiled. "But we sure laid a beating on guys when we were defence partners, didn't we?"

"We surely did. Nobody parked in front of our net for free." Razzolini smiled at the memory, then his face grew serious. "Listen, Donny, I don't mind going into the corners for you, but I don't like getting sucker-punched. We clear on that? You need to start thinking like a leader, not a hero. OK?"

"You're right."

"Of course I'm right. I'm the damned Chief, remember?"

Donny laughed, opened the door and got out. Razzolini leaned over and rolled down the window. "I've got a meeting with the Division Commander tomorrow morning. I'll get you those statements and the communications log for Commissioners Street. It'll keep you busy for the next week as you ponder your sins."

"Thanks, Ratzo, that means a lot to me. I owe you."

"Yes, you do. And don't think I'll forget it, either. OK, some of us still have to work. I'll see you, slacker." He put the van in drive. Donny gave a mock salute and Razzolini flipped him the finger as he pulled away.

The next afternoon Ratzo dropped off a four-inch-thick pile of documents. It would keep Donny very busy indeed.

ELEVEN
Report from Toronto

"YOU'RE QUITE CERTAIN this Captain Robertson is not a serious concern?"

Brendan paused for a moment, then shook his head. "He has nothing, only his suspicions and perhaps some sense of guilt."

Brendan had spent the past several days in Toronto. For most of that time he had posed as a writer working on a story about firefighters and career risks. He had contacted many of the same people Donny had spoken with and gotten the same responses. He had also spoken with a few off-duty firefighters on other crews in Donny's district.

Yup, the Commissioners Street fire was a terrible tragedy, they admitted, as Brendan paid for a round of drinks. But it was all part of the job, they declared with bravado. Brendan listened politely and took notes as they boasted about other rescues, escapes and tragedies.

"What about the psychological effects?" Brendan asked. "That guy who survived Commissioners Street, how's he coping?"

Ah, poor Wedge, he seemed to have a bee in his bonnet about the Commissioners Street fire. It was only to be expected, they clucked sympathetically. That fire seemed to have messed him up mentally as well as physically.

"Was there something unusual? Aside from the tragic death of Captain Fitzgerald?"

It just went bad, they said, shaking their heads. Brendan bought another round, toasted Fitz and left them with their stories.

The next evening Brendan waited until Donny had gone out for dinner. People with illicit skills could always be found for the right price. The man opened Donny's back door silently in a matter of seconds, accepted Brendan's cash and disappeared into the darkness.

Brendan found what he was looking for in the living room. He examined the piles of paper scattered haphazardly on every horizontal surface. It was as Brendan had suspected: document after document, all pointing to the same dead end. He carefully replaced each pile of paper where he had found it. He slipped out, locked the back door and headed to the airport.

Now he sat in Catherine's suite in the Carlyle in New York.

"I recommend doing nothing," Brendan concluded. "Eventually he'll get tired, frustrated or bored. With any luck, he may even kill himself. He was recently injured rescuing some drug addict from a fire."

"Really? How very noble of him," Catherine smiled drily.

"Bloody foolish if you ask me. I wouldn't risk my neck to save some low-life junkie," Brendan scowled.

"No, I don't suppose you would." Catherine rose from the grand piano she had been playing when Brendan arrived and looked out at the lights of Manhattan. Neither would she, she reflected, but not for the reasons of cowardice and disdain that she knew motivated Brendan. There was simply no advantage in it.

Neither did there seem to be any advantage in pursuing Robertson further. There was the risk of things snowballing, and she didn't want to start a trail of bodies. Experience and Machiavelli had taught her it was best to be ruthless, but not reckless.

She turned back to Brendan and nodded. "Very well, we'll leave Captain Robertson to chase his tail."

Catherine was relieved. She was a builder, not a destroyer, she told herself. Youssef Aziz had sealed his own fate.

There was also, she realized, a sentimental quality to her relief.

That made her uneasy. Sentiment clouded good judgement. Robertson still needed careful watching.

She dismissed Brendan and retreated to the bedroom. She was exhausted. Even a couple of years ago she could work sixteen-hour days with no problem, but lately she just didn't seem to have the energy, and the headache that had plagued her off and on for the past several weeks had returned. It wouldn't get any easier as she got older, either.

Early the next morning she placed two phone calls: one to Washington, the other to her doctor.

THERE WAS A MESSAGE waiting for Commander Wilkins when he arrived at his office the next morning. It was a summons from his section head, Colonel Ed Gilford.

"Come in and close the door, Mike." Gilford returned the Commander's salute and leaned back in his chair. He was a short, slightly built man with a bald head and a large pointed nose. Wilkins was not the only one to think he looked a bit like Dobby from *Harry Potter*, in an Air Force uniform.

Gilford pushed a file folder across the desk to Wilkins. It contained a photo of Donald Robertson, Captain, Toronto Fire Department on top of a dossier of personal information. Wilkins had years of practice controlling his expression, but some trace of his surprise must have leaked through. Gilford noticed it immediately.

"You recognize this man?"

Wilkins was only momentarily taken aback. Gilford had spent his entire career in the intelligence community and he was nobody's fool. "Robertson came up in that alert a few days ago, sir, the one you said was a favour for one of our 'friends.'"

"Correct," Wilkins nodded. "I need that Spectrum watch expanded, with Robertson highlighted: phone, Internet, financials, whatever. I want this guy under a magnifying glass."

A magnifying glass could reveal fine details, Wilkins knew. And if it were held in just the right position, it could also vaporize whatever was at its focus.

Gilford noted the tension in Wilkins' neck muscles and frowned. "You got a problem with that, Commander?"

Wilkins shifted in his wheelchair. "No, sir, it's just… I know these people help us out in some very tough spots. It's just that returning a favour is one thing. These people seem to be taking it to a whole other level."

"Well, it sucks to be him, I guess. You know, Mike, I like to catch fish and I like to eat fish. I don't particularly like to gut and clean them, but that's part of the deal. I don't like this any more than you do, but it comes from the very top."

"May I ask how secure our footing is, sir?"

"What footing? I don't see any footprints, do you?"

Wilkins nodded. The National Security Agency had a long history of operating at or just beyond the boundaries of the law. The courts and Congress tended to practise a form of "don't ask, don't tell" when it came to the NSA, particularly in the post-9/11 world. That suited the NSA just fine.

"I'd like you to handle this personally," said the Colonel. "The fewer people involved the better. Report directly to me. I will pass whatever is relevant on to our friends. Any questions?"

"No, sir."

"Very well. Carry on."

"Aye aye, sir."

TWELVE
Dinner Conversation

DONNY HAD ASKED FRIENDS to recommend a romantic French restaurant. He had dug a suit he had not worn in years out of his closet, and gratified that it still fit, sent it off to the cleaners. And he had resolved, as he splashed aftershave on his cheeks, not to talk about Commissioners Street or any other fire.

He had arrived at the restaurant half an hour early just to be sure. His was not the only head that turned when Laurie walked in. She wore a scoop-backed dress of deep green silk that was just tight enough to emphasize her figure and flowing enough to leave something to the imagination. The pearls that hung from her neck and ears glowed in the candlelight against her caramel skin.

She looked fabulous, but Donny could tell by the time they ordered that there was something bothering her. He made what now seemed like the mistake of asking what it was.

"It's part of fighting fires, Laurie. People get hurt doing your job too. If we wanted to be totally safe, both of us would be driving desks. But I don't think either of us is like that." Donny smiled at her. He hoped it was enough of an explanation. It was not what he wanted to spend the evening talking about.

Their entrees arrived and they ate without speaking for a while. The clink of dishes and cutlery and the murmur of conversation at other tables only emphasized the silence. Laurie struggled to sort out her emotions. Her attraction to Donny was undeniable. She admired his courage in rescuing the woman. But…

"I shouldn't have had to read about it in the paper," she said tersely, spearing a piece of potato with her fork. "You should have called."

Donny shrugged. "I'm sorry, I didn't know we were at that stage."

"That stage?" Laurie put down her knife and fork and glared at him. "I didn't know you were keeping score. Exactly what stage do we have to get to before you have the common decency to let the people who care about you know when you wind up in the hospital?"

Donny picked up his napkin and wiped his mouth. "I'm sorry, Laurie, I didn't think… I mean, I didn't call anyone. The guys all knew already. I'm just not used to thinking that way. It's been a long time since someone cared about me like that."

"Is there enough room in your life for someone like that, Donny? Is it too much to ask for a little consideration?" It seemed to him there was more fear than anger in her eyes.

"No," he sighed, "it's not too much. But you need to tell me one thing. Are you mad at me because my job can be dangerous or because I didn't call you? Because if it's the first thing, we have a real problem."

Donny put the napkin down and leaned back in his chair. "I'm sorry about what happened to your husband, but I can't fix that. I can't change what happened in your past. And I'm not going to give up the fire department because of it."

"How dare you?!" Laurie spat. Now she was angry. She was quivering with rage. "I'm sorry I ever told you about Steve. All I asked from you was simple courtesy."

"I didn't mean it that way, Laurie." Donny searched desperately for some solid ground before the quicksand swallowed him. "All I'm saying is being a firefighter is part of who I am and that's not going to change."

"I never asked you to change anything — just a phone call, just a little space in your life. But maybe that's too much for a macho guy like you." Laurie pushed her chair back and stood up. "Goodbye, Donny. I hope that fire truck loves you half as much as you love it."

Donny sat stunned. How had it gone so wrong so fast? The conversations at the other tables slowly resumed as the waiter glided over to Donny's side. "Madam will not be returning?" he enquired.

"I guess not," Donny replied. He watched through the front window as Laurie climbed into a cab. "Just bring me the bill." He drained his wine glass, then reached across the table and drained Laurie's too.

DONNY LAY ON HIS back in the cockpit, watching the stars weave back and forth as *Red Bird* rolled gently at the dock. Was it his fault, or had it been doomed from the start? Should he have run after her like they do in the movies? He took another sip of whiskey. The ice cubes in his glass tinkled in counterpoint to the chime of the rigging on the mast. It didn't matter anyway, he told himself. It was better this way.

It was a lie, but he had told himself bigger lies in the past and believed them. Why couldn't he believe this one? To hell with it, and her too. He closed his eyes and tried to think of something else, but the sound of her laugh, the genuine warmth of her smile and the fabulous green dress filled his mind. He gave up and let sadness and self-pity wash over him.

"That was rude of me. I don't like to be rude."

Donny's eyes snapped open. He had been dimly aware of the sound of footsteps coming down the dock and assumed it was another boater returning from a night out.

Laurie leaned against the cabin cruiser next to *Red Bird*, the green dress shimmering faintly in the moonlight.

"Laurie, I…"

She held herself rigidly as she gazed down at him. "It was also presumptuous of you, and inconsiderate and clumsy." Her posture relaxed and her voice softened. "It was also, maybe, a little too close to the bone."

"How did you know where to find me?" Donny asked as he sat up.

"You're not as complicated as you think," she shrugged.

"Guess I deserve that. Will you come aboard?"

"I don't know." Laurie held on to the cruiser behind her. Her head was cocked slightly to the side in a way that Donny had come to know was uniquely hers. "Is there room for both of us?"

Donny stepped onto the dock and stood beside her. He had the good sense to keep his mouth shut and let her vent the remnants of her anger and fear.

"You were right. Your job makes me nervous. Why do I fall for guys that don't have the sense of self-preservation that God gave a gnat?" Laurie shook her head. "I don't want to change you, Donny. I wouldn't ask you to give up anything that was important to you. But I do need some understanding from you. And compassion. Can you do that?"

"Yes." He held out his hand, but she didn't take it.

"I'm not asking for a permanent commitment. But I'm not looking for a one-night stand, either." Laurie looked around the marina. Shards of moonlight danced between the boats bobbing at the docks. "I guess what I'm looking for is a safe harbour."

"Laurie, I don't know what to say…"

"Then shut up and kiss me."

Donny bent and brushed his lips softly against hers. Then as her lips parted he drew her close and kissed her deeply, fiercely and with a longing that surprised them both.

THE GREEN DRESS was draped across the table. Other articles of clothing were scattered around the interior of the boat. They lay nestled in the V berth.

"That was… delicious." Donny stroked her hair as Laurie rested her head on his shoulder.

"First-time sex coupled with making-up sex. It's a pretty powerful mixture." She turned her face into his chest, breathing in his scent and tasting the saltiness of his skin.

"Mmmm, that's nice," Donny murmured.

Laurie propped herself up on one elbow and grinned down at him. "Don't you go to sleep on me, mister. I'm not finished with you yet."

"You're a cruel and demanding woman." Donny rolled over on his side and admired her. "You're so beautiful."

"I'm chubby and I have stretch marks."

"Not like that; real beauty, the kind that comes from inside. Though I must say, I'm also extremely fond of the outside too, just the way it is." He traced the outline of her buttocks with his hand and bent to kiss her breast. "Why did you come back?"

"I don't know. It's complicated." Laurie flopped back down. "One thing I learned in my marriage is that good relationships don't just happen, you have to work at them. I think you gave up on that a long time ago. Maybe you're ready to live without it. I'm not."

"I don't think I've ever felt as lonely as I did after you left." Donny shook his head. "I didn't even know I was lonely before. Isn't that crazy?"

"I think you're a decent guy, Donny."

"Gee, thanks," he snorted. "Damned with faint praise."

"It's not faint praise. You asked why I came back: because the other thing you need for a good relationship is good people. You're a fundamentally decent person, Donny. Maybe you don't know how rare that is. OK, you can be an asshole at times, but that's hardly unique." Donny feigned a protest as Laurie poked him in the ribs. She silenced him with a kiss. "I guess I sensed something good in you when we first met. You're honest and loyal, maybe a bit obsessive and self-absorbed, but you have a good heart. Kevin and Daniel like you too, and that means a lot. Sometimes I trust their judgement more than my own."

"Hmm." Donny sat up and opened the hatch over their heads. The night air spilled in, with the smell of damp decay. He lay back down and pulled the sheet up over them.

He had forgotten about the boys. Somehow the idea didn't frighten him as much as he thought it might. He craned his neck to look at the clock by the nav station. It was still only tenthirty. "Can you stay, or do you need to get back for the babysitter?"

"You don't think a girl wears a dress like that without making arrangements, do you?" Laurie climbed on top of him and swayed her breasts back and forth across his face. "The boys are having a sleepover at my sister's."

She reached down and guided him inside her. "And you, Captain Robertson, are all mine until morning."

Their initial lovemaking had been awkward and frantic, an urgent response to biological imperative. This time it was slow, tantalizing and breathtaking. They revelled in the sight, sound, smell, taste and feel of each other until at last they collapsed, sweaty, sated and spent.

Laurie lay curled in the crook of his arm, snoring softly. Donny wasn't sure if they were his lucky stars that shone down through the open hatch, but he thanked them anyway.

THIRTEEN
Extra Hose

"YOU BROUGHT ANOTHER hose line around the back. That's what you wrote, Scooter."

Scooter Evans, Captain of Pumper 7, was about the same age and build as Donny. Big Billy, the Aerial Captain, was a bit smaller than Moose, but still lived up to his name. He was a crew-cut, grey-haired veteran. Billy had been Captain of Aerial 7 since shortly after Donny was a recruit. He was solid, tough and fearless on the fire ground. Scooter and Big Billy sat at their desks in the office of the Dundas station. Donny perched on one of the bunks facing them.

He had been going over and over the reports and statements from the Commissioners Street fire for weeks now, looking for something, anything that seemed out of place. He was getting nowhere. The blossoming romance with Laurie had begun to occupy more and more of his attention, while the Commissioners Street fire gradually seemed to become less important. He was about to give up when it had suddenly jumped out at him: *another hose line*. They drove over to Station 7 first thing the next shift.

"OK, if that's what I wrote. I still don't get your point, Wedge."

Donny held out the copy of Scooter's report. "You guys were the next to arrive after us. Billy, you and the Aerial crew went to the roof, right?"

Billy nodded "Yeah, we were going to cut some vent holes."

"Right, and the pump crew took a line around the back," Donny continued. "We went in through the front, so yours would have been the *first* line around the back, Scooter. How could it be *another* line? Was there a line already there?"

"Jeez, Donny, I don't know. It was over a year ago. There was hose everywhere, it was like spaghetti. You know how it gets."

"But not at the beginning, Scooter. Yours should have been the first. What was that other hose line doing there?"

"I don't know." Scooter shook his head. "I'm not even sure there *was* another hose. Anyway, arsonists light fires, Donny. They don't lay out hose lines for us. It doesn't make any sense.

"Honestly, Donny, I don't specifically remember. I'm sorry, but it got pretty hairy there after it flashed, you know. All anyone cared about was trying to get to you and Fitz." Scooter paused. "It seems like I'm doing a lot of that lately, and frankly, I don't like it."

Donny stared at him blankly. Scooter continued, "Like the Pembroke fire. I don't know what the hell is going on with you, Wedge, but you better fix it before somebody else gets dead."

"Since when do you have a problem with aggressive fire attack, Scooter?" Donny answered coldly. "You lose your taste for it?" he added with a sneer. He regretted the words as soon as they left his lips, but it was too late. Scooter rose slowly from his chair and stalked across the room to stand in front of Donny.

"You can save that crap for the rookies. I will not take that shit from you or anyone. I got balls big enough for both of us." He spat the words out and jabbed his finger at Donny. "You want to try me?"

Donny started to rise to his feet, but Billy moved between them and put a hand on each of their shoulders. "Whoa, that's enough. I don't need the paperwork that goes with you two morons beating the shit out of each other. Now, we all go back a long way, and nobody needs to prove who's the toughest firefighter. That's dipshit stuff."

Donny looked hard at the smouldering anger in Scooter's eyes. He sat on the bunk again and looked down at his shoes. "I didn't mean it that way, Scooter. I, uh… I just need some answers, you know?"

"The only difference between us," Scooter said as he walked back to his desk, "is that I check my ego at the door when I walk in each morning. And my number one concern all day is making sure my guys go home at the end of the shift. If you can't do that, Donny, then you better turn in that red helmet."

"Jesus, Scooter, I'm sorry, all right? What the hell do you want from me?"

"Hey, hey, that's enough. Both of you stand down." Billy walked to the door and held it open. "You got questions, Wedge? Then how about we get some answers for you? The guys are all down in the kitchen. Maybe one of them remembers an extra hose."

THE CREWS WERE IN the kitchen trading friendly insults and newspaper sections as the three captains walked in. "Captain Robertson wants to ask you guys about the Commissioners Street fire," announced Big Billy.

They looked at Donny like race fans wondering if they were about to witness an epic wreck.

"Was there a hose already there when you guys brought the line around the back?" Donny asked. The simplicity of the question seemed to surprise them.

"You know," Spike broke the silence, "now that you mention it, I think there was a line on the ground."

"Go on," urged Donny.

"Well, we were dragging a 65 — big fire, big hose, right?" He looked around the room for approval. "Anyway, we're hauling the 65 around the back and as we come around the corner there's this other line. I don't think it was charged or nothing, but I remember thinking, shit, if we'd known there was a line already laid out we could have saved ourselves a lot of work. But maybe it was only a 38. I don't know, it's kind of fuzzy."

"But you're sure the line was already there," prompted Donny.

"Pretty sure," Spike scratched his head. "I didn't really think too much more about it. I guess I figured you guys had just laid it out and dropped it. I don't know. I mean, things started to go bad pretty soon after that, and it all got kind of crazy."

Donny shook his head. "You guys were the first around the back. Someone laid it out, but it wasn't us."

"It still doesn't make any sense, Donny," exclaimed Scooter, waving his hands in the air.

"It means something, I'm just not sure what," Donny replied.

"Hose doesn't lay itself out," Big Billy agreed, effectively ending the debate.

"Captain Evans, you got a problem with Spike here putting that down on paper?" asked Donny.

Scooter shrugged and rolled his eyes. "Whatever you like. You want it official? You want me to amend my report too? Shall we call it 'The Mysterious Hose Conspiracy'?"

Donny swallowed hard and counted to three. "Not for now. Spike, just write down what you saw and what you remember about the extra hose."

"Sure, I guess," Spike said hesitantly. The tension between the two captains was palpable, and Spike glanced nervously from one to the other.

"You might want to see if anyone ended up with extra lengths," suggested Billy. "Nobody leaves hose lying around after a fire. Someone picked it up."

"What is this, the friggin' Hardy Boys?" said Scooter, making a dismissive sound.

Donny shot him a withering look, but resisted the urge to strangle him in front of his crew. "OK, thanks for your help, gentlemen. You too, Scooter."

"No problem, Wedge. Come again when you can't stay so long."

The Lombard crew traded one final round of collegial insults with the men at the table and walked out to their truck. Billy got up and walked with Donny, limping slightly on a bad hip. A gentle misting rain drifted from the featureless grey sky as the streetcars rattled by in front of the station. "I'll see to it Spike writes that out and sends it to you."

"Thanks, I appreciate it. What the hell is Scooter's problem, anyway?"

The older man put his hand on Donny's shoulder. They stopped and faced each other. "Donny, guys are talking. It's not just Scooter."

Donny opened his mouth, but Billy cut him off. "Just listen to me. I've known you since you came on this job. You ever know me to stab a man in the back? Ever?" Donny shook his head. "Then you know I'm telling you for your own good. You got something you need to do, then do it. But don't let it get in the way and don't let it affect your judgement. That's how people get hurt. This is a wakeup call, Donny. Nobody wants to be marching behind a pumper carrying your coffin or anyone else's."

Billy's face was serious, and there was a soft sadness in his eyes. Donny chewed his lip for a minute, then nodded. "OK, you're right. Thanks."

Billy patted Donny's shoulder. "That was a bad night. We were going to retire together, Fitz and me. The two old war horses, last of the dinosaurs and all that." Billy's voice trailed off. He looked back at the station.

He turned his leathery face to the grey sky and let the rain run down the heavy creases. "You know, my grandfather was on the job when they got rid of the horses."

"Yeah, I heard." Donny glanced over at the truck where his crew were waiting inside.

"They just sold them off. The dairies bought a few of them to pull milk wagons. But every time a fire truck went by with siren and bells ringing, the horses would charge off after them, milk bottles flying everywhere. It was all they knew, see? In the end a lot of them just went to the slaughterhouse. Grampa said when the guys heard about that, he never saw grown men cry so hard.

"That's me, Wedge. This is all I know, the only real job I ever had. But I'm all beat up now. Some days the hip's so bad I can barely climb into the truck. Fitz and me… Now it's just me."

"You're not a horse, Billy, you're a man, and one hell of a firefighter."

"Sometimes I wonder," Billy smiled. "Anyway, listen, I didn't mean to start whining. What I want to say is, I know I'm not the smartest guy on the job, but I know a fart when I smell one. That Commissioners Street fire never felt right to me either. Now there's this extra hose. Something don't add up. You got anything else?"

"Maybe. I'm not sure. I need to do some more homework. But keep that to yourself for now, OK?"

"Fair enough. But you let me know if there's anything I can do. It'd be a lot easier leaving the job knowing we'd done right by Fitz."

"You got it. Listen, the guys are waiting in the truck and we're getting soaked. I'll keep you posted."

Donny climbed up into the captain's seat. He looked back at Billy, framed in front of the apparatus doors, his grey bristles slicked down to his scalp by the rain.

"Take a good look, Susan," Donny called over his shoulder. "You're looking at the end of an era there." Billy smiled and waved as they pulled out.

"Oh, is this where I'm supposed to go all doe-eyed and say 'I only hope I can be half the firefighter Big Billy is'?" she quipped lightly. She had expected at least Moose to laugh, but he just looked quietly out the window as they rolled down Dundas.

Donny turned to face her for a moment, but then turned back to the front. He was tired of arguing, tired of explaining, tired of being angry. He stared at the wipers streaking the rain across the windshield. It was Eddy who broke the silence.

"You could do worse, probie, you could do worse."

⋅

YELLOW LIGHT CREPT in through the window of the captain's office. The rain had ended and the setting sun was doing its best to redeem itself, sending golden shafts through cracks in the overcast sky.

Donny was oblivious. He sat hunched over, staring morosely at the computer screen, muttering to himself and periodically stabbing at the keyboard with one finger.

Susan hesitated in the doorway for a moment, watching him. She wasn't sure exactly how to start this. She had tried to join in the jousting of friendly mockery that ran through this fraternity. So much of the interaction on the job seemed to consist of insulting each other. In some cases it was gentle ribbing, in others it stopped just short of character assassination. What would be classified as harassment in other places seemed to bind them together somehow. It was part of the black humour that shielded them from the death, destruction and mayhem that was their stock in trade. Yet somewhere she had crossed an invisible line and it had backfired on her. She felt bad about it, but she was also frustrated and tired of being the outsider in this boys' club. She had been making progress over the first few weeks, gradually earning her place; now it seemed she was back to square one.

Susan had been well respected in her old job with the City's Health and Safety branch. She was recognized as an expert in the field of chemical exposure. Her professors had encouraged her to consider graduate school and an academic career, but she had chosen a different path. Now here she was starting down another new path, and nothing she had accomplished before seemed to count for much.

She cleared her throat. "Excuse me, Cap, you got a moment?"

Donny looked up, startled. "Oh, Susan, yeah, sure, come on in. What's up?"

She decided to swallow her pride. Apologies didn't seem that common in the fire department way of things, but she decided to try one anyway. "I wanted to, well, say I'm sorry about the crack I made about Big Billy."

Donny pushed himself away from the desk, leaned back in the chair and looked at her. "Fair enough," he nodded. "Apology accepted." She stood there with her lips pursed. "Is there something else?" He motioned for her to sit down.

She moved to a chair beside the desk and dropped into it. "I feel," she began, "I feel sometimes like I'm walking through a minefield. I try to tiptoe, I try not to do anything stupid, then I step on a booby trap and I feel like a turd."

"Consider it closed." Donny tried to smile encouragingly.

"No, I can't, because tomorrow or next week it'll be the same thing again." She sat forward in the chair and waved her hands as the words spilled out of her. "One minute we're sitting in the kitchen there and everyone is trading shots. The guys from 7 are ripping Eddy apart about his cooking, and he's calling them a bunch of shit-eating Regent Park cockroaches and what would they know about good food anyway. Nobody thinks anything about it.

"Then I make one little crack, in the truck, when we're by ourselves and it's like… I don't know, like I committed blasphemy or something." She slumped back in the chair and surveyed Donny warily.

"It's a little different, Susan."

"How?" she challenged defiantly.

Donny steepled his fingers and tapped them together in front of him. "You mocked the man's firefighting skills, Susan. That's a pretty touchy area. You haven't earned the right to do that to Billy. I'm not sure there's anyone on the job who has earned it. He was fighting fires before you were born, and he's been in situations you can't even imagine. For that he deserves respect. As a judge of fine food, well, that's a different matter."

Susan sighed and looked out the window.

"Look, I know you didn't mean any harm, so let's just put it behind us."

"Until the next time I step on a landmine no one told me about?" she said wearily.

Donny got up, moved around the desk and sat on the chair beside her. "Susan, there are some things you can put in the Drill Book: maintenance procedures, hydraulic equations, stuff like that. There's other stuff you can't write down so easily. You have to absorb it, if you know what I mean. And that takes time.

"Out there," he gestured to the office towers outside the window, "it's all about 'What have you done for me lately?'. But in here and on the fire ground it's about experience and respect. That's what holds us together. It's what gets us through the bad times. It might even save your life one day. Maybe that makes us a little slow to accept new ideas and new people, but don't sell it short until you've had a chance to really appreciate it."

"And when do I get to stop feeling like a bug under a microscope?"

"When you've earned it," Donny stated simply. "You're not the first rookie to piss in the pool and you certainly won't be the last. We've all done it. You've got what it takes to become a good firefighter. You proved that at the Pembroke fire. The rest just takes time."

"OK." She wasn't sure his reasoning was entirely satisfactory, but she decided to take the gist of his suggestion and move on. Donny moved back around the desk.

"Now if you'll excuse me," he said, pointing to the computer screen, "I have about a thousand files to read though."

"Something to do with the extra hose at that fire?" she asked as she stood up.

"Yup," he said, squinting at the screen. "I'm going over the Lost and Damaged reports. See, if you break or lose something at a call you're supposed to fill out a report. Same if you find something, but in that case you check off the 'found equipment' box. It's kind of like the lost and found at school, just not as many mitts and scarves. But there are thousands of reports."

"I see," Susan said, and came around the desk to look at the screen. "What kind of search parameters are you using?"

"Excuse me?"

"Well, you're not reading each one, are you?" she asked. Donny nodded mutely. "You're kidding me. No? Well, there's got to be a way to filter the reports. Do you mind?"

Donny moved out of his chair and let Susan sit down. "You know how to do that?"

"I think most City departments use the same reporting software. It shouldn't be too different from Health & Safety." Her fingers danced over the keyboard and mouse. "OK, here we are. How about we search for anything with either 'hose' or 'Commissioners Street' for, what, about two or three weeks after the fire? Is that OK?"

Donny nodded. He regarded computers with a mixture of awe and dread. He was amazed at, what seemed to him like, her mystical knowledge. She pressed the "Enter" key and a second later the computer made a soft beep. He was more used to the derisive "blaat" the machine made on a regular basis when he hit an incorrect key.

"Here we are. Let's see: 12 Pump broke an axe. Next one, 7 Aerial lost a Stihl saw. How do you lose a power saw?"

"They probably left it on the roof when the mayday went out. Lost it when the roof caved in."

"OK, I guess so. Then there's one from — hey, that's us, Pumper 6. Three bunker suits with burn damage: you, Moose and Captain… oh," her voice trailed off.

Donny stared straight ahead at the screen. "Bean counters," was all he said.

"Uh, well, ah, the only reference to hose is also ours: three lengths of burnt 38. Replaced with new hose, blah, blah, blah… there's the serial numbers… That's it." She looked up at him. "Sorry. We could expand the search but I don't think it would net much more."

"No." He smiled weakly as she got up out of the chair. "I guess it was a long shot. But thanks for trying." His smile warmed "You saved me I don't know how many hours. You are now officially designated as the station IT guy, err, person. I mean IT person."

Susan laughed. "Whatever. As for the IT stuff, I'm not sure how much of an expert I am."

"Well, you know a lot more than any of us," he said, waving towards the kitchen. He held out his hand. "Thank you," he said, looking her straight in the eye.

She took his hand and shook it firmly. "You're welcome," she said, returning his gaze. She turned and walked smartly out of the office. If respect was the currency of the fire department, her account had just moved slightly into the black.

FOURTEEN
Phenol

THEY COULD SEE THE accident as they reached the top of the hill, where River Street dropped down into the valley to join Bayview Avenue. The truck lay jackknifed on its side, with the tanker trailer it pulled sprawled diagonally across the road. The rear of a crumpled car protruded from underneath. A stream of syrupy liquid ran from the ruptured tanker down over the car and formed a large dark pool around the accident scene.

"Pull it down to the bottom of the hill, Moose. Block traffic in both directions," Donny ordered. He reached for the mic. "Pumper 6 on scene. We have a tanker on its side and leaking, with a car underneath. Give me a Level 3 HazMat response. Also tell police we need all traffic blocked on Bayview from Queen to Bloor Street. Pumper 6 Captain will be mobile command."

"Roger, Pumper 6 Captain, you have a Level 3 HazMat response inbound. Be advised wind is from the southwest at twelve kilometres per hour."

"Roger," Donny replied. He turned to the crew "At least we have a tailwind. Eddy, set up a hundred-yard perimeter on the north side. Give it a wide berth on your way there — you're going downwind. I want all those cars turned around and out of here." He pointed to the cars that were backed up on both sides of the accident. Fortunately it was early Sunday morning and traffic was light. Most of the drivers were turning around on their own.

They stopped at the bottom of the hill and dismounted. Even with the wind at their backs, a pungent, sickly-sweet odour hit them as they got out of the truck.

"Mask up, folks. Let's not breathe any more of this shit than we have to." They slipped on their face pieces and turned on their air tanks. Eddy headed off at a trot through the park that ran down the hill beside them.

"Susan, you're the chemical lady — stay back but see if you can find any labelling on that tanker. Moose, set up a wash-down line for decon. Then we need to check out that car and the cab of the truck."

"Gotcha," Moose answered. He connected a length of 38 to an outlet on the side of the truck while Donny took the oxygen kit and a pry bar from a side compartment.

"I can see a placard, Cap," Susan called out. "Class 6, UN number 2312."

"How bad is that?" Moose asked.

"I'm not sure. I'll look it up." She flipped rapidly through the "Orange Bible," the hazardous materials reference guide each fire truck carried.

Eddy was almost parallel with the cab of the leaking tanker when he suddenly veered toward the truck and bent down beside a clump of bushes. What the hell was he doing? Donny wondered.

"The line's ready, Cap," Moose reported.

Eddy's voice came over the radio; he was breathing hard. "Wedge, I've got a guy down here. Big guy. I'm going to need some help."

Donny peered in his direction. Eddy draped a man's arm over his shoulders and pulled him up. There was blood on the man's forehead and arms, and white foam frothed from his mouth. "Shit, Moose, go give Eddy a hand with that guy."

Moose ran across the park as Donny thumbed his mic and held it to his face piece. "Pumper 6 Captain, I need paramedics at the top of River Street. I have one casualty, possibly more to come."

Donny turned to Susan. "When Moose and Eddy get back, get the oxygen on that guy, wash him down and get him up the hill to the medics. I'm going to check the car under that trailer."

Susan held up her hand. "No, you can't."

"What?"

"You can't go in there. It's phenol. Damn it, I thought I knew that smell when we pulled up." She held the Orange Bible out for him to see. "2312. It's molten phenol. You need a full chemical protective suit for that stuff."

"Thanks for the information, probie, but you don't give the orders here." He turned to go, but she grabbed him by the back of his tank and spun him around.

"Screw you, Donny! You may be God's gift to fire fighting, but this is my domain." She pointed towards the tanker, still spewing its contents. "That's molten phenol. It's toxic, corrosive and flammable. It poisons your liver, your kidneys and your central nervous system. It'll burn out your lungs if you breathe it and it absorbs right through your skin even if you don't."

Moose and Eddy arrived back at the truck and laid the man on the pavement. Eddy fitted the oxygen mask on the man's face as Moose directed a gushing stream of water over the man's body. They looked over as Susan and Donny squared off at the edge of the grass.

"Cap, listen to me," Susan continued. "The Nazis used that shit at Auschwitz because it was cheaper and quicker than the gas chambers. Anyone in that car is already dead. If you go in there you will die too. How quickly depends on how much you get on you, but you will die. Please trust me. I know this stuff."

They could all see Donny's jaw working inside his face piece. The radio crackled to life. "Chief 41 on scene, establishing command post at River and Dundas. Pumper 6 Captain, give me a report."

Donny looked at the growing pool around the tanker, then back at Susan. "Help Eddy get that guy up the hill to the ambulance. Moose, turn this truck around and get it out of here. We're going defensive."

He keyed the mic and spoke into it. "Chief, the product is UN number two-three-one-two, phenol, I repeat, phenol—poppa, hotel, echo, november, oscar, lima. One casualty incoming. We are retreating to your location. I have a crew member coming to give you a full briefing."

THEY BAGGED AND TAGGED their bunker suits for decontamination when they got back to Lombard. They borrowed gear from the off-duty shifts to wear for the rest of the day, then they showered. The showers couldn't remove what they had already absorbed through their skin, but it made them feel clean. No one felt much like talking.

Sunday afternoons were traditionally down time in the fire hall. Donny retreated to his office and shut the door. Eddy washed and waxed his car in the spare bay. Moose lay on his bunk and pretended to read, until soft snoring betrayed him.

Susan sat alone in the kitchen and wondered if she had made such a wise career choice. She looked around the room, at its collection of photographs and paraphernalia from years gone by. The men in those old pictures looked so proud: proud of the glossy coats on the horses, proud of the gleaming brass on their engines, proud of the neatly stacked coils of hose, proud of what it all stood for. She longed for her share of that pride.

She thought of the wide-eyed looks of admiration she saw on children's faces as the truck drove by — and on the faces of a few adults as well. Then she thought of the look of surprise and consternation she sometimes noticed when people realized she was a woman. She felt like Moses looking at the Promised Land, but forbidden to enter it.

"Damn it, I was right!" she told the circle of long-dead firefighters.

Chief Razzolini had seemed happy to receive her briefing and her advice, but then the HazMat team had shown up and assumed command. They had been told to clear and clean themselves up. And that was it.

"I was right, and I saved his sorry ass," she whispered to the indifferent ghosts.

She filled the kettle and put it on the stove, then turned back to face the black and white jury. "Well, you better get used to it, boys," she declared across the ages, "because I – am – not – going – anywhere!"

She sat back down to wait for the kettle to boil and wondered if she could live up to her bravado.

"Chief in the hall," Eddy announced over the PA from the floor watch. Everyone converged on the kitchen. Ratzo took his place at the head of the table.

"That was good work today," Ratzo announced after the customary greetings had been exchanged. "The guy you rescued was the truck driver. He's in serious condition but they think he's going to make it. What the long-term effects will be, who knows? Still, it was a good save."

Susan knew what the long-term effects were — kidney failure, heart and liver disease and emphysema — but she chose to remain silent.

"I really appreciated your input, Susan." Ratzo nodded in her direction. "We don't deal with this sort of thing every day, thank God. It was really good to have your expertise." Susan smiled weakly back at him.

"And good call setting up the initial perimeter and going defensive, Donny." Donny sat rigidly, holding a sheaf of papers in his hand.

"The Haz guys found two bodies in the car," Ratzo continued. "They probably died instantly. There was nothing you could have done for them. Seems like the car crossed over the centre line right into the tanker. Maybe the guy at the wheel had a heart attack. Who knows?

They're going to have to decontaminate everything before they can get the bodies out and do a full autopsy.

"So, how's everybody feeling?" Ratzo looked around the table. You didn't have to be psychic to pick up on the strain in the hall.

"Great, Chief," answered Eddy. "Like you said, it was a good save."

Moose looked at Eddy and nodded. Mostly they agreed they weren't about to rock the boat. Susan said nothing.

"I'd like you to sign these, Chief." Donny slid several sheets of paper over to Ratzo. He took them, but kept his eyes fixed on Donny.

Donny cleared his throat. "I'm recommending probationary firefighter Kozarovitch for a personal merit award. Her knowledge and action prevented serious injury and possible death to her crew. It was her recommendation we go defensive, Chief. I was going to walk right into that mess. She stopped me."

He looked over at Susan. "Thank you. Thank you for saving my life." He said it quietly and earnestly. She bit her lip and choked back her tears. Donny turned and stood up to get himself a cup of coffee.

Ratzo leaned back in his chair. "There is only one thing I really don't like about this job. You know what it is? Paperwork. But this is one set of papers I am very, very happy to sign."

"Gosh, Moose, pass the Kleenex. I'm so happy I'm going to cry." Eddy started wailing and honking his nose. Moose joined him.

They passed the box of tissues to Susan last. She dabbed at her eyes and started laughing. "You guys are absolute, complete assholes. And I love you."

Eddy stood up and spun on his heels. "She loves me! You heard it, boys. I'm sure she meant me."

Moose looked over and rolled his eyes. "Just remember, there's a fine line between love and hate."

Donny sat back down with his coffee and handed one to Ratzo as well. It was good to see them laughing and joking. He had wrestled with it this way and that, played it back and forth, and in the end he had done the right thing. For the first time it felt like they were melding as a crew. And for the first time, by giving in, he felt like he was worthy to be their Captain. He smiled at Ratzo and clinked mugs.

"Now there's a sound I love," said Eddy. "You know what this calls for?" He looked around the room. "A breakout!"

"I will heartily second that motion," declared Moose.

"Done!" Donny slapped his hand on the table. "I'll call around the district."

"Breakout?" asked Susan.

"Think of it as a group hug, fire department style," explained Moose.

"Thursday night at the Sparrow work for everyone?" asked Donny. There was agreement all around. "OK, Susan, line up a babysitter, bring your dancing shoes and cancel your Friday-morning appointments."

"I'M SORRY, DONNY, that's a school night for the boys and I have to work the next morning."

They sat on the sidelines with the other parents, watching the boys' soccer game. Though it was after seven, it was mid-June and the sun was still well above the horizon. The evening was warm and the air was fragrant with fresh-mown grass. Dogs romped and barked merrily in the off-leash area, a softball game was unfolding on the diamond across the park, and somewhere in the distance an ice cream truck patrolled the neighbourhood, playing its repetitive jingle.

It was a scene Donny had witnessed many times, but this time, though he was just a spectator at a soccer game, he felt like he was a part of it all, not just a distant observer. It was a feeling he liked. He took Laurie's hand.

"Good pass, Kevin," he called towards the field, then turned to Laurie. "That's too bad. I really want you to meet the crew. Are you sure? It should be a good party."

"I'll meet them another time," Laurie smiled at him and squeezed his hand. "We'll have a BBQ or something. Besides, it sounds like it's more of a work thing. I don't want to be the only outsider."

"You wouldn't be, but OK, whatever." He was disappointed, but he tried not to let it spoil the mood.

"God, you pout worse than Daniel," Laurie accused. "OK, I've got a surprise for you. I was going to save it for later, but maybe this will cheer you up. I figured out how you blow a water main without anyone knowing."

Donny whirled to face her. "Really? That's awesome! Tell me."

"I had kind of forgotten about the water main," Laurie confessed. "But when you told me about that extra hose thing I started thinking about it again. I realized I had been thinking about it all wrong. You don't blow it from the outside: you do it from the inside."

They stood and cheered with the other parents. Donny had no idea what he was cheering for — it was automatic. His attention was focused on Laurie.

"From the inside?" Donny asked when they sat down again. "That's impossible."

"No, it's not. It's actually pretty simple." Laurie explained. All you really needed were two things: an access point and some kind of an air lock. The access point was the easiest part. Every building had one where the water pipe entered the building. The industrial buildings on Commissioners Street had two- or three-inch supply lines, more than big enough to introduce a small charge. The rest was simple plumbing.

All you needed to create an air lock were some pipe and a couple of valves. There would already be one valve in place to shut off the building's water supply when needed. Install a second valve to keep the water in the building's pipes from flowing out, add a length of pipe between the two valves on a "T" joint, cap it, and *voilà*, you've got an air lock.

Getting the explosive charge in place was a little tougher, but still not rocket science. You could use some type of robotic device to crawl along the inside of the pipe. Oil and gas companies used them to inspect the insides of their pipelines.

"But that's tricky and expensive. Me, I like simple and reliable," Laurie said, patting Donny on the knee.

She smiled briefly and then was serious again. If you used a packing gland instead of a cap on the air lock, she explained, you could push the charge into place with a length of stiff, flexible wire, like a plumber's snake. The packing gland would seal around the wire the same way it does around the stem of a tap handle coming out of a faucet.

"Wouldn't water pressure be a problem?" Donny wanted to know. "We get up to 60 psi at a hydrant."

"Pressure isn't the problem, it's flow. There's almost fifteen pounds of air pressure in the atmosphere all the time, but if the air isn't flowing, there's no wind, and you and your precious boat aren't going anywhere."

"Hmm, don't I know it."

"Late at night there's very little water flow in those mains. That's when I'd do it, Donny."

"OK, smarty pants, how do you position the charge in the right place?"

"I wondered about that too," said Laurie. She twirled her hair around her finger as she thought. "There are a few possibilities, but I think I'd go with magnets. Those old water mains are cast iron, so magnets would be ideal. They're simple and reliable. Attach the magnets to the explosive charge in the orientation you want it to sit, then wrap it all up in a ball of twine."

She started counting the steps on her fingers. "Put the whole thing in the air lock, open the valve and push the charge out into the water main. Then let the current take it. The twine unravels until the magnets are exposed and the charge sticks in place. Rig a simple release on the string. Use a time delay detonator and pull all your gear back out of the system."

Donny looked over at her and nodded slowly. "It makes sense. You, Ms. Zhou, are an evil genius."

"Well, there are other possibilities, variations on a theme mostly, but that's how I'd do it. The engineering is pretty simple. It really doesn't take much genius. It's the evil part that worries me." Laurie looked at him with concern. "Isn't it time to turn all this over to the police?"

"Soon." Donny kissed her on the cheek. "But so far it's all still theory. I need proof, some kind of physical evidence before they'll take me seriously."

FIFTEEN
The Air Lock

THOUGH IT WAS HIS day off, Donny put on his uniform the next morning and headed out. He stopped for a coffee and a muffin at a local drive-through, then joined the lemmings in the morning commute. Most of the traffic headed into the downtown core. Donny kept going south, towards the Portlands, at the east end of Toronto harbour.

During the first half of the twentieth century, the Portlands had been one of the city's industrial hubs. There had been factories, foundries and warehouses, huge stockpiles of coal and the squat cylinders of petroleum tank farms. During the war years Munitions Street was lined with factories filling defence contracts. Ships from around the world tied up at the piers, unloading goods from exotic lands, and hungry for raw materials from Canada's heartland.

Most of that was gone now. A few lake freighters sat rusting along the concrete channels. Railway lines still crisscrossed the area, but trains rarely ran to the few remaining businesses.

As Toronto became a financial and business centre, the heavy industry in the Portlands withered away, and most of the area was now abandoned brown fields. Several plans had been proposed to redevelop the area as a prime waterfront residential and recreational area. However, the cost of cleaning up the contamination left behind had so far proved prohibitive. Despite their proximity to the city centre, the Portlands had become the industrial low-rent district.

Donny turned onto Commissioners Street for the first time since the fire. He pulled up in front of the empty lot that had been #54, turned off the engine and sat in silence, looking at the expanse of broken pavement and weeds.

What he felt more than anything was a curious emptiness. It was a place that had scarred him body and soul, yet it wasn't the same. It wasn't simply that the building was gone, nor the daylight that washed the scene, nor the wild greenery of nature reclaiming what man had abandoned. The geographical location was the same, but the pain and tragedy of that night were not anchored to something defined by latitude and longitude. They belonged rather to a locus in time, a sequence of events immutably etched in the past.

Memories of that night still echoed through his mind: blindly groping through the smoke, searching for the heart of the fire; the terrible heat, rising so quickly, flooding through his bunker suit into his soft, moist flesh; and the murky darkness blossoming into yellow-orange light all around as the fire swallowed him. He remembered these things, but they were like the rumbling of distant thunder, ominous but no longer threatening.

That realization made Donny feel somewhat better, but it left a troubling question in his mind. What was he doing here, in uniform, about to do something that could cost him his captain's bars or even his job?

The past was the past, right? Fitz wasn't coming back no matter what he did. Anna Fitzgerald had lost her husband and her children had lost their father, yet they had all moved on. Why couldn't he?

The more he thought about it, the less he understood. Better to simply do what he had come here to do. It seemed like the path of least resistance. Donny took one more look at the empty lot and drove on.

The next lot was also empty, and beyond that was Jake's Scrap Metal. Donny pulled into the driveway, parked the car and grabbed a clipboard with a pad of blank inspection forms.

A large bearded man with dirty coveralls and half a dozen earrings walked towards Donny as he got out of the car. Donny put on his best friendly firefighter smile. "Hi, I'm Captain Roberts… Saunders, Robert Saunders, Fire Prevention. How are you? Would you be Jake?"

The big man eyed him warily, but took Donny's proffered hand and gave it a greasy squeeze. "Jake was my dad. I'm Wayne. What can I do for you?"

"We're conducting sprinkler and water connection inspections in the area. It was one of the recommendations from the inquest into the fire. I think it was right around here, wasn't it?"

"Where them guys got killed? Yup, it was just down the road, right there." Wayne nodded in the direction Donny had just come from. "What a goddamn mess that was. Anyway, we ain't got no sprinklers. This is a scrapyard, buddy. No place to put 'em, unless you expect me to hang 'em in mid-air." The big man chuckled at his own joke.

"What about your water connection?" Donny asked, still smiling.

"Over there in the office," Wayne answered, pointing to a trailer in the corner of the lot. "The only things connected are the shitter and a sink for the coffee machine. You're welcome to have a look if you want."

Donny doubted the toilet would pass a public health inspection, but there was nothing irregular about the plumbing. He asked Wayne a few more questions, tested the smoke alarm in the office, and wished him a good day.

The next address was a recycling facility. The manager showed Donny around the plant, describing in intricate detail how they used magnets, air jets and human hands to sort the collected material into steel, aluminum, glass and various grades of plastic and paper. The sorted material was then bundled into large bales and shipped off to be turned into a seemingly infinite number of indispensable objects. The place smelled like garbage that should have been taken out the day before. Donny tried to look interested while suppressing a shudder at the thought of hundreds of tons of plastic catching fire.

He dutifully noted the pressures on the various gauges in the sprinkler control room. The manager proudly showed him the annual maintenance records from the company that serviced and tested their system. Nothing seemed out of the ordinary.

Donny thanked the man and congratulated him on running an exemplary fire safety program. He promised to highlight the company as a model corporate citizen in his report.

There was another empty lot and then what appeared to be an abandoned factory. The brickwork was crumbling in spots, the windows were covered with sheets of weathered grey plywood, and the corrugated metal roof was rusted and sagging. A high chain-link fence with a locked gate surrounded the place. There was no obvious way for Donny to gain entry without breaking in.

A small sign on the gate gave the name and phone number of a security company. Donny called and let it ring. He pressed 1 for English, then 3 for customer assistance and then several more buttons before he was finally connected to a person.

Donny gave his well-rehearsed speech and asked if there was some way he could inspect the empty building on Commissioners Street. The person on the other end said that they normally requested twenty-four hours' notice for such things but that she would see what she could do, and put him on hold. She came back a few minutes later and said someone would be by within the hour.

Forty minutes later a young man drove up in a car that was deliberately painted to resemble a police car — if the police drove seven-year-old rusty Hyundais, that is. He was skinny, with short hair, glasses and the pockmarked ravages of an unfortunate adolescence.

Donny walked over as the kid got out of his car. "Hi, thanks for coming," Donny said. "I'm Captain…"

"Saunders," the kid finished for him, consulting a notebook. "I'm Josh Findlay. Nice to meet you." A puzzled expression crossed the kid's face as he looked up. "You guys drive your own cars?"

Crap, why hadn't he thought of that? "Oh, that, the department car's in for repairs," Donny improvised. "You wouldn't believe the pieces of crap they give us."

"Tell me about it," the kid said, gesturing over his shoulder at the Hyundai. "They pay you mileage?"

"Forty-nine cents a kilometre."

"That's good, real good. You ready?"

Josh removed a large ring of keys from his belt, opened the gate, ushered Donny through and locked the gate behind them. "Gotta keep it locked up. We've had problems with tweakers and homeless guys."

The kid unlocked the door at the front of the building. A shaft of light framed their shadows on the dusty floor. Its angular brilliance made the darkness beyond all the more impenetrable, as though they might plummet into nothingness if they stepped beyond its sharp boundaries.

Years of moving through smoky blackness had sharpened Donny's senses. There was a musty odour of decay and rat droppings that spoke of years of neglect. The echoing silence told him they were in a single large room, the space over his head clear, likely to the roof. Experience told him the emptiness concealed deadly traps. There would be holes in the floor where hoppers and conveyors had once stood; there would be scattered bits of abandoned machinery and sharp-edged fragments of twisted metal that could trip, cut and impale.

Josh switched on his flashlight and excused himself to find the light switch somewhere to their left. A few seconds later a line of fluorescents flared into existence high overhead, confirming Donny's suspicions.

Donny made a cursory inspection of the place, making notes on his clipboard. There were no sprinklers, but there were standpipe connections, one on each of the two longer walls.

"I need to check the main water connection," Donny said when he thought he had made enough of a show.

"I don't know where that is," Josh replied.

"It'll be in the basement, probably somewhere on the wall closest to the street."

They moved to a set of stairs that descended into the darkness beneath them. They started down, Donny in the lead, carefully testing each step for its soundness. The damp mustiness was closer down here and there were scurrying sounds in the distance.

Josh swung his flashlight nervously from side to side. "I've never been down here before." There was an edge of apprehension in his voice. "Usually I just pop my head in upstairs, hit the lights and make sure no one's living inside."

"Don't worry," Donny answered his unspoken question, "the rats won't bother you. Just be careful of stepping into sump holes."

Josh found a light switch and Donny found what he was looking for in a cinder-block room in the southeast corner of the basement. There was an array of risers and a single pressure gauge. The glass on the gauge was fogged. Donny doubted it even worked any more, but he made a show of noting the reading. Then his eye was drawn to where the three-inch main came in through the foundation wall.

The pipes were all heavily rusted, but there, right behind the main shutoff, was a section that was obviously newer. There was a "T" joint, a second shutoff, and directly in line with the main supply, half a metre of pipe that dead-ended in a cap. A low whistle escaped Donny's lips.

"Something wrong?" Josh asked.

"Uh, no," Donny recovered, "everything looks fine. I can see someone's done a little repair work here. I'm just going to take a few pictures for reference."

Donny pulled his phone from his pocket and snapped a couple of photos of the new pipe. He checked to make sure the images were clear and then told the kid they were all done. They retraced their steps and emerged squinting into the daylight.

"Thanks, Josh. You've been very helpful." Donny held out his hand after the kid had finished locking the gate behind them.

"No problem," said Josh, shaking Donny's hand. He squinted up at the badge on Donny's uniform hat. "That your badge number? 1541? I gotta put it all in the occurrence report." He pulled out his notebook and made a quick entry.

Donny silently cursed himself for missing the obvious hole in his own cover story. He forced a smile. "Bloody reports, eh? The paperwork never ends. You should think about becoming a cop. You're, uh, very good with details," Donny suggested with a nod.

"That's my plan, but I got bad eyes. I gotta save enough money for the laser surgery."

"Well, good luck, and thanks again." Donny walked to his car and busied himself with his clipboard until the kid drove away. He waved goodbye, then pulled out his phone and looked at the pictures once again.

It was exactly as Laurie had described it. There was the air lock, connected with a "T" between the two shutoffs. Donny felt his pulse race. For the first time he had hard physical evidence. It might be circumstantial, but it was real, not just a feeling or someone's best recollection. He called Laurie's number.

"Laurie? I found it! It was just like you said. I couldn't believe my eyes!" He was breathless, almost wild with joy.

"That's great. I'm really happy for you. What are you talking about?"

"Jeez, I'm sorry, I'm kind of excited. I found the air lock!"

"Wow, congratulations. I'm always glad to make my man happy, even if it is just plumbing." He could hear her smile.

"It's the best news I've had in a long time. Laurie, you don't know what this means to me. It means I'm not crazy. It means someone did set this up. It means… You're incredible, you know that?"

"Yes I am, and don't you forget it. Hold that thought, OK?

Right now I've got a backhoe and a ten-foot hole in the middle of Greenwood Avenue. Come over tonight and we'll, uh, celebrate."

Donny drank in the soothing warmth of her voice. The memory of her welled up within him: her smell, her taste, her warmth…

"Donny?"

"Yes," he said slowly, "yes, I would like that very much. Sorry, I was just switching gears there. You make supper, I'll bring the wine."

It was, Donny decided as he put away his phone, if not the best day of his life, quite certainly the best day in a very long time.

IT WAS QUITE PROBABLY the worst day Catherine had ever had. She stared blankly at the Monet. It was one of the painter's water-lily series, one of the few that remained in private hands. It hung by itself on one wall of Catherine's private study, her inner sanctum.

It was a surprisingly small and simple room for a woman in her position. There were two comfortable armchairs, a small desk, an Oriental rug, some bookcases and a fireplace. The room's two focal points were the Monet and, in a case against the opposite wall, a copy of *The Prince* published in 1559, the year the book was banned by the Catholic Church.

Normally Catherine could lose herself in Monet's fluid azure depths. Now all she could think about was the almond-sized tumour growing on her brain stem. A glioma, the doctor had called it. To Catherine it sounded more like an Italian dessert than a life-threatening cancer.

The doctor had made all the typical reassuring statements. He had already sent her file to a neuro-oncologist in Zurich — the top man in the field, he assured her. There was every reason to be optimistic. But Catherine had not gotten where she was without being able to see through spin.

She had no illusion of immortality nor any wish to live forever.

The idea of lapsing into doddering decrepitude filled her with dread. But that should be years, even decades away yet. She was being cheated out of good, productive years. And no one cheated Catherine Rockingham out of anything.

She looked down at the tablet resting on the small table beside her armchair. It was the icing on the cake, the fitting conclusion to a wretched day. The message summarized the latest results from Spectrum: computer searches for extra hose, phone calls and pictures, and a security guard's report with Robertson's badge number.

She picked up the tablet and hurled it at the fireplace. Shards of plastic skittered across the floor.

Catherine recognized self-pity for the pathetic weakness it was, and hated it. Action was the key, decisive action. So be it. She was not ready to accept a death sentence, but she was more than willing to hand one out.

"Your assessment of the situation in Toronto couldn't have been more wrong, Brendan," she said curtly into the phone. "Contact our supplier and tell him I want the situation cleaned up. I do not want to deal with this matter again. Is that understood?

"After that, call the airport and have the plane readied. I want to leave for Zurich in two hours."

THE MAN IN THE shower enjoyed the way the hot water intensified the scent of smoke that clung to his hair. He turned the water off and reached for the phone when he heard its little melody. He quickly scanned the information as he stood dripping in the tub.

"Oh dear," he said to himself, putting the phone back down, "that isn't good."

But it wasn't all bad, either. He had really enjoyed the Toronto job. He brought his wet hair forward, cupped his hands over his face, and breathed in the lingering smoky scent.

He liked to make problems disappear, and he had the perfect solution for this one. He would return to Toronto first thing in the morning and set everything right.

SIXTEEN
Breakout

THE THIRSTY SPARROW WAS a pleasant watering hole that had weathered the test of time, as well as several generations of firefighters, cops and paramedics. It wasn't solely an emergency services bar as such; it was just that "civilians" who happened to wander in tended to feel they might be more comfortable somewhere else. Thus the Sparrow, as it was simply known, had avoided the twin fates of fleeting trendiness on the one hand and the slow descent into seedy obscurity on the other.

The Sparrow was like a pair of old slippers, a bit worn in places but with a comfortable, reassuring familiarity. The décor was more primal than retro. Like the Catholic Church, the Sparrow changed at a glacial pace. The pressed tin ceiling was original. The walls were lined with an eclectic assortment of pictures that spanned the city's history: the Great Toronto Fire of 1904 that had levelled twenty acres of the downtown core; a policeman pulling a woman and child into a boat during Hurricane Hazel in 1954; George Armstrong, captain of the Maple Leafs, hoisting the Stanley Cup in 1967. Wear and tear had necessitated occasional replacement of the Naugahyde upholstery, but it had been lovingly matched. A jukebox had finally been accepted sometime in the late '60s. More recently it had been refitted to play CDs instead of vinyl, but rock 'n' roll still outnumbered hip-hop by a wide margin.

The place was filled with sixty or so firefighters from the downtown stations as well as the regulars. "Come on and do the jailhouse rock with me…" Elvis did his best to make himself heard above the general hubbub of conversation and occasional eruptions of boisterous laughter.

Donny and Eddy sat at a small table in the back, with two pints of dark ale and several empty glasses between them. Donny took a long drink and continued. "So I went to the Hose Shop…"

Eddy nodded. The Hose Shop, otherwise known as Equipment and Technical Services, was responsible for repairing and maintaining anything on the job that didn't have wheels. "You figure they'd notice anyone who came in for pressure testing with extra hose?"

"Exactly," Donny said. He was drunker than he normally allowed himself to get, but he was feeling good. It was time to let off a little steam.

"And?" Eddy prompted.

"Nothing," Donny replied, taking another swallow. "Like they told me, who's gonna show up with extra hose in their inventory? It's gonna end up lining the edge of the dock at some guy's cottage, right?

"But," Donny put down his glass and waved an index finger in Eddy's general direction for emphasis, "one of the guys there had a great idea: aerial photography!"

"Sorry, Wedge, you lost me."

"Aerial photography, man! The news helicopters. They would have been there. You'd be able to trace all the hose lines from those pictures, see if there was an extra one."

"Hmm, I guess," Eddy shrugged, "but it still wouldn't tell you who put it there or why. You know what, Donny? I really don't want to think about that night right now. I want to have a good time. Maybe you should take a break from it too."

"I'm having a great time, Eddy. I mean, what could be better? I'm with my pals. I got a woman who thinks I'm… I don't know what she thinks, but she likes me, Eddy, she really likes me. You gotta meet her, Eddy, she's really something. Lemme buy you another drink."

"I still have most of this one. Maybe you should slow down a bit, Wedge. The evening is yet young and I have a little surprise for later on. I'm gonna go mingle for a while. I'll see you."

Donny watched Eddy move off towards the bar, shaking hands, clinking glasses and trading insults along the way. He moved with an easy social grace that Donny admired and envied. Donny was never truly relaxed at social events. He always had a sense of being removed, of wondering what the right thing to say and do was. Guys like Eddy never thought about that — it just came naturally. And that, of course, Donny knew, was the secret: not to think about it.

He could do that on *Red Bird*, when the wind was in his face and the spray washed the deck. He sailed as much by intuition as anything, sensing the boat respond as he trimmed the sheets. He could feel her bow cutting through the waves as if it were his hand slicing through the water. He knew her moods from the sounds of her rigging, and the way she heeled with the wind.

He loved the Norton for that reason too. On a warm summer day, on a winding country road, it was like dancing. Every road had its own rhythm, and when he found it, riding became seamless. There was no separation between him, the motorcycle and the road: they became one organic whole. Lean, clutch, shift, accelerate—no thought, just being, his senses full, the sun warm on his shoulders, the wind rushing around him, the road flowing up and through him.

It used to be like that at work, too, trusting his experience and intuition. Donny missed that confidence more than anything. Or was it overconfidence that had got him into this jackpot in the first place? If he had followed his instincts at the phenol spill last week, he'd be dead — or worse. He'd been through enough to know there were things much worse than death.

Donny shook his head and ordered another beer and a shot of Jack Daniels. If he couldn't drown his problems, he was going make damn sure they knew how to swim.

He sat back and watched the room through the warm glow of the whiskey. Eddy was leaning on the bar talking to a couple of guys from Front Street.

Susan was with a group from her recruit class that had also been assigned to stations in the district. They were laughing and pointing at various other groups around the bar. She caught Donny's eye, smiled and waved.

Ratzo was talking with a couple of cops. Donny didn't know their names, but he recognized them from various calls. That was Ratzo, always networking.

Moose was on the dance floor. Donny couldn't quite see who he was dancing with — maybe no one. He seemed absorbed in his own peculiar rhythm, something Donny thought resembled a cross between modern interpretive movement and the funky chicken.

Donny ordered another whiskey. It was good. He was with his people. He closed his eyes and let himself be washed by the all-embracing philanthropy of being with good friends and more than a little drunk.

"Hello, everybody! Can I have your attention, please?" Eddy's voice rose over the din of music and conversation. Donny opened his eyes and saw Eddy standing on a chair beside the jukebox. "Stu, can you turn the music down for a minute, please?" The bartender did as Eddy requested. The room quieted down slightly.

"OK, everyone. It's good to see you all here. I just have a couple of things to say…"

"You suck, Eddy," a voice called from the back.

"Yeah, and so does your sister, Scooter, but I guess everyone's got the right to make a living," Eddy replied without missing a beat. Everyone laughed and the room quieted once again.

"Now, as we all know, the Academy recently turned out another batch of whale shit. Ah, look at them," Eddy pointed to Susan and her classmates, "aren't they cute? So bright-eyed and bushy-tailed. Let's raise our glasses and drink a toast to our new probies!"

They all raised their glasses and a chorus of "Fuck you!" echoed around the bar.

"Probie Kozarovitch, front and centre!" Eddy ordered. Susan looked around nervously as her classmates pushed her towards Eddy. She made her way forward through the applause and whistles.

Eddy motioned for silence before he went on. "As you doubtless know, Probie Kozarovitch is the first person of the female persuasion ever to be assigned to Lombard. This is no small thing." There was a smattering of applause, mostly from Ratzo. "Thank you, Chief, for that politically correct response.

"Now, at the risk of being serious for a moment, it's been a bit of an adjustment for us, and for her too. It's not easy being the first at anything.

"However, I am pleased to announce that she has performed more than adequately. Despite the bad influence of the training academy she has proven adept at learning how fire fighting works in the real world. She has also shown herself to be an astute judge of fine cuisine." There was a chorus of boos as Eddy took a small bow.

"And of course, being a woman, she has a natural affinity for cleaning and does a wonderful job stoking the hall." At this Susan reached over and punched Eddy in the ribs.

"You all saw that. Assaulting a senior firefighter!" Eddy protested.

"Didn't see a thing, Eddy," Ratzo called, and everyone shook their heads.

"Ah, traitors, all of you," Eddy accused, pointing dramatically around the room.

"Anyway, as you all probably know by now, Susan brings some special talents to the job from her previous life as a science nerd. That proved particularly handy last weekend at the chemical spill on Bayview, where she prevented some of us from being personally fitted for body bags.

"As a result, Wedge and Ratzo have written her up for a

commendation. And…" He waited for the applause to die down. "Yes, that's very nice, but far, far more important than any award: I would like to take this occasion to promote Probie Kozarovitch from whale shit to pond scum. Ladies and germs, raise your glasses to Susan Kozarovitch, pond scum!"

"Pond scum!" they all cheered. It was Susan's turn to take a bow.

"Thank you. Thank you very much," she smiled.

"Shut up and drink. Pond scum doesn't have vocal cords." Eddy handed her a glass that Stu had placed on the bar.

"Now, one more thing." Eddy waved his hand over his head. "As Senior Man it is my right, my GOD-GIVEN RIGHT, to name this probie!" There were a few hoots and cries of "Amen!" Eddy waited, letting the expectation build for a few moments. Susan looked up at him, not knowing quite what to think.

"Now I have given this a great deal of thought," Eddy said to the hushed room. "She's smart, there's no arguing that. 'Spock' came to mind, but I didn't like that. Besides, she's a lot better-looking than Leonard Nimoy. But I did kind of like the whole science/*Star Trek* thing. And she's also a bit different from what we've encountered before, being from the female continuum. Then there's the crazy scientist guy in James Bond. So…" He motioned to Moose, who pressed a few buttons on the jukebox. A snare and cymbal began to tap out a familiar rhythm, joined by a thrumming bass.

"Ladies and gentlemen, I give you…" Eddy paused for effect. "She's smart! She's sexy! She's the future! I give you… Q!!"

"Oh Suzie Q!" John Fogerty's voice rose from the juke box and cut through the chorus of cheers. "Oh Suzie Q! Baby, I love you, Suzie Q…"

Eddy started singing along and clapping his hands. Suzie pulled him down off the chair he was standing on and they started to dance. The crowd began singing, clapping and cheering them on. Moose cleared a swath through the crowd as he boogied up to Suzie and dropped to his knees in front of her. The three of them abandoned themselves to the music and the cheering. Moose tilted his head back and howled, swaying back and forth on his knees; Eddy sang, clapped and stomped while Suzie shimmied and shook her way around the circle that had been cleared for them.

She was searching for Donny. He was standing at the back, leaning against a post, singing and clapping along with the rest. She beckoned to him. He grinned, raised his glass to her and took a long drink. Suzie, however, was not going to be denied. She slithered through the ring of people, took his hand and led him, weaving drunkenly, back to the centre.

"Ohhh, Suzaay – Kewww!" Fogerty wailed as Suzie took her place in the middle of the circle. The men moved around her, each dancing in his own unique style and rhythm. It was a euphoric, primal moment and everyone was caught up in the magic. The crew of Pumper 6, A Platoon, danced as their tribal ancestors had done, welcoming a new member into the Lombard clan.

They collapsed into each other's arms as the song ended, laughing like maniacs. Donny bought a round of drinks for the house. Everyone agreed that it was a fabulous evening and that the "Suzie Q Breakout" would probably attain legendary status.

Eventually things began to wind down. People said their goodbyes and headed out into the cool night air. Suzie hugged them as they left, whether she knew them or not. Donny was back at his table, his head laid on his arm, humming to himself "mmm Suzie Q… mmm Suzie Q…"

"What are we going to do with our fearless leader?" Eddy asked.

Moose shrugged. "I'd give him a ride, but I'm heading the other way."

"He lives up in Don Mills, right?" Suzie asked.

"Yup."

"It's on my way. I could split a cab with him and drop him off," she suggested.

"Are you sure?"

"It's the least I can do," Suzie declared with inebriated emphasis. "As Q, I would normally instantly teleport us there, but my amazing powers are a little teensy bit impaired." She giggled at her own extraordinary wit.

Eddy hailed them a cab and gave the address to the driver. Moose helped Donny to his feet and poured him into the cab.

"Yer awright, Q," Donny slurred as the driver did a U-turn and headed north. He was slumped in the corner of the rear seat. "I really mean zhat."

"Thanks, Cap, I appreciate it."

"I din'n wansh you at first, ya know. Bud I wash wrong."

Suzie remained silent.

"I wash wrong, Q. I admiddit. Bud I'm nod a bad guy."

Suzie smiled over at him "No, you're not, Donny. You're not a bad guy at all."

He grinned drunkenly back. "Now Fitz, he wash a grade guy. I wish ya coulda known 'im."

"I wish I could have too."

Donny smiled at her again then closed his eyes. In a few seconds he was snoring.

Suzie laid her head back and looked out through the window. The stars struggled to be seen amid the city's glare, but they stayed fixed as the lights of the office towers and condos rushed by.

SHE WOKE DONNY AS the cab came to a stop in front of his house. She hadn't noticed the blue Toyota as they had driven up. It was parked at the end of the street with its lights off. Nor had she noticed the man sitting in the driver's seat, his lighter vanishing and reappearing as it moved from hand to hand. The man pressed a button on a small grey box when he saw Donny get out of the cab and wobble up the driveway. A signal passed silently and invisibly through the air, and in Donny's basement a relay closed and a valve opened.

Donny stood fumbling with his keys at the front door. He stumbled sideways, tried to regain his balance, but toppled when he stepped into the soft earth of the flower bed.

"Wait here," Suzie instructed the cab driver, handing him a twenty. "I'll only be a few minutes. I just need to get him inside."

"Sure thing, lady."

She walked over and helped Donny up. She brushed what dirt she could off him, took his keys and opened the front door.

"I'm awride."

"Come on, let's get you inside." She put his arm over her shoulder.

The light switch was just inside the door. She looked around briefly, noting the place could use, at the least, a good cleaning and would probably benefit from a complete makeover. For now, though, her main concern was to find Donny's room and get him to bed. She moved down the hall, half supporting, half dragging him towards the back of the house, peering through doorways left and right.

"Where's your room, Donny?"

"It'sh 'ere." He lurched to the left just past the bathroom, and fell over a pile of clothes.

"OK," Suzie said, helping him up again, "let's get you into bed before you kill yourself."

She steered Donny towards the unmade bed and released him. He sprawled in a final surrender to gravity.

"Geez, Donny, I got a cab waiting. Come on, help me out a little bit here, eh?" She managed to tug his shoes off, then started on his jacket.

"Ah, Sushie, we can'd. No, no, itsh nod ride…"

"Hmmph," she snorted. "You should be so lucky. Now be a good boy, get your pants off and crawl under the covers. I'll see you at work."

Donny fumbled with his belt as she tugged at the cuffs of his jeans. Suzie wrinkled her nose, "Aw Christ, Donny! You didn't, did you?"

"Whad? I didn' do nossing."

Suzie sniffed again. "Wait a minute, that's not you. That smells like gas. Donny, I think you got a gas leak."

"Gas leak?" The words stabbed through the drunken fog like a siren. He struggled to sit up and sniffed. His eyes opened wide. It was every firefighter's nightmare. You can fight fire, but you can't fight an explosion.

He grabbed at Susan. "We godda get outta here!" They ran down the hallway towards the front door, Donny bouncing off the walls.

The cab driver was amazed as they emerged running from the house; Donny dressed only in his socks, underwear and shirt. They had almost reached the street when the house miraculously disappeared in a flash of blinding light. Donny and Susan rose into the air as if lifted by the hand of God, silhouetted against the light, just an instant before the windows on the cab shattered and the car flipped onto its side.

The noise came later.

SEVENTEEN
Suspended

ALCOHOL AND SHOCK HAD helped to numb his injuries at first. Now the dull throb of a whiskey hangover was the rhythmic accompaniment to a symphony of pain. His whole body hurt. Donny felt like he had gone fifteen rounds with an angry gorilla. He wondered if a friendly gorilla would be any better.

Dawn was bleeding into the charcoal sky. It seeped in through the window of the small treatment room. Donny was oblivious to it. His mind was chasing its own tail, trying to comprehend what had happened.

The doctor finished wrapping Donny's broken left arm in fibreglass and stepped back to admire his work. "That will harden up in a few minutes. In the meantime, keep that arm still. You're a lucky man, Mr. Robertson."

Why did doctors always say that? Was it something they were taught to say in medical school, no matter how grave the patient's injury? Donny could imagine the pathologists down in the morgue saying it as they began the gruesome work of an autopsy: snip, snip, out comes the heart, "You're a lucky man, Mr. Smith," whir, zip, out comes the brain, "Yes, very lucky indeed."

Donny felt many things, but lucky was not one of them. He did his best to focus on what the doctor was saying.

The cast could come off in six weeks; the cracked ribs would take about the same time to heal. Aside from rest and Tylenol, there was not much that could be done for the ribs. They would be very sore for awhile and he should try not to cough or sneeze.

He would have to take antibiotics so the gash in his calf didn't get infected. The stitches there and on his chin could come out in ten days. The rest of his cuts and scrapes had been cleaned and bandaged. Some were from flying glass; most were from where he had bounced on the pavement.

"It could have been much worse," the doctor continued. "I'm not one to advocate drunkenness, but sometimes being loose like that can prevent more severe injury."

"How's Susan?" asked Donny.

"The woman who was with you? Your wife?"

"No, a friend. We, uh, we work together."

"Oh, I see. You're… close friends?"

The doctor raised an eyebrow, but Donny ignored the innuendo. "We work in the same fire station. We're family. How is she?"

The doctor paused a moment to take Donny's measure. "She's in surgery right now. Her spleen is ruptured; they have to take it out. Other than that her most serious injury is a couple of fractured vertebrae—a broken back, but there doesn't seem to be any neurological damage. We'll know for sure in a couple of days."

Donny looked down and shook his head. Q was lying there under the knife because of him. This was his fault. He sat for a moment studying the floor tiles, then gingerly stepped down off the gurney, testing his weight on the injured leg and wincing at the pain in his ribs. "I need to call someone to pick me up and bring me some clothes."

"Mr. Robertson, we'd like to keep you for twentyfour hours' observation. Individually your injuries aren't life-threatening, but all together, your body has been through a significant trauma." The doctor was standing, blocking the doorway of the treatment room.

"I'm OK, Doc. I'm sore, but I'm OK. I appreciate what you've done, but I've had my fill of hospitals in the last while."

"So I noticed from your records. Perhaps you should consider a change of career, Mr. Robertson," the doctor said in an officious tone.

Donny took a step forward, and then paused to get a grip on his temper. "Doc, my goddamned house blew up. This has nothing to do with my work." Somewhere in the back of his mind he wasn't sure that was true. "Now I've got a crew member in surgery, everything in my house is gone, I've got a ton of shit to do, and I need you to get out of my way."

The doctor didn't budge. "Please," Donny added grudgingly.

"And they say doctors are the worst patients."

Donny promised to rest, let his wounds heal and have someone stay with him for the next day or two. They both knew it was a lie. The doctor shook his head and pointed Donny towards the nurses' station.

IT WAS MIDMORNING when Ratzo arrived at the hospital. "Jesus," he said, looking at Donny's face, "you lose a fight with a lawn mower or something?"

"That's what I love about you, Ratzo: you always know the right thing to say to cheer a guy up."

"Don't get me wrong, I am very glad to see you on the green side of the grass." Donny changed into the fatigues Ratzo handed him. "Sorry, Wedge, it was all I could find in your locker at the station."

"No problem, I got civvies on the boat. Let's get out of here." The Tylenol 3s had taken the edge off his hangover and his various aches and pains. "I could use a cup of coffee and something to eat, if you've got the time."

"I was going to suggest the same thing," Ratzo said. He handed Donny a cane. "It was my father's. You can give it back when you're done with it."

Donny nodded his thanks and they walked out to Ratzo's car, Donny leaning heavily on the cane. He gave Ratzo directions to a diner not far from the marina. They compared notes on what they had learned about Suzie's condition. Other than that, the two men didn't speak much. Each was absorbed in his own thoughts.

Donny stared glumly out the passenger window as they drove. He still had *Red Bird*, but just about everything else was gone. His wallet and all his ID were in his pants; that would all have to be replaced. He'd have to rent a car. There was insurance to deal with. There were all the records from Commissioners Street he had gathered…

A handful of tables huddled by the front window of the diner. A row of booths ran to the back, flanked by the lunch counter and the open grill behind it. Donny and Ratzo took a booth in the back. They studied their menus in silence, though each already knew what the other would have: a Western omelette with brown toast for Ratzo, scrambled with rye for Donny. The waitress brought them coffee without asking and they ordered.

"Sorry, I'm going to have to ask you to get me those records for the Commissioners Street fire again," Donny said. "I'm pretty sure they're gone with everything else."

Ratzo shook his head. "That's not going to happen."

Donny looked at him with a quizzical expression. Ratzo stared at him, his jaw clenched. "There's no easy way to say this, Donny. You're suspended."

"Excuse me?!" Donny exclaimed, wide-eyed.

"This thing's all over the news, Donny. You were found half naked with a female probie. The political correctness police are on the warpath. They want your head!"

"Oh Jesus, Ratzo it wasn't like that! I mean, I was drunk. She was just helping me…"

"You know that, and I know that, but the rest of them? If it was just that, we could probably take care of this when Q gets back on her feet. But Donny," Ratzo leaned forward and spread his arms, "what the hell were you doing in uniform, using a fake name, masquerading as a fire inspector on your day off?"

"I… I don't…" Donny stammered.

The waitress approached to refill their coffee, but turned on her heel when Ratzo slammed his mug down on the table.

"This is no time to play dumb, Robertson. I spent half an hour on the phone with the Fire Chief before I came to pick you up. He is madder than hell, which, let me tell you, is not my favourite way to start my day. Your badge number is on the security guard's report and the description fits you to a T, right down to your cute little pink scars." Ratzo pointed to the puckered skin on Donny's neck. "Maybe we could have smoothed this over if we could have kept it in house. But that property is owned by Korvan Developments. They're a big-time player, Donny. When they found out about your little game, they went straight to the mayor's office."

"Ratzo, whoever set the Commissioners Street fire used that building to blow the water main."

"What are you talking about?"

"There's this air lock thing, see?" Donny explained Laurie's theory to Ratzo and told him what Donny himself had seen. Their orders came and they began to eat.

"And you can prove this?" asked Ratzo between mouthfuls.

Donny's eyes opened wide in sudden realization. "Damn it! My phone! It was in my jacket, in the house, and… Shit, shit, shit!" He winced, but then began again excitedly. "But hey, there's that extra hose, right? What about that? And… and why would those guys go to the mayor over a little inspection if they had nothing to hide, eh? What about that?"

Ratzo chewed thoughtfully as he looked at Donny. "Buddy, you have a hearing at headquarters next week. Right now you need to focus on keeping your job. I'm telling you this as a friend, Wedge."

Donny poked at his eggs with his fork. He looked towards the window at the front of the restaurant, at the people walking by, at the streetcars chasing their schedules along Queen Street, at everyday life going on as if everything was normal; as if Q wasn't lying in a hospital bed with a broken back and an incision in her belly; as if his house wasn't a smoking hole in the ground; as if…

It was the first time he had allowed himself to face the reality of the thought.

"I think someone's trying to kill me, Joe. I think they blew up my house because I'm onto something." Donny put down his fork and took a long drink of water. He was exhausted from the pain and the lack of sleep. Now, the impact of this new idea staggered him.

Ratzo frowned. No one on the job ever called him Joe. "Donny, water mains break. Buildings catch fire. And every once in a while, thank God it's not more often, but every once in very long while, houses blow up because of a gas leak. That doesn't mean they're all part of some big conspiracy. It just doesn't make any sense. In all of this you've never been able to tell me why anyone would do this."

"I don't know why, not yet…"

"Let me finish." Ratzo cut him off gently but firmly. "Now, there's probably some perfectly reasonable explanation for everything. But for now, let's just say you're right."

"I know I'm right."

"OK, but isn't that all the more reason to hand this over to someone who knows what they're doing? Instead, you go and get yourself into deep shit — and I do mean very deep shit — over some bogus inspection. For Christ's sake, we're firefighters, not detectives, Donny."

Donny raised his hands in a gesture of surrender. "You're right. I screwed up. And I appreciate what you're trying to do…"

"What you need to do, Donny," Ratzo continued insistently, "is call the union and concentrate on this hearing next week. If Q backs you up, I'm sure the human rights thing will go away. She seems like good people. The phony inspection thing, maybe we can work the stress angle on that. But you gotta keep your nose clean. No more Sam Spade, OK?"

"Sure."

"You're a lying sack of shit, Robertson."

Donny blew out his breath in a long hissing stream. "I will not just drop this, Ratzo. I will not let them run me off. And don't ask me why, 'cause I really don't have a good answer. But I'll talk to the guy from the fire marshal, Edwards or whatever his name is. If he'll take it on, so much the better."

They agreed by silent consent to drop it there. They finished their breakfast, argued briefly over the bill, then shook hands and went their separate ways.

Donny crossed the street and limped through the cool leafy green of Kew Gardens towards the boardwalk that ran along the beach. With its manicured lawns and flower beds, the park was one of the city's little gems. It was the trees, though, the massive, stately oaks, that Donny loved. They were the remnants of an ancient forest, now captive in an urban park. Silent sentinels, they stood looking out over the lake like the Moai of Easter Island. As seedlings, they had borne mute witness to the lives of the Wendat and Seneca people. They had been spared when the white men came and carved their imaginary lines across the land. They would continue watching the passing of the seasons, drawing life from the sun and soil, long after Donny had returned to the earth.

The thought comforted him. He needed something that endured. He sat on a bench in the peaceful shade and looked out over the water, searching for some clue on the distant horizon. It seemed, however, that there was a desperate shortage of omens in the city that day.

There was so much to deal with… chaos and confusion, forces pulling him this way and that. There were so many things he needed to do. But for now he needed to sit and be quiet. He watched the timeless ballet of the waves washing the sand and tried to let his mind go blank.

After a few minutes he gave up. He was no Jedi master. The only thing he had in common with Yoda was the cane Ratzo had given him. Donny heaved himself painfully to his feet. Leaning on the cane, he limped along the boardwalk toward the marina.

He stopped at the phone booth beside the marina office and called his voice mail. There were messages of concern from Eddy and Moose. There was a short call from Fire Chief Allan Stevens saying he was suspended from duty pending an investigation and that a formal written notice would be mailed to him. There were several calls from reporters. Micah Edwards from the Fire Marshal's office wanted to talk to him. That was interesting. Finally, there was a message from John Aldrich. The message he had hoped for wasn't there.

He called Aldrich back. It was reassuring to hear the old man's voice.

"Thank God you're alive, Donald, and the woman too! Where are you staying?"

"I'm heading over to the boat. I just wanted to let you know I'm OK, and, you know, say thanks for calling…"

"That won't do, Donald. You can't be climbing all 'round that rigging in your condition. Not as long as I have spare rooms. You'll come and stay with me. And there'll be no arguing. That's an order."

It hadn't been Donny's intention to invite himself as a house guest, but it was comforting to connect with something solid from the past. He agreed after only a momentary pause.

"That would be nice. Thank you. The doctor said I shouldn't stay by myself for a day or two anyway. I just don't want to be any bother."

"Nonsense. I'm a lonely old man in an empty house. I'll be glad of the company. Now where are you?"

Donny told him, and Aldrich said he would come by to pick him up in half an hour. Donny said goodbye and hung up. Then he dialed again.

"Hi, Laurie? It's Donny."

"Jesus! Donny, what's going on?"

"My house blew up," he said, marvelling at the simplicity of the short phrase and all that it implied.

"I know. It's front page. Are you all right?" There was the sound of jackhammers and machinery in the background. There was obvious concern in her voice, but something else too.

"Yeah, I'm fine. Well, I got a broken arm, some stitches and stuff. And, oh yeah, cracked ribs, it hurts to breathe. But aside from that I'm just great." He tried to laugh but the spasm of pain quickly ended it.

"I'm sorry I didn't call, but I didn't know where to get hold of you." She was silent for a moment. "The news said there was another, uh, person too." She tried to keep the suspicion from her voice without success.

"Suzie? It's not what you think. I'm not like that, OK? You've got to believe me. I got really drunk. And that's not like me either. It was so stupid. Suzie was just helping me get home. She's my probie and I wouldn't do that. I mean even if… I wouldn't do that to you. And now she's lying in the hospital and… oh my God!" Donny slumped against the clear plastic wall of the phone booth.

"OK, OK, calm down. I believe you. I didn't think… I mean, I just wondered, you know? And… the truth is I was afraid. You know, after what happened to Steve… I didn't want to put myself through all that again."

"I understand, really. It's OK. You're absolutely right, nobody needs that."

"We need to talk, Donny. I'm at work and it's really busy. What hospital are you in? I'll come see you."

It hurt but Donny tried to take a couple of deep breaths to regain his composure. "I signed myself out. I don't like hospitals."

"Are you retarded?! No one likes hospitals."

"I'm going to stay with my old captain for a couple of days. I'll be OK."

She turned and yelled something Donny couldn't make out to the men working in the background, then put the phone back to her mouth. "Well, that's good, better than staying alone. When can I see you?"

Donny closed his eyes. He could see her smile, that wonderful smile. He remembered the feel of her body nestled against him, drifting into sweet sleep with his arm draped around her, his hand cupping her breast.

"No!" he said emphatically, but mostly to himself. "Laurie, my house blew up."

"I know," she said impatiently.

"It's not safe. I don't know what they'll do next."

There was a pause before she responded. "You think someone…"

"I'm sorry," he cut her off. He couldn't bear to hear her say it. "I'm sorry I got you into this whole mess. For your own good…"

"I can make up my own mind about what's good for me. You say you're not 'that kind' — well, I'm not the kind that takes off at the first sign of trouble either. I mean, yes, I was afraid, but I'm not going to run." She was fiercely defiant and he loved her for it.

His voice was barely more than a whisper. "You're not thinking straight, Laurie. You said it yourself, these guys are pros. You have kids. You need to protect them." She said nothing. "You know I'm right. I'm sorry. Goodbye, Laurie. I… I…" He hung up before he made it any worse.

The wave crested and broke: Laurie, Suzie, his house, the job, his whole life was spinning crazily out of control. He staggered to the bench beside the phone booth. That was where Aldrich found him, the phoenix on the shoulder patch of his fatigues rising and falling as his shoulders heaved and the tears ran down his face.

EIGHTEEN
Bubble

"DISAPPOINTED, BRENDAN? Disappointed? You have no idea how disappointed I am." Catherine gave a short, humourless laugh. "I told you I didn't want to deal with this again."

The Gulfstream was luxuriously outfitted with silk and leather upholstery and hand-woven carpets. A Picasso sketch hung on the bulkhead behind the walnut table. A bottle of Château Margaux '95 sat breathing as the plane climbed to cruising altitude, and wonderful smells were wafting from the galley. Despite all of this there was almost nowhere Brendan wouldn't rather be. He knew that disappointing the woman in the hand-tailored Armani suit and custom-fit Prada shoes was not something one did lightly. There was, however, nowhere to escape.

"I'm terribly sorry, ma'am," Brendan stammered. "It was a bit of bad luck, I believe."

"I wanted this cleaned up quietly; now we have front-page news and we're no further ahead. It's simply unacceptable. Bad luck or incompetence, I will not tolerate either."

"No, ma'am."

"This needs to be contained. Use whatever influence we have to ensure that happens, and purchase more if needed. Inform the supplier that I consider it his responsibility to set this straight. There will be no more excuses. Is that understood?"

"Yes, ma'am."

"I'm going to lie down. Call me when Henri is ready to serve."

Brendan stood as she left. He cursed softly to himself, then pulled out his laptop and began making arrangements.

The aircraft's bedroom was equally well appointed, but Catherine felt suffocated in the tiny room. She lay and stared at the cabin ceiling curving over her head. Is this what it would be like to lie in her coffin? she wondered. It would be no less luxurious, she was certain, fitted with the finest silks and rare woods. But what did any of that matter?

Catherine enjoyed the comforts her success had brought, but she recognized them for what they were: the reward of hard work, attention to detail and the razor-sharp instincts of a predator; the spoils of victory. They were not, as her feckless children seemed to think, some sort of entitlement.

David, second eldest of her grandchildren, showed signs of promise.

Time. She needed more time. Time to nurture that spark, to teach him that money and privilege were not ends in themselves but the tools of power, levers to be used to achieve…

Inoperable. That's what the neuro-oncologist in Zurich had said. The tumour was too closely entwined with her brain stem, which controlled so many basic life functions. But, he said with professional sympathy, it was relatively slow growing. With appropriate therapy Catherine might enjoy two, maybe three more years before she lost the ability to speak, to walk, to breathe…

She had been betrayed by her own body. Some rogue gene, some treacherous molecule, some traitor of a cell had started a process she was powerless to stop. That was what really galled her.

She could be charming, persuasive, ruthless, generous, or demanding, as the situation required. She was a shrewd negotiator, a passionate motivator and a consummate manipulator. She was determined. She was a winner. And she made the decisions, damn it!

She didn't fear death any more than she welcomed it. She accepted, however reluctantly, its inevitability. Just not yet. She wasn't finished. She had yet to complete her crowning achievement.

Edison had launched many great innovations, but without the light bulb he would be just one more obscure inventor. The Aziz project would assure her legacy.

And not a death like this; not being taken hostage by some tiny assassin and suffocated inside her own body.

He would lay out a program of radiation and chemotherapy for her, the specialist had said. And there were also some promising experimental therapies if Catherine were willing to consider them.

She recognized these for the pitiful offerings of desperation they were. But what choice did she have?

COMMANDER MIKE WILKINS wheeled himself over to the window and allowed himself the luxury of a few moments of reflection. The Maryland countryside was sizzling hot, though it was still early morning. His shirt had pasted itself to his back during the short trip across the parking lot from one air-conditioned bubble to another.

His life, it seemed, was a series of bubbles. In one he was a suburban Dad, cooking burgers in the backyard, going to parent-teacher nights, another anonymous cog in the Byzantine governmental machine that churned around the Beltway.

Here, at the NSA, he was in a different sort of bubble, floating high above, unseen, but seeing all that was laid out below. Yet in so many ways he was powerless. He put his hand against the glass barrier between him and the sweltering heat outside.

Among the Spectrum alerts waiting for him that morning were several news stories from Toronto regarding a natural gas explosion. Wilkins had another look at the Robertson file. The broad outline was easy to see and it wasn't that hard to fill in the blanks. Robertson was innocently enough, perhaps even naively, trying to figure out how and why his friend had died. What Robertson didn't understand was that someone had a significant interest in keeping that information private. Someone, it seemed, who was willing to go to any lengths to do that.

"I'm sure you're right, Commander," Colonel Gilford had responded when Wilkins reported the latest results and voiced his concerns. "But it doesn't change anything. This is a 'big picture' matter. Carry on."

Maybe the explosion would scare Robertson off and that would be the end of it. Wilkins wanted to believe that, but he knew it wasn't true.

He took his hand off the window and retreated inside the bubble to his desk. It might be a necessary evil in a dirty little world, but it was an abuse nonetheless. It put Wilkins in a foul mood. Such was the curse of the Tree of Knowledge.

THE MOOD WAS NO better in the hotel room in Toronto.

"…Donald Robertson, the owner of the home, was treated and released. An unnamed woman remains in hospital in serious but stable condition…"

The man in the hotel room muted the TV and cursed when his phone rang, but answered it when he saw the number. He said little other than "yes" and "I understand." Then he hung up and cursed again.

At least they had given him another chance. He had had a very successful career in a profession that did not tolerate failure. He would show them. He would wrap it all up in one nice neat little package. For that he needed something special, something truly inspired.

"Yes, Captain Robertson, something very special, just for you." The Zippo materialized in his hand. He thumbed the wheel and watched the cascade of sparks rush toward the wick. With a wave of his hand, the lighter vanished, and then reappeared only to melt into the ether once again. The lighter winked in and out of existence, but always there was the shower of sparks and the dancing flame. He did it over and over, the simple repetition clearing his mind as it had done so many times before.

NINETEEN
A Small Crater

THEY STOOD IN FRONT of a line of yellow police tape, looking at the rectangular crater that yawned where Donny's house had once stood. The two houses on either side were heavily damaged as well: the closest walls were blown in and portions of the roofs were gone. Across the road and down the street on either side, neighbours were repairing shattered windows and cleaning debris from their yards. Some of them looked over at the two men, but none of them came to speak.

Donny stood transfixed. The area before him was littered with blackened splinters of wood, fragments of furniture, crystalline shards of glass, bits of insulation, and the chalky monotony of drywall — the humpty dumpty pieces of what had been a home. His home.

Looking at the scene of utter destruction, he was amazed that he and Suzie had survived.

He'd seen devastation before, more times than he could count. A home, a place where people raised their children and stored a lifetime of memories, all reduced to sodden ashes. And death, he'd seen lots of that.

Sometimes he would cheat death and bring them out a little singed, gasping and stinking of burnt hair, but alive. Those times almost made up for the others. They helped quiet the wails of hysterical grief that echoed in the dark corners of his mind.

And then there were the little miracles: a photo album that

somehow survived, tucked deep in a back closet; a teddy bear or grandma's quilt, some talisman of all that had been lost. Joy would blossom in the midst of desolation. They would clutch their keepsakes and thank him, with tears streaming down their cheeks. Donny would turn away, embarrassed by their gratitude, ashamed that all he could offer were these trinkets.

Now it was his turn.

He felt curiously indifferent about the house itself. It had been for him just a place, a comfortable abode, somewhere to keep his things, but little more. He had lived here almost twenty years, but it had never fully become a home. He did feel shock that it had all been wrenched away so suddenly, but little else. Perhaps he would feel different if it were *Red Bird* that he had lost. He had put so much more of himself into refitting the boat. But even then the real emotional attachment was to the art and craft of sailing. It was a state of mind, a way of being, rather than a physical thing.

If there was grief in his heart, it was not for this house; it was for the brief glimpse Laurie had shown him of what a home might be. How laughter and companionship, joy and sorrow could work their alchemy to change four walls into something much, much more. That, more than anything, was what he had lost.

"… about six feet high?"

Donny shook his head and turned to face Micah Edwards. "I'm sorry, what did you ask?"

Micah was a bit shorter than Donny, with broad shoulders and thick powerful arms. His dark blue coveralls were smeared with soot. His large head was topped by a white hard hat emblazoned with the Fire Marshal's crest, and the broad face beneath was framed by a neatly trimmed beard. Their previous encounter, on the phone, had not gone so well. Now here he was standing beside Donny. He had hoped to meet with the investigator, but this was not what he had had in mind.

"Your basement — the ceiling was about six feet high?" Micah asked, his soft, lyrical Caribbean accent a contrast to the scene of devastation around them. Donny nodded and Micah scribbled rough calculations in the small notebook he carried. "So roughly five thousand cubic feet. Let's say a 5% mixture, that's the lower explosive limit of natural gas. That's roughly equal to… about a hundred and twenty-five sticks of dynamite."

"Holy shit," Donny said softly.

"You got a good solid foundation. It focused most of the blast force up instead of out. Damn near launched your roof into orbit." Micah pantomimed the process with his hands in case Donny didn't quite appreciate the fact that his house had blown up. "Pieces came down two blocks away, but that foundation saved your life. You're lucky."

"So everyone keeps telling me," Donny said, poking at a piece of charred wood with his cane.

"You're alive, aren't you?"

Donny said nothing.

"OK, I need to ask the usual questions for the record." Micah asked if Donny had done any work on the furnace or water heater. Had he or any neighbours dug up or damaged any gas lines? Had he ever smelled gas in the house before? Donny answered "no" to all of the questions.

"I didn't think so," Micah continued, "but I had to ask. Aren't you curious why I'm here?"

Because it's your job, Donny was about to say, then thought better of it and closed his mouth.

"A man calls me and tells me he's suspicious about a fire. A couple of weeks later his house blows up. Now isn't that funny?"

"Yeah, hilarious," said Donny, unable to resist the combination of sarcasm and self-pity.

"I specifically asked for this case, Donny. I think maybe you pissed somebody off. If that's so, I want to catch them. If I can connect this with Commissioners Street, I'll charge them with murder one."

"That… that would be good." Donny's face brightened for the first time since he had arrived at the scene. "Listen, I'm sorry. It's been a lousy couple of days."

"So I hear." Micah gave a deep chuckle. "Sorry if I was a little hard-assed last time we talked. Why don't we start fresh?" He held out his hand and Donny grasped it firmly. "We need to talk. Let's go sit in the van."

They turned their backs on the crater and walked to the white van parked a couple of doors down the street. They sat in the front seats facing the hole in the suburban landscape. "All right. Let's start with how you managed to get yourself suspended," Micah said when they were seated.

Donny looked surprised. "You heard about that, eh?"

"Come on, it's the fire service. Besides, it's my job to know." Micah made notes as Donny recounted the events of the past couple of weeks.

Micah pursed his lips and looked at Donny. "You know why they recruit police detectives to become fire investigators, instead of you guys? Huh? Because we know how to collect evidence and we know the law."

"Yeah, I kind of realize that now. But you weren't exactly helpful when I called you the last time."

"True. However, the problem, aside from you getting yourself in shit, is that anything you saw regarding that air lock is probably inadmissible. That was an illegal search. Now, I can try to talk my way back into that building, but I doubt I would ever be able to get a search warrant now. You've more or less poisoned the well."

"Sorry."

"It's a setback," Micah said, "but it's not the end of the world. I'm going to try to track down the security guard. He was there legally, so his testimony might be untainted. I'll have to talk to a prosecutor about that. Now, how close are you with this Laurie Zhou woman?"

"Christ, is there anything you don't know?"

"I talked to your crew. Donny, I'm an investigator. I need to know all the angles."

Donny shrugged. His instinct was to try to protect Laurie. "I took her sailing. We went out a couple of times. It didn't work out." He tried to look like it didn't matter, but he knew it was a thin disguise.

Micah glanced at him sideways and made another notation. "OK. It shouldn't matter anyway. Her testimony about the water main may be important, though.

"Now, this business about the extra hose is interesting. I like the idea of looking at the aerial photography. I'll contact the TV stations, get copies of their footage and have our video guys take a look at it. We'll see if there's anything there."

Micah turned and reached behind him for a clear plastic bag labelled "evidence." Inside the bag was a thin metal tube about the thickness of a straw and about two centimetres long. A broken wire extended from the end of the tube. He held the bag up to Donny. "You know what this is?"

Donny shook his head.

"This is a thermocouple," Micah explained. "That tube sits in the flame of the pilot light in your furnace. As long as the pilot light burns, the thermocouple stays hot. It sends a signal through the wire to a safety valve that says it's OK to supply gas to the furnace.

"If the pilot light goes out, the thermocouple gets cold, the safety valve closes, and the gas gets shut off. You follow me?"

Donny nodded and Micah continued with his explanation.

"This collar at the base of the thermocouple fits into a holder that keeps it in the flame of the pilot light. There's no damage on this collar, so it wasn't torn free by the explosion. I think it was detached beforehand."

"But wouldn't that shut off the gas?" Donny asked.

"Ordinarily, yes, but see that other little piece of wire?" Donny looked closer. There was a fragment of wire about a centimetre long stuck to the side of the thermocouple.

"I think that piece of wire got welded on during the blast. I'm sending it in to the lab for testing. If it comes back as a chromium-nickel alloy, then that wire was part of a heating element."

Donny sucked his breath in through his teeth. "So you mean you stick the thermocouple in a toaster or something, that heats it up and opens the gas valve?"

"It's possible," Micah said, nodding. "I have to look at the other pieces of your furnace and gas system, but this is a lead."

Micah turned in his seat to face Donny squarely. "If I'm right about this, someone has gone to a lot of trouble to make this look like an accident. And the same at Commissioners Street, assuming they're connected. Someone is trying to cover their tracks. This isn't your run-of-the-mill fire bug."

"Yeah, I kind of figured that already." Donny slumped in his seat. "Where do we go from here?"

"*We* let *me* do my job, OK?" Donny started to object, but Micah cut him off. "Donny, you're out of your depth. This is what I do and I do it well. You messing around is what got us here. Now, there may be one thing you can help with."

"What? Do I get to make the coffee and sandwich run?"

"That's not a bad idea, but I was thinking you could talk to Leila Aziz — you know, the widow from Commissioners."

"I tried that back when I started all this." Back when I had a house and a job, Donny thought to himself. "She wasn't real helpful. She more or less hung up on me — kind of like you did, come to think of it."

"Yeah, but look at us now, just like old buddies." Micah gave him a broad smile. "Listen, she wasn't very talkative with me either. She might open up a bit to you if you play the sympathy card. You know: 'my house blew up, Suzie's in the hospital,' that sort of thing."

"I don't know. That seems a bit cheesy."

"Donny, in this business you use whatever angle will work. The cane's good too. People like to help cripples."

"Gee, thanks."

"It's a psychological fact. Use it."

Donny nodded. "OK. What should I ask her?"

"Anything she can tell us about Aziz Energy Systems would be good. The main thing, though, is to get her to start talking. Once you open the door, I can see where it goes. You got her contact information?"

"No, I kind of lost everything. You might remember there was this explosion?" Donny gestured towards the empty space that had been his house.

"Ha ha. Just a minute." Micah reached for his laptop. He wrote the information on a piece of paper and handed it to Donny.

"Thanks," Donny said, shoving the paper into his pocket. "I'll get on that. In the meantime, I want to swing by the hospital and see how Suzie's doing."

"How do I get hold of you now?" Micah asked.

Donny held up a new cell phone. "Same number as the old one. I'm staying at my old captain's place for a couple of days." He recited Aldrich's contact information and Micah wrote it down.

As Donny reached for the door handle, Micah put a hand on his shoulder. "If we're right about all this, Donny, we're dealing with some dangerous people."

"You think I don't know that?"

"Yeah, well, just be careful. I don't think anyone's going to gun you down or anything. They seem to want to keep a low profile. Just look both ways before you cross the street, OK?"

Donny wasn't sure how you went about protecting yourself from "accidents" without lapsing into paranoia. He left the van and walked past… what was it now? Not a house, that was certain.

The blackened rim of a motorcycle wheel peeked out from under a pile of rubble. The Norton was nothing but burnt, twisted metal now. He thought of the Buddhist he had dated briefly many years ago. She had told him that being detached from his material possessions would bring happiness. So much for that theory.

DONNY STOPPED AT A flower shop on the way to the hospital and chose a bouquet of yellow roses. That was friendship, wasn't it, yellow roses? He was about to leave the store when he turned around and headed back to the counter.

"Do you deliver?" he asked.

"Of course," the woman at the counter said with a smile.

He wanted to ask what colour of roses meant "My life is completely messed up. I wish things could be different and I'm sorry for ruining everything. I miss you so much it hurts to breathe." Though the last part might be the cracked ribs.

"Can I help you with something?" the woman prompted.

"Hmm, I wish you could," Donny said ruefully. He picked a dozen red roses and gave the woman Laurie's address.

"Would you like to include a card?"

He thought for a moment. "Maybe you could just write 'I'm sorry' for me and leave it at that."

HE GOT SUZIE'S ROOM number from the hospital information desk and took the elevator to the fifth floor. There were voices coming from Suzie's room. He stopped short of the doorway and listened.

"Ryan can stay with Elaine and me as long as you need, Sue. It's not a problem." It was a man's voice Donny didn't recognize.

"Thanks, Rob." Suzie's voice sounded weak and sleepy.

"Are you going to be a fireman again, Mom?"

"You bet, sweetie, just as soon as I get better."

"Will you get blowed up again?"

"No, this was just an accident, muffin. I'm going to be fine."

Donny made his way to a chair on the other side of the wide corridor, and sat. He could just see diagonally across into Q's room. She was facing away from him. A framework of padded plastic cradled the back of her head and circled her chin. Metal rods connected this to a rigid brace that covered her shoulders and continued under the covers. An IV bag dripped into her arm.

Rob sat facing her in a chair by the window. He looked like the country club type: polo shirt, chinos and Topsiders that had most likely never seen the deck of a boat. He had a square jaw and perfect hair. The latter was probably surgically enhanced, Donny thought — maybe both.

Ryan sat on the foot of his mother's bed, wearing a fire department T-shirt that was three sizes too big for him. He was looking alternately at his mother and the various pieces of equipment that were attached to her. His expression was one of curiosity mingled with concern.

They could both see Donny sitting there if they chose to look, but to them he was just another visitor sitting across the hallway. Words and phrases drifted out of the room, but Donny wasn't paying much attention. He simply watched the tableau and let his mind wander.

Each of us makes a thousand choices every day: simple choices, mindless choices. Most of them disappear unnoticed into the chaos of everyday life. The "big" ones, the ones we agonize over, rarely have the impact we imagine. More often it's the "butterfly effect": it's some arbitrary selection, a seemingly trivial decision, lost in the noise of day-to-day living, that, amplified by time, changes the course of our lives.

And so the four of them had come to this place at this time: a woman lay in a hospital bed and tried to comfort the comforters; a man watched her, torn between his concern for the mother of his child and his longing for his beautiful young wife; a child grappled for the first time with the concept of his mother's mortality; and a man sat in a hallway, clutching a bouquet of slowly dying roses and wondering what, if anything, it all meant.

Donny left the roses with a short note at the nurses' station. He walked out of the hospital feeling like he was searching for something he wasn't sure he could recognize, and wondering why.

TWENTY
Exile

"YOU KNEW IT WOULD be like this, didn't you? *'A sadder but wiser man'* — isn't that what you told me at the cemetery?" They were sitting in John Aldrich's back yard in the late afternoon heat, listening to the hum of the insects and the whisper of the sprinklers.

Donny's meeting with the union had been a dismal end to a dismal day. He had been given his pick of two bad choices. If he were willing to sign an apology to Korvan Development admitting trespass and fraud, and agree to give up anything to do with the Commissioners Street fire, he could keep his job. He would be demoted and assigned to a desk job. It was the Fire Department equivalent of being exiled to Siberia. Take it or leave it, he had been told; it was the best deal the union could negotiate.

His only alternative was to face dismissal for gross misconduct. The union would grieve his dismissal, of course, but given the circumstances they held out little hope of success. They gave him four days to make up his mind.

"I believe the exact quote is *'A sadder and a wiser man,'* but never mind." Aldrich picked up the crystal tumbler beside him and raised it to Donny. "Here's comfort to the living and peace to the dead."

Donny raised his glass, clinked it with Aldrich's and took a long sip of the amber fluid. He closed his eyes and savoured the smoky warmth. "That is some very fine scotch."

"This isn't just scotch. This is Glenmorangie 25, twenty-five years in the cask, and just about the finest thing you'll ever put in a glass. Like the kiss of an angel, isn't it?"

"With the kick of a mule."

"Well, the angel did dislocate Jacob's hip, didn't he?" Aldrich looked at Donny, who merely shrugged. "Do you not know your Bible?"

"Perhaps not as well as I should."

"Well, it's worth reading, whether you're a believer or not, Donny. There's a lot of wisdom in it. You see, Jacob was a man with a heavy conscience. And there were some folks who wanted to kill him as well. Sound familiar?"

"Does he have an albatross too?" Donny asked, taking another drink of the whisky.

"No," Aldrich replied, looking over his glasses, "but his opponent did have wings. It's a complex story with many parts. In this part Jacob spent a whole night wrestling with an angel. Some say it's Jacob wrestling with his own conscience; others believe he's wrestling with God's will. In the end it's a bit of a draw. The angel dislocates Jacob's hip and he limps for the rest of his life, but he earns the angel's blessing. Jacob is a changed man after the encounter, but he still retains the free will that God gave Adam."

Donny said nothing. He drained his glass and held it out for a refill. Aldrich looked at him for a moment, then poured him another drink. "The answer to your problems is not in that glass. And by the by, this is very expensive single malt whisky. If it's guzzling you're after, I'll get the blended stuff."

"Sorry. I'll sip."

Aldrich settled back in his chair and watched the leaves of the big maple at the end of yard tremble in the breeze. "We all wrestle with God in one way or another, struggling to understand the incomprehensible."

Aldrich looked directly at him, but Donny refused to meet his eyes. "Trying to unscramble the egg has destroyed a lot of good men on the job, Donny. Don't be one of them."

"Fine words, Cap, but it's not so easy."

"What is best is rarely easy, Donald. Fitz wouldn't want to see this — you almost killed and Susan in the hospital, your house gone, losing your job. He would be appalled to think it was because of him."

"It's not just for him," Donny protested. He stared up at the deep blue well that stretched above them. Did any of it matter? The house? The job? Their pathetic lives spent scrambling for answers to questions they couldn't even articulate? Was there, as Aldrich believed, some master plan? Some invisible hand moving the pawns, decreeing who should live and who should be sacrificed for some inscrutable strategy? That seemed somehow even more cruel than the indifference of random chance.

"You told me back when I was new that we stood for something. You said that firefighters weren't saints, that some of us were even rogues and scoundrels, but that when we put on our gear and climbed aboard the truck we made a sacred covenant: a covenant to stand together, a covenant to save the lives and property of strangers, no matter who they were, even if it meant risking our own lives. You told me that in a world of greed and convenience, we stood for something noble and pure."

"You remember that, do you?" Aldrich smiled. "It's something my first captain taught me."

"And it's something I've tried to pass on to every new guy I meet on the job," Donny nodded. "Fitz believed it. I need to believe it too."

The harsh glare of day was softening into the golden light of evening. The low sun bathed the world in a warm light that made even seemingly inanimate things glow with life, and the lengthening shadows gave an extra dimension of depth.

How nice it would be to simply sit here drinking Aldrich's

expensive whisky and discussing theology, philosophy and other things he knew nothing about. To simply sit and smell the flowers, listen to the insects drone and watch the birds flit from branch to branch. How nice it would be to ignore the dead end that faced him with nothing but bad choices to make.

"Everyone thinks I should give up: Ratzo, Micah, the union… even you think I should break the covenant," Donny said sadly.

"Do you remember backing out of a fire when I was Captain?" Aldrich asked.

"Once or twice. No more than a handful of times that I can remember."

"But we did it. Do you know why I gave the order to pull back?"

"Because we were going to get our asses fried if we stayed. Like that place on Sumac Street, remember that?" Donny asked with a smile.

"Perfect example," Aldrich replied. "The fire had a hold on every floor. The roof would have come down on our heads if we'd stayed in there. We lost that house, but we saved the ones on either side. Did I break the covenant by pulling us out?"

"Well, no, but…"

"There is no 'but,' Donny. There is no shame in resigning from a fight you can't win."

"So you think I should sign the papers, put my tail between my legs, and give up on the whole thing."

"At least you'll keep your job and your pension. That's no small thing. And you wouldn't be giving up on anything. This Micah Edwards sounds like a fine fellow. Let him carry the ball. It's his job. You've done enough."

Aldrich poured them each another dram of whisky. "Lay pride aside, son. Listen to your heart."

Donny sighed heavily. "I told Micah I would do one more thing. He wanted me to talk to the widow of the other guy who was killed."

"Then you had best do it in the next four days."

Donny nodded and gazed into a space somewhere between the trees and infinity. Aldrich rose and stretched. He took his glass but left the bottle.

"I'm heading inside. Enjoy the sunset."

Donny sat in Aldrich's backyard as the day faded, until at last he was submerged in the comforting anonymity of darkness. The outcome was never really in doubt, but still he turned the decision this way and that, like a dog worrying a bone. Finally, exhausted, he went inside and put Aldrich's whisky on the kitchen counter. The bottle was still a little less than half full.

He awoke the next morning from a deep, dreamless sleep. For the first time since the explosion he felt refreshed. Perhaps it was because he was not the type who watched his life pass in the rear-view mirror. Perhaps it was because he felt he could trust Micah. Perhaps it was because he had little real choice.

Aldrich was already up, sitting in the breakfast nook off the kitchen, reading the paper with his morning tea. Donny decided that as a gesture to new beginnings he would change things up a bit, and poured himself a mug of the dark steaming brew. He was surprised and pleased by the rich, smoky and slightly nutty flavour, and he murmured his approval.

"It's Russian Caravan," Aldrich said over the paper. "I have it blended for me at a little tea shop downtown. Nothing Russian about it these days, but it got its name from the days when they would carry the tea by camel caravan and dog sled from China across Mongolia and Siberia to Moscow. It was a journey of terrible hardship. Sometimes it took a year or more."

"All that for a cup of tea?" Donny exclaimed.

Aldrich harrumphed. "Wars have been fought and nations have risen and fallen over tea."

Donny enjoyed the brew, but declined when Aldrich offered to share his toast and Marmite. The latter, Donny decided, should be classed as a biohazard, based on smell alone. He opted for strawberry jam instead.

They shared the tea and traded sections of the paper in silence.

"Heading out?" Aldrich enquired as Donny rose from the table to put his mug and plate in the dishwasher.

"I need to look after a few things. I can stay on the boat until the end of October, but I need to see about finding a place to live. And I need a new car, some clothes. All my ID's gone. There's a lot of stuff to do," Donny sighed.

"That sounds like a full day," Aldrich said, nodding. Donny had deliberately avoided mentioning anything to do with his decision, and Aldrich decided to return the courtesy.

"I thought I might drop by the hall, too, and see what's for lunch," Donny brightened. "Check how Eddy's doing being in charge."

"I'm sure the boys will be glad to see you. Just remember a crew needs only one captain at a time. Eddy's competent, and no one likes people looking over their shoulder."

"THIS FEELS WEIRD. You want to sit over here?" Eddy was sitting behind the big oak desk in the captain's office. Donny sat facing him.

"Nope, you're in charge now," Donny said, leaning back. "I felt the same way at first. You'll get used to it."

"In that case, get your damned feet off my desk."

"It's what you always did," Donny protested.

"That was different."

They both smiled and Donny swung his feet to the floor. "So how do you like it?"

"It's the same but different, you know?" Eddy shrugged. "We haven't had anything real serious yet: some first aid calls, one little kitchen fire, the usual. The job's the same, I guess; you just look at it different, being in charge. I don't want to screw up and make a mistake."

"That's why you get the big bucks."

"Yeah," Eddy laughed, "that, plus all the glory and respect. So how long is my evil reign of terror going to last? Linda likes me getting the acting pay, but I'll be glad to see you back."

"Yeah, well, that's part of what I wanted to talk to you about." Donny recounted his meeting with the union and spelled out the ultimatum that had been presented to him.

"Are you serious?" Eddy asked in disbelief. "After all the stunts guys have pulled on this job, they want to can you for having a look in the basement of an abandoned building?"

"They're playing hardball with this one," Donny explained.

"Well, I think it's completely unfair," Eddy exclaimed, jamming a finger in the air. "That really sucks."

"Hmm, thanks for your professional opinion, counsellor. I'll be sure to use that one in my defence: Eddy the Ladle says it sucks." Donny looked down at his fingernails. "I came to clean out my locker."

Eddy looked stunned.

"Lunch up!" Moose's voice came over the PA.

"Moose is making lunch?" asked Donny, grateful for the change of topic.

"The key to effective leadership is knowing how to delegate," Eddy explained. "And besides, how bad can you screw up soup and grilled cheese sandwiches?"

They made their way to the kitchen. Eddy and Donny jockeyed briefly for the captain's seat at the head of the table, until Donny moved down the side and sat across from the two guys from Front Street who were filling in.

Moose asked Donny how he was feeling. Assured that his injuries were healing, they all went on to speculate on what new and interesting way Donny would find to kill himself next. They discussed the latest department gossip and rumours. It sounded like the usual fire hall banter, but there was a strain in the undertone.

The alarm went off when they were halfway through the meal. It was almost a relief as the crew got up from the table and disappeared one by one down the pole hole.

Alone in the kitchen, Donny listened as the big doors opened, the truck started up and the siren faded into the distance. He took another bite of his sandwich and dumped the rest into the garbage.

He returned to the office and piled the contents of his locker into the empty boxes he had brought with him. He sealed the boxes, then wrote his name and "Admin" on them. The boys would see that they were delivered to headquarters.

He looked around the office one last time.

It would be better if he was gone before the crew got back. He turned around and made his way out to his rental car without looking back. He stopped the car briefly in front of the station to gaze up at the big red bird perched in its nest of sandstone flames. He slammed his cast into the steering wheel again and again, welcoming the jolt of pain it brought each time. Then he drove off, cursing God, the fire department, and most of all himself.

TWENTY-ONE
Leila

DONNY FELT LIKE A cartoon character with a tiny perfect angel perched on one shoulder and a little red devil on the other. There were no visual hallucinations, but he could certainly hear the two voices warring within him. He just wasn't quite sure which voice was which.

It wasn't his fault to begin with. She could have talked to him on the phone, but she had hung up, several times, and then refused to even answer the phone. That was simply rude.

But people were entitled to their privacy. It was a free country, after all, and she had no legal obligation to talk to him.

Legal aside, she had a moral obligation. Had he not risked his life? Been seriously injured? Lost his best friend, his house and so much more? All trying to find out what had killed her husband? He was doing this as much for her as for himself.

He was in enough trouble as it was, and this would only make matters worse. Hadn't she threatened to call the police before she hung up the last time?

Nonsense. If she were going to call the police, she would have done it by now. There was no fraud this time; he wasn't abusing his uniform or misrepresenting the Department. There was nothing illegal about sitting in his car, parked on the street.

Donny, this is stalking!

OK, maybe he did know which voice was which. He turned on the radio, hoping the music would drown out the noise in his head.

His coffee was cold. He drained the last of it and crumpled the cup into the litter bag. He looked again at the house, yawned and wondered how cops withstood the mind-numbing boredom of a stakeout. Maybe, he speculated, it was one of the reasons so many of them were a little off-kilter.

Yeah, right, as opposed to firemen who lose arguments with themselves sitting in parked cars.

He looked at his watch. It was almost tenthirty and the morning paper was still sitting on the front step. Surely she would come out and get it eventually.

It was a pleasant-looking, sixties vintage, split-level home with a well-groomed yard, in the Guildwood neighbourhood of Scarborough. The street ended a hundred metres south of the house in a park that ran along the top of the Scarborough Bluffs. Lake Ontario could just be seen through the trees, glittering in the distance.

Not a bad neighbourhood, Donny thought. Maybe he would contact a real estate agent and see what was available in the area. He could move *Red Bird* to the nearby Bluffers Park Marina.

He was considering this when a car pulled into the driveway and two smartly dressed women got out. The older one was shorter and more matronly, with salt-and-pepper hair neatly coiled into a bun at the back of her head. The driver was younger, in her late twenties, early thirties perhaps. She was a head taller, with a slender build and long black hair that spilled over her shoulders.

Donny had been expecting someone to come out of the house. The arrival of the car so surprised him that he sat momentarily stunned as the women walked up to the front of the house. He threw the car door open and limped across the street as quickly as he could, waving his cane like a lunatic and calling out.

"Hello! Hello, Mrs. Aziz? Please wait a second. I'm Donny Robertson."

The older woman stepped behind the younger one, clutching her purse in front of her like a shield. "That's him!" she hissed, "the one I told you about. Call the police, Adina!"

Donny stopped in the middle of the front lawn. His leg ached from the limping run and he was breathing heavily. "No, please don't do that. Look at me," he pleaded. He held up his cane and the cast on his arm. "I'm no threat. I only want to talk to you. Just a few minutes, I swear, and I won't bother you again."

"Mama?" the younger woman asked. Leila Aziz continued to glare warily at Donny through narrowed eyes, but said nothing.

Adina turned back to face Donny. "You're the fireman? You were there when Papa died?"

Donny nodded.

"And this…" She ran her finger over her own neck, but meant the puckered pink skin that disappeared below Donny's collar. "You got this trying to save my father?"

It wasn't strictly true, but it was close enough. "Yes, I was burned and my Captain, my best friend, was killed trying to save him." He felt dirty using Fitz's death and his own injuries as leverage, but he was desperate.

Adina turned to her mother again. The two began a heated exchange in a language Donny didn't understand, but it was easy enough to tell what was going on. The argument was brief but intense. Finally the older woman turned in disgust, fitted her key into the lock and went inside, leaving the door open.

"My mother asks you to come inside, please, Mr. Robertson," Adina said, trying to save face.

Donny doubted the invitation was quite that polite, but he accepted graciously. "Thank you. After you." He bent painfully to pick up the newspaper and closed the door behind him.

Adina ushered him into the living room. It was a light, airy room with a big picture window that looked southwest towards the park and the lake. The décor was a curious mixture of East and West. A fine Persian carpet of rich scarlet and gold covered the centre of the floor, and a numbered Robert Bateman print of a snow leopard hung over the overstuffed leather couch. A pair of recliners framed the fireplace, over which hung a beautiful parchment of illuminated Arabic calligraphy.

"Please, sit and make yourself comfortable, Mr. Robertson. Will you have tea or coffee?" Adina asked.

"Whatever you're having is fine," he replied, taking a seat on the couch.

"Tea then," she smiled, and disappeared into the back of the house. Donny heard the argument resume, interspersed with the clatter of china. Adina reappeared a few minutes later and sat on one of the chairs beside the fireplace, facing Donny.

She was beautiful. Not the made-up, contrived beauty of Western fashion magazines, but rather a natural elegance. She had a long face, fine high cheekbones, and delicate hands. She moved with a ballerina's grace. Her manner was a combination of modern chic and Old World charm. Her voice was a rich contralto, made all the more exotic by just a trace of a Middle Eastern accent.

"Please excuse my mother, Mr. Robertson. She is a very nervous woman," Adina apologized.

"So it seems," he smiled. "Please call me Donny."

"And I am Adina, as you may have gathered." She smiled briefly, then her face became serious again. "My parents came here as refugees from Iraq. They had a very bad time under Saddam. They were put in prison and tortured. These things, they stay with you always. My mother doesn't trust anyone from the government, especially anyone in uniform."

"She doesn't seem to have any problem with calling the police," Donny commented.

"You don't understand. For her the police are not for protection — they are a threat, perhaps the worst threat she can make to you."

"May I ask why your father was imprisoned?"

"My father was a professor of engineering, a very brilliant man. In 1982, when the war with Iran started to go very badly, they took my father from the University of Baghdad and ordered him to work on Saddam's chemical and biological weapons. He refused, so they put him in prison and did terrible things, unspeakable things to him. Still he refused, so they put my mother, my brother and me in the prison. They did things to my mother and made my father watch. I don't remember it. I was less than a year old. My brother died of pneumonia in that prison. He was three. My mother watched him die. There was no medicine, no help…" Adina's voice trailed off.

Donny folded his hands on his lap and bowed his head slightly. "I'm very sorry. It must have been awful."

"The loss of a child leaves a wound that never heals. My father gave in after that. He would rather have died himself, but to save me and my mother, he helped to make those terrible weapons. He knew what was happening at the front, but when he saw the pictures from Halabja, he had a breakdown. By then, though, it was too late. Do you know of Halabja?" Adina asked.

"No," he confessed.

"It is the name of a Kurdish village in northern Iraq. In 1988 the weapons my father helped to build were used as part of Saddam's campaign against the Kurds. More than five thousand people died that day—men, women and children. Thousands more died later from the after-effects. It was more than my father could bear."

"That would be, uh…" Donny tried to find the right words. "That would be hard to live with."

She went to the mantel and picked up a picture of her father, a middle-aged man with a bushy moustache and a shy smile. She ran her fingers around the frame. She spoke with her back to Donny. "He tried to kill himself, but even the Devil did not want him, he once told me."

She turned to face Donny again. "After the first Gulf War, my father made contact with the UN weapons inspectors. The Americans helped to arrange our escape. They were very interested in my father, but they had also supported Saddam before he invaded Kuwait. The Americans had supplied some of the equipment needed to make the chemical weapons and they had refused to condemn Saddam when he used them. Papa answered their questions, but he refused to live in America" — she spread her hands wide — "and so we came to live in Canada."

"Yes, Canada, the land of great freedom." The words dripped with contempt. Donny turned to see Leila Aziz bringing in the tea tray. Her voice was rougher, her accent thicker than Adina's. She set the tray on the coffee table in front of her daughter, then took hold of the turquoise pendant that hung from her neck. As she straightened up she held it up to Donny to ward off his influence. "You bring evil into this house."

"Mama!" There was another sharp exchange of Arabic. The old woman dismissed Adina with a wave of her hand and went to sit on the other side of the room.

Adina's cheeks flushed as she bent to pour the tea. "I am sorry. This is unforgivable. You are a guest in our house."

"It's all right. I'm the one who should apologize," Donny said, accepting a cup. He took a sip and set the cup down. He turned to face Leila. "I probably shouldn't have come, but I didn't know what else to do. You wouldn't talk to me on the phone."

"No," Leila said simply, staring hard at Donny. She waved away the cup of tea Adina offered her. "But here you are anyway. And now it is too late."

He could apologize all day and get nowhere. Donny decided to forge ahead. "Can you tell me anything about your husband's company?"

"Ask her, she's the scientist." Leila nodded towards her daughter, then crossed her arms across her chest.

"I'm a medical researcher, not an engineer," Adina corrected. She steepled her fingers and listened for the echoes of past conversations.

"My father," she finally said, "felt he needed to redeem himself. That was partly why he encouraged me to become a doctor. He himself became a proponent of green power. He had seen so much of the evil caused by oil: greed, war, pollution and so on. He thought a world free of oil would be a better, safer world, and so that became his passion.

"He designed and sold conventional solar panel systems. That was the core business of AES, and it was successful in a small way. But my father's long-term goal was to move solar power from the fringe into the mainstream. There are several problems preventing that."

"Like, for example, the sun doesn't shine all the time," suggested Donny. He took another sip of his tea. It was delicious, minty and slightly sweet.

"Yes, and so you need some way to store energy for when there is no sunlight." She sat forward in her chair and began to illustrate her points with her hands. Donny suspected the gestures were those her father had used when explaining the principles to a young Adina.

"There are also problems with the cost and efficiency of the solar panels, but my father decided to focus on the storage problem. Do you know what a fuel cell is?"

"It uses hydrogen to make electricity?" Donny ventured.

"Exactly. The problem with batteries is that they're heavy and expensive, and they don't store enough energy. That's why electric cars have only a fraction of the range of gasoline engines. Hydrogen, on the other hand, has three times the energy density of gasoline, by weight.

"So here is my father's dream." She stood and pointed to the imaginary components of the system. "The roof is lined with solar panels generating electricity. During the day your lights are off, maybe you're away at work. Your house isn't using much power, so the electricity is used to split water into hydrogen and oxygen. That's what water is, H_2O. The hydrogen is stored and the oxygen is released into the air. At night the stored hydrogen is fed into a fuel cell that generates the electricity to run your house. The hydrogen becomes water again. Everyone becomes their own electrical utility. Perhaps you would siphon off some of the hydrogen to power your fuel-cell electric car. No need to go to the gas station anymore."

Leila was looking at Adina now. There was a hint of admiration on her face, but her posture was no less rigid.

"That's the 'hydrogen economy,' right?" Donny asked. "I remember reading something about it in a magazine."

"Yes, it's part of it. As I said, there are several barriers relating to cost and efficiency. My father believed that the safe and efficient storage of hydrogen was one of the keys. As you know hydrogen is flammable and explosive."

"Like the space shuttle."

"Exactly," Adina said, taking her seat again. "More tea?"

"No, thanks," Donny smiled, "but it's very good. What happened to your father's research?"

"Most of it was destroyed in the fire. I'm not sure if there was anything here in the house." Adina turned to her mother, but the old woman looked out the bay window and said nothing.

"Would it have been worth killing your father for?" Donny posed the question to Adina, but it was Leila's reaction he was watching.

"It was an accident. The autopsy… Everyone said it was an accident, right, Mama?"

Donny watched as a storm of pride, pain and anger flashed across Leila's face.

"There have been a lot of accidents since I started looking into this." Donny kept his eyes on Leila but she refused to meet his gaze. She pulled her prayer beads from her pocket and began to finger them, her lips moving silently.

"You know, don't you?" Donny rose and stood over her. "A man died trying to save your husband. I have a crew member lying in the hospital right now because I've been trying to bring your husband some justice. Who did this, Mrs. Aziz? You owe me!"

Leila had determined earlier to say nothing, to wrap herself and her family in the protective cloak of silence. Now her own fear and grief had breached that defence. It was too late. The anger faded from her. She looked out the window toward the lake and spoke in a voice barely loud enough to hear.

"The week after Youssef's funeral, two men came to the house…"

"Mama! What men? You never mentioned this."

"No, I didn't," Leila said defensively. "I said nothing — to protect you and the children. Because I have seen men like this before: men in expensive suits, smiling men with teeth as white as wolves' and souls as black as Satan. They said they represented Youssef's investors, and how sorry they were. They had come to collect his research. I would be compensated but they needed all of it. They were very insistent. I knew it was not an offer of kindness, it was, how you say, an ultimatum."

Donny returned to his seat. He had succeeded and forced a crack in the dam. He had his victory. He watched Leila twist in misery and felt like an axe murderer.

"I told them there was very little in the house," Leila continued. "Youssef had kept most of his things at the office. That was all right, they said with their smiling teeth, they would help me find whatever there was. They went from room to room. They took some boxes from the basement, the computer, some files, notes and reference books from Youssef's study.

"When they were satisfied, they handed me a cheque for half a million dollars and said it would be best if I told no one about their visit. It was not a suggestion." She continued to stare out the window, her mouth working silently.

"Mama," Adina said softly, "you took this… this blood money?"

"Yes, and it sits in the bank, every penny of it. I took it because I had to, because if I didn't… if I didn't…"

"You should have gone to the police, Mrs. Aziz. This is not Iraq. This is a free country, where the rule of law…"

She whirled on him, the anger erupting once again. "Oh yes, a free country with liberty and justice. A pleasant illusion, until you come up against those who have the real power. It is the same thing everywhere. Here the leash is longer, but the chain bites just as deep when you come to the end!" She held her hand to her throat.

"Who were these men? Who sent them?" Donny asked as gently as he could.

"I don't know. What does it matter? They were the sons of darkness," Leila answered in a tired voice.

"Ask them yourself. They will come back for you because you ask these questions." Her voice was calmer, more matter-of-fact. She rose and took a couple of steps towards him, holding the turquoise pendant in her hand. "And now you have brought Death to our door. God curse you for this, Donald Robertson."

She spat at his feet and left the room.

THE MAN IN THE blue Toyota had parked his car at the bottom of the street. He sat on a park bench in the dappled shade, reading his book and chatting amiably with the dog walkers passing by. He had a good view of the Azizes' house. He had seen the two women arrive and Donny go into the house with them.

My, my, he thought, this was disturbing. But perhaps he could adapt his plan and turn this to his advantage. By the time Donny left the house thirty minutes later, the man had worked out the details in his head. There were only a few small items to look after and then he could take care of this business once and for all.

He took the Zippo from his pocket, flipped the lid open and

watched the sparks spray from the thumb wheel. He snapped the lid down. Not yet, but soon. A smile crept across his face. Yes, very soon, and it would all be such good fun.

TWENTY-TWO
And Those Who Make the Rules

HE HAD EXPECTED TO feel some sense of completion. Not that it was all over by any means, but he had anticipated a certain satisfaction that his part was done, that he could turn the whole business over to Micah and let him put the rest of the puzzle together. Instead he felt a chill he couldn't shake. Adina had apologized profusely for her mother once again as she showed Donny to the door, but the old woman had unsettled him.

Donny started the car and headed downtown. "You can't always get what you want…" the oldies station crooned. Donny snapped the radio off. The last thing he needed was synchronistic pop philosophy.

He drove to the union office and signed himself into exile.

Sometimes, after Fitz died, the sadness would almost crush him. Gradually the spaces in between got longer. In the end what was left was not quite grief and not quite acceptance. There was simply emptiness and a nagging hunger for the truth. Now he had signed away even that.

A spanking westerly was whipping up whitecaps out on the lake, and Donny briefly considered taking *Red Bird* out. He'd singlehanded her in worse weather than this, but that was with two good hands and ribs that didn't ache with every exertion. He opted for a beer instead.

He would put it all behind him, he decided, the whole damned mess. Maybe he would leave the entire rat-infested, screwed-up city behind, and all the deal-making, pus-sucking maggots with it. Maybe he'd just take early retirement and sail off into the sunset. It was a mental tantrum, he knew, but it felt good.

He pictured himself aboard *Red Bird*, anchored in the turquoise water of a tropical lagoon. Behind a beach of pure white sand, palm trees waved in a soft, warm breeze. Sunning herself on the foredeck was a woman who looked amazingly like Laurie…

His phone rang.

"Hey, Micah," Donny answered, jolting himself back to reality. "I was going to call you."

"Good. We need to talk." Micah's voice was carefully neutral.

"I met with Leila Aziz and her daughter this morning. I didn't get much, but there were some interesting…"

"You know," Micah interrupted, "I think it would be better if we did this in person."

"Uh, sure, whatever you like."

"Where are you right now?"

Donny gave him directions to the marina. "See you when you get here."

MICAH ARRIVED AN hour later. Donny met him at the foot of the dock and showed him aboard. Micah looked around with an appreciative eye.

"Nice boat," he said. "My father was a shipwright in Grenada."

"Really? I could have used him when I was refitting this baby. I did most of the work myself," Donny said, patting the hatch cover.

"You did a good job, then. My father would have approved."

"Thanks. You want a beer?"

Micah looked at his watch. "Technically I'm still on the clock, but sure. I told them I'm not coming back to the office this afternoon."

Donny got them each a beer and set a bag of chips on the cockpit table. "Cheers. So what's up? You sounded a bit odd on the phone."

"Why don't you tell me how it went with Leila Aziz first," said Micah, settling back and taking a swig of his beer.

Donny decided to skip over the part about his stakeout/stalking.

"You know AES was into fuel cell research, right? But did you know why?" He began with Adina's story of the family's background and her father's passion for green energy. He ended with Leila's curse.

"She was angry, but I think she was more afraid than anything. I guess I would be too if I had been through that," Donny concluded.

"That's a bad thing where I come from—a grandmother's curse." Donny was surprised at the seriousness in Micah's voice.

"Yeah, like I need any more bad luck. This has not been a good day." Donny decided to change the subject. "What about the cheque? It shouldn't be too hard to trace half a million dollars."

"Up to a point, no, it shouldn't be. But I'm pretty sure it will come to a dead end at a numbered Swiss account or something similar. This thing is bigger than you or I imagined." Micah took a handful of chips.

Donny's eyes narrowed, but he said nothing. Micah chewed for a moment before continuing. "Your idea about looking at the helicopter video for the extra hose was a good one. It was a real pile of spaghetti, but you can trace all the hose lines back to the trucks — all except one. With a little enhancement it stood out like a sore thumb. It must have been brand new hose, it was so clean and so much brighter than the others. You know where it ran to?"

"Tell me," Donny said, leaning forward. Micah pulled a sheet of paper from his back pocket, unfolded it and handed the image to Donny.

"One end was at the office window in the back of the building, here." Micah pointed to the spot on the paper. "The other end was here, beside the hydrogen tank behind the parking lot."

"But I thought hydrogen exploded."

"It can; it depends how you handle it. Take propane: if you rupture a propane tank you get an explosion, but if you feed it through a hose you get a barbecue. You know what you get when you burn hydrogen?"

"Water?" Donny suggested.

Micah nodded. "Exactly. It's the perfect accelerant. No residue, no traces."

"Holy shit!" Donny exclaimed "And when it's over the firemen pick up the hose for you. No evidence."

"You need some technical expertise, an adapter to go from the hydrogen tank to the fire hose, some fittings and stuff, but it's the perfect plan. When you guys show up they simply disconnect their gear and leave the hose behind. You've got to admit it's brilliant."

"Talk about hiding in plain sight." Donny leaned back and shook his head. "I knew it. I knew that fire had help."

"It looks that way. It's one more piece of the puzzle. Now, you need to ask yourself who would do this. We can rule out insurance fraud, a family feud or anything like that. At first I thought maybe Aziz borrowed money from the wrong people. But those guys like to leave a calling card. They don't want to hide, they like to make an example of someone. And they don't come back later to collect computer files.

"Then I thought maybe it was a business rival. But would a guy like that go to all the trouble to build an air lock, track you down and blow up your house and all that? And how would he even know you were looking into it? That's the real key."

"I don't know. You're the expert, remember?" said Donny. He took another swig of his beer, set the bottle down and wiped his mouth with the back of his hand. "So where does that leave us?"

"There's more." Micah took a deep breath and looked around the marina, trying to find a way to say what he needed to. "A lot of things have happened in the last couple of days."

"What kind of things?" Donny asked, noting the worried tone in Micah's voice.

"Remember the thermocouple? It's gone."

"What do you mean, gone?"

"I called the lab," Micah explained, "to tell them what I wanted. When they went to pick it up from the evidence room yesterday, it was missing. Sometimes stuff gets misplaced, but they had a good look and the thermocouple is gone."

"Shit!"

"It gets better," Micah said wryly. "I called Korvan to see if they would allow me into that empty building with the air lock. Like I told you, we'd never get a search warrant after your little adventure."

"Sorry about that."

"Spilled milk, Donny. Anyway, that was two days ago. They said they would get back to me. I drove by there this morning, and there's construction hoarding all around the property. So I called them back. Sorry, they told me, the building's being demolished."

"That building has been sitting empty for over twenty years and they got a demolition permit in less than forty-eight hours? You can't even get a dog licence from the city that fast. It's obviously a coverup!" exclaimed Donny.

"It's all legal. The only one who broke the law is you, my friend. The fact that Korvan is also one of the top contributors to the mayor's campaign fund is just a coincidence, I'm sure."

Micah picked at his fingernails. He looked up briefly at Donny, then turned his gaze back to his hands. Donny barely knew the man, but he could tell there was something bothering Micah deeply.

"What else?" Donny asked.

"There's no easy way to say this. I'm being taken off the case," Micah said at last.

"What? That's bullshit!" Donny exploded. "How can they do that?"

"Keep your voice down." Micah looked around nervously again. "They can do it by making it look like a promotion. I'm being given the Chief Investigator's job in Thunder Bay."

"And you're going to take it? You're just going to walk away?" Donny was incredulous. "I didn't think you were a quitter, Micah."

"Do you think I like it?" Micah challenged.

"Then why are you doing this?" Donny asked more softly.

Micah put his beer bottle on the table. He stood, took hold of the aft stay and stared out at the endless march of waves beyond the harbour entrance.

"What have I been telling you? Open your eyes and look at the big picture." Micah sighed and sat on the aft rail facing Donny. "This is not some solitary fire bug or an insurance fraud amateur. Whoever is behind this is a pro, a real pro with very powerful connections.

"When I was growing up in Grenada, even as a little kid I knew there were two types of people: those who live by the rules and those who make the rules. Things aren't so different here."

"You sound like Leila Aziz," said Donny. He was unable to hide the disappointment in his voice.

"Think about it. Who drops half a million dollars in hush money? Who would have the sophistication to sabotage a water main and rig up a hydrogen feed like that? Who can blow up a house, make it look like an accident and then make the one shred of evidence disappear? Who gets a demolition permit in a day and a half? How come every time I pick up the phone to arrange something I find a roadblock?"

"You think they're listening in on your phone?"

"Why do you think I wanted to see you in person?" Micah asked.

"But that's crazy," Donny protested. "You're a cop, or the next best thing anyway. Who's going to tap your phone?"

"The same people who somehow knew you were looking into this whole thing in the first place. Didn't you ever wonder how that happened?"

"I never really thought about it," Donny shrugged.

"You should. They can get me promoted and they can make people go away. You remember that kid Josh Findlay, the security guard, who let you into the empty building?"

Donny nodded.

"I went to find him yesterday to see if he'd back up what you saw. Well, it seems he suddenly quit his job and nobody knows where to find him."

Donny stared at Micah with his mouth open. "No, no, they wouldn't…"

"Maybe he was just paid to disappear. That's the simplest thing and it's happened before. Let's hope so. It leads to fewer questions than killing someone. But if you keep pressing and try to find him, odds are he'll end up dead and so will you."

Micah sighed heavily. "This thing is way bigger than you and me. Donny, you can't win when the game is rigged. These are very powerful, very dangerous people, and I can't take the chance. I have a wife and family, Donny. I'm sorry, I am really and truly sorry."

Donny opened and closed his mouth several times, not knowing what to say. "So what am I supposed to do?" he finally managed.

"You want my advice?" Micah raised an eyebrow. "Turn your back on this whole thing and forget about it.

"They'll assign someone else to the explosion at your house. In a couple of days they'll probably find something like a corroded joint in the gas line or some defect in the meter. If you're smart you'll say, 'Yes, that must have been it.' And you won't say anything about the things we discussed.

"Then, after a week or two, they'll probably close the case on the Commissioners Street fire. And you should raise a toast to Captain Paul Fitzgerald, a good man and a brave firefighter. Then swallow that bitter pill and walk away. It's your only chance."

HOURS LATER, DONNY was still sitting in the cockpit where Micah had left him. He had neither the will nor the energy to move. The sun was creeping towards the horizon behind the office towers downtown. It looked fake, like a cheap black cut-out of the city skyline silhouetted against a brassy background.

It was all fake, wasn't it? The people in those towers made millions trading things that didn't even exist—futures and derivatives and things like that. Billions flitted around the world as electronic impulses, but no one ever held a nickel in their hands. It was all smoke and mirrors, a puppet show with invisible strings.

Micah was right: there was nothing he could do anymore. Exhaustion rolled over him like a wave. Regret, anger and frustration were faint echoes dying in the distance. He felt helpless and drained. It was all he could do to heave himself upright, go below and collapse in the V berth.

TWENTY-THREE
We've Been Expecting You

DONNY WAS TOO TIRED to sleep. He lay in the berth listening to the soft noises of the boat pulling on her mooring lines and the fenders rubbing on the dock. He wasn't sure how long he had been lying there when his phone went off. It was a text from Leila Aziz:

I want to apologize. There's something I need to tell you. It's important. Please come to the house as soon as you can.

That's a bit odd, thought Donny. The old girl didn't seem like the texting type. Maybe she was too embarrassed to speak on the phone. Or maybe, like Micah, she was worried that someone was listening in.

Should he call Micah? This might rekindle his interest. But Donny knew it was an empty hope. Micah had shut the door. His family's safety was priority number one, and who could blame him?

Powerful and dangerous, Micah had said. *Turn your back and walk away.* He briefly considered rolling over and ignoring Leila's message, but he knew it would nag at him. And what was the harm in listening to what she had to say? At the very least she might lift the curse. A man who put himself at the mercy of the waves could never be too careful.

Donny rolled off the bunk. This is it, he told himself in the mirror as he splashed water on his face and brushed his teeth. This was the final act. He would sit and listen to what the old woman had to say, then he would do what everyone had been telling him to do: he would put the past behind him and leave the dead to their rest.

HE PULLED INTO THE Azizes' driveway. No need to hide this time. The living-room drapes were closed, but light glowed behind them. He got out, walked to the front door and knocked.

Donny was startled when a man opened the door. He quickly checked the number on the doorpost to see if he had the right house.

"Captain Robertson?" the man asked politely. "Please, won't you come inside? We've been expecting you."

Donny recognized the hallway. It was the right house. He stepped in. The man smiled at him and closed the door. He appeared to be in his early forties, with short dark hair and vivid green eyes. Aside from the eyes and an athletic build, he looked quite unremarkable. He was well dressed, with a camel hair sport coat over a white polo shirt and dark slacks.

"You must be wondering who I am," the man said amiably. He seemed genuinely pleased to see Donny.

"I was expecting Leila."

"Of course. I'm sorry, please allow me to introduce myself," the man smiled and offered his hand. Donny reached out his own, but before he could grasp the handshake, the man drove his fist hard into Donny's solar plexus. His ribs erupted in pain as the breath exploded out of him. He dropped to the floor and clutched his arms across his abdomen.

"I'm the man you've been looking for." He stood over Donny and made a slight bow. Donny reached up for the front door. The man with the green eyes kicked, catching Donny under the chin, snapping his head back. The taste of blood filled Donny's mouth. The man stepped over him and locked the front door. "Please come into the living room. Leila's waiting."

The man picked up Donny's cane and prodded him with it. The tip of the cane felt like a hot poker stabbing into his injured ribs. Donny struggled for breath as he crawled down the hall. The man shepherded Donny into the living room.

"I believe you two already know each other," he said, pointing to Leila with the cane.

Leila was seated beside the fireplace in one of the recliners. A large welt showed on her left cheek, and a thin ribbon of blood flowed from beneath the gag in her mouth. Her ankles were bound with handcuffs; her hands were behind her, presumably bound the same way. Leila's eyes darted back and forth from Donny to the dark-haired man.

Donny crawled to the centre of the room and lay there, groaning and holding his ribs.

"That's fine, Captain Robertson. Why don't you rest right there? We've got a big night ahead of us and you'll want your strength," said the dark-haired man as he settled onto the couch. "Now I hate clichés, but I'll say it anyway: please don't do anything stupid. I'm faster, better trained and obviously in better condition than you.

"If you insist on trying something heroic, I will quite literally beat the shit out of you. And no one really wants that, do they? It will be very unpleasant for you, I assure you, and rather smelly for the rest of us. Do we understand each other, Captain Robertson?"

Donny sat on the rug, still panting and stared at the man on the couch. His mind was racing, trying to detach itself from the pain. His eyes scanned the room for some avenue of escape.

"You're so obvious," the green-eyed man sighed. "I would be on you long before you made it to the window, much less through it. Now reach into your pocket and put your phone on the coffee table there, beside Leila's."

Donny did as he was told. The man held the cane ready to swat the phone from his hands if he tried to call 911.

"Very good, thank you. Did you know Leila had never sent a text message before? I had to show her how. As they say, we learn something new every day." The man smiled and a shiver ran down Donny's spine. He was hopelessly out of his depth. He'd been out of his depth from the beginning but only now did he realize it fully.

"You set the fire on Commissioners?" Donny's voice was ragged. His tongue was swollen and still bleeding where he'd bitten it. It was hard to talk, and he spat blood and saliva as he spoke. "You killed Fitz and Aziz?"

"Well, yes, I already told you that, didn't I? Of course, Youssef was the target. Captain Fitzgerald was just an unexpected bonus. You, on the other hand, have been a rather troublesome annoyance."

"Sorry to have bothered you," said Donny, rallying some spirit.

The man on the couch raised an eyebrow. He stood and stepped towards Leila. Then in a flash he whirled and slashed the cane across Donny's head, sending him tumbling to the carpet again.

"Your apology lacks sincerity, Captain Robertson. I will hand it to you, though: you're a hard man to kill. Now, while I do enjoy a challenge, you have caused problems for my employers and tarnished my professional reputation. But we're going to fix all that."

He was standing beside Leila now. "You know, I never did properly introduce myself. You firemen all have such cool nicknames: Wedge, Moose, Eddy the Ladle. I do like that one. Frankly, I'm jealous. I know: why don't you just call me the Spark?"

He reached over and pulled the Zippo from Leila's ear. Then, with a flourish, a coiled length of wire suddenly appeared in his other hand.

"What next?" Donny asked, raising himself again. "You going to do card tricks or tell fortunes?"

"Impertinent to the end, but yes, as a matter of fact, I am." He looked sideways at Donny as he uncoiled the wire. It was a little over a foot long when it was straightened. "It seems you're going to die relatively young."

The Spark stomped down hard on Donny's bad leg, ripping open the stitches. Donny felt the wet warmth of blood soaking his pant leg as he writhed on the floor. The man flipped open his lighter. Sparks flared and the flame danced. "Beautiful, isn't it? And it all starts with one tiny little spark."

He held the tip of the wire in the flame until it was red hot, then touched the glowing wire to Leila's face. She jerked her head violently from side to side, her screams muffled by the gag.

The Spark sat on the arm of the chair beside Leila. She stared at him unblinking, her eyes wide with terror. He turned to Donny. "Let me explain how this works." Donny struggled to sit and leaned back against the coffee table.

"First of all, I am going to kill you, Donny. There's no way around that, and to tell the truth, I'm going to enjoy it. However, Leila here doesn't necessarily need to die. I'm going to ask you some questions. If you lie to me, I'm going to use this wire on her." Leila started to moan and jerk her head again. The Spark reached over and stroked her hair. "If you really make me angry I will kill her. I will kill her very slowly and painfully right in front of you. Understand?"

"People will know. You can't kill them all. People will know!" Donny wanted to rage, to scream, to find some way out of this nightmare.

"People like who? Like Adina?" The Spark smiled at Leila. "I had a lovely visit with Adina before I came over here. I gave her some pictures I had taken of her children. Such lovely children, so full of life and hope. No, I don't think Adina will be any problem. I think Micah has seen the writing on the wall too. So let's start with him, shall we, Donny?"

He started heating the wire again, and Leila made muffled squeaking sounds. "What were you and Micah talking about this afternoon?"

"He told me he was leaving, going to Thunder Bay," Donny sputtered. "He warned me to quit too. He said there was nothing I could do, no way to win." His eyes were riveted on the wire, willing it away from Leila.

"Very true. That's good advice, if a bit late for you. What else did he say?"

"That they're demolishing the building on Commissioners Street and something about donations to the mayor's campaign fund."

"That's it?" the man with the lighter asked nonchalantly.

"Yes."

"You're lying, Donny." He pressed the red-hot wire to Leila's forehead. Her squeaks turned into a steady high-pitched wail.

"Oh God, stop, please stop!" Donny sobbed.

"The next time you lie to me it will be her eye, not her forehead. Understand? Now, what else did Micah tell you?" He put the wire back in the lighter's flame.

"The thermocouple, he found the thermocouple you doctored. Micah sent it in for analysis and he said it disappeared."

"That's true. What else?"

"He had the news helicopter video analyzed to show how you used a fire hose to feed hydrogen in to the fire. I knew there was extra hose and he figured out how you used it."

"That's very impressive. Anything else?"

"No. I swear to God, that's all," Donny pleaded. He hugged his knees and started to rock back and forth.

"I believe you. There, you see how easy that was?" The voice was sweet and silky smooth but full of cruelty. "Still, I think I'll keep an eye on Mr. Edwards. Maybe I'll take some photos of his children as well.

"Now, what about your crew? What do they know?" He began heating the wire again.

Donny looked up with horror. It finally dawned on him that everyone he knew was a target. What had he done? These people were ruthless and seemingly able to operate with impunity. "They know I was looking into the fire. That's about it. And the extra hose, but they have no idea what it was for. Aside from that, all they know is that I think someone tried to blow up Suzie and me."

"Well, I think the official investigation will reveal some rather ordinary cause for the explosion. Of course, conspiracy theories are always popular, but that's part of what makes life interesting, don't you think?" The green eyes twinkled as he smiled again. "Then there's John Aldrich. You two have become very chummy lately."

"Please leave him alone. He's just an old man. He just keeps telling me it's all God's will."

The smiling man grasped Leila's chin in a vice-like grip and brought the wire up to her face. "I want to believe you, Donny, really I do."

"Please, he doesn't know anything more than the guys on the truck. I swear it."

The wire slid across Leila's eyelid. She bucked wildly, and the Spark put a knee on her lap to keep her in the chair.

"It's the truth! It's the truth!" Donny wailed.

"I know. Believe me, I know when you're lying. That was just a reminder." He gave Donny an evil grin.

"You sick bastard!" Before Donny knew what he was doing he had launched himself, but the Spark was too fast. He pivoted and sent Donny crashing into the fireplace. Donny crumpled to the floor again and then the Spark was sitting on him, crushing his ribs and pinning Donny's arms under his knees.

"'You sick bastard'? Is that the best you can do? Come now, Donny, where's that cutting fire hall wit?" The polite veneer was gone; there was pure venom in the voice now. "You're not the first person to say that. A psychiatrist once called me that. Well, first he said I had a psycho-sexual disorder."

He waved the hot wire in front of Donny's face. Donny wriggled but couldn't get free. The pain in his ribs was unbearable.

"It made me angry. So I burned his house down around him, while he was still alive. But he was right. I was angry because I was fighting against it. I've come to accept myself since then. It's true what they say: the truth, once you accept it, will make you free. We're lucky, you and I, Donny. We both enjoy our work so much. It's a real blessing, isn't that what Aldrich would say?"

He began heating the wire once more. "Now, where was I? Oh yes, that leaves Laurie Zhou. What to do about Laurie Zhou? Maybe I'll just kill the bitch for the hell of it." He thrust the red-hot wire up Donny's nose. Donny writhed and screamed. The Spark grabbed one of Leila's shoes from beside the chair and jammed the toe deep into Donny's mouth, gagging him as he screamed.

He pulled the wire out and stood up. Donny rolled onto his side and threw up on the hearth. The Spark moved to the couch, unwrapped a toffee from the crystal candy dish on the end table and popped it into his mouth. Leila sat shaking in the chair and making little mewing noises.

Donny finished vomiting and brought his good hand to his nose. There was pain everywhere, and his leg was soaked with blood. He struggled to raise himself and looked at the evil gleam in those green eyes.

"Please leave Laurie alone," Donny rasped. He barely recognized his own voice.

"I did warn you not to do anything stupid, now didn't I? I hope you've learned your lesson." The jovial mocking tone was back in his voice.

"I'll do whatever you say. You can do anything you want to me. Just please leave Laurie alone."

"I'll think about it," replied the Spark. "Well, I'd say we could all use a breath of fresh air after that mess you made, Donny. It stinks in here. How about we all go for a car ride? You drive, Donny. I'll snuggle in the back seat with Leila. And remember, we don't want anything bad to happen to Laurie, now do we?"

TWENTY-FOUR
Reduce, Reuse, Recycle

DONNY WAS DRIVING ON auto-pilot, following instructions from the back seat. Half of his mind was dealing with the pain that started in his ribs, spread through his whole body and crescendoed inside his nose.

The other half was thinking of Laurie. They had known each other only a short time. How little he really knew of her, yet the thought of anything happening to her and the boys was unbearable.

He was driving to his own execution. Instead of fear, the certainty of his death filled him with an overwhelming feeling of regret. His life, it seemed to him, had been a pathetic charade. He had been a good firefighter and an adequate sailor, but he had amounted to little else. Of the rest — love, family, devotion, the things that comforted Aldrich in his sunset years — he knew only the names and their outline on a distant horizon.

For him the fruit had withered on the vine, until Laurie had brought with her the promise of a second chance. Now, not only had he squandered that chance, he had placed them all in danger as a result of his obsession.

He was jolted back to the present when he was told to turn down Leslie Street toward the Portlands. It suddenly dawned on him where they were going. The man in the back seat noticed Donny stiffen.

"Did you just figure it out? I thought you were smarter than that,

Donny. Yes, the wheel comes full circle. Well, almost — unfortunately, you can't burn the same building twice.

"We could have done it back at Leila's house, but neighbours have this annoying tendency to call the fire department. We'll have a little more privacy down here. I've prepared something very special for you. I think you'll really warm to it."

They turned onto Commissioners Street and then into the entrance of the recycling plant Donny had visited only a few days before. The place was dark and quiet except for a few floodlamps that washed the front of the building with an orange glow. He was told to park around the back. A blue Toyota was already parked there.

Donny turned the car off and got out first, as he was instructed. Leila emerged unsteadily, and held onto the car for support. The Spark got out last. He kept a gun trained on Leila. "You're good with doors, Donny. There are tools in the back of the other car. Get them."

The Spark pressed a button on a remote in his other hand. A beep sounded from the Toyota and the trunk lid opened. Donny retrieved a pry bar, a K-tool and a sledgehammer. The Spark pointed to the back door of the building. It was awkward with his cast, but after a couple of tries, Donny popped the lock cylinder out of the door.

"Good. Now put the tools down and get the duffel bag." Donny got the bag out of the blue car and opened it as he was told. Inside were his bunker suit and an SCBA.

"You see, I brought you a present, Donny," the Spark smiled, keeping his gun pointed at them. "I thought you might like to die in uniform. I took it while the boys were out at one of those annoying false alarms. Go ahead, put it on."

Donny didn't move. He looked at his gear, then stared in quiet defiance at the Spark. "Put it on or I will shoot Leila and let her bleed out on the ground."

Leila, who had remained silent up to this point, collapsed to her knees and began to chant quietly in Arabic: "*Lā 'ilāha 'illallāh,*

Muhammad rasūlu-llāh." She repeated the phrase to herself over and over. Donny looked at her and began to dress. One arm of his bunker coat had been slit to accommodate his cast.

"Now the mask," said the Spark, pointing at the SCBA. Donny bent slowly and grabbed the straps. He considered whether he could swing the tank quickly enough to knock the gun out of the man's hand.

The Spark stepped back and sneered. "You are so transparent. The way you're holding the straps gives it all away. I read you like a book, Robertson."

Donny grimaced, slung the tank onto his back and snugged the straps. The harness hurt his ribs, but the familiar burden was somehow comforting. These were his vestments, his armour, his tools. Leila's soft, rhythmic chanting was almost soothing. He felt a calmness germinate within. His breathing slowed and the pain receded, if only a bit. There had to be something, some way…

"After you." The Spark motioned towards the open door.

The interior of the recycling plant was dimly lit by the few security lights that were left on at night. Donny remembered the smell of stale garbage. They made their way past conveyor belts, sorting machines and bins of glass, paper, plastic and metal. No one spoke.

They arrived at the warehouse area, where bales of sorted recycled material sat waiting to be shipped. They moved between two stacks of baled cardboard on the wall opposite the shipping doors.

"That's far enough," the Spark instructed.

"You're planning to burn me? You see those things on the ceiling? They're sprinklers, you moron," Donny declared, making no effort to hide his fear or anger. "You'll barely get a fire started and this place will be drenched."

"Are you trying to goad me, Donny?" replied the Spark disdainfully. "What should I do? Run to turn off the sprinkler control valve? And you're thinking, that will activate the tamper alarm and the cavalry will come charging to the rescue. Do you really think I'm that stupid?"

He shook his head at Donny. "You see, I was here earlier today. It's amazing what you can do with a laptop and a good laser printer. I made myself an ID card for the alarm company and came to make a 'service call.' I bypassed the tamper alarm and the smoke alarms and shut down the sprinkler system. You see, I've gone to a great deal of trouble for you, Donny."

He waved his hand at the bales of plastic and paper. "This place will burn all night. Now kneel and face the wall."

It had been worth a try. Donny wouldn't give up yet. Obviously by giving him his bunker suit, the man didn't want to kill him right away. Donny turned and faced the wall as he was told. The Spark moved in behind him and raised Donny's cast alongside a steel conduit.

"Do you know what she's been chanting?" he asked Donny as he secured the cast to the conduit with a heavy nylon cable tie, the kind riot police use to tie the hands of protesters.

"A prayer, I suppose," replied Donny.

"Close. It's the Shahada, the Muslim creed, 'There is no God but God and Mohamed is his prophet.' It's something they do when they're facing death. I heard it quite a lot when I was working in the Middle East. Do you follow any particular set of superstitions, Donny?"

"The fear of God is the beginning of wisdom!" Leila spoke before Donny could answer. She looked the Spark directly in the eyes for the first time Donny had seen. "But you, you have no wisdom. You live in darkness. And the darkness will swallow you!"

"Something much brighter is going to swallow you, my dear." He hit her hard across the mouth. He yanked her arm up as she collapsed and took a pair of handcuffs from his pocket. He secured one end around Leila's wrist and the other around the steel conduit.

"No! Let her go!" Donny pulled on his cast but the arm wouldn't budge. "She won't talk. Will you, Leila? Adina's children, remember? You said you would let her live."

"Did I say that? Well, sometimes I'm prone to exaggerate a bit."

The Spark smiled, stepped back and admired the scene. "No, I'm sorry. Leila has to stay with you to make it all look right."

He tucked away his gun and sat on a bale of cardboard. "It seems, Donny, you blamed Youssef for poor Captain Fitzgerald's death. Something inside you must have snapped. So you brought Leila here, handcuffed her to that conduit, and set the place on fire."

"I'm not an arsonist. No one will believe it!"

"No? I think they will. There are all those harassing phone calls you made to Leila. There'll be a record of that, you know. And everyone says you've been absolutely obsessed by Fitz's death lately. Why you even visited this place a few days ago, during your little masquerade. Oh yes, I think they'll believe you sabotaged the alarm and sprinkler systems and then set the building on fire. Unfortunately you didn't make it out alive. Maybe you got lost in the smoke, maybe you couldn't live with the guilt. Who knows?"

He held an empty hand out to Donny, then turned it over, and the lighter appeared at his fingertips. He thumbed the wheel. "Just one little spark, that's all it takes." He tore a piece of cardboard from the bale he was sitting on, lit it and tossed it in Donny's lap.

He laughed as Donny squirmed and swatted at the burning cardboard. The sound made Donny's skin crawl. "Here's how it's going to work. I'm going to set the fire at the other end of the building, so it will take some time for the fire to get here. Of course the smoke will get here sooner. That's what's going to kill you, Leila… and Donny, you get to watch her slowly choke and suffocate."

Leila began her soft recitation again.

"Of course, you've got your SCBA, so you've got a choice," the Spark continued. "Now, I'm guessing the survival instinct will win and you'll use it. Regardless, the fire will eventually get here and that nylon strap holding your arm will burn away. I couldn't use handcuffs on you. I mean, why would you handcuff yourself?

"Anyway, by the time it's hot enough to melt the nylon strap, the place will be blazing and I'm afraid it will be too late. They'll find your two bodies: the firefighter turned arsonist, caught in his own twisted plot for revenge, and his poor innocent victim. A tragic story, isn't it?"

He got up from the bale and stood in front of them. "Well, that's it. Any questions? No?"

Donny tugged briefly at his arm, and the Spark kicked him in the ribs one last time. "I've really enjoyed our time together. You two kids behave yourselves, now."

The Spark laughed and turned on his heel. A few moments later they saw a flickering orange light reflected on the ceiling.

Donny held his ribs and struggled to catch his breath. He had to think, to detach himself from the pain and clear his mind. They had only a few minutes at most, depending on how fast the fire spread. He was close enough to Leila that they could buddy-breathe, sharing the air in his tank, for as long as that lasted. Then what?

Leila had stopped her chanting. She was sniffing the air. There was an acrid tang of burning plastic now. He yanked again at his arm, but the nylon strap went around his wrist, the narrowest part of the cast, and held it fast.

"Mr. Robertson, Donny, will you forgive me?" Leila asked softly.

Donny turned to look at her. He could just make out her features in the dim light. There was a sort of noble sadness; the terror and the anger were gone. "Forgive you? For what? I got us into this mess."

"I spoke to you in anger this morning. I blamed you and cursed you because I was afraid. I would not go to God with this on my conscience. Will you forgive me?"

"Of course, yes, of course. You were right anyway. It's all my fault. I should be asking you."

"Thank you," Leila nodded. "I blamed poor Youssef too. I blamed him when our son died and for the things they did to me in prison. I even blamed him for his own death. All because I was afraid. Fear is a terrible thing. It is the Devil's whip. But God is merciful. I am not afraid now. Do you believe in God, Donny?"

The smell was unmistakable now. It caught in the back of his throat. This was not the time for a theological debate. They needed a plan, and they needed it quickly.

"I don't know. Maybe. I'm not sure God believes in me."

"He does whether you know it or not. God sees us all and knows our hearts. You asked me to forgive you and I do, but there is no need." Leila coughed. "You were looking for the truth. Those who seek truth and justice are the servants of God."

She was starting to annoy him and he tried to tune her out. On the other side of the warehouse, a hundred feet away, he could make out the red glow of an exit sign. So close, yet it might as well be a hundred miles away. Donny's mind was racing. He could picture himself and Leila pressing the crash bar of the emergency exit and walking out into the fresh, cool air.

They were both coughing now. The air they were breathing was a toxic brew that their lungs instinctively tried to reject. The coughing brought new waves of pain from Donny's ribs. He reached behind him with his free hand and turned on the valve of his air tank. He brought the mask to his face and took several deep breaths, then held the mask to Leila's face. Air hissed away as he passed it over. "Quickly, hold this tight to your face. Don't waste air. Take two or three deep breaths, then hold it. We'll take turns."

They passed the face piece back and forth. The smoke was getting thicker. The red exit light was getting harder to see, their only hope fading away. Again he pictured them crashing through the door, drinking in the sweet night air. The image played through his mind over and over.

The heat was beginning to rise now too. The bunker suit covered most of him, but he could feel it on his bare face and hands. The smoke stung their eyes. Filmy soot from the burning plastic began to drift down on them like black snow.

"God damn it! I will not die like this!" Donny roared, and pulled again at the arm that kept him anchored to the wall. Long ago he had accepted that he might one day die in a fire. But not like this, not as someone's pawn, taking the blame for a fire and murder he didn't commit.

"You should pray," Leila said between breaths.

The suggestion took Donny by surprise. "I don't know how," he replied angrily, when it was his turn with the mask.

"Then I will pray for both of us."

A firefighter turned arsonist. It was rare, but when it did happen they all felt tainted. It was the ultimate betrayal. From now on, if they spoke his name it would always be with shame.

"That bastard!" Donny muttered. "God damn him."

"That man? He knows nothing of God. He is the Devil's toy. But God will break him. God will smash him like an egg."

Smash him like an egg. A new image formed in Donny's head, like something from *Monty Python*: God's hand reaching down from the clouds and squashing the Spark, arms and legs splayed from a red smear. Donny even managed a quiet chuckle. The two images alternated in his mind: the exit door and God's fist.

Wait — there was something new, something he hadn't noticed before. He could see it in his mind's eye. There: a small red box beside the door. A pull station. It had to be there. The fire code required a pull station beside every exit.

Smash him like an egg.

The Spark said he had bypassed the tamper and smoke alarms but he had said nothing about the pull station. Even so, like the door, it might just as well be on the moon.

Smash him like an egg.

The two mental images merged and it came to him in a flash. Donny loosened the straps of the SCBA and slipped his free arm out of the harness. He slid the tank off his back and around in front of him.

"What are you doing?" asked Leila.

He didn't bother answering. One strap was still around the arm that was tied to the conduit, but he had enough room to swing the air tank. He drew back and swung it as hard as he could against his cast.

Donny screamed as a lightning bolt of pain shot up his arm. Leila held the mask out to him and he gulped greedily at the air. He handed the face piece back, swung the tank against his cast and screamed again.

"Donny, in God's name, what are you doing?" she asked.

"I'm going to get us out of here," he said through clenched teeth. He pounded the air tank against his cast over and over again, screaming with every blow. But it was working. The cast was looser now, he could feel it.

It was no longer his arm, it was a living incarnation of pain grafted onto his body. He hammered at the cast until it was a pulpy mass. He put the tank down and clawed at the cast with his free hand. He tore pieces away until at last the nylon strap slipped over his hand.

His arm fell heavy and useless to his side. He rolled against Leila as she held the air to his face. He wanted to rest, to let that sweet life-giving air carry him to a place where there was no pain.

No! Feel the pain, Donny, he told himself. Use it. Let it keep you focused. Almost there now, just a little more.

Donny handed the mask back to Leila, then took off his bunker coat and draped it over her. He could really feel the heat now.

"I can't get the handcuffs off you. There's no way to do that, but I'm going to get help. I'll pull the alarm at the door. The fire trucks will be here in a few minutes."

"Yes, you must go."

There was so much he wanted to say, but he had neither the time nor the words. He wanted to tell her he would come back once he had pulled the alarm, but he knew he would never make it. He had to leave the air tank with Leila, and without it this was a one-way trip.

"Hang on, Leila." He pressed the red emergency button on the PASS alarm built into the SCBA's shoulder strap. A high-pitched wail pierced the smoky darkness. "The guys will follow this sound and they'll get you out."

"Go quickly. It's very hot now."

Donny took a series of deep breaths from the mask. The smoke was blinding. He oriented himself against the wall behind him and tried to picture the exact position where he had seen the exit sign. He took one deep final breath, passed the face piece back to Leila and hauled himself to his feet.

"God be with you," she said. "Tell Adina I love her."

Donny didn't answer. He needed to save his breath. The toxic smoke was so thick now he would be unconscious in a matter of seconds if he tried to breathe.

He focused all his attention on one thing. Straight, he told himself, walk straight. Everything hurt; he could no longer distinguish one injury from another. He was a singularity of pain. He used his body like a machine, forcing one foot in front of the other. The path had been relatively clear as he remembered it. Now, blinded by smoke, he stumbled over unseen obstacles. How much further? His lungs were aching. Hadn't it been only a hundred feet? Was he off course?

At last he reached the far wall, but there was no door. Somehow he had gone astray, but which way, left or right? He couldn't see anything. His eyes watered uselessly in the murk and it felt like his chest was about to burst.

Most people unconsciously turn to the right, he remembered from a search and rescue seminar. He had probably done the same and wandered too far right. He knew had only one chance. He turned left and groped his way along the wall.

Something gave way under Donny's hand. He sprawled on the

ground. Black smoke belched from a rectangular hole in the wall above him. He had found the door, pressed the panic bar and fallen out without even knowing it. The air was cool and delicious. He gasped, filling his lungs with it. He lay on his back, revelling in the simple joy of breathing as the stars twinkled silently overhead.

Silence. He hadn't triggered the alarm yet. He had to get up. No, it was impossible.

He grabbed the door frame with his good arm, and mustering the last ounce of his strength, he struggled to his knees. His legs threatened to buckle. There was no way he could make it to his feet. Leaning against the door frame, he groped inside for the pull station. Bells began to ring as he fell to the ground again. He could move no more.

A signal raced along wires. Alarms sounded and firefighters slid down poles into boots and jackets. Lights flashed and trucks roared out into the night.

Time both expanded and contracted. Donny lay there alone for an eternity as smoke spilled from the doorway, black on black in the night sky. Then, in an instant, they were there. Bodies poured off trucks, grabbing hoses and equipment. A figure was running towards him.

"Holy shit, Wedge! What are you doing here?" It was Eddy. Good old Eddy. But there was no time for reunions.

"There's a lady inside." Donny's throat was raw from the smoke, but he had to get the words out. "She's handcuffed to a pipe straight across from the door. Follow the PASS alarm. She's on air, but you gotta get her quick."

Eddy stared at him in stunned silence for a moment, then turned back to the truck and yelled, "Moose, we need that line right now. Spike, bring the bolt cutters and a halligan."

It was a jumble of images when he tried to remember it later. One moment he was sitting there propped up against the doorway with a hose line running across his legs; then they were loading him onto a stretcher. He thought he caught a glimpse of Moose carrying something. Someone was yelling, "VSA!"

Not me, he thought. I'm breathing, aren't I?

Then it was dark.

TWENTY-FIVE
Consequences

ONE OF THE KEYS TO success was recognizing an opportunity when it presented itself. When Youssef Aziz had applied for a research grant to develop a revolutionary hydrogen storage technology, Catherine had recognized the spark of genius.

When the theoretical became the practical, Aziz had come back to her, asking for more money to bring the technology to market. The other key to success, Catherine knew, was timing. Aziz was an eccentric and brilliant engineer, but he was not a businessman.

Catherine had tried to explain to him that the world was not yet quite ready for hydrogen power. She had tried to charm, persuade and cajole him. She had made a magnificently generous offer to buy the technology. But the harder Catherine tried, the more adamant Aziz had become.

Not only wouldn't he sell, he had threatened to place the technology in the public domain, available free of charge to anyone, in order to "free mankind from the tyranny of oil," as he had put it. It was noble, idealistic and absolutely unacceptable.

Over her career Catherine had transformed her company, taking it from the regional arena onto the world stage. Aziz's system was a once-in-a-lifetime opportunity to become a dominant global player. It would be her crowning achievement, a legacy for all time. All it would take was one decisive, surgical strike.

Or so she had thought.

"This is intolerable!" Catherine roared. The chemotherapy had left her feeling sick and irritable. The latest news from Toronto was the last straw. Fury was a luxury Catherine rarely allowed herself. It clouded one's judgement and usually led to decisions one later regretted. She decided to indulge herself anyway and turned the full bore of her wrath on Brendan. "This was to be done quietly, discreetly. But instead of results, all I get is one front-page catastrophe after another, a trail of bodies, and Robertson still alive!"

"I'm… I'm sorry, ma'am. This was completely unforeseen…"

"Your pathetic apology is totally unacceptable. What a mess!" Catherine sighed and swivelled in her chair. The office was part of a sumptuously understated personal suite that occupied most of the top floor of the building. It looked out over the Houston skyline and across the sprawling suburbs that faded into the smoggy distance. The view did nothing to improve her mood. She hated Houston in the summer.

"You have bungled this from the very beginning, Brendan. Did you hire a contractor or a psychopath?" she asked acidly.

"He came highly recommended as one of the best in his line of work," Brendan stammered.

"I don't give a damn if he's Rembrandt, Einstein and Tolstoy rolled into one. He's turned this into a bloody circus!" Brendan jumped as Catherine slammed her hand down on the desk. He was a contemptible, spineless thing. However, unlike most of the bombastic, posturing apes she had known, Brendan was efficiently reliable. Most of the time.

"I am holding you responsible for ensuring that this is cleaned up once and for all. You will terminate our relationship with this person. Terminate it permanently. Do I make myself clear?" She skewered him with her gaze. Brendan tried unsuccessfully not to cringe, something she found immensely gratifying. It felt good to release some of her anger and frustration. It felt good to lash out. There were consequences for failure, and someone was going to pay the price.

"Absolutely clear, ma'am. It's just that there may be complications, and, uh, additional expenses, you see…"

"I — don't — Care. This has already become far too expensive and even more annoying. You will see to this personally."

"Of course. The, uh, situation may not be as bad as it seems, ma'am. Robertson is being investigated for the death of the Aziz woman. The details are in the report." He laid the folder on her desk and retreated as far as he dared.

"Well, that's something, at least," Catherine said contemptuously, ignoring the folder. "Make sure we do whatever we can to facilitate that."

"I'll see what we can do about that."

"Don't see about it. Do it!" she said in a tone of calculated malice.

"Yes, ma'am."

"Robertson won't be much of a threat while he's under suspicion. Once he's behind bars we can make other arrangements. I understand jail is a very dangerous place."

"That's quite true, ma'am."

"Good. You have the briefing notes for this afternoon's board meeting?"

"Right here, ma'am." Brendan handed another folio across the desk, relieved to be able to offer something she would accept. "The main items are revisions to the third quarter projections, mostly positive; there are some minor changes to the terms of the Chinese coal deal that require approval; and there's the Great Lakes wind power project."

The Great Lakes wind power project… At least that would get her out of Houston and back on the water again.

HE SLEPT UNTIL MIDDAY. He always slept well after a job. He yawned, stretched, and hopped into the shower. Room service brought his breakfast as the plastic personalities of the 24-hour news channel chattered mutely on the TV.

When the picture changed to flames leaping high into the night sky, he put down his toast and turned up the volume.

"… at a recycling plant in the Portlands. One person, an off-duty firefighter, was rescued from the fire and taken to hospital. A second person was also rescued but later pronounced dead. Thick, toxic smoke from burning plastic poured from the plant for over five hours as more than a hundred firefighters struggled to extinguish the blaze. Police have yet to identify the two people or explain what the off-duty firefighter was doing at the scene. The fire is under investigation. In other news…"

He turned off the TV and slumped in the chair. It was impossible. How could Robertson have survived? The man was worse than a damned cat. This was a real disaster. There were going to be some very unhappy people, and in his business, unhappy customers were a serious liability.

He could kill Robertson in the hospital. It would be relatively simple, but it would draw too much attention, and that was exactly what his clients were trying to avoid. It would only make his situation worse. He was reviewing his choices when his phone buzzed.

"Please remain in Toronto," the message read. "We need to meet and reconsider our options."

"Reconsider our options": he didn't like the sound of that. Whatever those options were, he suspected he was not part of them.

He thought of running. It was a natural instinct, but he knew better than anyone that there was no place to hide. He could survive for a few weeks or perhaps months, constantly looking over his shoulder, skittering from one dank hole to another, trying to stay one step ahead. But eventually they would find him.

There was no sense going anywhere. There was really only one choice.

He called the front desk and extended his stay. He also ordered a bottle of Dom Pérignon. He would know soon enough, and there was no sense being miserable.

HE SAW THEM ARRIVE the next morning. He recognized the short, nervous-looking one: Benson, Preston, something like that.

He also recognized the other man, though he had never seen him before. Most people would pass him on the street as simply another nameless, faceless cubicle dweller. It was the eyes that gave it away, though. One always recognized one's own. It was time to face the music. He got up from his seat in an out of the way corner of the hotel lobby and headed to the elevators, while the two men tarried at the reception desk.

Brendan was relieved when his companion declined his offer of assistance, even though he burned with shame at the man's obvious contempt. The man knew that Brendan would be more of a liability than an asset. Brendan retired to the hotel's café as the man disappeared into the elevator. He ordered breakfast even though he wasn't hungry, and pretended to read the paper even though he couldn't concentrate.

A text arrived ten minutes later. "It's done. Come have a look for yourself if you want. I need to dispose of some trash."

Brendan paid for his uneaten meal and rode the elevator up. The door to the suite was ajar. He cautiously slipped inside and stood there, paralyzed in horror. He bent over double and retched until he could retch no more. He had just enough sense to check the hallway for witnesses before he bolted for the stairs.

"WHAT'S YOUR RELATIONSHIP with Derek Spangler?"

Spangler? That was a name Mike Wilkins hadn't heard in years, and he wasn't particularly happy to hear it now. Colonel Gilford noticed Wilkins' jaw tense and his grip tighten on the rims of his wheelchair.

"You're probably aware, sir, that we were in the same SEAL class," Wilkins said as calmly as possible.

"Yes, I have his service record: regular Navy, survived hell week, made it through BUDS, and then dropped out. That's a bit unusual." Gilford paused and looked over his glasses at Wilkins.

"Spangler had issues, sir. He was unsuitable."

"But not too unsuitable for the CIA."

"That's not for me to judge, sir." Wilkins tried to relax his shoulders and back. He knew Gilford was measuring his responses.

The Colonel drummed his fingers on his desk. "Is it true that your last SEAL mission was to extract Spangler from southern Iraq?"

"Sir, if you have access to that file, you already know the answer. Otherwise I'm not at liberty to discuss the details of any mission," Wilkins answered mechanically.

"Come on, Mike, who do you think you're talking to here? He's the reason you're sitting in that wheelchair, isn't he?"

Wilkins shifted his weight. "May I ask what this is about, Colonel?"

Colonel Gilford got up, walked around to the front of his desk and sat on the corner facing Wilkins.

"Spangler's dead," said Gilford, watching Wilkins' reaction. Did he see relief? Happiness? Surprise?

Gilford pressed a remote and the video screen on his office wall flared to life. It showed images of a grizzly crime scene. Wilkins watched the images. Gilford continued watching Wilkins. "It came in from the Toronto Police as a John Doe. They found a body with no head and no hands, in a hotel room. Someone obviously didn't want the body identified. The cops lifted a couple of partial prints from the room and put them out on the wire looking for an ID. Our people ran them as a matter of procedure, and they match what we have on file for Spangler. The room was registered under the name of David Bowden. That's an ID Spangler used when he worked for the Agency. He'll remain a John Doe as far as the cops are concerned, but we're fairly certain it's him."

Wilkins raised, then lowered his eyebrows, but he said nothing.

Gilford continued, carefully watching Wilkins' reactions as he spoke. "Spangler was one of the feeds we gave out from the Spectrum file on Robertson. You were pretty unhappy about that operation, weren't you, Mike?"

What exactly was Gilford after? Things weren't always what they seemed in the world of shadows, and he didn't like operating in the dark. He decided the best defence was a good offence.

"No, sir. I made it pretty clear how I felt about it, but I had no idea Spangler was involved." Wilkins straightened in his chair. "However, if you think I had anything to do with Spangler's death you'd best call the MPs."

"Screw the MPs. You Navy guys are so formal." Gilford waved the idea away. "Put yourself in my shoes, Mike. Two people have an unhappy history; then chance brings them together again around an operation one of them doesn't like very much. The other one ends up dead. Now, I'd be mighty pissed off if someone put me in a wheelchair. Not that there aren't a few who wouldn't like to try."

Still Wilkins said nothing.

"Listen, I don't give a rat's ass about Spangler," Gilford continued. "I do care about people on my team going freelance. That bothers me a lot. I also need to know if this has any chance of coming back on us. So why don't you tell me about you and Spangler?"

Wilkins took a deep breath and closed his eyes. When he opened them he noticed Gilford had carefully adopted a neutral, listening posture. Wilkins knew better than to think that having nothing to hide meant he was safe. He decided to take a chance anyway.

"Spangler dropped out of SEAL training during the close quarters combat course. I don't think anybody was sorry to see him go. I certainly wasn't. Rumour was he got recruited by the Agency. I forgot about him after that.

"Six years later my team got assigned to extract a CIA operative from Basra just before the second war started. It was Spangler." Wilkins' eyes lost their focus and Gilford knew he was reliving the mission as he told it. "Spangler was sent in to look for information about Saddam's nuclear and chemical weapons program. There was a lot of pressure from the White House to find evidence for WMDs. The Agency was willing to go to just about any lengths to get it, but they got wind that Spangler was completely off the rails and they wanted him out.

"He had connected with some local anti-Saddam elements and they set up in a villa outside of Basra that was owned by some oil company executive. There was a big private compound, nice gardens, the whole deal. Upstairs everything looked normal. The basement was… it made Abu Ghraib look like kindergarten." Wilkins remembered the sour smell of sweat, urine and fear; the whimpering of a woman cowering in the corner of an improvised cell; the battered bodies of two men, not quite dead and not quite alive.

"I think the locals were into it for revenge. Spangler, he just enjoyed it. The intel was only a bonus for him." Wilkins closed his eyes again and shook his head, trying to clear away the images. "I'm not squeamish, sir. I've conducted my share of interrogations, but this was offside. This was way offside.

"Spangler wasn't exactly happy to see us when we arrived, particularly when I told him what was going to be in my report. We argued, but he saw we weren't leaving without him. Then he said something to his people in Arabic and they started to leave. I wasn't happy about that, but he said they needed to get away clean before the chopper came for us, and I couldn't stop them without risking a firefight.

"We were running out to the Black Hawk when we started to take small arms fire." Gilford's office melted away. The shadowy hulk of the helicopter hovered, a darker shade of night at the back of the compound. The rotor wash flattened the neatly tended flowerbeds, mixing the scent of jasmine and roses with the dusty desert air. Muzzle flashes flared in the darkness as the wasp sting of bullets bit into the plaster and marble of the villa.

"I'm sure it was Spangler's people but I can't prove that. He tried to take off when the shooting started, but I tackled the son of a bitch." Wilkins felt himself running, his legs moving, driving, and then launching himself at Spangler. He felt his arm drawing back and his fist smashing into the side of Spangler's head. He felt the burning in his lungs as he dragged Spangler across the compound towards the chopper. The ground seethed as he ran, spitting up sprays of sand and dirt as bullets plowed the soil.

Almost there. Thirty yards. His team were spread out in front of the chopper, returning fire. Twenty yards. He could hear the cries of wounded Iraqis behind him. Ten yards. Something hit him from behind. There was no pain, just a sledgehammer blow in his lower back, and suddenly the carefully choreographed rhythm of arms, legs, heart and lungs was all out of kilter.

It was a kaleidoscope of motion. He was falling; dirt filled his mouth and nose. Hands were lifting him, then something larger was raising him into the night air. Through the chopper door he could see the tiny lights of cars and houses fading in the distance as other twinkling lights spun overhead. The vision faded with Wilkins' memory.

"That's the last time I saw Spangler. I took a round in the back as we were loading him in the chopper." Wilkins blinked and wiped the back of his hand across his mouth. "Am I glad to hear that piece of shit is dead? You bet. But I had nothing to do with it, and I had no idea he was connected to the Robertson matter. The last I heard, the Agency let him go. No one there was interested in pursuing it any further, and I had enough on my plate."

Gilford was silent as he considered Wilkins' account. It squared with everything he had been able to discover on his own.

"Fair enough," the Colonel announced. "As I said, Mike, my primary concern is for the organization. The last thing I need is for some hotshot Congressman or reporter to get hold of this and try to make a name for himself."

"I understand, sir." Wilkins was relieved, but now he was curious. "So Spangler set the original fire and then blew up Robertson's house?"

"It looks that way. Spangler went freelance after the Agency let him go. He popped up on the radar every now and then." Gilford pressed the remote again. The images on the screen changed. They showed Spangler sitting in a café, hailing a cab, walking through a market… "He did some work for the Israelis, the Algerians and the Saudis. Then it seems he went mostly private. This fits his MO, though. Seems he liked to play with matches."

Wilkins pursed his lips. He could tell Gilford wanted this wrapped up and buried, but it was worth a try. "Are you aware, sir, that there was another fire two days ago? The Aziz widow was killed, and Robertson escaped. The details are in the latest Spectrum files. Based on what you've said, it seems likely that Spangler arranged that too. The police are investigating Robertson, though. Spangler probably set him up as the fall guy. Any chance we could link Spangler for the cops? Anonymously, of course."

"Absolutely not." Gilford crossed around behind his desk again. The video screen faded to black. "That's too bad for Captain Robertson. Let's hope he gets a good lawyer. I want the Spectrum file on him terminated immediately. We've done more than enough for our friends and this has become way too messy. I want anything that connects us to Robertson or Spangler, or them to each other, swept clean. Understood?"

"Aye aye, sir." Wilkins spun his wheelchair to go, but Gilford stopped him.

"I'm sorry, Mike, sorry I had to put you through that. I had to be sure. It's always awkward when there's a personal element. But we need to keep this in perspective. This is a molehill that's become too much of a mountain. It needs to disappear."

SWEEP IT CLEAN, that's what Gilford had said. It wasn't such an unusual request and it didn't bother Wilkins that much. What did bother him was wondering who else would be cleaning up loose ends. That's what Robertson had become: one big walking loose end. Wilkins wondered if the people behind this would be content with having Robertson in prison for life for a murder he didn't commit. Probably not.

And who were these people anyway? Until now they had just been "friends," people with intimate connections in the corridors of power.

Spangler was dead and he was still destroying people's lives. That was what really stuck in Wilkins' craw.

Wilkins had gotten on with his life. He had successfully rerouted his career; he had married and started a family. He could have been the poster boy for the disabled community. But still, deep down he carried a hatred for the man who had put him in his chair.

Wilkins was no naïve rookie. He knew first-hand that there was no black and white. Innocent people sometimes got hurt along the way, but he tried to let his moral compass and the oath he had taken as an officer guide him towards the greater good. There might not be any such thing as absolute right, but he was pretty sure he could recognize absolute wrong.

It wasn't really a matter of disobeying orders, Wilkins rationalized to himself; it was more a matter of interpretation. He wasn't sure Gilford would see it that way, but with any luck the Colonel would never know. He would shut down the Robertson file and clean up, but he couldn't stand idly by without lifting a finger. That would make him Spangler's accomplice, and that was a thought Wilkins couldn't stomach.

First he would track down the identities of the other feeds from the Robertson Spectrum. Then he would locate Robertson himself. Once the Spectrum was shut down it should be fairly safe to make one call on a secure line. At the very least, Robertson deserved to know what he was up against.

TWENTY-SIX
One Of Those Days...

ONE OF THE BEST THINGS about being in the hospital was that it gave you time to think. It was also one of the worst things. Donny was alone with his thoughts and it felt like he was trapped behind enemy lines.

It had started with the phone call, probably the strangest phone call he had ever received.

"Hello. Is that Donald Robertson?" The voice was tinny and distant.

"Yes," said Donny somewhat hesitantly. Oh God, he thought, how the hell could telemarketers track him down in the hospital? Normally he would have hung up, but he was bored.

"I need you to listen very carefully to what I have to say." That was not the usual telemarketing script.

"Who is this?"

"Sorry to sound clichéd," said the voice, "but that really isn't important. However, what I have to tell you is. Do you want to hear it?"

"Yes."

"Good," said the voice. It was hard to tell if it belonged to a man or a woman. Donny suspected it had been altered.

"First of all," the voice continued, "the man who tried to kill you in the recycling plant, the one who blew up your house and killed Captain Fitzgerald, is dead."

Just like that? It was over just like that? After all he had been through, all he had suffered and lost? How could that be? Donny's mind reeled at the news. He was relieved and yet afraid to believe.

"Really? Are you sure?" he asked. "How do you know all that?"

"Because it's my business to know things. And yes, I'm sure," the voice answered.

"OK. Well, that's good."

"Yes and no. He's dead because he failed to kill you. However, you're still in a great deal of danger. The people he worked for will try to have you convicted for Leila Aziz's murder first, but I doubt they'll stop there."

"But I didn't do it! I tried to save her," Donny protested. It was not the first time he had said that.

"Do you think you'd be the first innocent person to go to prison?"

No one believed him. The police didn't seem to. The Fire Department hadn't terminated him yet, but that was just a formality, waiting for the conclusion of the police investigation. It was a wild tale, he had to admit: an evil green-eyed man, a conspiracy that Donny insisted was real but couldn't explain. A few people gave him the benefit of the doubt — Aldrich, Eddy and Moose, perhaps a few more — but no one that really mattered.

Now this voice, this unknown, unidentified person from nowhere, knew the whole story, but said it didn't matter anyway. He was going to prison.

"What do you want from me?" Donny felt an edge of panic creeping into his voice.

"I don't want anything from you, Captain Robertson. I simply want to tell you the truth."

"How do I know that? How do I know what you say is true?"

"You don't. But maybe the fact that I haven't asked you for anything is an indication."

"You could stop them," suggested Donny. He couldn't help the desperation in his plea. "Please, if you know all these things, you could tell the police."

"No, that's impossible. I'm taking a risk just calling you. That's all I can do. The only person who can stop this is Catherine Elizabeth Rockingham. Have you got that?"

"Catherine Elizabeth Rockingham," Donny repeated. "Who is she?"

"She's the president, CEO and majority shareholder of Sovereign Petroleum."

"What am I supposed to do? Send her an email saying 'please stop trying to kill me'?" He was getting hysterical. Donny swallowed hard and tried to get control of himself. "I mean, I don't understand. What's this all about?"

"I'm not entirely sure," said the voice. "Catherine Rockingham is the only one who really knows. I don't know if you can reach her, or if she'd even listen to you, but she's the one pulling the strings."

"Just tell me what the hell is going on!" Donny yelled into the phone.

"I've told you as much as I can. Good luck, Captain Robertson."

The line went dead. Donny punched *69 into the phone to try to retrieve the number. There was no "that number is unavailable," there was simply nothing. It was as if the mysterious phone call had never happened.

DONNY WAS STILL replaying the conversation in his head when Laurie appeared in the doorway. He was too busy mentally chasing his own tail to notice her standing there.

She looked at him lying in the hospital bed. An IV ran into the back of his good hand, just behind the thumbnail he was chewing. The other arm was held in a framework of metal bars and wires. Staples ran along the incision where they had screwed and plated the bones back together. The black eye was obvious. The broken ribs were covered by the blue hospital gown, but the pain showed every time Donny shifted in the bed.

It shocked her to see the confident, easygoing skipper she had seen at *Red Bird's* helm replaced by this battered and frightened man. Laurie considered whether she should stay or go. In the end she decided on "Hi!"

Donny started, then winced and held his ribs with his good hand. "Jeez, Laurie, you shouldn't sneak up on a guy like that."

"Sorry," she said, hoping the fragility of her smile didn't show. She crossed to his bedside and put a box on the side table. "Here, these are for you. Eddy said you liked peanut butter cookies. Daniel and Kevin helped me make them. They made the card too."

She showed him the card. It was a child's drawing of a big yellow sun, two puffy clouds and four smiling faces on a sailboat.

"You spoke to Eddy?" Her sudden appearance had jarred him. He felt like he was living on several planes simultaneously. The ghosts of the past, disembodied voices on the phone, and the name of a woman he had never met seemed more real than Laurie standing there holding the card out to him.

"Yes, I called the station. Eddy told me you were here." She wanted to reach out, to stroke his hair, but he seemed so far away. She put the card down on the table beside the box of cookies, sat in the visitor's chair by the window and tried to smile again. "He said you could use a friendly face."

Donny closed his eyes and tried to force himself fully into the present. "You shouldn't have come here."

"Can't I even visit you in the hospital?" she asked, leaning forward in the chair.

"No. It's for your own good."

"For my own good? Do you have any idea how condescending you sound?" She didn't want to show her frustration, but she couldn't help it. "I guess that's why you have so many get well cards, eh? It's the same old Donny. If anyone tries to get close to you, you just push them away."

He looked around. Aside from the cookies and card she had brought, there was one card from the guys at Lombard and another from Aldrich.

"It's not like that." He winced as he struggled to raise himself. He wanted to explain to her, but how could he explain something he didn't understand himself? Anything he did tell her would only put her in more danger. "I'm sorry, Laurie, but you need to forget about me."

"Did I mean anything to you? Am I supposed to pretend that this…" she couldn't hide the hurt, "that we never happened?"

"This isn't about you and me. Please, Laurie," Donny pleaded, "you're killing me. This is hard enough. Forget about us. Forget about the water main, the air lock and everything. It's for the best, really."

"Fine. If that's the way you want it. I'm sorry I wasted your time." She got up and walked around the bed to leave. He reached out and grabbed her arm as she passed. She spun angrily, yanking her arm free. Donny grunted with pain. She glared at him, angry that he had touched her, sorry she had hurt him and angry at herself for caring.

"Tell me what the hell is going on." She stood with her arms crossed and glared at him.

"They think I killed that woman. They haven't charged me yet, but I can tell." That much was safe to tell her.

"Yes, Eddy kind of mentioned that." Laurie's face softened and she shook her head. "You're an asshole, Donny, but you're not a murderer."

"Thank you for believing that." Donny smiled faintly, then his face grew serious again. "Now if the cops ask you any questions, tell them you met me, but put as much distance between us as you can. Don't say anything about explosives in the water main or air locks or anything like that, OK? That's really important."

"Why?"

"Don't you see what's going on? You said it yourself: these guys are pros!" He loved her for her stubborn, bull-headed loyalty, but it was making him crazy. Donny took a deep breath and continued. "They blew up my house and they tried to kill me in the recycling plant fire. And it's all connected to Commissioners Street. Anyone who talked to me about it or helped me is in danger. That's why Leila Aziz is dead, and the people who did this are going to make it look like I killed her. There's nothing you can do to help me. You've got to protect yourself."

She leaned against the wall by the door. "Let's just go to the cops and tell them everything."

It was Donny's turn to shake his head. "It won't work. No matter what we say or prove, they'll just fix it. The less you know, the safer you are. You have to trust me."

"And that's it?"

"There's no choice." He turned and looked out the window. "I couldn't live with myself if anything happened to you. If you won't do it for yourself, do it for the boys." When he looked back she was gone.

Two men in suits got off the elevator at the end of the corridor. They passed Laurie, looking at room numbers as they went. She stopped and watched as they disappeared into Donny's room. She turned and walked back the way she had just come, stopping a few feet from Donny's door to listen.

"Donald Robertson, you are under arrest for the murder of Leila Aziz. You have the right to retain and instruct counsel without delay. A lawyer can be referred to you free of charge if you do not have your own lawyer. You are not obliged to say anything, but anything you do say can be used in court as evidence. Do you understand?"

Silence.

"Mr. Robertson, do you understand?"

There was another pause and then Donny's voice, "Not really, but I sure as hell wish I did."

TWENTY-SEVEN
The Weight of Evidence

"THEY'RE WILLING TO consider a claim of diminished responsibility. It's a generous offer, Donny: manslaughter, and seven years. I may be able to bargain them down to five, and with early parole you could be out in three. The crown seems really eager to put this behind them. A lot of people don't want the publicity of a trial and the damage it would do to the Fire Department's reputation."

Donny sank down in the leather armchair and said nothing. He stared at the bookshelves that lined the office.

"Donny, a conviction for murder means an automatic life sentence." Still Donny said nothing. Larry Miller threw his hands in the air. "The right to remain silent is not a good strategy with your own lawyer."

Larry Miller was a short, heavyset, balding man. It was obvious he made his living with his mind rather than his hands. When Donny was arrested he had called Aldrich, not knowing where else to turn. Aldrich had called Larry, his son-in-law's brother, and Larry had agreed to be Donny's lawyer.

A video link was set up and the arraignment was held in the hospital. Aldrich agreed to be Donny's surety and put up his house as collateral for Donny's bail. From there the wheels of justice had begun their slow grind. Donny was released from hospital a week later.

That had been a month ago. His arm was still in a sling, but physiotherapy was helping him regain strength and function. His ribs no longer hurt with every breath, but sneezing and coughing were still to be avoided if possible. He walked with a slight limp, and there was a haunted look around his eyes that told of wounds that had no other outward sign.

They were seated at a small coffee table, Larry on the couch and Donny facing him in the armchair. Two thick stacks of files sat on the table between them.

"Look, Donny, here's what we know the prosecution already has." Larry leaned forward and began counting off the points on his fingers. "They have your phone record, with nine calls to Leila Aziz in the two days before the fire. They have the daughter's statement that you were harassing Leila. You admit you were there, and in addition to obvious signs of a struggle they have blood splatter from both of you in the living room. Your rental car was parked at the scene of the fire. There were forcible entry tools in the back seat, with your fingerprints all over them. Most of all they have you at the scene, in your bunker suit with an SCBA."

Larry picked up a file from the coffee table. "And now they have a coroner's report that says there was enough Valium in Leila Aziz's bloodstream to render her helpless."

"That's pure bullshit!"

"That's not really an argument I can use in court against a coroner's report," said Larry. He offered the coroner's report to Donny, but he waved it away. "That pretty much shoots down our defence that you were too badly injured to overpower her."

"I suppose I branded the inside of my own nose and shattered my own arm for fun?" Donny asked. Larry shrugged. "She wasn't drugged. He wanted her to suffer."

"Donny," Larry leaned forward with his hands on his knees, "I can't go into court and just call the coroner a liar."

"They must have paid off the lab technician or switched the samples or something."

Larry sat back and put his hands in the air. "And I can't just tell the jury there's some wild conspiracy, without anything to back it up."

"You don't believe me either," Donny said with resignation.

"That's not what I said. What I said was that a jury isn't going to believe us without some kind of evidence and a plausible story. Right now the weight of the evidence is all stacked against you."

Donny sighed and shook his head.

Larry got up and went to his desk, opened the bottom drawer and took out two glasses and a flask. "Truth serum," he said as he poured a measure into each glass. He returned and set one glass in front of each of them.

"Cheers," said Larry, raising his glass.

Donny sniffed at his and took a sip. "Rye?"

"I think so. Either that or very bad brandy." Larry set his glass down and looked Donny squarely in the eye. It was a speech he had to make to most clients at one point or another.

"I've been in this game a long time, and I can tell when people are lying to me. I don't think you are. I believe there was someone else there, someone who assaulted you and Leila and tried to kill both of you. People don't make up the kind of details you told me. That hot wire up the nose thing, that's just creepy." Larry shuddered.

"However, I don't think you're telling me everything, either. As I said, the right to remain silent is a bad policy with your lawyer. You need to tell me the truth, Donny: the whole truth, and nothing but the truth. Otherwise I can't help you. Now is the time to come clean."

Larry sat back, picked up his drink and waited. It sometimes took a few minutes, but it usually worked.

Donny rubbed the back of his neck. "I've told you as much as I can."

"Anything you tell me is privileged information," Larry said soothingly.

Donny got up and started to pace. It was all becoming clear to him. The whole legal process was a ritual dance, but it would have no effect on the final outcome. The only question was how many people he would take down with him.

"I don't think you can help me, Larry, but not for the reason you think. You see, it doesn't matter what evidence we come up with: they'll find some way around it." Donny pointed to the files stacked on the coffee table. "Like that crap about Valium in the coroner's report."

"Donny, listen…"

"No, you listen, Larry. Five years, seven years, life — it doesn't matter, because I won't survive the first year. I know you think I'm half-crazy or paranoid, but when you hear I've hung myself or I've been shanked in the prison yard you'll know I was telling you the truth. And you'll be glad I didn't tell you any more."

DONNY STOPPED AT THE public library on his way back from the lawyer's office. He had been using the computer terminals at the library to look into the affairs of Catherine Elizabeth Rockingham and Sovereign Petroleum. His final conversation with Micah and the mysterious phone call in the hospital had left him feeling slightly paranoid. Part of him knew that the library was a feeble attempt at anonymity, but it made him feel better nonetheless.

The world's largest oil companies, such as Saudi Arabia's Aramco, were government owned. Of the independents, Sovereign ranked number seventeen, well down from the giants such as ExxonMobil, Royal Dutch Shell and BP. But thirty years ago Sovereign hadn't even been on the map.

Their operations were global in scope, with oil and gas leases in central Africa and Indonesia, as well as Canada and the U.S. Like the big players, Sovereign had branched out into different areas of the energy business: they had controlling interests in coal mines in

Australia and South America, and they had recently developed a green energy division, with investments in wind and solar power.

Catherine Rockingham had a degree in petroleum engineering from Stanford and an MBA from the London School of Economics. Her father had died when Catherine was twenty-nine, and she had taken over the reins of the company. Over the next thirty-five years she had transformed Sovereign from a local drilling and exploration company into an international player.

Catherine Rockingham was also recognized as a leading art collector and an accomplished sailor. It was the latter fact that most attracted Donny's attention. In her early twenties she had twice been a member of the U.S. Olympic sailing team, and she was one of the first women skippers to win her division in the Chicago-Mackinac, the world's longest freshwater sailing race. Donny noted that several commentators remarked on her "aggressive tactics" in both business and sailing.

Donny had been going through the material for weeks now, following link after link. A lot of it was repetitive, listing the same corporate milestones and personal accomplishments. He wasn't sure what he was looking for, other than some way to get to Catherine Rockingham. "She's the one pulling the strings," the voice had said.

Donny seated himself in front of a terminal and logged in. As always, he started with the Sovereign Petroleum homepage. His eye was drawn to a new item on the side: "Sovereign Petroleum announces the world's largest wind power initiative." He clicked on the link.

Sovereign Petroleum and its subsidiary, Sovereign Energy Alternatives, are pleased to announce their commitment to build the world's largest wind power project.

Spread over five sites around Lake Michigan, Lake Huron and Georgian Bay, this project will generate almost 5,000 megawatts of clean renewable energy in the United States and Canada.

"Sovereign is more than an oil company, we're an energy company," said Sovereign Petroleum President and CEO Catherine Rockingham.

"*As an experienced sailor, I have always known the immense power of the wind. We are committed to green sustainable energy solutions, like wind power, now and for the future.*"

Ms. Rockingham will participate in the kickoff celebrations for this exciting wind power initiative at Tobermory, Ontario and Bay City, Michigan. Powered by the wind, she will travel to each site on her sailboat, Sovereign Seas.

Tobermory, with its rocky bluffs and cold, clear waters dotted with windswept islands and treacherous shoals. It was the graveyard of dozens of ships.

Donny had visited there on *Red Bird*'s first long cruise after he finished the refit: up the Welland Canal from Lake Ontario to Lake Erie; north past Detroit into Lake Huron; then around Tobermory, at the tip of the Bruce Peninsula, and into Georgian Bay; finally back south along the Trent-Severn canal system to Lake Ontario again.

It had been a glorious month-long voyage as boat and skipper had gotten to know each other's quirks and capabilities. There had been big cities, quaint ports and quiet bays, winds fair and foul, and the hammer blows of the Great Lakes' infamous squalls.

Donny smiled at the memory of the voyage up Lake Huron to Tobermory in a brisk nor'wester, *Red Bird* close-hauled and double-reefed, heeling hard to starboard, her bow plunging through the waves and the spray washing his face. He had tested the boat and his seamanship and found them both to be, if not perfect, quite pleasingly adequate.

Now this woman, this captain of industry, this threat to him and all he loved was coming to those same waters in her boat. She would arrive in barely four weeks.

Donny googled *Sovereign Seas* and soon had an image of the ship in front of him. She was a 155-foot gaff-rigged Grand Banks schooner, built in Essex, Massachusetts in 1908. She had begun her life as a fishing schooner out of Gloucester. Most of her kind were nothing more than memories now. *Sovereign Seas* had escaped by becoming the plaything of the ultra-rich. The pictures Donny saw took his breath away. She was tall and graceful. Only someone like Catherine Rockingham could afford to restore, maintain and crew such a vessel.

An idea blossomed in Donny's mind. It sprang fully formed into being like Venus rising from the waves. It was simple, daring and desperate. It was the only sort of plan that had any chance of success.

Donny logged off the computer and called Larry Miller.

"**IN SUMMARY, YOUR HONOUR**, this is most irregular. Mr. Robertson is charged with murder. In most such cases the accused is held without any bail. Now Mr. Robertson asks to able to wander at will. The Crown strenuously opposes this application."

The judge made some notations on the pad in front of her, then looked at Larry Miller and Donny and raised an eyebrow.

Larry stood and gestured to his left. "Your Honour, my learned friend for the prosecution is given to some degree of exaggeration. While I will admit that the application is a bit unusual, we are hardly asking the court to allow Mr. Robertson to 'wander at will.' We ask only that he be allowed to travel on his sailboat within specified waters in southern Ontario. Mr. Robertson is quite willing to abide by whatever conditions the court may impose to allow this to happen.

"As to the seriousness of the charge against my client, I can only wonder: if the Crown feels Mr. Robertson is such a danger to the community, why would it make an offer of manslaughter and minimum sentencing?"

"We have made no such formal offer, Your Honour!" said the prosecutor, leaping red-faced to his feet. "We have merely initiated some preliminary discussions with the defence, in the interests of, uh, a speedy and efficient resolution of this matter."

"Seems a bit like splitting hairs to me, Mr. Davison," replied the judge. "However, your concerns are duly noted, and I assure you that I do not take murder charges lightly. Do you have anything else, Mr. Miller?"

"Only to point out the relevant precedents from case law which I included with my earlier submission. I would also remind the court that Mr. Robertson has been an upstanding member of the community. He has never before had anything more serious than a traffic violation, and he has been decorated several times for bravery as a firefighter. We have supplied numerous references as to his character. And I would point out that Mr. Robertson has scrupulously obeyed all the conditions of his bail to this point.

"Finally, if Mr. Robertson were a serious risk for flight, a sailboat moving at five knots on an inland waterway is far from the ideal means of escape." The judge smiled for a second as Larry sat down.

"There are precedents, but this is a very unusual request nonetheless." The judge paused while she leafed through some of the papers both sides had submitted. "Mind you, there are many unusual aspects to this case. Would you care to explain the reasons behind this request, Mr. Miller?"

Before Larry could respond, Donny pushed himself up from his chair. "May I speak, Your Honour?"

"You're certainly free to address the court, Mr. Robertson," the judge replied. She was surprised but not unfriendly. "However, one of the reasons you retain counsel is that they are experienced in dealing with legal matters."

"I just thought I could answer your question, that's all. I'll leave the legal stuff to these two gentlemen." Donny indicated the two lawyers. "I'm not as good with words as they are, so I'll just speak plainly, if that's OK."

"Please do, Mr. Robertson." The judge set down her glasses and fixed her gaze on Donny.

"Keep it simple," Larry whispered to him.

"I know this isn't the time or place to argue my case, so I won't do that." Donny chewed his lip for a moment, then held out his hands, palms up. "In the last couple of months I've lost just about everything I had. I guess you know my house blew up. I lost my job and a bunch of other stuff too. All I have left is my boat, and no matter which way this goes I'm going to have to sell *Red Bird* to pay my legal bills. A friend of mine is a yacht broker up in Midland. I'd like to take her for one last cruise on Georgian Bay before I drop her off there.

"I'm not asking for pity, Your Honour. I know everyone here is just doing their job — you, the prosecutor, everyone. What I am asking for, I guess, is a little understanding.

"That's it. Thanks for listening to me. I hope it made sense." Donny sat down and Larry patted him on the shoulder.

"What kind of boat is *Red Bird*, Mr. Robertson?" the judge asked.

Donny scrambled to his feet again. "An Island Packet 35, Your Honour."

"That's a nice boat." The judge made a few more notations on her pad, then she straightened her robes and cleared her throat.

"I will grant this application based on the following strict conditions. First of all, Mr. Robertson, you will be restricted to the waters of Lake Ontario, the TrentSevern system, and Georgian Bay. You will radio your location to the Canadian Coast Guard at noon each day. Furthermore, you will be required to stay at least ten nautical miles from the American border at all times. Do you understand and accept these conditions?"

"Yes, Your Honour, I do," Donny nodded.

"Is Mr. Aldrich in the court?" The judge looked out to the gallery. The old man rose to his feet. "Mr. Aldrich, do you consent to continue as Mr. Robertson's surety and do you agree to accompany him on this voyage?"

"I'm not that fond of boats, Your Honour, but I agree."

"That's very good of you, then, Mr. Aldrich." The judge smiled at him. "Both of you will be required to present yourselves in person at the nearest Ontario Provincial Police detachment every Monday, Wednesday and Friday during the trip. Is that understood?"

Donny and Aldrich looked at each other and nodded.

"All the other conditions of your bail," the judge continued, "will still apply: the surrender of your passport, the prohibition from owning weapons and so on. All this changes is your ability to travel aboard your boat based on these conditions.

"Let me be perfectly clear about this, Mr. Robertson. If you stray from these conditions in the slightest, you will be apprehended and you will spend the rest of your time awaiting trial in custody."

"Yes, Your Honour. Thank you," Donny replied. The prosecutor scowled and shook his head.

"And Mr. Davison, I will thank you to stop shaking your head at me in my courtroom. This hearing is closed." The judge banged her gavel and everyone rose as she left the chamber.

"Thanks, Larry," Donny said, shaking the lawyer's hand. The prosecutor brushed by and gave them a foul look.

"He's a rather unpleasant fellow, isn't he?" remarked Aldrich, watching the prosecutor leave. "The judge forgot to mention one more important thing."

"What's that?" asked Donny.

"If you expect me on that boat, you'll need a bottle of good whisky. A bottle of Glenmorangie 25 would serve well."

"Glenmorangie 25? Very nice. Perhaps you should take legal counsel with you," suggested Larry.

"Sorry, Larry," Donny apologized. "Lawyers and anchors are too much of a temptation. I'm in enough trouble already."

TWENTY-EIGHT
Trent-Severn

THEIR DEPARTURE FROM Toronto was uneventful. They had a schedule to keep and were forced to run the engine most of the way. Donny cursed the light wind, but Aldrich was just as glad.

They arrived in Trenton by mid-morning on the second day. This was where the Trent-Severn waterway began its traverse from Lake Ontario to Georgian Bay. The minimum bridge clearance on the canal was twenty-two feet and *Red Bird* with her mast up measured forty-eight feet. Moose and Eddy drove up from Toronto to give them a hand taking the mast down. They arrived with a bundle of two-by-fours strapped to the roof of Eddy's minivan, and cobbled them together into a cradle to hold the mast on deck.

They worked quietly and efficiently under Donny's direction. It was good to have the help. Donny's injuries were mostly healed, but he still didn't have much strength in his left arm. Everyone was just as happy to keep their hands busy and not have to think too much beyond the task at hand. When they were done, *Red Bird* looked like she was ready for a nautical jousting match, with her mast laid horizontally in the improvised cradle, hanging over the bow and stern.

The trip up the canal was scheduled to take a week. Donny and Aldrich would do most of it on their own. The plan was for the Lombard crew to join them in Orillia for the last two days.

They shook hands, Eddy and Moose cast off the lines, and *Red*

Bird headed up the Trent River under the July afternoon sun. Eddy and Moose got in the van and headed back to Toronto.

"What do you think he's doing?" asked Moose.

"Going sailing on Georgian Bay. That's kind of the whole purpose of having a boat. *Capisce?*" replied Eddy, pulling out to pass a truck.

"No, I mean what do you think he's doing?"

Eddy glanced over at Moose. The big man wore a concerned, thoughtful expression. "I don't know. Maybe he just needs to get away. Christ, if it was me I'd probably find a nice quiet place to drown myself."

Moose knit his brow for a moment. "No, you wouldn't. You're not the type. I don't know about Wedge, though. I worry about him."

"You're thinking too much, Moose. It doesn't suit you. Better stop before you blow a gasket. Besides, he didn't do it, so it's going to be fine, right?" Eddy tried to sound convincing, but he didn't even believe himself.

RED BIRD WAS FOLLOWING the ancient waterway that Native people had used for thousands of years. It was a network of lakes, rivers and gorges created by meltwater from the last ice age. Fur traders had used the route as a shortcut to and from Georgian Bay and to avoid the dangerous open water of the Great Lakes. Lumber barons had built the first dams. In the mid1800s, locks gradually replaced the portages, allowing commerce to flow through the rough landscape. With the advent of railroads and highways the commercial boat traffic had all but disappeared, and the Trent-Severn Waterway was now the playground of cottagers and recreational boaters.

Donny and Aldrich simply let the landscape flow past them. Farms, marshes and woodlands drifted by as they travelled upstream. Summer was at its height and the countryside was bursting with life. It was an idyllic pastoral scene viewed close up and at a pace slow enough to appreciate the subtle details: the hundred different shades of green among the fields and forests; the scent of fresh-mown hay and wild flowers and the rich odour of decay from the swamps; the myriad melodies of unseen songbirds; the mirrored symmetry of a twisted tree on the shoreline, reflected in still water and framed against the sunset.

They spoke little as they made their way. What little they did say had mostly to do with the details of navigating the locks, what threat, if any, the weather might pose, and the small details of daily life. Their active attention was focused on the tasks at hand. Their other thoughts they kept to themselves.

They reached Balsam Lake on the fourth day, the summit of the waterway. Here they would transit from the Trent system, which drained south into Lake Ontario, to the Severn, which flowed north to Georgian Bay.

There were thunderheads building all around them as they crossed the lake, and Donny decided to anchor in a protected cove behind an island to ride out the storm. The anchor bit deep into the sandy bottom and he let out extra scope to make sure it didn't pull loose.

Thunder rumbled as he made one final tour of the deck to ensure that everything was secure. The first fat raindrops fell as Donny closed the hatch. The two men settled into the cabin; Aldrich put the kettle on for tea, and Donny dug out the cards and the cribbage board and began shuffling the deck.

"I guess you want to make sure your anchor is well set in a storm," Aldrich mused. The rain was pounding hard on the cabin roof now and gusts were rocking the boat.

"Yup," Donny replied, "otherwise you end up on the rocks."

"You've some rough water ahead of you, Donald." They hadn't talked about the court case. Aldrich had hoped that Donny would bring it up, but he hadn't. This seemed as good an opportunity as any.

"You could say that." Donny cocked his head slightly. What was the old man getting at?

Aldrich went to his berth and retrieved an old leather-bound Bible. He held it out to Donny. "Please take it. My grandfather gave it to me when I was seven or eight. I didn't have much use for it as a young lad, but it's come to mean something to me since. I'd like you to pass it on to my grandchildren when the time comes, but for now I want you to have it."

Donny hesitated. He didn't want to hurt Aldrich's feelings, but he didn't want to take the Bible either. "Gee, that's really kind of you, but it's sort of an heirloom. I really shouldn't…"

"I'm not asking you to believe anything or agree to anything. I'd merely ask you to keep an open mind. When the storms of life blow it's good to have something solid to hang on to. It would mean a great deal to me if you'd take it."

Donny pursed his lips, then reached out and took the Bible. "I'll make sure your grandkids get it."

"Thank you." Aldrich sat at the table and Donny dealt the cards. They played a couple of hands as the kettle came to a boil and the tea steeped.

"There's one more thing," Aldrich said as he poured the tea. "I haven't asked you why we're really making this trip."

"No," Donny answered. "It's probably better that way."

"I assume it's more than a pleasure cruise." Aldrich set two mugs of tea in front of them. He sipped his and looked at Donny over the rim of his mug. "There's a certain air of urgency about you and this schedule you insist on."

The rain had brought a slight chill after the day's heat. Donny wrapped his hands around his mug and thought for a moment. "As you said, there's a storm heading my way, and I think this is my one chance to dodge it. It's pretty slim, but at least it's a chance."

"I assume you don't want to explain what it is."

Donny shook his head.

"Then promise me one thing." Aldrich put down his tea, reached over and placed Donny's hand on the Bible. "Promise me you'll not harm yourself or anyone else."

Donny frowned and lifted his hand. "Cap, you have to understand: these people are playing for keeps. I don't want to hurt anybody, especially myself. If everything works out, maybe I won't have to. But I have one chance to fix this and I won't back down. Now, is it your crib or mine?"

Aldrich sighed and dealt the cards.

THEY MADE AN EARLY start the next day and were in Orillia by late afternoon. They checked in with the police as per Donny's bail conditions and then called Lombard to confirm the rendezvous. Eddy said they'd be leaving straight from the station when their shift ended in the morning.

Eddy's van pulled into the parking lot at the Orillia town dock just after nine the next day. Donny and Aldrich waved from the boat.

"Hi, Donny, how are you?" Eddy's wife was the first one out of the van.

"Fine, Linda, how about you? This is a pleasant surprise."

"Don't worry" Linda said as she circled around to the driver's side. "Kyle and I are headed up to my mother's in Parry Sound."

"You're welcome to come along." Donny spread his hands in invitation. "I'm sure we could make room."

"You hear that?" Kyle looked at his mother hopefully. "Uncle Donny said I could go with them."

"Get in the van," Linda said, all trace of pleasantness had disappeared. "You're going to visit your grandmother, and you're going to act like you're having a good time if it kills you. Understand?"

Kyle slouched into the passenger seat, plugged in his ear buds and stared morosely at the dashboard.

"Look who we found on the roadside," Eddy said as he and Moose unloaded bags of food and beer. Suzie stepped out stiffly from the side door of the van.

"Good thinking — bring the probie as a galley slave," Donny answered as they carried the supplies aboard the boat.

Aldrich extended his hand to help Suzie aboard. "Pay them no mind. They were raised by wolves, the lot of them. I'm John Aldrich. It's a pleasure to finally meet you."

"Likewise. I'm Susan Kozarovitch," Suzie smiled brightly. "Thanks for the hand. I'm not very nimble in this back brace. It's like wearing an iron maiden."

"Have fun," Linda called as she backed the van out of its parking spot. "If Eddy doesn't behave, Suzie, you have my full permission to beat him."

Donny smiled. He was tired of thinking and brooding. Things would never be the same again, he knew that, but for today, at least, it felt like old times.

It was a perfect day, just hot enough to feel like summer without being stifling. A cooling breeze shepherded flocks of puffy clouds across a limitless blue sky. The boat was more crowded with five adults on board, but everyone found a spot and settled in to enjoy the cruise. Eddy sat with his legs dangling over the bow, waving to other boats they passed in the channel, especially those with women aboard. Suzie sat on the cabin roof, chatting with Moose as he knit. Aldrich stretched out in the cockpit as Donny steered the boat.

"How's the Walrus working out for you?" Donny called forward.

"OK," replied Eddy. "We've had a couple of fires with him. He keeps his cool. It's not the same as having you there, but… You know."

"I'm glad it's working out. I've known the Walrus for a lot of years. I figured he'd fit in OK." Donny was still technically under suspension until after the trial, but they had already replaced him as Captain at Lombard. He was glad the guys had gotten someone good, someone they could count on, but it still made him sick at heart.

"Is he as big as ever?" asked Aldrich.

"He's slimmed down a lot," answered Moose. "I'd say he's lost thirty or forty pounds."

"What'd he do, trim that moustache?" suggested Donny.

"Nah, that's still as big as ever," Eddy chuckled. "Hey, how about someone pass me a beer?"

"Sorry," Donny answered, "no drinking while we're underway. The cops tend to frown on it."

Eddy was undeterred. "So pour it in a coffee mug or something. It's thirsty work waving to all these girls."

"Can't do it, Eddy. Sorry, I'm on a short leash. You're going to have to hang on till we drop anchor."

"Jeez, you're already a criminal, Wedge. How much worse can it get?"

There was silence aboard except for the hum of the engine. They all stared at Eddy, except for Donny, who kept his gaze fixed on the channel ahead.

"Do you have any last words, Eddy?" Aldrich asked.

"What? What?" Eddy protested.

"Moose, do you mind taking out the trash?"

"My pleasure." The big man handed his knitting to Suzie, walked to the bow, picked Eddy up and held him over the side of the boat.

"No, Moose, it's me! We're buddies, remember? I don't swim so good."

"That's a shame, Eddy. Bye-bye." Moose gave a mighty heave. Eddy landed with a large splash and started thrashing in the water.

Donny grabbed a ring buoy and tossed it off the stern in Eddy's direction. Eddy clung to the buoy with one arm and gave them the finger with the other. Suzie glanced nervously behind them, but everyone else kept their eyes fixed resolutely ahead. "Don't the cops tend to frown on throwing people overboard too?" she asked.

"Not so much, really, unless the bodies become a hazard to

navigation," Donny quipped. It had been nice to forget about it all for a while, to pretend that life was normal and they could all go back to the way it was. But he'd also known it was only a matter of time until someone mentioned the elephant. The key was not to let it ruin the time they had together.

"But Eddy does have a point. You're sailing with an accused murderer." Donny switched to his best pirate voice. "Yer all marked as outlaws now, me hearties. It'll be the gallows for the lot o' ya, if they take us alive."

"Arr, it's Cap'n Wedge and his scurvy crew!" cried Moose, pumping his fist in the air.

"How silly of me to forget my eye patch," said Aldrich.

"Are we going to turn around?" Suzie asked, watching Eddy recede in the distance.

THAT WAS GREAT lasagna, Eddy." Aldrich wiped his mouth. "One of the things I miss most is the meals."

"Thanks, Cap. It's a pleasure to have a gentleman at the table for a change."

"What do you think he means by that?" Moose asked as he mopped the lasagna tray with a piece of garlic bread and shoved it, whole, into his mouth.

They were anchored just short of Port Severn and the last lock before entering Georgian Bay. The five of them were crowded around the table in the cabin. and the warm light of the long summer evening flooded in through the windows and hatches.

The rest of the day had passed pleasantly enough. They had fished Eddy out of the river and subsequently threatened to throw him back when he complained. They all knew this was more of a wake than a holiday, but having accepted the fact, they determined to enjoy it as best they could.

It wasn't often you got the chance to speak at your own wake, and Donny resolved to say a few words. He waited for a lull in the conversation.

"I'm really glad you could all come. This means a lot to me." For once no one tried interrupting with a wisecrack. "We've been through a lot together — even you, Q, in the few short months we've know each other. We put our lives in each other's hands every day and that creates something special. You guys are about as close to family as anything I've got.

"I'm gonna miss that. I'm gonna miss that more than anything." There were murmurs of denial around the table. "No, listen, that's the way it is. These are the cards we've been dealt and that's how we gotta play them.

"You're going to hear a lot of bad stuff about me during the trial. Some of it's pure bullshit, some of it is just me being in the wrong place at the wrong time. A lot of people, even guys on the job, are gonna think I'm guilty." There were more protests. "Thanks, I appreciate that, but let me say what I got to say.

"The important thing to me is that *you* know that I would not, that I could not kill an innocent person, and certainly not like that, not in a fire. Anyone who's been burned wouldn't wish that on their worst enemy. If other people talk crap about me, well, there's nothing I can do about that, as long as you all know I'm not guilty."

"Donny, there's not a person here who thinks you are." Eddy put his arm around Donny's shoulder. They all agreed.

"Thanks. There's one more thing. I'm sorry for the shame this is going to bring to the station. Maybe it already has. From the first day I walked into Lombard, all I wanted was to measure up to the guys in all those old pictures. I guess that's not going to happen. But don't let anyone run down our job or our station because of what's happened to me. Because who we are, what we do and what we stand for, that stuff is bigger than me or any one of us. It's important to remember that and to honour it."

Donny stood and raised his glass, looking at each of them around the table. "Here's to the phoenix and to the crews of Lombard past and present, the toughest firefighters who ever stood at the wet end of a hose."

They all stood, clinked glasses and drank the toast.

"And here's to Donald 'Wedge' Robertson," Aldrich proclaimed, "a man of courage, principle, and all the best the phoenix stands for."

They cheered and drank again. There was a lump in Donny's throat.

"Since you're all in such a good mood," he said, "I'll let you guys clean up." He climbed out of the cabin and went to sit at the bow.

IT WAS DARK WHEN Suzie joined him an hour later.

"Mind a little company?" She sat before Donny had a chance to respond.

"The party breaking up?" he asked.

"Can't you hear? They've got the dominoes going. I thought I'd get some fresh air." Donny had been absorbed in his own thoughts and blocked out the slap of the tiles on the table until now.

They watched the stars dance on the water's surface. A crescent moon quivered nervously and then shattered into a hundred pieces as a fish jumped in the darkness.

Donny spoke without turning to face her. "Listen, Q, I want to say how sorry I am you got hurt. It was all my fault."

"Stop, Donny. Stop right there. It was not your fault."

"Yes it was," he said quietly. "I didn't plan it, I didn't intend it, but this all happened as a result of my actions. If I hadn't been so drunk, you wouldn't have been there."

"Maybe I was supposed to be there, Donny. I'm not sure you would have made it out alive if I hadn't been there."

Donny harrumphed, "You and Aldrich! 'It's all part of God's plan,' eh?"

"I don't know about that," Suzie replied, "but I do think things happen for a reason."

"I would certainly like to know what that reason is, then, 'cause I'll be damned if I can figure it out."

"It was the same guy, wasn't it?"

"Who?" Donny asked, even though he knew what she meant.

"The same guy who blew us up, set the fire that killed that woman." She stated it as a fact.

"Yeah? How do you figure?"

"It only makes sense. It's all tied to the first Commissioners Street fire, isn't it?" Suzie asked.

"Did I say that? Maybe you should forget whatever I told you." He was tired of avoiding questions he couldn't answer and irritated that she could so easily deduce and accept something he had no way of proving. "It's really none of your business anyway."

"None of my business? In case you've forgotten, I've got some skin in this game too, you self-righteous bastard!" Suzie glared at him. "What exactly is your problem? One minute you're all warm and fuzzy, giving the big pep talk, and the next you're clammed up tighter than a drum."

"I meant every word I said in there," Donny protested.

"Including the part about us being the closest thing to family you've got?" She could just make out the muscles in his jaw working in the dim light that spilled from the hatches, but he said nothing. "Or is that only true when it's convenient?"

"Let me give you a little advice." Donny turned to face her. "There are some things on the job you don't want to let get close to you. The whole reason I'm in this mess to begin with is because I cared a little too much."

Suzie threw her hands in the air. "You're right. Why the hell should I care? I forgot: self-pity isn't a team sport. I hope you have a great time in prison while that guy walks scot-free."

"He's not walking scot-free. He's dead." Shit, Donny thought, he hadn't meant to say that.

"Dead? How do you know that?"

"Trust me. And no, I didn't kill him." Though Donny dearly wished he had.

"You met him, though, didn't you." It was a statement, not a question. Donny said nothing, but Suzie's intuition and the venom in Donny's voice told her it was true. She was silent for a few seconds. "There's got to be some way…"

His frustration boiled over. "Don't you think I've been over this a thousand times? There is no way! I don't know his name, or even who killed him. As for the rest of it, I have no proof, no evidence, nothing except for a wild story I can barely believe myself!"

The noise from the cabin stopped for a moment, then slowly resumed. Suzie got up without speaking and made her way to the cockpit. Why the hell couldn't she be like those buffoons in the cabin, slapping their dominoes and whistling through the graveyard? Why the hell did she want to scream, cry, shake him by the shoulders and rock him in her arms?

Donny lay back on the deck and looked up at the pinpoints of light sparkling in the inky mantle of darkness. He could navigate by those stars to any place he chose to go, across the sea or around the world. If only they could steer him now to some safe harbour.

TWENTY-NINE
Tobermory

THEY DOCKED AT A marina after they had passed through the final lock. With so many helping hands it wasn't long before the mast was raised and rigged. It had been a pleasant enough trip motoring up the canal, but Donny was happier now that *Red Bird* was a sailboat once again. He knew she was only fibreglass, wood and metal, but in his heart he felt that *Red Bird* was happier too.

Donny topped up the fuel and drinking water tanks, and pumped out the sewage tank. Eddy, Moose, and Suzie unloaded their gear. There were the ritual hugs, goodbyes and best wishes, followed by a period of awkwardness as they waited for Eddy's wife to pick them up again and take them home. When it became too uncomfortable Donny called Aldrich aboard. They motored out of the channel, raised the sails and headed out to the open water of Georgian Bay.

"Maybe I shouldn't have come," Suzie said sadly as she watched them sail away.

"What are you talking about?" said Eddy.

"I don't know, it's like I'm always irritating him somehow. Nothing I do ever seems right or good enough."

"He's got a lot on his mind, Q. It's not you," Moose explained.

"If he didn't like you, he wouldn't talk to you," Eddy added.

Moose draped a big arm around her shoulders and smiled down at her. "I'm glad you came, anyway."

Eddy gave him a curious look, and Moose blushed and pulled his arm back.

"I mean, we're all glad, right?" Moose pointed to the boat dwindling in the distance. "Donny wouldn't let us come unless we promised to pick you up, you know."

"Really?" Suzie asked in disbelief.

Moose nodded. "Wedge said you were just about the finest probie that ever came to Lombard. Didn't he, Eddy?"

"That he did," agreed Eddy.

"Goddammit! How come he never said anything? Why didn't he tell me?" Suzie twisted the handle of her bag.

"How long were you married?" asked Eddy.

THE PASSAGE TO Tobermory would take just over twenty-four hours. They made up for the lack of wind they had had on Lake Ontario with a steady westerly and six-foot waves. Medication helped Aldrich's seasickness, but he felt thick and his mouth was constantly dry. He slept most of the afternoon.

Towards sunset the wind decreased and the waves gradually diminished. Donny furled the sails and started the engine.

"I need a few hours of sleep," he told Aldrich. "The autopilot will hold our course and I've set the radar to alarm if anything comes within half a mile of us. I just need you to stand watch. Think you can do that?"

"It's been awhile since I did floor watch, but I think I can handle it," Aldrich said with a wink.

"Call me if the weather changes or you see anything you're not sure about; otherwise, wake me up in four hours. OK?"

It was a starless night and the world disappeared as the twilight faded. It was darker than anything Aldrich could remember. There was nothing but the boat and the faint circle of water illuminated by their navigation lights. His other senses sharpened. He heard, really heard the wash of the water along the hull and the wind in the rigging. He felt each subtle motion of the boat as she moved through the waves. No wonder sailors had imagined all manner of beasts and monsters lurking in the deep.

Aldrich felt something else he couldn't quite identify: a mixture of fear and excitement, and something more besides.

It was awe, he realized — awe at his own tiny, fragile mortality and awe at the vast, incomprehensible power of the world around him. They were a speck sailing over a primordial sea towards the unknown, their wake disappearing behind them into the nothingness.

"The earth was without form, and void; and darkness was upon the face of the deep. And the Spirit of God moved upon the face of the waters."

The words repeated in his mind. Aldrich understood the verse as never before and a sense of deep reverence filled him.

The hours passed without incident, and he let Donny sleep an extra hour before waking him.

"Now I understand why you love this," he said as Donny put the kettle on. "It gives a man… perspective."

Donny smiled at him sleepily. "That it does."

"I won't be buying a boat anytime soon, mind you, but I do understand. Thank you for bringing me along."

"I literally couldn't have done it without you," Donny shrugged. "Go ahead and turn in. I've got it from here."

Donny checked their course and position, then set the sails and cut the engine. *Red Bird* heeled and stiffened as her sails filled, bracing her against the waves. He poured himself a coffee, sat back in the cockpit, hummed a little Jimmy Buffett and let himself merge with the boat, the water and the darkness.

TOBERMORY WAS THE sort of village for which the word "quaint" had been coined. It was perched at the tip of the Bruce Peninsula, sandwiched between two national parks, surrounded by water on three sides, and blessed with two small craft harbours. Tobermory had some of the clearest water in the Great Lakes. That, together with the numerous wrecks, made it a mecca for scuba divers. Kayakers patrolled the shore line beneath the limestone cliffs, naturalists hiked the forest trails, and boaters explored the region's bays and islands.

Small Tub harbour was home to the dive and tour boat operators. The waterfront streets were lined with ice cream stands and craft shops selling made-in-China Mountie dolls and moccasins, alongside the works of local artisans. Donny rented a slip at a marina in the somewhat quieter Big Tub harbour.

Having spent over a week together in close quarters, Donny and Aldrich decided to go their separate ways on shore leave. Aldrich poked through the craft stores and side streets, looking for gifts for his grandchildren, while Donny patrolled the docks.

There were power boats from all around the Great Lakes. Some of the sailboats had come from even further afield, including one from Denmark and another from Australia. None of them, however, were attracting as much attention as a boat too large for any dock in Tobermory: the 155-foot *Sovereign Seas* lying at anchor in Shoal Bight.

She was breathtaking, from the lines of her hull to the spiderweb of her rigging. Varnished wood and polished brass gleamed in the sun. Like a vision from another age, she floated on the sparkling water of the bay, the perfect blend of form and function. She was, Donny thought, the most beautiful boat he had ever seen. And her owner, he reminded himself, wanted him dead.

He stopped in at a waterfront bar, ordered a beer and listened to the conversations around him. It sounded like those people who weren't interested in *Sovereign Seas* herself, were talking about the reason she was here. The bar was abuzz with the debate over the wind farm that was to stretch for several kilometres along the Lake Huron shore west of town.

"What do you think?" Donny asked the burly man tending bar.

"Anything that brings jobs and money to the area is all right with me," said the bartender as he wiped the counter. "Most of them that don't want it are cottagers, not folks from around here. They all want their green power but they don't want their view spoiled. You know, the sort that are all against mining but never stop to think where the steel and nickel for their hybrid SUVs come from."

"Vegetarians who wear leather shoes," Donny chuckled.

The bartender nodded. "You got that right. Toronto yuppies, most of them. Where are you from, buddy?"

"Toronto," Donny said, looking the man straight in the eye.

"Sorry, I didn't mean no offence."

"None taken. I'm not a vegetarian anyway," Donny said with a grin. "I'm a sailor. I'm more interested in the schooner." He pointed out the window across the harbour.

The bartender followed his gaze. "Ain't she a beauty? My great-grandfather skippered a boat like that out of Canso. Her tenders are proper dories too, but not like any working boat I ever saw. They're too pretty to be landing cod in. I think each one is worth more than my house. You should take a look. There was one tied up just the other side of the glass-bottom tour boat, if it's still there."

Donny finished his beer, thanked the bartender and walked around the harbour to the town dock. Sure enough, there behind the tour boat was a twenty-two-foot dory. The outside of its hull was painted the same deep blue as the schooner, and inside were the same flawlessly varnished wood and polished brass.

A flawlessly varnished folding stool sat on the dock beside the dory, and perched on it was a flawlessly varnished crewman. Or so it seemed to Donny. The man looked like he had stepped off the cover of *GQ*, with his square jaw, perfectly coiffed blond hair, expensive sunglasses and crisp white uniform.

Donny instantly hated him. Or envied him. Or maybe both, he couldn't quite decide. Putting on his best poker smile, he walked over to the man.

"Mind if I have a look?" he asked.

"Help yourself," the man said indulgently. "Just please don't touch anything."

"Of course," Donny agreed obediently. He took out his phone and snapped a few pictures of the dory. "Do you row her?"

"There's an electric motor under the rear seat. The batteries are under the midships bench. It's all run with that little joystick on the starboard side aft." The man in uniform pointed.

"You're with the schooner, I guess?" Donny asked.

The man nodded and indicated the *Sovereign Seas* logo on his shirt.

"Sorry, I guess you get a lot of that. It's just that my great-grandfather skippered a boat like that out of Canso," Donny said, hoping the bartender hadn't already used that line. "Me, I've just got an Island Packet 35."

"That's a nice boat," the man said, thawing a bit. "When I was starting out, I crewed on a delivery job for an Island Packet 45 from L.A. to Honolulu."

"They're a good boat in bad weather, that's for sure. What's it like sailing the schooner?"

"What's not to like?" the crewman said with a note of pride. "She's a classic with all the mod. cons.: sat nav, electronic sail handling, the best of both worlds really. We sail her with a crew of five most of the time. The owner only uses her a couple of weeks a year. We sail the boat to where she wants it — the Caribbean, the Med, South Pacific, whatever."

"Sounds pretty sweet. I envy you," Donny grinned ingratiatingly.

"Say, I don't suppose it would be possible to get a tour, would it?"

"Sorry: she is a private yacht, not a museum," the man said with a condescending smile.

"Of course, just thought I'd ask. Would it be OK if I took my dinghy over to get some pictures?"

"You're welcome to take pictures. We just ask that you keep a respectful distance. The morning would be your best bet. If you want to get a shot of us under sail, we'll be weighing anchor and heading out about five or six tomorrow evening."

The radio clipped to the man's belt squawked to life. "The plane just landed, Tony. We'll be back at the dock in ten minutes."

"Roger," Tony answered. He turned back to Donny "If you'll excuse me, I need to get ready."

"Sure. Listen, thanks for your time." Donny held out his hand. Tony shook it, then folded his stool and stowed it in the dory.

Donny walked across the street to the ice cream store, bought a cone and sat at one of the tables on the patio, where he had a clear view of the parking lot and the dock.

A panhandler sat on the park bench at the end of the parking lot. Donny watched him muttering to himself and shaking his cup at passersby. He was filthy, with a scraggly beard and a pair of taped-together women's sunglasses askew on his face. Though it was a warm summer day, the man was dressed in heavy winter clothes with a hood drawn tight over his head.

Donny thought about the separate catastrophes that had brought them both to this place at this time. Had the panhandler once had cherished dreams and ambitions? What unseen forces had shattered his life, ripped away his loved ones and replaced them with menacing shadows?

He was indistinguishable from the countless other homeless people Donny had seen, but something about the man was familiar — Donny wasn't sure what. Maybe he had seen him once on the streets of Toronto.

Maybe it was just that now, with his world in tatters too, Donny could see that the gulf between them was in fact only razor-thin.

A few minutes later a limousine pulled into the lot. The driver got out and opened the door. A slim lady wearing a cream-coloured blouse and a pale apricot suit emerged. She had shoulder-length salt-and-pepper hair. It was hard to make out her features from this distance, but it was unmistakably Catherine Rockingham. Donny had seen enough pictures to be sure of that.

Donny's heart was pounding. He could rush across the street and tackle her, smash her head into the pavement. He could throw himself at her feet and beg for his life. He could scream and cry out for justice.

He did none of those things. Instead he sat and watched her walk down the dock, as ice cream dripped onto his shorts. A younger man followed behind her, carrying a small bag and a briefcase. She got into the dory without speaking and sat in the front seat. The younger man sat behind her.

The man in the white uniform undid the lines and the dory slid silently away from the dock.

"I'M SORRY, WHAT DID you say?" Donny asked. He and Aldrich were having supper at the marina restaurant. Donny was distracted and there had been little conversation. Aldrich assumed Donny was brooding about his future. He was right, though not in the way Aldrich imagined.

"You plan on staying here two more days, right?" Aldrich asked again.

"Uh, yes. Why?"

The plan, as Donny had explained it to Aldrich, was to lay over a couple more days in Tobermory, then spend the next two weeks cruising the North Channel to Killarney and then back south through the Thirty Thousand Islands. They would finish in Midland, where Donny would list the boat for sale with the broker.

"The couple I was telling you about, the ones I met from Aberdeen? They invited me to go hiking and birding with them tomorrow. I'll be gone most of the day, if that's all right," Aldrich replied. He and Donny would have plenty of time together during the coming weeks, and given Donny's present mood, Aldrich was just as happy to leave him alone to make whatever peace he could with his fate.

"Sure, that would be fine," Donny smiled. "I was just going to work on the boat anyway, change the engine oil, that sort of thing."

In truth, one of the things Donny had been thinking about was how to get rid of Aldrich. He had considered inventing some sort of engine or rigging problem and sending Aldrich off to find parts. This was better. Donny and *Red Bird* would simply be gone by the time Aldrich returned.

He hated the idea of leaving the old man like that without saying goodbye. Aldrich had opened up his home and his heart, and he and the rest of the Lombard crew had stood by Donny when so few others could or would.

Now Donny would slink away like a thief in the night. It wasn't right, but it had to be done.

THIRTY
Mayday

THE NEXT MORNING, after Aldrich left, Donny wrote two letters. The first one he mailed. It was a set of instructions to his lawyer. The second letter he left in the marina office together with Aldrich's clothes and other belongings.

A schooner like *Sovereign Seas* would be twice as fast as *Red Bird*. That meant Donny needed to leave by midafternoon to get into position. It also meant he had most of the morning to reflect on the sheer folly of his plan.

He was getting ready to cast off when he noticed the panhandler he had seen the day before, walking down the dock towards him. The heavy winter clothes were gone, as was the shambling posture. The man carried a gym bag and walked with purpose and confidence.

"Hello, Donny," he smiled as he tossed the broken sunglasses into a trash can.

Donny froze. That voice, those green eyes — it couldn't be!

Donny looked around for help, but it was midafternoon on a weekday; there was no one else on the docks, and there was nowhere to go except to dive into the water. And then what? Fear and fury competed for control of his mind.

"Mind if I come aboard?" the man asked. He took hold of one of the shrouds and stepped onto the boat amidships. Donny backed away, brandishing a boathook.

"I'm not here to hurt you, Donny. I will if you force me to, but that is not my intention."

"Get off my boat!" Donny growled.

"This is nice, very nice," the Spark said with an appreciative look around *Red Bird*. The green eyes came to rest on Donny.

"Get off my god-damned boat, you piece of shit!" Donny said, his voice rising.

The Spark pulled a silenced gun from his bag. A bullet hissed into the water beside Donny. "If I wanted to kill you, you'd be dead already," he sighed. "My name, my real name, is Derek Spangler. Not many people know that. I give it to you as a sign of trust. Now, we can go through round two, but do you really think it would work out any different than the first time? So why don't you at least hear me out before you do something stupid?"

Spangler walked to the cockpit and stepped down. Donny edged warily away from him, still holding the boathook. "What the hell do you want?"

"The same thing you do," Spangler waved his hand toward where *Sovereign Seas* lay at anchor, "to get at Catherine Rockingham. As the saying goes, 'the enemy of my enemy is my friend.'" Spangler set his bag down and sat.

"Friend?" Donny exclaimed. "After what you did?"

"The point is we have a common purpose. I'm not here for your understanding or forgiveness. I'm here to solve a problem, the same problem you have: Catherine Rockingham."

Donny was confused. "But she sent you to kill me."

"Yes, she did. And I failed. Twice. Catherine Rockingham is not the sort of person who tolerates failure. As for what happened between us, that was business. It's a business I enjoy, but I have nothing personal against you, Donny. You can choose to accept that or not, I don't care," Spangler shrugged.

"What are you going to do?"

Spangler sat forward. "The question is, what are *you* going to do? I assume you're planning some kind of intercept out on the lake. And then what?"

"I… I'm not sure," Donny confessed. "I was going to play it by ear."

"Oh, that's brilliant! That will catch them totally off guard," Spangler laughed. He set his gun down beside him. "Catherine Rockingham isn't the sort who takes prisoners, just in case you were planning to plead for mercy."

Donny flushed and tried to reclaim some of his dignity. "Maybe I'll kill her."

"You? No, I don't think so. But I could." The façade of casual indifference disappeared. "Any fool can kill someone if they're willing to sacrifice themselves. The tricky part is getting away and not leaving a trail. I've been here for days looking for a way to do that. Then you show up. I think you're my best shot for getting aboard that boat."

"What makes you think I'd do anything to help you, you murdering son of a bitch?" Donny's loathing dripped from every word.

"Because with Catherine Rockingham around, neither of us has a future. You get me on that boat and I'll look after it." Spangler picked up his gun again and rested it on his lap. "We can help each other, Donny. But one way or another I'm taking your boat. If you want to live, then cast off and you can tell me about your plan."

DONNY STEERED SOUTHWEST along a straight-line course between Tobermory and Bay City, Michigan. The Sovereign Petroleum website had said Catherine Rockingham was due for another press conference there the next afternoon, and Donny was betting *Sovereign Seas* would follow a direct course.

The day was warm and the wind fresh. From a distance they looked like two friends on holiday, not would-be assassins. Spangler sat on the windward rail with his feet dangling.

"An interesting idea," Spangler nodded. "It's not something I would have come up with, but I like it. We just have to make them believe it's real. But that's the key to any trick, isn't it?"

The Zippo appeared and disappeared in his hands. His gestures were smooth and effortless. The sight of the lighter filled Donny with revulsion, but he was spellbound nonetheless.

"Planning a second career as a magician at children's parties?" Donny asked, trying to cover his fascination with sarcasm.

"I saw a magic show when I was eleven years old. It was the most amazing thing I had ever witnessed." It was the first time Spangler had ever talked about himself, and it shocked Donny into silence.

"We all knew it was tricks, but we wanted to believe. He simply led us there, with his smooth patter and his magic wand. That was the real magic: the way he drew the audience in and made them believe. I was hooked right then and there. I sent away for a magic kit I saw advertised in a comic book.

"My father didn't like it. It was the Devil's work, he said. God was the only one who could perform miracles. He was a real Bible thumper, you see. When he wasn't drinking, that is. He tried to beat the Devil out of me. He liked to do that drunk or sober. But the funny thing was, the more he beat me, the more I practised and the better I got."

Spangler glanced over at Donny. "You're thinking, 'Ah, that explains it. That's what went wrong with him.' But that's not the point. You see, the old man taught me about the power of fear, pain and desire. I wanted to learn magic more than I was afraid of the beatings. The first step is learning to conquer your own fear. Then fear and pain become powerful tools.

"This was his," Spangler said, holding up the lighter without looking at Donny. "It was the last thing he saw on this earth.

"Magic taught me a very important lesson." He cocked his wrist and the lighter vanished. "It takes a lot of practice and dexterity, but that's not enough."

He turned around to face Donny at the helm. "The real key is that people want to believe. Fear, desire and the willingness to believe: those are the most powerful tools there are, Donny. Learn to use them and you can do anything. That's the first lesson priests, rabbis and every other sort of con man learn."

A large echo showed on the radar, fourteen miles to stern, following the same course and gaining on them at six and half knots. Donny altered his course fifteen degrees to south. They couldn't be too obvious, and the adjustment would put *Sovereign Seas* about four miles away as she passed.

"Coming back from the dead is a pretty good trick." Donny tried to sound nonchalant.

Spangler's eyes narrowed. "How'd you hear about that?"

"The same way I found out about Catherine Rockingham. How I heard doesn't really matter." The revelation seemed to have surprised Spangler, and Donny enjoyed that small victory.

Spangler got up and went below. He came back with two beers.

"Someone's dead," Spangler replied, handing one of the beers to Donny. "She sent another contractor after me, but he was careless. I cut off his head and hands and left the body in my hotel room. Like I said, you just have to lead them there. Most people will arrange the puzzle pieces to make the picture they want to see." He said it as if he were explaining a well-played bridge hand.

"How do you live with yourself?" Donny asked.

"What, are you going to give me some Boy Scout lecture on morality?" Spangler snorted.

"Sounds like it's a little too late for that."

"The Aztecs and Incas made human sacrifices to their gods. The Christian invaders thought that was barbaric and slaughtered them by the thousands." Spangler fixed the full intensity of those green eyes on Donny. "Who were the real barbarians, Donny? Ethics? Morality? They're nothing more than a myth, something created for convenience and manipulated as the situation requires. And so torture becomes 'enhanced interrogation.' The list goes on and on. You see me as a psychopath, but I'm just a realist. At least I'm honest — grant me that much."

Donny didn't feel like granting him anything. And he didn't want to think about it, either. They sailed on in silence.

TWO HOURS LATER the radar echo was almost abeam. Donny did a final gut check, took a deep breath and put his plan into action.

He doused the sails and then pulled the inflatable dinghy they had been towing alongside. He and Spangler tied a rope underneath the dinghy from one pontoon to the other. Donny tossed in the "ditch bag" he had prepared. It contained some dried food, water bottles, flares and other emergency supplies.

A last look at the radar showed *Sovereign Seas* dead even with them, just over four miles away. Donny swept his binoculars along the starboard horizon. A bank of thunderheads lined the southwest. To the northwest, a large sailboat was silhouetted against the low sun. It was impossible to tell for sure if it was *Sovereign Seas*, but any normal-sized sailboat would have been little more than a speck.

"It's them. You better get ready," Donny told Spangler. "Thunderstorms are moving in, too."

"A little drama just makes the trick better," said Spangler as they climbed down into the cabin.

Donny opened the access hatch to the engine compartment. There were two large hoses that drained water from the scuppers in the cockpit out through the bottom of the boat. Donny closed the valves on the through-hull fittings and disconnected the hoses. He did the same with the engine cooling water intake.

Donny pulled his head out of the engine compartment and wiped his hands. Spangler was changing into a wetsuit. Donny sat at the nav station and took hold of the microphone for the VHF radio. His mouth was dry and his heart was pounding. He set the mic down and got a drink of water. He steadied himself, checked the GPS and picked up the mic again.

"Mayday, Mayday, Mayday. This is *Red Bird*, *Red Bird*, *Red Bird*, Mayday. My position is 44 degrees 48 minutes north, 82 degrees 6 minutes west, approximately thirty miles southwest of Tobermory. *Red Bird* is a thirty-five-foot sailboat with a beige hull and white deck. I've collided with a submerged object, and am taking on water. I'm alone on board and preparing to abandon ship in a yellow inflatable dinghy. Over."

"*Red Bird, Red Bird, Red Bird,* this is Sarnia Coast Guard Radio, Sarnia Coast Guard Radio," came the reply. "We have your position, thirty-five-foot sailboat, sinking with one soul on board. Have you collided with another vessel? Over."

"Negative. I think it was a shipping container. I didn't get a good look at it. There was almost nothing showing above the water. I have a huge tear in the hull. The water is pouring in and the bilge pump can't keep up. I need to launch the dinghy and abandon ship. Over."

"Roger, *Red Bird*. Good luck. Help is on the way. Attention all stations, attention all stations, this is Sarnia Coast Guard Radio. Mayday *Red Bird*. All vessels in the vicinity and able to render assistance, position is as follows…"

CATHERINE ROCKINGHAM was enjoying the late evening sun and the feel of the wind on her face. The press conference had gone exceedingly well. The local and federal politicians had been suitably deferential while vying for their share of the limelight. The protesters had been politely restrained and kept far enough away so that they weren't a distraction. The first news stories were already posted online. They were for the most part quite complimentary, lauding her and Sovereign Petroleum for their investment in green power research and development. "Visionary" was how one reporter had described the project.

Her self-satisfied smile faded as she heard Brendan's footsteps approaching from behind.

"I thought I told you I didn't want to be disturbed," she said crossly, without bothering to look at him.

"I'm sorry, ma'am, but the skipper reports he's just picked up a Mayday from a sailboat four miles southeast of us. The boat's name is *Red Bird*. I took the liberty of tracing the registration. It belongs to Donald Robertson. I thought you would want to know."

"Really? Now that *is* interesting. What do you suppose he's playing at?" She was talking more to herself than to Brendan.

"I'm not sure, ma'am. Robertson claims he's sinking. The skipper would like to know if he should respond."

Catherine closed the book she had been reading and put it down. She looked out over the port rail, searching for a clue on the featureless horizon. How had he found her? It was public knowledge that she would be at the two press conferences; that wasn't the issue. How had he discovered the connection between them? The mouse had presented himself to the cat. How could she refuse?

Brendan stood at the rail, waiting. Catherine turned to him. "Tell the skipper to plot an intercept course. Tell him to advise the Coast Guard that we're responding. He's to inform them when we have Robertson's boat in sight, so that they'll call off the search. After that I think we're going to develop communication difficulties. Is that understood?"

"I'll inform the skipper right away." Brendan turned to go but she stopped him with a gesture.

"I'm going below. Bring him to me when you get him aboard. But be careful. You were supposed to kill him, Brendan, and you left him wounded. There's nothing more dangerous than a wounded animal."

RED BIRD'S RADIO CRACKLED to life. "Sarnia Coast Guard Radio, Sarnia Coast Guard Radio, this is *Sovereign Seas, Sovereign Seas, Sovereign Seas*. We are experiencing radio difficulty. Do you read? Over."

"*Sovereign Seas*, this is Sarnia Coast Guard Radio. You're slightly broken up, but we are able to read you. Are you able to offer assistance? Over."

"That's affirmative. *Sovereign Seas* is a one–hundred-fifty-five-foot schooner. We are underway to the last known position of Mayday *Red Bird*. Our ETA is twenty minutes…"

The message died as *Red Bird*'s radio shattered into shards of plastic and electronic components. Spangler tucked his gun and several clips of ammunition into a waterproof bag.

"That's enough. Do it," Spangler ordered.

Donny opened the valves on the through-hulls, and water gushed into the engine compartment with surprising force. He looked around the cabin one last time. He thought of the years he had put into refitting the boat and all the miles they had logged together. There were almost six hundred feet of water under her keel. No one would ever know that he had deliberately sent *Red Bird* to her watery grave — no one but him and Spangler. There was an aching sickness in Donny's chest.

He climbed out to the cockpit and into the dinghy. Spangler was already waiting there, dressed in his wetsuit, the waterproof bag slung over his shoulder.

Red Bird was settling by the stern as the engine compartment flooded. Four tons of lead in her keel were pulling her to the bottom. The sun crouched on the horizon, painting the approaching bank of thunderheads with pumpkin hues. Hopefully the storm would miss them or they would be picked up before it hit. A six-foot dinghy would be an uncomfortable place to ride out a thunderstorm.

He was about to undo the lines that held the dinghy to the sinking boat when he suddenly remembered Aldrich's Bible. It was still in the V berth.

"I forgot something. I'll be right back," he told Spangler.

Floating debris filled the cabin. The water was already hip deep and cold. The bow was pitched up, though, and the V berth was still dry. He found the Bible on the shelf where he had left it and made his way back through the cabin. A box of ziplock bags floated by. Donny took one, shook off as much water as he could and sealed the Bible inside.

The boat was sinking more quickly now, and waves were spilling over the transom. Donny threw himself into the little yellow rubber boat. Spangler scowled at the Bible. They undid the lines that held them alongside and drifted away.

Donny looked away, but he could hear the noises coming from the boat — groaning and hissing as water pressure competed with the air trapped in various compartments; the rattle of things shifting as the boat tipped up, reaching into the airy realm for a rescue that would never come. He looked back just in time to see *Red Bird*'s bow rail slip beneath the waves.

It was an impressive sunset. The thunderheads had moved in closer; towering pillars in every shade of orange, red and purple surrounded them. There was a breathless calm broken by the ominous rumble of what was to come. Donny shivered in his cold, wet clothes, staring at the angry clouds that billowed overhead. He had scuttled his own boat and betrayed the gods of wind and water. They seemed very unhappy. Soon they would unleash their fury on him.

Donny dug into the ditch bag for the flare gun, loaded it, and sent a ball of red fire arcing into the crimson sky. He counted to sixty and then fired another. He heard the distant bellow of a ship's horn answer. It was faint but distinct above the rumble of thunder.

The storm hit when the schooner was still half a mile away. The wind slammed the dinghy like a sledgehammer, and raindrops the size of grapes pelted them. Spangler slipped over the side as lightning streaked across the sky and stabbed into the water. Good, maybe he'll fry if it strikes close enough, Donny thought to himself. The lake churned and the dinghy bucked like a bronco. Spangler rode it like a cowboy in an upside-down rodeo. He clung to the rope they had slung underneath, his snorkel tucked tight against the dinghy's pontoon and almost invisible.

Sovereign Seas circled at a hundred yards to approach Donny upwind. They had furled her sails in preparation for the storm and were making their way with the ship's powerful diesel engine.

Three men in foul weather gear were standing on deck. One of them made ready with a heaving line as they approached. He made a perfect throw, compensating just enough for the wind. Donny seized the line as the man on deck made his end fast to a cleat.

Donny pulled the dinghy alongside. He noticed one of the men looked like the man he had seen getting out of the limousine with Catherine Rockingham.

"Thank you," Donny said, repeating the line he had rehearsed. "Am I ever glad to see you guys! My name is Paul Halls."

"Pleased to meet you, Captain Robertson," Brendan replied. He gestured to the sailors. One lowered a rope ladder, the other trained an assault rifle on Donny. It was the sailor Donny had talked to on the dock yesterday. He looked less pleased to see Donny now. "Tie off the dinghy, bring your bag and come aboard. Keep your hands in view at all times or Tony here will put a hole in your chest."

THIRTY-ONE
Sovereign Seas

"**SURVIVAL SUPPLIES, FLARES,** and a Bible," said Brendan, indicating the contents of Donny's ditch bag spread out on a table.

"Not even so much as a knife?" Catherine asked. Brendan shook his head.

"You're rather woefully underprepared if you've come as an assassin, Captain Robertson." Catherine smiled mockingly at him. "Or perhaps, armed with your Bible, you've come to induce me to some sort of repentance? I didn't realize you were religious. We missed that on your profile somehow."

Donny stood shivering in his wet clothes with his hands tied. Tony stood by the door, his rifle trained on Donny's back. His plan was a shambles. He could only stare sullenly at Catherine. But no matter what, he told himself, he would not whimper, he would not beg.

"The Bible belongs to a friend. It's a family heirloom. I didn't want to lose it," Donny mumbled.

Catherine was seated at a Queen Anne desk in the corner across from him. She was smaller and older-looking than he had expected, but imposing nonetheless. She was the sort of person who radiated authority, not through any conscious effort but through her own confidence in who and what she was.

She was casually dressed in slacks and a plain white blouse. She had piercing ice-blue eyes under the shoulder-length salt-and-pepper hair. There were wrinkles around her eyes and mouth, but rather than detracting from what must once have been a flawless complexion, they gave her an air of regal grace and authority. She was utterly at ease.

Donny had expected her to look hard and cruel. She didn't. Under any other circumstances he would have described her as charming.

She followed his gaze around the room. The salon was panelled with mahogany and teak, with accents of rosewood, cherry and exotic woods Donny didn't recognize. Brass lamps with raw silk shades suffused the room with warm light. To Donny's left were a loveseat and two wingback chairs, upholstered in burgundy leather. Between them was the inlaid coffee table that held the contents of Donny's ditch bag. A large painting of a sea battle hung over the loveseat, and a pair of crossed naval sabres adorned the opposite wall.

"Lovely, isn't it?" she smiled at Donny. "Pity I don't get to spend more time here. Thank you, Tony, you can leave. Untie Captain Robertson's hands, Brendan; he won't harm anyone."

"Are you so sure?" Donny challenged her.

"Oh yes, quite sure," she said matter-of-factly. "A sculptor can look at a block of marble and see the shape that lies within. Any master craftsman intuitively senses the potential of his tools and materials. It's my business to know people, and I am very good at my business. You're simply not a killer."

Brendan untied Donny's hands and stepped back against the door Tony had just left through. The ship rolled in the storm, and thunder reverberated through the hull. Donny wondered how much of the noise was the work of someone who *was* a killer, a remorseless predator whom Donny had made his ally.

Catherine moved to one of the wingback chairs and indicated the loveseat across from her. "Please, sit down."

"What are you going to do with me?" Donny asked, not moving.

"That's a good question. To be honest, I haven't decided. We've yet to inform the Coast Guard whether we found you alive or dead."

A bottle of wine and two glasses rested on the small table beside her. "Some wine? It's really an excellent vintage."

Donny stared at her stonily. "You threaten to kill me and then offer me a drink?"

"It's no reason not to enjoy a glass of good wine," she taunted. "I should think that someone in your profession, who faces death on a regular basis, would learn to live for the moment."

She poured a glass for herself and held it to her nose, savouring the rich bouquet. "This wine is like you in some ways: unorthodox, complex but unpretentious. It's from an obscure little vineyard in the Barossa Valley called God's Hill. So many wineries these days focus on cookie-cutter consistency. They let the grapes speak for themselves at God's Hill. The results are quite remarkable." She poured a second glass and held it out to him.

"Do you actually think I'm going to drink with the woman responsible for the death of my best friend?" Donny folded his arms across his chest.

"Can we dispense with the petulant sulking? I know you hate me and I don't care. It's irrelevant. Now if you prefer, I'll have you thrown overboard and we'll inform the Coast Guard that we found your dinghy empty. You might last an hour or two, but you won't survive the night in that water. You decide."

Donny hesitated for a moment, then moved to the loveseat and took the glass. She was right: the wine was outstanding. And she was gracious enough to ignore this small victory.

"Now, I need to know how you found out about me. The truth, please — I'll know instantly if you lie." Donny had heard that warning before, and he unconsciously reached for his nose.

"And I suppose you'll do the same for me?"

"Of course," Catherine answered without hesitation. "What reason would I have to lie when I hold your life in my hands?"

She smiled and took a sip of wine. "Who told you?"

Donny took a deep breath. "I don't know. I got a phone call when I was in the hospital. There was no caller ID, nothing, just a voice. But he knew everything. I'm not even sure it was a man — the voice sounded filtered."

"Really? How did he know all these things?"

Donny shook his head. "I asked that too. He just said it was his business to know things."

"Aha, that's interesting." Catherine crossed her legs and took another sip of wine. "So you found out about the press conferences, I suppose?"

"From the Internet," Donny nodded.

"And you scuttled your own boat, just for a chance to… what, confront me?" There was a sneer in her smile.

"I didn't think you'd give me an appointment if I phoned," Donny sneered back. "Maybe I just needed to meet you, to see what kind of person does this sort of thing."

Catherine laughed. "And am I the monster you imagined?"

"Worse, maybe, because you look so normal." Donny watched as she refilled their glasses. "Why? Why did you do it?"

"You were sticking your nose in where it didn't belong. However, I assume you're referring to the beginning of this whole affair." Donny nodded and Catherine settled back in her chair.

"First of all," she said, "the death of your colleague was a regrettable accident. It served no useful purpose."

"Your compassion is underwhelming," Donny said derisively. His exhaustion and the wine had begun to work on him. He tilted his glass back.

"If you expect me to collapse in a fit of guilt, I'm afraid you're going to be disappointed," she countered. "Now, as to Youssef Aziz, I gather you know he was working on the hydrogen storage issue?"

Donny acknowledged this was so and Catherine continued. "I offered to buy the patent on his work. It was a very generous offer, I might add. Aziz refused."

"You killed two men simply because one of them wouldn't sell you his idea?" It was unbelievable.

"Yes," she said with pitiless ferocity. She leaned towards Donny, her eyes hard and unblinking. "Because a breakthrough in one area will catalyze breakthroughs in other areas. Aziz's work could spur a revolution in the green energy industry, even more wide reaching than the communications revolution."

"And the problem with that is?" Donny asked, feeling confused. "What about all these windmills you're building?"

She looked at him as if she were being forced to explain things to a small child. "The wind generators are a trifle. They're a drop in the bucket compared to the total energy demand. The problem is not green energy: the problem is who controls it and how quickly things change. It needs to be carefully managed. Revolutions tend to be very messy. A lot of people get hurt, and not just those on top."

"So you're saving us from ourselves? How noble of you."

"Not at all, so save your sarcasm. That technology is worth a fortune in both money and opportunities. We will license it, at the right time and for the right price. But that time is still many years away. In the meantime, do you have any idea how much oil is still in the ground?"

Donny shook his head.

"About twelve hundred billion barrels," she informed him. "Close to a hundred and fifty trillion dollars' worth. And that's just the proven reserves. Do you think anyone is going to be allowed to mess with that kind of wealth? If I hadn't got to Youssef Aziz, someone else would have. I was merely the first one there."

"So this is all just about money and oil?"

"Of course. What do you think the two wars in Iraq were about? It's really a bit of a pity. Iraq used to be a rather nice country, aside from the government. I had a villa just outside of Basra, with gardens full of jasmine and roses." Catherine smiled wistfully. "But wars have been fought over much less."

Catherine was topping up their glasses when a shot sounded outside the door and a fountain of red mist erupted from Brendan's forehead. Catherine dropped the bottle and stared wide-eyed as Spangler shouldered the door open, pushing Brendan's body aside. His wetsuit glistened with drops of water and blood.

"Sorry to break up the party, but it's time to go, Catherine."

She looked from Donny to Spangler and back again. "You are full of surprises, Captain Robertson." She tried to regain some of her composure, but the fear in her voice was unmistakable.

"Let's go! Up on deck." Spangler gestured with his gun. Catherine and Donny got up and moved towards the door. Spangler turned and shot Donny in the leg. "Wait here, will you? I have something special planned for you."

Donny fell to the floor, groaning and clutching his thigh.

THE STORM WAS DYING down when they reached the deck, though the ship was still rolling in the waves that had been whipped up. Two bodies shifted lifelessly on the deck, and Catherine assumed there were others spread throughout the ship. Spangler held a lifejacket out to her.

"Put it on," he said simply.

"You're the contractor Brendan hired?" Catherine asked as she donned the lifejacket. "I'm sure we could come to some arrangement," she said hopefully.

"It's a little late for that. You shouldn't have tried to kill me. Now move to the rail."

Catherine stood her ground.

"I would prefer it if they found your body and assumed the ship sank in the storm," Spangler resumed. "And I would think the sleepy cold of hypothermia would be preferable to the slow, painful death of being gut shot, but it's your choice." He fired a shot into the deck and Catherine jumped. "That was your only warning. Now move."

Catherine moved to the side of the ship and climbed over the side. She clung, feet braced and hands locked on the rail. Her eyes pleaded with him. Spangler brought the butt of his gun down hard on the back of her hand. Catherine screamed and dropped into the cold black water.

HIS LEG WAS BLEEDING, but the blood wasn't spurting. The bullet hadn't hit an artery and seemed to have missed the bone as well. It hurt like hell, but he wasn't crippled. And he couldn't lie there waiting for Spangler to return.

Donny pulled himself painfully to his feet and looked around. He scooped up the flare gun and shoved several of its shotgun-sized shells into his pocket. He looked at Aldrich's Bible. Belief be damned, he needed all the help he could get. He shoved it into his other pocket. As he limped towards the door, his eye caught the sabres hanging on the wall. He limped over, took one of the sabres down from the wall and swung it. It left a deep gash in Catherine's chair. He thought ruefully of the old adage "never bring a knife to a gunfight," but any weapon was better than none at all.

Donny made his way to the door, turned a corner and headed aft, away from the direction he had seen Spangler go. He tried a couple of the doors he passed, but they dead-ended in cabins. He needed to get up on deck; then maybe he could get to his dinghy and drift away with the storm.

The corridor ended in a hatch and a ladder that led down, not up.

"God damn it!!" he heard Spangler's voice from the salon. Donny had no choice. He tried to ignore the pain in his leg as he hobbled down the ladder.

The blood trail was obvious, and Spangler raced to follow. A bullet slammed into wall just over Donny's head as he ducked down the ladder. There was a short corridor at the bottom and only one door.

Judging by the noise, it led to the engine room. There were a couple of drums of engine oil secured to the wall of the corridor, but they wouldn't provide much cover. Donny opened the door.

The engine room was noisy, hot and dark. Donny limped to the other end and took what cover he could behind the big marine diesel engine. He raised the flare gun and fired when he saw Spangler's silhouette in the doorway. Flare guns are not designed for accuracy, though, and the ball of red fire bounced off the door frame and lay fizzling on the floor.

Spangler emptied his clip in a deafening barrage, and the dark compartment was strobe-lit with muzzle flashes. Donny crouched as bullets ricocheted around the machinery. In the silence that followed, he could hear the sound of running water and smell diesel fuel. He scrambled to reload the flare gun as Spangler reached into his bag for a fresh clip.

Donny tried to correct his aim, but the flare bounced uselessly off the wall again. This time a pool of flame sputtered to life as the flare hit the floor. One of Spangler's bullets must have hit a fuel line.

Spangler peered cautiously around the door frame, trying to draw a bead in the flickering light and compensate for the ship's rolling. He smiled as he saw the fire growing quickly on the engine room floor. There was a rapid rise in heat and the taste of oily smoke.

"Fine, have it your way, Donny. I was going to copy your plan, open the sea cocks and let her sink. But I like this better." Spangler slammed the engine room door shut, dogged the latch and secured the handle with his belt.

Starved of fuel, the engine shuddered to a halt. Donny backed away, coughing in the greasy smoke. But the fire also gave him light to see. There was an extinguisher hanging on the wall beside him, but it was too late for that now — flames were already licking across the ceiling. But there, beyond the extinguisher, was another ladder leading up. Of course: the engine room would have to have a secondary, emergency exit.

Donny seized the courage of a man who had abandoned all hope. He climbed the ladder, the throbbing in his leg a counterpoint to the familiar pain of burning heat.

The emergency hatch opened into a dimly-lit storeroom. Donny's first instinct was to close the hatch and contain the fire. Screw it, he thought, let it burn.

He looked around. There were spools of rope, spare sails neatly folded, cans of varnish and solvent, all the things needed to keep a classic boat like *Sovereign Seas* going. He used the sabre to cut a long strip from one of the sails, wrapped it around his leg several times and tied it tight. He had lost a lot of blood and he needed to control that. Then he opened two of the solvent cans and tipped them onto the floor.

Yes, let it all burn.

The storeroom door led to a service corridor that seemed to run the length of the ship. The fire flared in the storeroom behind him as Donny made his way towards the bow.

He poked his head out of the forward companionway. Spangler was crouched on the deck, undoing the straps that secured one of the dories, preparing it for launch. He had set his gun down beside him, on top of his ammo bag, while he worked on the dory. Donny had dropped the flare gun in the engine room, but he still had the sabre and the element of surprise. Spangler would not expect him to come from that direction, if he expected him at all.

Donny crept along the opposite side of the deck. The sound of the wind and waves was enough to muffle his progress. He moved to the main mast when he was directly behind Spangler. Donny gathered himself, flexing his fingers on the sabre's hilt. He timed the rolling of the ship, and then, with every ounce of the remaining strength in his good leg, he launched himself.

Spangler saw him at the last moment. He whirled, reaching for the gun. Donny slashed, but the blow missed Spangler's neck and caught him just below the elbow, cutting him to the bone. Spangler cried out in pain as Donny crashed into the side of the dory.

The gun clattered across the deck to the rear of the ship. Spangler scrambled after it and Donny crawled back towards the mast for cover. Spangler fired, but he was forced to use his left hand and his aim was off.

"You're a hard man to kill, Donny, I'll give you that. But it's over now." Spangler was breathing hard, but his tone was matter-of-fact.

"Screw you!"

"Come on now, Donny, there's no place left to run. Come out and I'll make it quick. Or you can go over the side like Catherine if you like. Your choice, OK?"

He's right, Donny thought: there's no place left to run. He'd never make it back to the forward companionway, and smoke was rising from the aft companionway. The fire was spreading rapidly below decks.

"If I have to come after you, Donny, I'll make you wish you had never been born."

Donny laid his head back against the mast. The clouds were parting and the stars peered coldly down through the rigging.

The rigging! He had one chance.

"You want me, asshole? Come and get me." Donny poked his head around the mast. Spangler took two quick steps towards him and fired. Donny heard the bullet whiz by his ear.

"What's the matter, tough guy? That little scratch bothering you?" Donny peeked around the mast again, checking Spangler's position. Just a few more feet. Splinters erupted from the mast in front of Donny's face, and he ducked back.

Donny listened for the sound of Spangler's steps and then rolled around the mast, slashing upwards with all his might.

Spangler squeezed off three shots before he realized what was happening. A bullet creased Donny's shoulder and sent him sprawling, but it was too late. One of the lines Donny had managed to cut was the topping lift. The massive weight of the boom and the four thousand square feet of sail it carried crashed onto Spangler, crushing his legs to the deck. He kept firing wildly as Donny rolled back behind the mast, until there was only the clicking of an empty chamber.

Donny peered around the mast. Spangler had discarded the useless gun; he was groaning, trying to shift the boom off his legs, but it was impossible. Donny put down the sabre, picked up the empty gun and limped over to where Spangler had left his ammo bag beside the dory. Spangler glared at him, hatred burning in his eyes.

Donny inserted a fresh clip, cocked the gun and stared down at Spangler.

"Congratulations, you win," Spangler hissed through the pain.

The gun trembled in Donny's hand. He tried to will himself to pull the trigger, then looked away and lowered the gun.

"No," Donny said grimly, "you lose."

Spangler followed Donny's eyes to the flames beginning to lick out of the companionway.

"You can't do that! No!" Spangler cried, as Donny threw the gun overboard.

The ship's lights flickered and went out. The fire must have reached the main electrical panel. There would be no power for the davit to launch the heavy dory now. Donny limped to the wooden boat and removed the box labelled "Emergency."

"You can't leave me here like this, Donny!"

Reaching into the ammo bag once more, Donny pulled out Spangler's Zippo and tossed it to him. "Try some magic. Maybe you can make me believe."

He climbed down the rope ladder to the rubber dinghy.

"You're a fireman, Donny — you can't leave me here to burn!" Spangler called. He clutched the lighter, but the sabre had sliced through nerves and tendons and he couldn't control his fingers. Spangler roared and threw the lighter after Donny. The magic was gone.

The Zippo landed with a soft splash behind him as Donny rowed the dinghy away from the burning ship. Spangler's curses drifted after him. When he was far enough away, he opened the emergency kit and bandaged his leg and shoulder as best he could. Then, wrapping the thin emergency blanket around himself to try to stop his shivering, he looked out over the dark water.

A flash caught his eye. Was he seeing things? No, there it was again: an orange light. He knew what it was: the light from the burning ship bouncing off the reflective strip of a lifejacket.

He should leave her there; by all rights he should just leave her to fade away. But he knew he wouldn't. Despite everything that had happened, he knew that he couldn't do that and hang on to what was left of himself.

And she was still the only one who could keep him out of prison.

Gritting his teeth against the pain, he began to row towards the light. The ship had travelled less than half a mile from the spot where Catherine had been thrown overboard before the engine had stopped.

"Climb in," he said when he reached her.

"I… I can't," she said, her teeth chattering. "My hand is broken. I'm so cold… no strength. Please, help me."

Donny reached over and grabbed her by the wrist. He braced his good leg against the dinghy's side and heaved. Catherine slid up onto the pontoon like a seal beaching itself. He grabbed her belt and rolled her onto the floor of the dinghy. She curled into the fetal position, shivering uncontrollably. Donny moved beside her and wrapped the thin emergency blanket around them both.

The rowing had warmed him up some, and his meagre heat seemed to revive her. Catherine struggled to sit up and huddled in tight against him.

"Thank you," she said simply.

Donny didn't answer. He was listening to the crackle of the distant flames and the screams of a man being burned alive. The wind was blowing the smoke away from Spangler's face, feeding him fresh air as fire spread across the deck, consuming his flesh inch by inch.

Donny knew that pain all too well. Tears ran down his cheeks as he listened to the man's dying cries borne away on the wind.

"That's him?" She heard it too.

"Yes."

"And you feel sorry for that bastard?"

The screams crescendoed and then stopped.

"No," said Donny as he wiped his cheeks. "I don't feel sorry, not one little bit. And I have to live with that."

They watched in silence until the fire burned to the waterline and her ballast took what was left of *Sovereign Seas* to the bottom.

"You shouldn't have come back for me. Why did you do it?"

Donny looked down at her, huddled against him like a child and deadly as a snake. She was still shivering, but she seemed to have regained some of her strength. It was only then that he noticed her head. "Your hair! What happened to your hair?"

"Oh, that." Catherine ran a hand absently over her bald head. "If you still want to kill me, I'm afraid you'll have to get in line. There's a tumour that's way ahead of you. At most you've probably given me a few more years. Not that I'm ungrateful."

"But if that's so… I mean, why… All that stuff about an energy revolution, you'll never live to see it," Donny spluttered.

"Perhaps not. The doctors are trying some experimental therapies. We'll see. I haven't given up. Why did you come back for me? After all, you brought him along to kill me, didn't you?"

"I *didn't* bring him along to kill you," Donny protested. "At least, that wasn't my… Never mind, it's a long story."

"It seems we have some time together."

It spilled out of him as they huddled together, lost in the darkness.

He told her everything: his hope, fear, anger and pain. He held back nothing, from Fitz's death right up to the boom crushing Spangler's legs. Catherine listened quietly until he had finished.

"So why did you come back?" she asked again.

"Because I'm not like you," he said passionately. "Because I need to believe that there are things more important than money and power, or nothing I've ever believed in makes any sense."

Catherine sat there, pressed against him, soaking in his warmth, saying nothing. What a fool he had been to think things would be any different. Still, he couldn't bring himself to plead for his life, for justice, for what was rightfully his.

"So what now?" he said bitterly.

"Have you read Machiavelli, Donny?"

"No," he answered. "But I heard he wasn't a very nice guy."

"He got a worse reputation than he really deserved," Catherine explained. "Regardless, Machiavelli wrote that men should either be treated generously or destroyed utterly. You've proven to be remarkably indestructible. Perhaps, after what we've been through, I should be generous."

"What we've been through? What *we've* been through?!" Donny pulled away. He could just make out her features in the starlight. "All *you* went through was a cold bath. I've lost everything. You destroyed every good thing in my life!"

"Not everything, Donny. You sank your own boat, remember?"

That one hurt. He made no reply.

"Very well, then. I think the police are going to find out that someone else set the fire that killed Leila Aziz," Catherine concluded.

"Just like that? Like throwing scraps to a dog?"

"If you'd prefer, you can spend the rest of your life rotting in prison."

"No!" Donny exclaimed quickly. She was offering him what he wanted, what he had barely dared to hope for. And yet it rankled. "What gives you the right to play with people's lives?"

"Play? I never play. As for the right, the fact that I *can* gives me the right. I claim that right because I dare to!" Catherine said tartly. "I am a wolf in a world of sheep and I make no apology for that."

"And I'm just supposed to pretend nothing happened?"

"What did you expect, Donny? Some road-to-Damascus conversion? Some fairy-tale justice? I'm offering you your life."

"Why should I trust you?"

"You shouldn't. Never trust anyone, that's the first rule. Unless, like you, you don't have a choice." Catherine had regained some of her strength and all of her imperious manner. Donny grabbed her roughly by the front of her blouse.

"I could throw you back and let your drown!" he growled, holding her over the edge of the dinghy.

"You could," Catherine replied, unfazed, "but I'm the only one who can keep you out of prison."

Donny shoved her away. She picked up the emergency blanket and wrapped it tightly around herself.

"I'm quite untouchable by someone like you. You understand that now, don't you?" Catherine didn't wait for him to answer. "Spangler is dead, and cancer or not, I won't live forever. Most of the trail is clean enough that you will seem like just another crazy conspiracy theorist. However, if you do persist in pursuing the matter, I assure you someone will find you irritating enough to kill."

"I still don't understand. If you knew you were dying, none of this makes any sense. Why kill Aziz in the first place?" Donny asked.

"I didn't know it at the beginning, of course. I only found out after you had already become a problem." She ran her hand over her smooth scalp. "We are what we are. Once you're a wolf, it's hard to give up the hunt."

"You… insane," Donny said hesitantly.

Catherine laughed, a deep, throaty laugh. "And this from a man who runs *into* burning buildings."

THE COAST GUARD HELICOPTER found them shortly after dawn the next morning. Catherine explained that she had caught one of her crewmen red-handed, stealing her jewelry, shortly after they had rescued Donny. The man had gone berserk: he had set fire to the ship and shot the rest of the crew. Donny had been wounded trying to save Catherine as they escaped in his dinghy. It was a wild tale, but she was Catherine Rockingham and whether they believed it or not, no one questioned it.

THIRTY-TWO
Lombard

SHE APPRAISED HERSELF in the mirror, turning this way and that. Whether the treatment worked or not, she was a survivor, she decided, and she wasn't going to hide the fact any more. Catherine tossed the wig aside. She had worn her hair shoulder-length for almost twenty years before the treatment. It was time for a change. The hair that had started to grow back was about an inch long now, and completely silver. She liked it, she decided. It made her look a bit like Judi Dench.

She turned from the mirror to the video screen on the other side of her office as the story changed.

"Thanks, Wendy. In Toronto, a firefighter has been cleared of all charges in a bizarre arson-murder case. Captain Donald Robertson had been charged with the death of Leila Aziz…"

Catherine smiled to herself. The exercise of power was a satisfaction in itself. Sometimes it was even more satisfying when it went unnoticed.

"The Chinese delegation is waiting in the boardroom, ma'am," her new assistant said deferentially from the doorway.

"Let them wait," Catherine said, turning back to the mirror.

MOST PEOPLE RELEASED from custody simply leave the courtroom and try to resume their lives. Some celebrate with friends and family. A few go so far as to hire a limo. This was the first time anyone in the courthouse could remember someone being picked up in a fire truck.

Moose sounded the air horn as Donny and Aldrich walked down the courthouse steps. Eddy leaned out the passenger window. "You guys need a lift?"

"You're in my seat," Donny replied.

"Is that so? Well, until you're officially back on the books, you ride in the back with the peasants."

Suzie opened the back door and Donny and Aldrich climbed in. "Welcome home," she said, giving Donny a hug.

They chattered at him as Moose drove back to the station. Donny simply looked out the window as the last leaves of autumn drifted to the ground. It was a dull, grey day, with the sun struggling to break through low, heavy clouds, but even this was a feast to his eyes.

Donny had spent the last three months in jail for violating his bail. The prosecution and defence had spent the time arguing as new evidence came to light. An anonymous tip identified the headless body found in the hotel room as Derek Spangler. Sources at Interpol revealed that Spangler was known to be a hired killer. A re-examination found Spangler's prints on Donny's car and at the Aziz house.

Finally, a newspaper story quoted unnamed sources claiming that Spangler had been hired by remnants of Saddam's regime to kill the Azizes. It was a wild story, but it seemed to satisfy most people and it fit well enough with Donny's claims. The charges against him were finally dropped.

Catherine Rockingham had kept her word.

"OK, one thing I don't get," Moose said as he drove. "These guys, these mookha… whatever they are."

"Mukhabarat," Aldrich interjected. "It's Arabic for 'secret police.'"

"Why don't they just say secret police?" Moose asked.

"'Cause they speak Arabic, not English, you moron," said Eddy.

"Then they should learn," Moose declared, pleased with this gem of infallible logic. Donny chuckled, and the others rolled their eyes. It was good to be back — very, very good.

"Anyway," Moose continued, "how come those guys were going after Aziz after all these years?"

"Some people hold grudges for a long time," Suzie suggested, "especially in that part of the world."

"Why didn't they just do it themselves, then?" Moose pressed.

"Because," Eddy explained, "some people like to have others do their dirty work for them. Besides, a bunch of Iraqis running around setting fires and blowing up houses tends to raise people's suspicions. Right, Wedge?"

Saddam's henchmen were no angels, to be sure, but after the nightmare of what he had gone through, the notion of turning an entire nation into scapegoats bothered him. He should speak up. He should say, no, it wasn't the Iraqis, it was Catherine Rockingham and Sovereign Petroleum. It was the whole rotten system where corporations could buy and sell justice…

"Listen, can we change the subject? I'd kind of like to put all that stuff behind me, if you don't mind," Donny said without looking up.

"What, you didn't like jail?" Eddy asked. "Free room and board, plus all the sex you can handle?"

"You know, Eddy," Suzie scowled, "as an acting captain, you're OK. As a human being, you leave a lot to be desired."

Moose reached across the cab with his free hand and began to twist Eddy's arm at an unusual angle.

"Ow, ow! Moose, I need that arm! Q, call your boyfriend off!"

"You can hurt him, honey, but don't cripple him," Suzie said casually.

"What?? Did I miss something?" Donny exclaimed, looking around the truck. Suzie shrugged and Moose blushed deep red.

"We figured you had enough trouble without having to deal with the traumatic mental image of these two making the beast with two backs," Eddy explained, massaging his shoulder.

They all got out as Moose backed the truck into the station. Donny looked up at the phoenix poised on its sandstone perch. Once again he had been reborn.

They were about to close the door when the alarm went off. Eddy and Suzie climbed back aboard. Donny and Aldrich stood in front of the station and watched as the truck pulled back out onto Lombard and roared off. "I wish I were going with them," Donny sighed.

"You'll be back soon enough." Aldrich patted him on the back. "Ratzo said it would take about a week for the paperwork to go through. Me, I'm stuck on the sidelines permanently now."

"Do you still miss it?"

"Every day, son. I'm like those old horses every time I hear that bell." Aldrich smiled wistfully. "Enjoy it while you can, Donny. It all goes by so quickly."

They listened to the siren fading in the distance.

"So," Aldrich said, turning back to Donny, "do you want to tell me what really happened out there on the water?"

"My boat sank."

"And?"

"There's an old saying, 'the sea keeps her secrets'. Maybe it's best left that way." They headed into the station.

"How's that albatross?" Aldrich asked as they climbed the stairs.

"I think he left when the ship went down," Donny said.

"Are you satisfied?"

Donny paused on the landing. "Satisfied? That's a strong word."

He reached into the bag he had brought with him and pulled out a leather-bound Bible. "I think this is yours. Thank you, John. Thank you for everything you did. I wouldn't be here without your help."

"You're welcome." Aldrich took the Bible and ran his fingers over the cover. "Did you read it?"

"There's nothing but time in jail. You can pass it on to your grandchildren now."

"Fair enough. I've got a surprise for you too." Aldrich smiled and clapped him on the shoulder as they reached the top of the stairs. "Someone heard you were getting out. They're waiting in the kitchen."

Aldrich turned and headed to the office. "I'll give you some time together."

Donny had spent the long months in jail trying to picture each intricate detail of her face and desperately trying not to, certain that he would never see her again.

He opened the kitchen door. She stood silhouetted against the window, with the sunlight diffracting in rainbow hues from her jet-black hair.

"Hi," Donny said shyly.

"Hi," Laurie answered. "Any new scars?"

"Yeah, a couple." He moved to take her in his arms. "How about you?"

"Nothing that won't heal," she said, wiping her tears on his shoulder. "Nothing that won't heal."

THE END

ACKNOWLEDGEMENTS

THIS BOOK COULD NOT have come into being without the encouragement and assistance of many people. Foremost among them is Dean Cooke, who recognized in the first draft the bones of a good story, though the body was flabby and misshapen. Dean patiently read each major rewrite and gave me the detailed critical feedback I needed.

I am also indebted to my other first readers for their comments and suggestions. Thanks to Dave and Anne Bowden, Kathy Jennings, Eva Montville, and Clea and Andreas Wood.

I am grateful to Iman Abdel Wahed, Dr. Nancy McLinden, Bill Hiscott of the Ontario Fire Marshal's Office, and Pat Campbell of the Office of the Chief Coroner of Ontario for their research assistance. Any errors are entirely my fault.

Many people have directly and indirectly, in ways large and small, encouraged and assisted me in completing this project. Among them are Norm and Gaynor Reader, Teresa O'Kane, Helen Douglas, Christie Cowling, Charlie Scalzi, Peter McFawn, Robert Manson and Terri Ottaway.

My deep thanks go to Diana Tyndale of Piranha Communications (www.piranha.net) for her expert editing, to Laura Brady of Brady Typesetting (www.bradytypesetting.com) for the beautiful cover and interior design, and to Steve Bennett and the staff of AuthorBytes (www.authorbytes.com) for the killer website design.

Thanks also to the Ocean Wave Fire Company and Fire Chief Les Reynolds for allowing me to use their facilities for shooting the author photo and for their warm welcome on many other occasions.

For almost a quarter century it has been my privilege to work with and learn from some of the finest firefighters on the face of the earth. It would take another book to list them all. Thanks, all of you , for sharing with me your love of the job and its rich heritage.

Finally, I wish to express my deep love and gratitude to my wife, Liz Krivonosov, for reading draft after draft, for putting up with my obsessive preoccupation, and most of all for providing unflagging support even when I was lost in doubt.

Made in the USA
Charleston, SC
25 August 2014